A Shared Dream

JAYNE ANN KRENTZ

A Shared Dream

MIRA®

ISBN 1-55166-817-3

A SHARED DREAM

Copyright © 2001 by MIRA Books.

The publisher acknowledges the copyright holder
of the individual works as follows:

DREAMS PART ONE
Copyright © 1988 by Jayne Ann Krentz.

DREAMS PART TWO
Copyright © 1988 by Jayne Ann Krentz.

Visit us at www.mirabooks.com

Printed in U.S.A.

CONTENTS

Dreams

Part One

1

He'd had enough of the mating dance. He wanted her, and he was almost certain she wanted him. They weren't kids. They were mature adults. There was no need for games. He swore to himself that if she put him off again tonight, he would walk out the door. And this time he wasn't going to go back.

Even if she did make the best stir-fried vegetables in the entire state of Oregon.

Damn.

He was kidding himself and he knew it. He'd see her again tomorrow, if she politely showed him the door tonight. He'd make another date, and another one after that, until he finally got through her bedroom door.

Something about Diana Prentice fascinated him.

No, it was more than fascination. Diana Prentice was beginning to become an obsession with him, almost as much of an obsession as his writing.

He conjured up an image of her and felt the instant response of his body. At forty he shouldn't be having this kind of problem, he told himself as he shifted his position a bit to ease the sudden tightness in his jeans.

Then again, it was vaguely reassuring to know he could still suffer like this.

But why Diana Prentice?

It wasn't as if she were some young, tall, bosomy, centerfold honey pot. Diana was thirty-four, a little on the short side and built along rather compact lines.

Firm, straight nose. Assertive chin. High cheek bones. She had a smile that held a warmth of feminine secrets and a hint of mischief.

The only really spectacular thing about her was the color of her eyes. Colby was deeply intrigued by those eyes. He'd spent a lot of time trying to determine their exact shade.

He'd finally settled on the approximate description of hazel. As a writer he should have been able to do better than that, and he knew it. But it was tough to come up with a word that covered the curious blend of turquoise, green and gold that characterized Diana's faintly tilted eyes. They made him think of some exotic, mysterious feline. Sensual but untamable. She might choose to give herself to a man, but she would never be coerced or taken by him.

Her hair was an easier matter. Tawny. Definitely tawny. Pale gold layered with rich brown. Colby had been wanting to get his hands into the thick, sweet-smelling stuff for weeks. He envisioned using such a grip to hold her gently captive while he pulled her down onto a carpet of green grass and made love to her until she no longer had the strength to push him away.

Until she no longer had the energy to keep him dangling.

Until she surrendered completely.

She had to surrender to him. Why didn't she realize it? She was his. She had always been his. She could not fight him forever.

He scowled, feeling uneasy about the odd turn of his thoughts. It wasn't like him to think of a woman with such urgency and possessiveness.

The hell with it. He was brooding again.

Colby Savagar groaned and opened his eyes to study the fading light of the setting sun. Soon the mountain valley would be in deep shadow. The boulder on which he was lying was rapidly losing the heat it had been soaking up all day.

A bird wheeled overhead, searching for one last meal before seeking its nest in a towering pine nearby. Colby listened carefully and thought he heard the creature's mate calling to it, but he couldn't be sure. It was hard to hear anything up here above the waterfall. The constant roar of the foaming white water cascading down the cliff below covered most sounds.

Colby shifted position on the huge boulder, turning on his side and propping himself on one elbow. He drew up one leg to balance himself, and then he leaned over the edge of his perch to stare down at the plunging water. It was almost time for the daily light show. He didn't want to miss it.

Below him, Chained Lady Falls tore its way out of the cliffs, emerging from some mysterious source deep in the heart of the mountain. The wild water created a heavy, glistening white wall for over three hundred feet as it fell straight down to the river.

But Colby knew from previous experience that, for a few minutes, just as the summer sun set, the pristine veil would turn blood-red. The strange effect of twilight on the falls had never failed to mesmerize him.

He waited as the first tinge of color appeared in the mist that always hung around Chained Lady Falls. The sun dipped a little further behind the mountain. Brilliant gold, orange and yellow splashed across the sky. The billowing white plumes of water caught the delicate shades and reflected them. For a moment or two, gold poured from the cliffs.

The gold turned to fire a few seconds later.

And then the fire turned to blood.

Colby sat up and hooked one arm around his knee as he stared intently at the long fall of crimson water. Time hung suspended.

Then the sun disappeared completely and the falls returned to normal, pale and glistening in the evening shadows.

Colby raised his head and gazed out over the water to the roofs of the small town that clung to the banks of the river.

Maybe it had been a mistake to come back after all. What had he expected to find here? Nothing had changed in Fulbrook Corners in the past twenty years.

The falls still turned to blood at sunset just as they always had and Colby had discovered that he still hated his hometown as much as he always had.

The only thing different this summer was the presence of Diana Prentice. At the thought, Colby got to his feet and made his way over the jumble of massive rocks that marked the top of Chained Lady Falls.

Diana would be waiting for him. She had invited him over for dinner, and he had promised to bring the wine.

Colby wondered gloomily if he was doomed to spend another evening in a state of frustrated sexual tension. Then he wondered again why he was tolerating the situation.

That question was as unanswerable as the one about why he had come back to spend the summer in Fulbrook Corners.

"Relax, Specter, you're going to get your dinner. You've never missed a single meal since you moved in with me, and you know it." Diana Prentice laughed affectionately at the huge brindled dog sitting expectantly beside her chair. She reached out to scratch the creature's ears and he leaned closer so that he could rest his heavy muzzle on her thigh. "Honestly, you'd think he lived on the edge of starvation."

"Maybe he did before he met you." Colby eyed the big dog with wry disgust. There was no love lost between him and the monster, and both parties knew it. They were polite enough to each other when Diana was around but that was the extent of their relationship. "Or maybe he's got a bottomless pit for a stomach. That's the ugliest dog I've ever seen in my life, Diana. No charm. No cute personality. Doesn't do any tricks. Nothing to recommend him at all. And I happen to like dogs."

Diana smiled benignly, her eyes alight with humor. "He speaks very highly of you when you're not around."

"I'll just bet he does. He'd as soon rip out my throat as look at me." Colby grinned briefly, showing his own teeth. "He tolerates me because he's afraid to offend you. He's probably worried you'd cut off his rations if he gets in the habit of tearing apart your dinner guests."

"If he's smart enough to have figured that out, then you can hardly call him a dumb dog."

"I never said he was dumb. Just very uncute."

"No," Diana agreed thoughtfully, "He's not what you'd call cute. But, then, I've never gone for cute." If I had, she added silently, I wouldn't be entertaining you here in my summer cottage, Colby Savagar.

Colby was anything but cute. Like Specter, he was strong, street-smart and no doubt dangerous when provoked. But the truth was, she didn't know much more about Colby's past than she did about her dog's. She knew Colby had an apartment in Portland, that he was forty years old, and that he looked his age. There were a number of uncompromising lines in his face.

Colby's nearly black hair was streaked with silver at the temples. It would have made him look distinguished if he'd had the kind of pleasant, regular features of most successful businessmen, doctors or lawyers. But Colby didn't have that kind of features, and the net effect of the silver in his hair was to make him look a lot like a battle-scarred wolf.

In the few weeks she had known him, Diana had never seen Colby dressed in anything but jeans, faded denim or khaki shirts and well-worn running shoes. The uniform suited him in some undefinable way.

"Where did you get the monster?" Colby asked casually, as he helped himself to more of Diana's stir-fried vegetables.

"I found him in the pound." Diana smiled, remembering. "We took one look at each other and knew it was fate."

"Uh-huh. More likely he took one look at you and knew a soft touch when he saw it. My guess is, there was probably a damned good reason why that dog was in the pound in the first place."

"He'd been abandoned." She smoothed the dog's rough fur, and Specter leaned more heavily against her leg. His watchful brown eyes looked up at her with open adoration.

"Somehow, the fact that someone had enough sense to abandon him doesn't surprise me. What is he, anyway? I mean apart from half-dragon?"

"I'm not sure. The lady at the pound said she thought he had some Rhodesian Ridgeback in him, but she didn't know what the rest was."

"I'll bet he earned his living as a junkyard dog before you got him."

Specter grinned savagely, and then tried to hide it behind a doggy yawn.

"What did you earn your living at before you became a writer?" Diana asked suddenly. Her curiosity about Colby was growing daily. She knew she was deeply attracted to him but she didn't like the idea of being attracted to what she did not understand. Diana was accustomed to being very much in control of herself and her life.

"Anything and everything that came along. I was in the army for a while. Construction work mostly after that. Then the writing started to sell."

She knew he was impatient with her questions. This was one of the few he had bothered to answer. Diana savored the small tidbit of information. "Would you like some more rice?"

"Thanks." Colby took the bowl with alacrity. "No offense, but is stir-fried vegetables and rice the only thing you know how to make? You've served the same thing every night I've been here."

Diana grinned. "It's my one and only company dish. I've never really had time to learn how to cook for guests. Besides, vegetable dishes suit me. I like to keep my weight under control."

"I guess it's a good thing I like vegetables, too." Colby sprinkled soy sauce on a fresh heap of greenery.

"Obviously Specter's not the only one around here with a hearty appetite."

"I've got an excuse," Colby said around mouthfuls of rice. "I did some climbing this afternoon."

"You climbed to the top of Chained Lady Falls again?"

"Yeah."

"You're really fascinated with those falls, aren't you?"

"One of these days I'll take you up there at twilight. It's a hell of a sight. The water catches the sun in a certain way and turns the whole thing the color of blood."

Diana shuddered. "Is that where you got the idea for the title of the book you're working on?"

" Blood Mist? Yeah." His hooded, gray eyes moved assessingly over her face as he put down his fork and reached for his wineglass.

Savagar's gaze had a disconcerting effect on Diana. It was one of the reasons she had been careful to keep him at arm's length since she had first met him at the post office in town a few weeks earlier. She had sensed something obscurely dangerous in that gaze, yet she had been unable to resist when he had practically invited himself over for dinner a few days later.

One dinner had led to another, and now here she was, almost a month later, playing a reckless game of sexual hide-and-seek with a man she couldn't quite fathom. Common sense warned her to sever the relationship before she was caught, but Diana found herself unable to do that. She was too attracted, too curious, too intrigued. She felt compelled to take the risk of learning more about her summer neighbor.

"What did you do today?" Colby asked, as if sensing the direction of her thoughts and wanting to distract her.

"The usual." Diana smiled and fed Specter a bite of broccoli. The dog wolfed it down as if it were a choice piece of steak. "Had breakfast, typed up some more résumés and letters to my job-hunting contacts, picked up the mail, took a long walk with Specter and read a few more chapters of Shock Value."

"Sounds like you're having one hell of a summer vacation, aren't you? What made you choose this burg in the first place? How come you didn't go to the coast?"

Diana shifted restlessly. She'd privately asked herself that same question more than once. "I'm not sure what made me choose this part of the state. I wanted someplace quiet. One day when I was looking at a map, I spotted Fulbrook Corners and something just clicked. I made the decision on the spot."

"And now you're stuck feeding me and trying to get through one of my novels. Fate works in mysterious ways, I guess. It's not exactly a compliment to my writing that you're taking so long to finish that book, though." Colby's mouth curved wryly upward at one corner.

Diana looked up from popping another tidbit between Specter's huge jaws. "I can't take too much of it at a time," she said honestly. "It scares me to death."

Colby shrugged. "Probably because you've never read much horror fiction before."

"I'll admit it's not my first choice of reading material. After finishing half of Shock Value, though, I now know why I've had the good sense to avoid the horror genre all these years. Your stuff gives me nightmares if I read it right before going to bed, Colby."

"I guess I can take some pride in that," he replied smoothly. "Scaring people is what I get paid to do."

Diana frowned. "How can you write that kind of thing? Doesn't it bother you? Don't you frighten yourself with your own fantasies?"

"When my fantasies succeed in scaring me, I know the writing is going well."

Diana shook her head, aware of a curious sense of frustration. "I doubt if I'll ever completely understand how your mind works."

"Is that a problem?" Colby asked softly. He leaned back in his chair, stretched out his legs under the table and swallowed the last of his wine. His gaze was sharp and questioning under half-lowered lashes. "Is that why we're playing this look-but-don't-touch game? You're trying to figure out how my mind works before you'll let me take you to bed?"

Diana became very still. Under her palm Specter came to attention. The dog glared at Colby with accusing eyes as if daring him to make any further offensive moves.

"I wasn't aware we were playing a game," Diana said, mustering the sort of composure that had always served her well in the business world. "I thought we were becoming friends. If you feel I'm playing games, perhaps you'd prefer to leave."

Specter didn't growl, but his lips retracted just far enough to show his teeth.

Colby glanced down at the dog and then back at Diana. "Forget it," he said, sounding half-amused. "You're not getting rid of me that easily. But I'm not going to let you off the hook, either. You know damned well you've been doing your best to keep me dangling since the first day we met. You let me get just so far and no farther."

Diana surveyed him, rapidly growing annoyed. "I see. You're not interested in developing a friendship, then? You've been inviting yourself over for dinner several times a week because you're restless and bored? You think things might be a little more amusing here in Fulbrook Corners this summer if you had a convenient bed partner?"

Colby eyed her for a long moment. "For the record," he finally said carefully, "I have never found Fulbrook Corners amusing, with or without a bedmate."

Diana flushed, sensing the savage intensity behind the words. "Then why did you come back here after being away for nearly twenty years?"

Colby leaned forward and folded his arms on the table. "I've already explained why I'm here. I have to make a decision about what to do with Aunt Jesse's house, and I needed a quiet place to finish Blood Mist. I decided to kill a couple of birds with one stone this summer."

"I think there's more to it than that."

Colby shook his head slowly. "You can think whatever you like. But I'm warning you, Diana. I have no intention of letting you entertain yourself this summer by trying to see what makes me tick."

"No problem," she retorted. "I'm sure I can find better things to do with my time, anyway. I've told you I've got some major career decisions to make this summer and I will no doubt be much better off if I concentrate on them instead of on you. Let's just call it quits here and now. We both made a mistake. Our judgment was off. It happens, even at our ages." Her smile was all challenge as she got to her feet and began collecting the dishes. "Dessert?"

"Yeah, I'll take dessert." Colby's voice was a low growl as he surged to his feet directly in Diana's path. He reached for her, pulling her roughly into his arms.

"Colby." She spread her fingers across his chest as she fell against him. Her eyes flashed with anger.

Specter gave a fierce, disapproving whine as Diana struggled to find her balance.

"Call off your dog," Colby ordered, his mouth hovering an inch above Diana's.

"Why should I? He's only trying to protect me."

"You don't need protection from me. You can take care of yourself. Tell him to get lost."

Diana hesitated momentarily, dazed by the implied threats, both human and canine, that seemed to cloud the air around her. Then common sense took hold.

"Easy, Specter," she said firmly. "That's a good boy. Go lie down, Specter. Everything is fine. Go on, boy. Lie down."

The big dog looked unconvinced. He studied his mistress as she stood locked in Colby's embrace. Then the animal swung a deeply suspicious gaze on Colby.

"Go on," Colby said. "You heard the lady. Go lie down. I'm not going to hurt her."

With one last, complaining growl, Specter turned reluctantly and slunk off toward the corner of the room. There he obediently settled down, but he didn't take his eyes off Diana.

"You're making him nervous," Diana said. "You're also making me nervous."

"We're even. You've been driving me crazy for the past few weeks." Colby slid his fingers into her hair, tugging the tawny mass free of its knot. "I've been wanting to do that for a long time," he added in satisfaction as Diana's hair tumbled down over his hands. He bent his head as he used his thumbs to tip up her chin.

Diana was suddenly breathless. The dark, mysterious fate she had been tempting for a month had finally cornered her. After putting off the inevitable for so long, she was awash with a reckless desire to surrender to it, to experience it completely.

Colby groaned as Diana lifted her arms to encircle his neck. "That's it, honey. Now you're catching on. That's the way it's supposed to be. Why the hell have you been so damned stubborn and elusive this past month?" His mouth came down on hers with swift eagerness, and he crushed her against the lean, taut length of him.

The kiss was exactly what she'd been expecting and yet stunningly unexpected. The intimate caress was exotic, almost alien, yet the most natural thing in the world.

It was as if Colby were some strange new masculine life form she had just encountered. Yet it was as if she'd known him well in some other time and place-had known him and feared him. And fought him.

He tasted the way Diana had known he would taste, and at the same time his mouth was new and strange and beguiling. He was as demanding as she'd guessed he would be, but she discovered within herself a rash need to meet his demands with a few of her own.

Colby's arms tightened around her and Diana felt the hardness of his lower body thrusting against her softness. He wanted her and he was making no secret of it. Something snapped within her, and the fiery kiss threatened to roar out of control. It was as if she had been waiting for this man and this kiss all her life.

Diana was only dimly aware of the sliding, gliding, exploring movement of Colby's hands as he moved his palms down her body to her hips. She felt his fingertips brush the curve of her breasts en route, and a sensual warmth filled her. When he cupped her buttocks and brought her more tightly against his hardened body, Diana shivered and cried out softly.

He freed her mouth with slow, drugging reluctance and began talking to her as he tugged her shirt out of her trousers.

"I knew it would be like this with you," Colby muttered as he inhaled the fragrance of her hair. His hands were trembling with the force of his desire. "Hot and sweet and frantic at first. I feel like I've been waiting for you for a long, long time."

"Oh, Colby, I wish"

"Shush. Don't try to talk. Not now." He drew a thumb across her parted lips and his eyes burned as he looked down into her questioning face. "This first time is going to be fast and hard and wild. But later we'll take it slow and easy, I promise. Hell, later we'll become connoisseurs. But not this first time. I'm too hungry for you this time." His hands were moving up beneath her shirt now, seeking the gentle curves of her breasts.

The tiny snapping sound of her bra fastener as it came unhooked was what pulled Diana back from the brink. She blinked rapidly, trying to unfog her mind. She was aware of a curiously scattered sensation as if important parts of her were spinning wildly, uncontrollably. She wondered fleetingly if this was how the moth felt when it approached the flame.

Primitive, feminine instincts took over, jerking her back to safety.

"No." Her voice was a soft, beseeching thread of sound. "No, Colby," she said again, this time more firmly. "Not now. Not tonight. I don't...I'm not ready. I want to think. This isn't what I—"

He silenced her with an impatient kiss and his palms covered her taut nipples with deliberate possessiveness. "I want you."

"That's not enough."

"You want me."

"That's still not enough. Please let me go, Colby."

For an instant Diana wasn't sure he would release her. She knew with unnerving certainty that if he did not, she would be drawn back to the edge of the abyss, and this time she would go over into the velvet darkness with him.

She wasn't ready for that. Not yet. There was too much she did not know or understand about him.

And then, without any warning, she was free. Colby swung around and strode violently away from her, one hand raking through his dark hair. He halted in front of the cottage window and stood staring out into the night.

Specter watched him closely but didn't move.

"What is it with you, lady?" Colby said without turning around. The rigid line of his broad shoulders gave undeniable evidence of his volatile mood. "Why the constant come-on and then no follow-through? That's an adolescent's game. You're no kid."

Diana closed her eyes. "No, you're right about that. I'm not exactly a kid." She opened her eyes, and gazed at his back. "But, then, neither are you. Why the heavy pass followed by the macho temper tantrum when I fail to put out, as the kids say? You're forty years old, Colby. Too old to be acting like a teenager who isn't getting what he wants in the back seat of a car."

Colby whipped around, gray eyes lit with an unreadable combination of emotions. "Sorry," he said laconically. "Guess I misread the signals."

"I guess you did," she snapped, her heart sinking. This wasn't the way she wanted the evening to end.

He didn't move. For a long moment they simply stared at each other, neither offering a graceful way out of the highly charged situation.

"What do you want from me?" Diana finally asked helplessly. "A couple of quickies? A one-night stand?"

"Do I look stupid? Nobody with a brain larger than a cockroach's does one-night stands these days."

"True," Diana agreed readily. "So what do you want?"

"Isn't it obvious?" He shoved his hands into the back pockets of his jeans, and began to pace restlessly back and forth across the small room. "I want an affair with you."

"A few days? Weeks? Maybe the whole summer?"

He shot her a glowering look. "Yeah, maybe the whole summer. Maybe longer. As long as it lasts, for pete's sake. As long as it's good for both of us. Damn it, who the hell can answer that kind of question? Do you always have to have answers?"

Diana laced her fingers together and glanced down at them. "I'm a businesswoman," she explained with soft apology. "I like answers. I tend to look before I leap."

"Do you grill every man who takes an interest in you? Do you have to analyze everything to death? Get all the answers before you take any risks? No wonder you're not married."

Diana's head came up swiftly as fury arced through her. "Get out of here, Colby."

He stopped his pacing as the raw anger in her reached him. He grimaced. "Sorry," he muttered brusquely. "That was out of line."

"Yes, it was. I want you to leave. Now."

He ran his fingers through his hair again. "Look, forget I said that last bit, okay? I had no right."

"No right at all. Now leave before I sic my dog on you."

Specter growled obligingly and got to his feet. He watched Colby carefully, anticipation in every line of his massive body.

"Don't threaten me with your damn dog." Colby shot Specter a grim glance and then stalked toward Diana. "If you want to kick me out, do the job yourself."

"I'm trying."

Colby stopped a few steps away from her, regarding her with frustrated male anger and something else—something that might have been desperation. "I said I was sorry."

Diana raised her chin. "Why bother to apologize? I'm sure you meant every word."

"No, I didn't mean every word," he exploded. "Believe me, I sincerely regret every word. I wish I'd kept my mouth shut."

Diana walked to the door and opened it. "Good. Now please leave."

"Diana, wait. I want to talk to you."

"There's nothing left to talk about."

He moved slowly toward the open door. "I wonder if you're going to regret this as much as I will."

"Probably not," she said dryly. "I have nothing to regret."

"Lucky you." He strode past her, out into the night.

Diana closed the door behind him and leaned back against it. Outside in the yard the engine of Colby's black Jeep roared to life. Diana listened to it for a moment. Then she drew a deep, steadying breath and looked at Specter.

"I think," she said to the dog, "that I may have just made one of the biggest mistakes of my life. Either that or I had an extremely close call."

Specter came and leaned against her, offering silent comfort. Diana stroked his fur with an unsteady hand. "He scares me sometimes, Specter. But he fascinates me, too. I can't shake the feeling that I know him from some other place or some other time. Part of me says he's dangerous, but I can't figure out how I know that. And why do I have this strange feeling that he needs me? Worse yet, why do I need him?"

2

Scarlet mist and thundering red water roared past him. The waterfall had turned to blood.

High above him yawned the black depths of the cave. Hidden in its deep shadows lay the entrance to the small grotto. The wrenching sense of longing and desperation that lapped at him in painful waves originated in that secret place.

He was working his way up the path behind the falls, knowing he would not be free until he had satisfied whatever lured him from within the cave. He could not leave until he had done what was required. But he also knew he could not do it alone. He needed her, but she must come to him willingly this time or they would both be trapped forever.

Colby snapped awake, shuddering as the last of the dream fragment faded. It was getting worse. He'd had the dream many times during the past twenty years, but it had never been as intense, as real and disturbing as it was this summer.

He sat up and swung his legs over the side of the bed. He started to switch on the lamp and changed his mind at the last instant. He didn't need light to show him that his hands were shaking. He could feel the faint shivers in his palms.

Annoyed, he got to his feet and padded, naked, downstairs to the old-fashioned kitchen. He opened the aging refrigerator, and stood contemplating its contents in the weak glow of the appliance light.

He had his choice of leftover tuna salad, sliced cheese, or pickles and beer. He chose the tuna and the beer. Closing the refrigerator door, he carried the bowl and the bottle over to the scarred oak table where he had eaten his haphazard meals as a boy.

Aunt Jesse hadn't been into cooking, either for herself or for the small nephew who had landed on her doorstep after the death of his mother. She'd been far more interested in her doomed career as a poet. Colby had learned early to keep food stocked in the refrigerator. If he forgot to do the grocery shopping, he and Jesse didn't eat.

Looking back he realized the kitchen experience had been good, practical preparation for the future. He owed Jesse for that much, at least.

Now, at forty, it was easier for him to feel a certain sympathy for Aunt Jesse's eccentric ways, her poet's ravaged temperament, her tendency to wallow in long bouts of depression and her desire for privacy. She had never wanted or needed anyone else, but she'd been stuck with Colby.

His hands were steady again. With a quick, practiced movement, Colby opened the bottle of beer. He took a long swallow of the brew and thought about how badly he'd screwed up earlier that evening.

He'd probably gotten exactly what he deserved.

What the hell had happened to him during the past few weeks? He'd been unable to get Diana Prentice out of his mind. She'd been haunting him in almost the same way the dream fragments had. But he'd figured he could do something about Diana, even if he was helpless against the dream. He could take Diana to bed and satisfy his obsession with her.

But tonight he'd gone too far. He'd blundered uncontrollably through the delicate spider web of a situation, and the whole thing had disintegrated in an instant.

He'd behaved like an idiot.

But what was done, was done. Colby was used to putting his mistakes behind him. Lord knew he'd had enough practice. The problem now was to figure out a way to recover all the ground he'd lost by trying to jump on Diana tonight.

Because somehow he had to find a way to make her see him again.

"You want the windshield washed, Miss Prentice?"

Diana smiled through the dusty glass at the lanky young man

dressed in jungle fatigues. Eddy Spooner waited, poised with a rubber-bladed squeegee.

"Please, Eddy. It needs it."

"You bet. One thing we get plenty of around here during the summer is dust. You waiting for Colby to hit the post office?"

Diana's smile turned wry. Apparently everyone in Fulbrook Corners knew she and Colby had been dating. "That's right. Have you seen him yet this morning?"

"Nope." Spooner squinted past the pumps toward the small post office building on the opposite side of the main street. "No sign of him yet. You're a little early."

"Yes," Diana admitted softly, "I am." She'd driven into town early this morning precisely because she hadn't wanted to miss Colby when he showed up to collect his mail.

Diana considered the post office neutral ground. It seemed safer to try reestablishing the lines of communication with Colby there where they had first met, rather than taking the risk of going to the old, decaying house where he was staying.

Spooner stared at her through the windshield as he slowly raked the squeegee across the glass. Spooner did everything with a lethargic lack of interest. "You and Colby are hittin' it off pretty good, I hear."

"Really?" Diana made the response very cool. The last thing she wanted to do was talk about her relationship with Colby. Especially to a gas station attendant.

"It figures Colby would take a crack at the first classy broad we've seen around Fulbrook Corners in a month of Sundays. He always did go for the fancy ones. Folks said he had no business aimin' as high as he did. But I always told him-what the hell, go for it, man. What do you have to lose? Me and him used to spend a lot of time talkin' about women."

Diana took a closer look at the man who had been filling her gas tank once a week for the past few weeks. For the first time, she realized that Eddy Spooner was about Colby's age, maybe a year or two older. It struck her that these two men must have been contemporaries while they were growing up here in Fulbrook Corners.

That realization came as a surprise. Eddy Spooner looked as if he came from a different world than the one Colby inhabited. It wasn't just the jungle fatigues and heavy old military-style boots Spooner wore that gave that impression. Nor was it the thinning blond hair that fell to his collar. It was something else, something to do with the expression of lingering bitterness that marked what had probably once been a handsome face.

Spooner was the kind of man who would spend a lifetime blaming others and an unkind universe for everything that went wrong in his world. He looked like a man who'd seen a lot of dreams go up in smoke.

"You and Colby were friends as kids?" she ventured.

"Sure. Me and him used to hang out together. Sort of lost track of him after he left town. I spent a few years in the army and then came back here. But Colby, he lucked out. He didn't come back until this summer. Wonder why he bothered to now? He never did think much of this town and after what he did, most people in town sure don't think much of him."

Diana started to ask another question. Her curiosity about Colby was running rampant again. But before she could open her mouth, the familiar growl of a Jeep's engine caught her attention.

"There he is now. Looks like you timed things just right." Spooner dropped the squeegee into a bucket and came around to Diana's window. "Ten bucks even for the gas."

"Thanks, Eddy." Diana reached for her purse, one eye on the black Jeep that was coming to a halt outside the post office.

Spooner took the money and stared at Specter, who was sitting in the passenger seat watching attentively.

"That's sure some dog you got there."

Specter yawned, showing a lot of teeth. He was used to such observations.

"He's a comfort to have around at times," Diana murmured, patting Specter's shoulder.

"Yeah, a lady livin' alone needs a dog. I used to have me a dog. Real nice Shepherd. But he died a couple years back." Spooner turned his head to watch another car, an aging blue Cadillac, pull into the post office parking lot.

"I'd better be on my way," Diana said, turning the key in the ignition.

"If I was you, I wouldn't go rushin' into the post office just yet," Eddy advised. "Not unless you want to wind up in the middle of a real mess." There was a twisted smile on his face, as if he was taking a perverse pleasure in a secret knowledge of whatever was about to happen.

"Is something wrong?" Diana asked bluntly.

"Probably. See that big blue Caddy that just pulled up out front?"

"Yes." Colby had disappeared into the post office. Apparently he hadn't noticed her car parked across the street yet. Or if he had, he was choosing to ignore it. This was not going to be easy.

"See that old lady gettin' out of the Caddy?"

"What about her?" Diana asked impatiently. She briefly switched her gaze to the aging, gray-haired woman with the regal bearing who was getting slowly out of the passenger side of the Cadillac. She was being assisted by her driver, a large, beefy man of about forty-five whose potbelly strained the buttons of his shirt.

"That's Mrs. Fulbrook herself. Fulbrooks have owned just about everything in this town ever since my great grandpa's time."

"Is that right?"

Spooner must have sensed her lack of interest. He flattened one greasy palm on the roof of Diana's Buick and leaned down to look at her through squinted eyes. "You don't know nothin' about the high and mighty Mrs. Margaret Fulbrook, do you?"

"What should I know about her?"

"Well, for starters," Spooner said, drawing it out as slowly as he could, "She's Colby Savagar's mother-in-law."

"His mother-in-law!"

"Yup. And I'll tell you somethin' else. She hates his guts." Spooner stepped away from the car, apparently satisfied that he'd finally gotten her full attention. "See you next week, Miss Prentice. Nice talkin' to ya."

"Goodbye, Eddy." Diana pulled away from the gas station feeling dazed. Colby's mother-in-law? But Colby wasn't married.

She was sure he wasn't married. He couldn't be married.

He would have told her if he'd had a wife. Colby Savagar wouldn't play that kind of game.

But there was a lot she didn't know about Colby Savagar, Diana reminded herself as she parked her Buick next to Colby's Jeep. It was precisely that lack of knowledge that had kept her from going to bed with him last night.

She turned off the ignition and slipped out of the car. A small voice was urging her to turn around and drive away from what promised to be an unpleasant little scene. But the need to know the facts proved a far stronger motivation.

"Stay here, fella," she advised Specter. "I'll yell if I need help."

Specter was busy exchanging cold stares with the man who had driven the Cadillac. Diana took one glance at the overweight driver and then looked away. The man's heavily jowled face was marked with the cruel, not overly intelligent lines of a natural bully. Diana was willing to bet that this was the kind of man who had amused himself as a child by tearing wings off flies. She hurried toward the post office.

The tension in the lobby hit her like a tidal wave when she pushed open the glass doors. The silence was unnatural. Several people stood as if nailed to the floor. Instead of exchanging gossip and observations on the weather as usual, they were all mute, all staring with rapt attention at the scene that was unfolding before them.

Colby was just turning away from the counter, a bunch of mail in his fist. He glanced toward the door and saw Diana. For an instant he fixed her with his brilliant gray eyes, but a second later he jerked his attention back to Margaret Fulbrook who had planted herself directly in his path.

"Harry told me you'd come back this summer, Colby Savagar." Mrs. Fulbrook's voice had the carrying power of a woman who'd spent a lifetime commanding others and the situation around her. She wore her nearly seventy years with icy, rigid pride. Her hair was anchored in a queenly bun and her fine brown eyes were piercing. "I was inclined not to believe it at first. But then I recalled that the one thing you never lacked was the devil's own nerve."

Colby gave the older woman a chilling look. "Sometimes nerve was all I had. Excuse me, Mrs. Fulbrook. Someone's waiting for me."

"Who? That Prentice woman? I pity her. I've heard about her, too. Does she know what kind of man you are?"

"No, but then, neither do you," Colby said with soft savagery.

"You bastard," Mrs. Fulbrook hissed.

"You aren't the first to suggest that possibility and you probably won't be the last. But you sure can't say that about my son, can you? In fact, if I ever hear you say anything at all about my son, I'll"

"Good morning, Colby." Diana unstuck herself from the floor and went forward with her best corporate smile, just as if she hadn't overheard a word. "I wondered if I'd see you here today. I was going to give you a call later and remind you about that trip to the falls you promised me." She switched her smile to the postal clerk behind the counter who was watching the confrontation with a gaping mouth. "Got anything for me today, Bernice? I'm in a hurry."

Bernice closed her mouth, her eyes darting from Colby to Mrs. Fulbrook to Diana. "Just this one letter." She handed it over the counter.

"Thanks." Diana took a quick glance at the familiar masculine scrawl and then dropped the envelope into her purse. She took Colby's arm in a casual gesture, aware of the battle-ready tension in his muscles. Then she smiled at the grim-faced Margaret Fulbrook. "You'll excuse us, won't you? Colby has been promising me this little outing for days. I've packed a lunch and everything."

"You're as big a fool as my daughter was. But at least you're no young, innocent girl. You look old enough to make your own mistakes. And mark my words, any woman who gets involved with Colby Savagar is making a serious mistake." Mrs. Fulbrook turned and swept disdainfully out of the lobby.

Instinct compelled Diana to urge Colby along in the other woman's wake. It was difficult to stage an exit if your intended victims did not take it seriously. Diana wanted to make certain no one in the post office assumed Colby was taking this scene to heart.

"It's going to be hot today," Diana remarked chattily as she crowded Colby through the swinging doors. "I was thinking of taking a swimming suit along on our picnic. Oh, and I'd better pick up some chips at the store. What's a picnic without potato chips? Have you got a cooler we can use?"

She fell silent as they stepped out into the bright morning warmth. The man in the Cadillac got out with ponderous slowness to assist Margaret Fulbrook into the passenger seat. When he threw Colby a vicious glare, Diana steered her charge in the opposite direction.

"Okay," Colby said quietly as they reached his black Jeep. "The rescue operation is over." He leaned against the fender and tapped his bunch of letters against one palm. "Should I thank you?"

Diana shaded her eyes and watched the Cadillac pull out of the parking lot. "I suppose that depends on how badly you wanted rescuing."

"Badly enough. It's been twenty years since I've gone toe-to-toe with that old bat. I'm out of practice. But I think I could still take Harry if I had to. He's really put on the weight. Looks slower than ever."

"Harry being the driver, I take it?"

"Harry Gedge being Margaret Fulbrook's odd job boy. He does whatever she tells him." Colby lost interest in the pair. "Were you serious about the picnic or was that just camouflage for the rescue effort?"

Diana drew in her breath and braced herself. "That depends on whether or not Margaret Fulbrook really is your mother-in-law."

Colby's brows rose sardonically. "Somebody sure filled you in fast."

"It was Eddy Spooner at the gas station," Diana admitted.

"Good old Eddy. Well, he was partly right. I married Margaret Fulbrook's daughter twenty years ago." He shifted his gaze to the disappearing Cadillac.

"Well?" Diana prompted.

"Well, what?" Colby looked back at her.

Diana sighed. "Are you still married?"

"No."

Diana hid her sense of relief behind a reproving shake of her head. "If I waited to get answers from you, I'd wait until hell froze over, wouldn't I?"

He smiled faintly. "And you like answers, don't you?"

"I need a few before I go to bed with you," she retorted evenly.

Colby didn't move. His expression was alive with sudden, searching intent. "Are you still considering the possibility of going to bed with me?"

"Yes."

Exultant relief flashed in his gray eyes, but he only nodded once. "If you come through with a real picnic this afternoon, I'll come through with some answers about Margaret Fulbrook."

"It's a deal." Diana turned to start toward her car.

"I'll pick you up in an hour. And wear a pair of sport shoes," Colby called after her. "It's slippery up there around the falls."

"I acted like an ass last night. You have my apology, for what it's worth." Colby stretched out on his side with unconscious masculine grace. One knee was bent, his upper body braced on his elbow. His brooding gaze was on the town far below.

Diana was sitting cross-legged on the blanket, listening to the dull roar of the water. She followed Colby's gaze and studied the pictur esque scene below. The road that paralleled the river through the gorge was a narrow, twisting ribbon. She could see the old bridge across the river that linked the two halves of Fulbrook Corners. Her cottage was just barely visible on the same side of the river as Colby's place.

Specter, having given up on the possibility of getting any more po tato chips, was sprawled behind her on a sun-warmed rock.

"Maybe you did act like an ass," she agreed after a moment. "But part of it may have been my fault. I didn't handle the situation very well. I did a lot of thinking last night after you left. I've come to the conclusion you're right. I have been giving out mixed signals."

Colby's eyes shifted slowly from the scene in the valley below to her face. "Signals?"

Diana fiddled with a small weed she had picked. "Yes, signals. You know what I mean."

"I know what you mean, all right," he agreed roughly. "If nothing else, it's a relief to know I wasn't imagining things."

Diana's mouth curved in gentle amusement. "I expect that with an imagination like yours you have to be a little cautious about how you interpret things."

Colby picked up his beer can and took a long swallow. His eyes met hers over the rim. "I can control my imagination. Most of the time."

"I see. It's your hormones you have trouble controlling?"

His eyes gleamed in the sunlight. "I can control those most of the time, too. But around you they seem to go a little crazy."

Diana gnawed briefly on her lower lip and then opted for total honesty. "I think a part of me was thrilled to know that," she admitted very softly. "Because I was having the same kind of trouble controlling my, uh, raging hormones around you." She looked away, unable to meet his steady gaze. "I don't have that kind of problem normally. It's been a very long time since I felt on the edge the way I do around you."

"So maybe we should take pity on ourselves," Colby said dryly. "Let's go to bed together and work it out of our systems."

Diana gave a disgusted exclamation and leaned back on her elbows. "You're such a flaming romantic," she complained sarcastically.

"I write horror, not romance."

"That's no excuse," she snapped.

"It's time both of us stopped behaving like a couple of teenagers and started acting our ages. Neither of us needs a repeat of last night."

"I'll make another deal with you," Diana said. "If you don't mention last night again, neither will I."

Colby shrugged. "Whatever you want, so long as you're not trying to put an end to whatever it is we have going between us. Any more potato chips?"

"I think Specter ate the last of them."

"Figures." Colby threw a disgruntled glance at the sleeping dog. "One of these days, that monster and I are going to have a serious talk."

"Speaking of a serious talk"

"Yeah?"

"Tell me about Margaret Fulbrook."

"I did promise you a few answers, didn't I?"

"Yes, you did."

Colby took another swallow of beer. "There's not all that much to tell. I was married to Cynthia Fulbrook. Technically, that made the old battle-ax my mother-in-law."

"What happened to Cynthia?"

"She died."

"Oh. I'm sorry."

"Margaret Fulbrook has always blamed me for Cynthia's death, among other things." Colby's mouth tightened. "I should probably take this from the top."

"I'm listening."

He drew a breath and shifted his eyes back to the little town below the falls. "My mother and my Aunt Jesse were both born in Fulbrook Corners. They came from the wrong side of the falls, as folks around here like to say." He smiled grimly and indicated a handful of rooftops on the left-hand side of the river. "They were stuck here all of their lives. My mother worked in a local café and dreamed of marrying some man from the other side of the river."

"And your Aunt Jesse?"

Colby's eyes softened slightly. "Aunt Jesse dreamed a lot, too, but not about marrying and moving to the right side of town. She poured out her dreams in an endless stream of poems and short stories that almost never got published. She considered herself a writer, even if no one else did, and she felt obliged to live up to the image. She was eccentric, unpredictable and erratic. She seemed to be in another world most of the time. But after Mom died, she didn't hesitate to take me in. Aunt Jesse was good to me in her own strange way. And she taught me things."

"What things?"

"How to take care of myself, mainly. She did it by leaving me to my own devices most of the time. It worked. I grew up knowing the only person you can count on is yourself."

"What about your father?" Diana asked cautiously.

"What about him? I sure as hell never had the privilege of meeting him. He worked for a lumber mill near here for a while-just long enough to get my mother pregnant-and then he took off."

"Oh."

Colby looked at her. "Yeah, that's about all you can say about it-`Oh.' At any rate, to make an excruciatingly long, boring story short, I grew up with Aunt Jesse. And I guess I ran a little wild. I was the dangerous young hood from the other side of the falls. Always in trouble. Always blamed when there were missing hubcaps. Always the one people pointed at when there was a fight at the school dance. Always the one who got picked up when Sheriff Thorp heard about a midnight drag race out on River Road."

"And you were always perfectly innocent, of course?"

His lips twitched with a small smile. "Of course-except when it came to drag racing on River Road."

"In short, the kind of boy our mothers warned us about," Diana replied with a flash of amusement.

"Afraid so." Colby rolled onto his back and cradled his head on his folded arms.

"Well, that makes sense," Diana said calmly. "That was always the most interesting kind of boy, naturally. I always wanted to meet one."

Colby blinked lazily. "But you never did?"

"Unfortunately, no. I was never the type boys like that found fascinating. I wasn't very pretty for one thing, and I was much too serious for another. From my first day in school, I knew I had to make something of myself. I always had my head in a book. By the time I was out of high school, I was on the fast track to college and a career."

"And the kind of boy who swiped hubcaps, drove too fast and wore his hair too long wasn't interesting any more, was he? That kind of guy wouldn't have had any place in your up-and-coming life-style."

Diana refused to let him bait her. "I don't know if he would have fit in or not. I told you, I never got a chance to meet him."

"Be grateful. You might have wound up pregnant at eighteen, the way Cynthia Fulbrook did."

Diana hesitated a moment, absorbing that information. "You got Margaret Fulbrook's daughter pregnant?"

"Yeah."

Diana became irritated. "Well? Don't just stop there. How did it happen?"

He gave her an odd look. "The usual way."

"Colby, stop it. You know perfectly well what I mean."

He exhaled slowly. "Cynthia Fulbrook was the princess of Fulbrook Corners. She was the richest kid in town, the prettiest girl and the best-dressed student at Fulbrook Corners High. She got a brand-new red convertible from her parents the day she turned sixteen, and she had her choice of any boy in school. She was a year younger than me and I'd been as dazzled by her as every other male in town."

"How did she feel about you?"

"She found me interesting. But her parents kept a close watch on her."

"Ah, the old forbidden fruit syndrome."

"On both sides," Colby admitted. "But nothing happened between us until after I went into the service. I saw the army as a way out of Fulbrook Corners, and I took it the day I got out of high school. Eddy Spooner went with me. The summer of my nineteenth year I came home on leave and there was Cynthia, just graduated and getting ready to go off to college. She took one look at me and decided to find out what forbidden fruit tasted like."

"And you took one look at her and decided to see what it was like to go to bed with a genuine princess?"

"That's about it. But neither one of us were quite as grown up as we thought we were. I thought I knew all about taking precautions, and Cynthia thought she knew all about safe times of the month and other mythical means of avoiding pregnancy. The net result was that we took some chances we shouldn't have taken."

"And Cynthia got pregnant."

Colby nodded grimly. "There was hell to pay. Cynthia was scared to death. Her mother was screaming at her, and her father was threatening to have me put in jail or shot. They both agreed the pregnancy should be taken care of as quickly and quietly as possible. The last option anyone considered was allowing Cynthia to marry me and have the baby."

"So you ran off with her," Diana concluded.

"We thought we were in love. Or at least, I did. I also thought I had to protect her from her parents. I don't think poor Cynthia was thinking at all. She was a nervous wreck, torn between angry parents and the guy from the wrong side of the falls. I took charge, packed her up and drove her out of town before she had a chance to reconsider. We got married in Reno, and then I took her to the army base where I was stationed. She had Brandon seven months later."

"Brandon?"

"My son."

Diana smiled at the quiet pride in his voice. "What happened to Cynthia?"

Colby tossed a handful of pebbles out over the falls. "Cynthia's parents decided they could force her to come home if they threatened to cut off her inheritance. They never let up the pressure. And Cynthia did not take well to motherhood. She hadn't wanted Brandon in the first place. The whole thing had been a stupid accident, and she decided she shouldn't have to pay for it the rest of her life. Maybe she was right. Hell, I don't know."

"Who does at that age?"

"Yeah. Who knows? Cynthia and I fought a lot, and one day I came home to find her gone. She'd left a note for me telling me Brandon was at a neighbor's and that she couldn't take it any more. Her life had been ruined. She was going home to her parents. She wanted to start over. I never saw her again. She was killed in a freeway smashup on the interstate. Her parents never forgave me. At the funeral they told me they never wanted to see me or Brandon again. I was happy to grant them their wish."

"And you never married again?"

Colby shook his head. "I figured I'd seen enough of marriage to last me a lifetime. Besides, I was busy with my son. I raised Brandon by myself. Made a lot of mistakes along the way, but the kid turned out okay." Colby's eyes warmed with paternal satisfaction. "He just finished his first year in college in Eugene. Did great, too. Thinks he wants to be an engineer."

"Congratulations," Diana said softly. She folded her elbows on her drawn-up knees and rested her chin on her forearms. "It must have been rough at times."

Colby grimaced. "You don't know the half of it. Like I said, I made a lot of mistakes. Sure as hell wouldn't want to go through it again. But Brandon and I both survived."

"And that's the great saga of Colby Savagar and the town of Fulbrook Corners?"

He looked at her. "That's it."

"I think I understand why you haven't bothered to return before now."

Colby's intent gaze never left her face. "I answered your questions."

Diana felt the warmth in her face. She glanced away. "Yes, you did."

"I've got a few for you, too," Colby said quietly.

Pleased that he was finally showing some real interest in her background, she glanced at him. "You do?"

"Most of them can wait."

"Oh." She was strangely disappointed.

"All except one." Colby reached out and gently tumbled her down across his chest. "And that one is a very straightforward question. All it takes is a simple yes or no to answer it."

Instinctively Diana struggled to find her balance, but she didn't pull away once she had braced herself. She sprawled on top of him, her face very close to his.

"Yes or no, Diana?"

The roar of the falls filled her ears and the warm fragrance of the sun-heated woods enveloped her. Gossamer plumes of mist, creatures of light and magic soared overhead. One of her jeaned legs slid between Colby's thighs and got caught there. His body was strong and hard and infinitely inviting. His eyes were pools of gray fire waiting to blaze.

Diana realized with blinding clarity that she was falling in love.

"Yes," she whispered and lowered her head to kiss him.

3

He had never felt so pulsatingly alive in his life. He was going to go up in flames at any moment. The blood beat heavily in his veins, and the ache in his loins was almost painful.

Colby held on to the woman in his arms with all his strength, afraid she would try to slip away from him again the way she had slipped away every other time he'd tried to make her his.

But this time she wasn't fighting him. This time she wasn't trying to edge out of reach. She was giving herself to him and his head spun with the wonder of it. All the hot, fierce questions his body had been asking would finally have answers.

"Diana. Honey, I've wanted you like this for so long. I've been going out of my mind."

She opened her mouth for him and he tasted her, whetting his own appetite even further. He cradled her legs between his own, anchoring her firmly against him. Then he slipped his hands under her shirt and traced the graceful line of her spine. She was supple and warm and very, very feminine. Colby groaned as desire raked him across hot coals.

He tugged the buttons of her shirt, pushing the garment off her shoulders with quick, impatient hands. Then he found the fastener of her bra and undid it. Her soft, gently curving breasts filled his palms and he lifted his hips, deliberately arching into her softness. Her skin was sleek and silky to the touch. He would never get enough of the feel of her.

"Colby, Colby, please. Yes, oh, please, just like that. You make me feel so good."

Captivated by her response, Colby grazed his palms again across her nipples. Tight, firm pebbles of desire formed beneath his hands. Touching was no longer enough. He lifted her higher along his chest until he could take the peak of one breast into his mouth.

"Yes," she breathed. A shiver went through her.

Colby tightened his hold on her and used his tongue to elicit another of the tantalizing little shudders of desire. The fact that he could make her react so fiercely only served to better fuel the fire that was burning within him.

She was scrabbling at his clothes now, unfastening buttons and pushing the denim shirt out of her way. Her fingers were as unsteady as his own. Her hands splayed across his chest, tangling in the rough hair there. When she lowered her head and touched the tip of her tongue to one of his own flat nipples, Colby groaned heavily.

He found the snap of her jeans and yanked at it. Then he fumbled with the zipper until he could slide his hand inside her flimsy panties. He snagged his fingers in the silky fabric that hid her secrets.

Diana writhed against him, crying out softly. He explored further and sucked in his breath when he felt the warm dew between her legs.

"Sweetheart," he muttered. "You want me. Say it. Tell me all about it." He probed gently with the tip of his thumb and her fingers clutched at his shoulders.

"I want you."

"Look at me," he urged, pushing carefully into her once more. "Open your eyes and say it."

Her long lashes swept up, revealing the gold and green and blue of her eyes. "I want you so much, Colby. I've never felt like this before in my life."

Her honesty almost shattered him. "It's the same for me," he admitted harshly. "I want you more than I've ever wanted anything in this world."

He pushed the jeans down over her hips and rolled her onto her back. Then he knelt, unbuckled his belt, and kicked himself free of his own denims. He hesitated a moment as she looked at him. An unfamiliar uncertainty flared briefly. He desperately wanted her to be satisfied. He wanted to please her. Then he saw the deep, feminine admiration in her eyes, and a sense of exultant relief rolled through his veins. She was pleased with what she saw.

"You're magnificent." Her eyes were glowing with soft, tremulous wonder.

"So are you." He drew his hand down the length of her from breast to thigh. "So are you," he repeated. "Oh, God, honey, you're perfect. Soft, sweet, beautiful. Perfect."

He parted her legs with his own and started to lower himself onto her. At the last instant a flicker of rationality went through his dazzled brain. He remembered the little foil packets he had optimistically put in his pocket before leaving the house.

"Just a second," he said hoarsely.

She nodded her understanding. He leaned down to give her a quick, hard kiss and then he reached for his jeans.

He took care of the small, crucial task with quick, efficient movements. Then he reached out to gather Diana back into his arms.

"Colby? I want you to know that I'"

He touched her mouth with his fingertips. "The last thing I want to do now is talk. I want you so much that unless we hurry this up, I'm going to explode before I ever get inside you. My self-control is shot to hell."

"Good," she said simply, mischief in her beautiful eyes. "I'm not in the mood for self-control either. Not now. Make love to me, Colby. Make it the way you said it would be the first time for us. Hot and wild and frantic."

He was enraptured by the siren song of her demand. And he was shaking with the effort it took to hold himself in check long enough to get himself into position. Then he was poised at the hot, damp core of her and he didn't have to wait any longer.

With a harsh exclamation of need, Colby drove himself into her soft, receptive core. He felt her quick, indrawn breath and the shudder that went through her. She was hot and tight. For an instant he feared his swift possession had hurt her. Her nails scored his shoulders.

Then she was clinging to him as if he were a lifeline, lifting herself to meet his demanding thrusts.

" Colby."

And the first time with her was just as he had known it would be. Hot, wild, frantic.

Perfect

"You're a screamer."

Diana raised her lashes halfway, aware of the hot sunlight filtering down through the trees and the heavy weight of Colby's leg as it lay across her bare thigh. "I did scream, didn't I?" she said, half-amused, half-bemused.

Colby raised himself on one elbow and grinned down at her. "Louder than Chained Lady Falls."

"Don't exaggerate. And don't look so damned pleased with yourself. Under certain circumstances, it could be highly embarrassing."

"It wouldn't ever embarrass me."

"Uh-huh. What if we'd been in a motel room or something?"

"What have you done in the past?"

"About the screaming?" She frowned slightly. "It's never been a problem."

"You don't spend a lot of time in motel rooms?" he asked innocently.

"I've never screamed before," she said quite seriously. She was not altogether certain she liked remembering that unmistakable evidence of sensual surrender. She was accustomed to being in control.

"Better get used to it," Colby advised. His eyes were brilliant with masculine satisfaction and anticipation. "You're going to be doing a lot of screaming in the near future."

"I am?"

He stroked a hand across her breasts and then bent over her. "Yes," he said softly. "You are."

"Colby?"

"Hmmm?" His arm tightened around her shoulders as he emitted a huge yawn.

"It's getting late. Won't be long until the sun sets. Maybe we should start back."

"We'll wait a little while longer. I want to show you something."

"The falls at sunset?" Diana sat up and picked up her shirt. The heat of the day was fading rapidly. "You said something about the water turning the color of blood. To be perfectly truthful, it doesn't sound all that terrific."

"You'll see. Where's that damned dog of yours?" Colby sat up and reached for his jeans.

Diana's glance got caught for a moment as she watched the smooth play of muscles under his skin. The strength in him was captivating. She had responded to it with more passion than she'd ever experienced. Colby saw her lingering look, and started to grin with lazy, come-hither sensuality. Diana quickly shifted her gaze to the woods, searching for her dog.

"Specter? Here, boy. Where are you? Specter? Over here, boy."

A soft, answering whine came from the trees. Diana smiled as the animal materialized from the woods. He appeared decidedly reproving. "Look at him. He probably wonders if we're finished acting like a couple of humans."

Colby chuckled. "I think we embarrassed him."

"I wouldn't be surprised. Specter has a great sense of dignity."

"Unlike you when you're going up in flames in my arms." Colby gave her a lingering kiss. "But it was good, lady. And I have a feeling it's going to get better and better." He got to his feet and tugged her up beside him. "Hurry up and get dressed. That sun will be in just the right position in another minute or two."

He helped her with the buttons of her shirt, and then she stepped quickly into her jeans and running shoes.

"Here we go. This is the best place to see the effect." Colby led her quickly to an outcropping of granite that gave a clear view of the thundering water. The mist boiled up into the air and settled lightly on Diana's tangled hair.

She looked down as the fading sun began to paint the sky. "It's beautiful," she said in surprise, as first the mist and then the cascading water turned a vivid gold. "I thought it would be red."

"Watch." Colby leaned forward intently, one foot braced on a chunk of rock.

Diana glanced at him curiously, wondering at his fascination. "You must have seen this hundreds of times."

"I used to come up here nearly every evening during the summer months when I was a kid." He didn't look at her. His whole attention was on the waterfall. "There. It's happening. See it? Like blood pouring out of the mountain."

Diana felt a distinct chill down her spine as she obeyed him and turned her gaze back to the falls. "My God, you're right," she whispered. "It's unbelievable."

"It's the blood of a dying warrior."

She wanted to ask him what he meant, but now wasn't the time. She stared in amazement, as fascinated as Colby was. The gold mist gradually shaded to orange and then to deep scarlet red. The effect lasted only a moment or two, and then the sun disappeared behind the mountains. The waterfall returned to its normal silver and white. Diana and Colby stood in silence for a moment. Then Colby reached out to hook an arm around her shoulders.

"Interesting, isn't it?" he asked a little too casually.

"It's weird," Diana retorted with feeling.

Colby laughed softly. "Yeah. Weird. Did I tell you there's a cave behind the falls? You can't see it because of the water, but if you know your way around down there, you can get to it."

"A cave?"

"Chained Lady Cave."

Diana leaned down to pick up the remnants of their picnic lunch. "How did the falls and the cave get that name? Chained Lady. It's strange."

"It's from an old legend." Colby folded the blanket and started to lead the way down the steep path to where the Jeep was parked.

"An Indian legend?"

He shook his head. "The Indians told it to the first settlers in the area, but they always swore the legend had nothing to do with their tribe. They claimed there was another race here before them. A fierce warrior people who had long since vanished."

"And the legend dates from that time?"

"Right."

"Tell me the story." Pebbles clattered under her feet as Diana hurried to keep up with him. She was suddenly keen to hear the tale of Chained Lady Falls.

"The way I heard it when I was a kid was that the warriors who inhabited this area had a habit of acquiring their wives through the time-honored procedure of kidnapping them."

"They sound like a typical bunch of male chauvinists."

"Don't look at me like that," Colby said with a sardonic glance over his shoulder. "I haven't kidnapped a woman in years. At any rate, it seems that one of the greatest of the clan's warriors decided he deserved the best. He wanted a woman who could give him a strong son. He hunted far and wide before he made his selection. Then he swooped down and grabbed the young lady one day while she was out picking berries. He carried her home and proudly installed her in his bed. But he'd made a slight miscalculation."

"The lady didn't like being kidnapped and carried away from her home and family?"

"She took strong exception to the whole situation. Under normal circumstances, her feelings on the subject would have been disregarded by all concerned. But in her case, her new husband couldn't totally overlook her opinion because she came from a very unusual clan. One in which the women were warriors. Not only that, but the females of the clan had learned how to control their reproductive cycles."

"Aha. In other words, she knew something about birth control and she refused to get pregnant. Good for her."

"Wait until you hear the end of the story before you start applauding."

Diana frowned at his back. "Is it going to have a happy ending?"

"No, it's not. Listen well, my sweet, and learn that female stubbornness doesn't pay off in the long run."

"Spoken like a modern-day chauvinist warrior type," Diana muttered.

Colby ignored her. "When several months of nightly effort on the part of our valiant warrior did not pay off, he finally realized his new bride was deliberately sabotaging his big plans to produce a mighty son and heir."

"And he was annoyed?"

"To put it mildly. He tried the usual beatings and threats, and when that didn't work, he decided the lady would come to her senses if she spent a little time alone in the cave behind the falls."

Diana's eyes widened. "He chained her in that cave you told me about?"

Colby nodded. "So the story goes." He leaped lightly down to another rocky ledge and had to dodge Specter who was bounding down the hillside ahead of him. "Out of my way, you dumb dog," Colby muttered through his teeth. Specter paid no attention.

"Stop maligning my dog, and tell me the rest of the story," Diana demanded.

Colby reached back to steady her. "Well, he stuck her in the cave and told her that she could come out only when she conceived."

"How awful."

"Every day just before sunset he came to her. He brought her food and made love to her and then he left her to face the darkness alone."

"You mean he raped her on a daily basis!"

Colby's eyebrows rose thoughtfully. "Yeah, that's probably what it amounted to, because the lady still refused to allow herself to become pregnant. And after a time she even refused to eat the food he brought her. All the while she was plotting, trying to figure out a way to get rid of her unwanted husband. One evening she saw her chance."

Diana looked up. "A chance to escape?"

"No," Colby said grimly. "A way to kill the warrior. She set a trap for him by pretending to surrender. He was so relieved to think he'd finally quelled her stubborn resistance that he apparently forgot just what kind of female he was dealing with. In his haste to get started on making a son, he got careless. Inexcusably careless, considering he was supposed to be a hotshot warrior."

"What happened?"

"The lady got hold of his hunting knife and she used it on him just as he was, uh, reaching the grand finale."

"She stabbed him to death while he was forcing himself on her," Diana concluded in awed wonder. "What a woman"

"This story isn't over yet," Colby warned. "I told you that it doesn't have a happy ending."

"Finish it," Diana urged, anxious to hear the conclusion.

"The warrior died at her feet, his blood running out of the cave entrance and mingling with the waterfall. With his last breath, he cursed the woman. Told her that her spirit would remain chained in the cave forever until a child was conceived and born there."

"Then he croaked, and she managed to get out of the cave?" Diana demanded.

"She was still chained, don't forget. She had no way to get free after she'd killed the warrior. She died there, and the legend says her spirit is still trapped in the cave. After all, what are the odds that a baby is going to be created and born in Chained Lady Cave?"

"Pretty poor, I imagine." Diana glanced back at the impenetrable veil of the falls, trying to envision a hidden cave behind the wall of rushing water. It made her uneasy even to imagine it. "So that's the end of the story?"

"More or less. But for as long as I can remember, kids from around these parts have always had a lot of fun scaring each other to death with rumors that the Chained Lady is still waiting inside the cave. They say she'll kill any other male who dares to enter. The theory is that she's still got her husband's knife, you see."

"What do the adults say?"

"For the most part they laugh the whole thing off, naturally. But whenever something strange or unsettling happens anywhere in the vicinity of Fulbrook Corners, you can bet someone's likely to blame it on the restless spirit of the lady in the cave."

"I can see you were one of those kids who got off on that story," Diana said with a rueful amusement. She paused. "Tell me something. Did you ever risk going into the cave?"

He flashed her an unreadable glance. "What do you think?"

She tilted her head to one side, considering the question. "Oh, I think you probably did. You wouldn't have been able to resist the challenge. After all, you were the toughest kid in town, right? You had a reputation to protect."

Colby's smile was ironic. "You're right. I spent a night in Chained Lady Cave once when I was in my teens. Eddy Spooner and I were supposed to do it together on a dare. But when evening came and the falls turned red, Spooner lost his nerve. He opted to spend the night at a campsite down by the river."

"But you stayed, of course."

"Had to," Colby said with patently false modesty. "Like you said, I had a reputation to protect." His smile came and went.

"Were you terrified?"

The smile vanished. "I'll tell you the truth. I've never told any other living soul, not even Eddy Spooner. I've never been as scared in my life as I was that night. The only other time that I even came close to being that terrified was the night Brandon ran a fever of a hundred and five, and I had to rush him to emergency. But even that fear was a different kind than what I experienced in Chained Lady Cave."

The quiet forcefulness of that confession startled Diana. She had the feeling she had just looked through a window into a very dark, very private corner of Colby's soul.

"Colby?"

But he had reached the flat terrain at the base of the falls where the Jeep was parked, and he had turned his attention to other matters. "Look at that idiot dog of yours," he said in disgust as he strode toward the vehicle. "Sitting right up there in the front seat as if he owned it. Talk about nerve."

"Love me, love my dog," Diana said lightly, unthinkingly. It wasn't until Colby glanced back at her with a level, searching expression that she realized just what she'd said.

"Let's compromise," he said with a slow drawl. "I will make love to you. I will tolerate your dog."

"Let's hope he's willing to go on tolerating you for a while longer. Specter is a very opinionated dog." Diana slipped into the Jeep, and pushed Specter into the back seat. The dog went willingly enough. She hoped the act of maneuvering the animal's large, furry body hid her faint flush.

How long would Colby want to continue making love to her? And how long would she fool herself into thinking that making love was close enough to the real thing to make the compromise worthwhile?

"Is this where you used to stage your midnight drag races?" Diana asked as Colby swung the Jeep out onto River Road.

"Yeah, this is it. I won a lot of cash out here."

Diana's brows drew together disapprovingly as she studied the narrow road that twisted and curved to follow the river. "But this would be a very dangerous road to drive at high speeds. If a car went out of control around some of these curves, it would wind up in the river."

"Diana, my sweet innocent, I hate to break this to you, but the fact that the road is a little treacherous is what made the racing exciting. It's also why I won most of the time. No one knew this road as well as I did. I made a scientific study of every curve and straightaway."

"Somehow I can just imagine you doing that."

"I knew exactly how fast I could go into every turn and when to start accelerating on the way out. The races always started about a mile from here and finished at the falls. If I hadn't managed to shake the competition by the time I reached that hairpin turn in the road near the bridge, I almost always lost them at the curve near the falls."

"Your teenage years were certainly a lot more exciting than mine were," Diana murmured. "But I don't want you to go to the trouble of recreating them for me. Mind slowing down a little?"

Colby flashed her an apologetic glance. "Sorry." He eased off the Jeep's accelerator. "Does my driving bother you?"

"Not really," she said honestly. "You always seem to be in complete control." That much was true. Colby drove with a smooth precision that struck her as unusual. "It's just that I'm accustomed to a slightly more sedate pace."

"You want sedate-you get sedate." He grinned at her. "This evening your wish is my command."

"So accommodating. Amazing what a little sex will do for a man's mood."

"The little sex we had this afternoon was the best I've ever had, lady."

Diana blushed warmly, aware of the lingering aftershocks that were still rippling through her. She'd flown into a whirlwind and survived but she didn't think she would ever be the same again.

Specter sat with his head hanging over Colby's shoulder for the entire drive back to Diana's cottage. The dog's tongue lolled between his teeth and moisture dripped from it in a steady stream. By the time the Jeep pulled into the small driveway, there was a large, wet patch on Colby's denim shirt.

"You know," Diana said, examining the wet shirt, "I think it may be a sign that he's beginning to accept you."

Colby glowered at the dog who stared back with an astonishingly innocent expression. "No, Diana, it's not a sign that he's beginning to accept me. It's a sign that he's getting sneakier about showing how much he hates my guts. He knows he's losing the battle so he's going underground to engage in guerrilla warfare."

"You're getting paranoid."

"I believe in never underestimating the enemy." He loped up the porch steps and opened the cabin door. "Going to invite me in for dinner?"

She laughed. "Has it occurred to you that you may be turning into as big a mooch as my dog?"

"Specter only loves you because you know how to open a can of dog food. I, on the other hand, not only like your cooking, limited though your repertoire may be, but I'm crazy about your body."

"Where does my fascinating mind come into all this?"

"Honey, two out of three ain't bad. I'm certainly not complaining."

"You chauvinistic turkey." She punched him playfully in the ribs and had the satisfaction of seeing him double up in exaggerated pain. "You want dinner here tonight? You can cook it."

"Getting tired of doing all the cooking, hmm? I was afraid it would come to this," Colby said with an air of resigned gloom. "I should never have let you seduce me this afternoon. I should have known that once you knew you had me well and truly hooked, you'd walk all over me, abuse me and generally take me for granted."

Diana stood on tiptoe and brushed her lips across his cheek. "Who," she asked softly, "seduced who this afternoon?"

"Whom," he corrected with a grin. "The question is who seduced whom. Pay attention. Us writers know all about grammar and stuff like that."

"I'm impressed, but that doesn't answer my question." Diana swept past him and switched on the light. If nothing else, the sensual encounter this afternoon had certainly put Colby Savagar into a playful mood. She realized she'd never seen him in quite this mood until now.

"Sorry. I forgot. What was the question?"

"Now you're avoiding it."

"Avoiding what?"

"The question."

"Speaking of questions, I've got one for you."

She paused at the kitchen door, aware that he had lingered behind her in the hallway. She glanced back curiously. Colby was eyeing the letter and envelope she'd left on the hall table beside the vase of flowers.

"What's your question?" Diana asked pointedly.

He looked up, much of the playfulness in his expression gone. "Who's Aaron Crown?" He gave the letter a flick that sent it skidding to the far end of the table.

"My boss," she said slowly. "Or, to be more accurate, my ex-boss."

Colby followed her into the kitchen. "Why's he writing to you?"

She shrugged, pretending to ignore the faint challenge in Colby's voice. She pulled a head of lettuce out of the refrigerator. "Two reasons, I suppose. One, because we've worked together for quite a while and we're friends, and two, because he wants me to come back to my old job at Carruthers and Yale as soon as possible."

"Doing that accounting stuff you were doing before you took a leave of absence?"

"Yes." Colby had not displayed much interest in her job. He had only a vague idea of what she did for a living and did not realize just how much her career meant to her. Perhaps he simply didn't care. "Let's see you put together a salad. I'll open some wine and pour us both a drink."

"I thought it was the man's job to open the wine and sit around watching while the woman washed vegetables."

"I'm giving you credit for being somewhat liberated." She maneuvered the corkscrew into the bottle.

Colby hoisted the lettuce, his gaze speculative. "You said you took a leave of absence from that job of yours because you didn't get the promotion you expected."

"That's right. I was going to resign outright, but Aaron convinced me to take some time off and think things over. He said I'd been working too hard for too many years."

"You never mentioned this Aaron Crown before."

"Didn't I?"

"No, Diana, you didn't. Stop playing games with me. I read the first couple of paragraphs of that letter out there in the hall. Crown is practically begging you to come back to work for him. Are you sure he isn't more than just your boss?"

Diana sat down in a kitchen chair and put her feet up on the chair across from her. She sipped her wine, patted Specter on the head and thought about Aaron Crown.

Good-looking in a corporate kind of way, well-dressed in a corporate kind of way, congenial in a corporate kind of way, Aaron Crown should have been able to go very far in the corporate empire of Carruthers and Yale. And he certainly had risen fast enough when he had Diana Prentice around to make him look good. It would be interesting to see how well he did on his own.

"No," she said quietly. "Aaron has never been anything more than just my boss."

There was silence for a long moment as Colby tore lettuce. "I'm beginning to realize something," he said finally.

"What?"

"There's a lot I don't know about you."

Diana smiled into her wineglass. "You mean now that you've had your wicked way with me, you're finally getting curious about me?"

"First things first, I always say. I'm very good at establishing priorities and believe me, making love with you was number one on my list. Where do you keep the olive oil and vinegar?"

"Second cupboard on the right."

When Colby opened the wrong door, Specter came to attention and produced a warning growl.

"What the hell's the matter with him now?" Colby demanded.

"You've just opened the cupboard where I keep his dog food. Maybe he doesn't trust you around his food."

"Maybe he shouldn't trust me. We're enemies." Colby smiled slightly and closed the cupboard door. "The only thing I care about is whether or not you trust me. Do you, Diana?"

She sipped her wine and studied him. "I still don't know you very well."

"You're trying to sidestep the issue." He leaned back against the tiled counter and picked up the glass of wine she'd poured for him.

Diana took a deep breath. "I must trust you on some level, or I wouldn't have spent the afternoon doing what I did with you."

Colby nodded in satisfaction. "Yeah, that's the way I figured it, too." He turned back to the lettuce. "Did I ever tell you I make the world's best Caesar salad?"

"No, I don't believe you ever mentioned it."

"Wait until you've tasted it."

"Where did you learn to cook?" Diana asked curiously.

"From books. I had a kid to raise, remember? I decided I owed Brandon something besides frozen dinners and pizza, although he would have been just as happy with that level of cooking. I learned a lot of things about raising kids from books. I also found out the books aren't always right."

"No, I don't imagine they are. Did you want a child, Colby?"

"Not at the age of nineteen, I didn't," he said with an ironic twist of his mouth. "But I didn't have much choice in the matter. One fine day Brandon arrived and that settled it. There wasn't time to worry about whether or not I wanted a kid. I had one. What about you?"

The intimate question surprised her. Colby didn't ask such questions. Diana stared into her wine. She had wanted him to be curious about her, but not on this particular subject. She was not prepared to give him a full and complete answer, so she hedged with a portion of the truth. "I used to think about it sometimes. But somehow the right time and the right man never came together."

"Never?"

"Well, there was a man once, back when I was just starting my career. I was about twenty-five. I thought perhaps he might be the one. Things were very good for a while. But it turned out that he'd been on the rebound when he came into my life. When his ex-lover showed up, he realized that she was the one he really wanted."

"He walked out on you?"

"I've always been extremely grateful the ex-lover showed up before the wedding instead of after it," Diana said dryly. "At any rate, after that I quit thinking about a family and concentrated on building my career. Now I'm thirty-four and I'm content with what I have."

"You don't wonder what you missed?"

"Not really. Not often. I've built a full life based on a successful career, good friends and a variety of interests. I don't think I would have made a really terrific mother, anyway," she added with an attempt at lightening the unexpectedly tense atmosphere. "I've never been overwhelmed by the cuteness of kids and the thought of trying to get a child through the teenage years would traumatize me."

"It can be rough, all right. You get through it by doing what has to be done. But now that I'm a qualified expert, I'm more than happy to retire from the field. Raising kids is a job for starry-eyed people in their twenties who don't know what they're getting into."

"That I can believe." She stood up. "After thirty, you're old enough to be able to see what an undertaking it really is. At thirty-four, I'd be absolutely horrified at the prospect of getting pregnant."

Colby glanced at her with sudden understanding. "It would throw your whole carefully structured life into chaos, wouldn't it? It would change everything for you."

"Yes, frankly, it would," she shot back, miffed by his tone. "You sound as if you think it might be a good thing for me to have everything changed in my life."

Colby sliced a blood-red tomato into small chunks. "Yeah," he said. "Having a kid would definitely change everything for you."

"Well, that's one thing I don't have to worry about, do I?" she said very firmly.

"No," he agreed. "That's one thing you don't have to worry about. But maybe there are a few other, less drastic changes you could make in your life."

"Such as?"

"Such as moving in with me for the rest of the summer. Being the generous man that I am, I'm even willing to take your stupid dog."

4

He hadn't liked her answer but he'd handled it with his customary cool. Probably because he was convinced it wouldn't take him long to change her mind.

Suit yourself, he'd said. *No need to make a decision this minute. We'll talk about it some other time.*

Diana thought about Colby's implicit assumption for a long time after he'd left that night. He was probably right. She was already sleeping with him. Why not move in with him?

For the summer.

Deep inside, Diana knew that was the part that grated. Colby Savagar wasn't looking any further ahead than the end of the summer. He was certainly honest enough about that.

Restlessly, Diana pushed back the covers and left the bed. Specter got to his feet as she put on a robe and found her slippers. He looked up at her questioningly.

"Want a midnight snack?" Diana asked.

Specter's large, floppy ears snapped forward with eager attention, and he crowded close as Diana went down the hall.

"No need to ask you twice, is there? You and Colby both respond well to the stimulus of food."

Specter probably didn't care to be lumped together with his archrival but he kept quiet about it. He watched alertly as Diana dug out a dog biscuit and handed it to him. Specter took it from her fingers with great delicacy and then proceeded to swallow the snack in one chomp and a gulp.

"My, what big teeth you have," Diana said as she found a cracker for herself. "Colby's right. Those teeth do make a person wonder what you did for a living before you got this cushy job as my pal."

Specter grinned in what he probably felt was an engaging manner. Unfortunately the canine smile only succeeded in showing more teeth.

"Don't do that," Diana instructed firmly. "You remind me of Colby."

She sat down at the kitchen table to munch her cracker. The copy of Shock Value Colby had given her a few weeks earlier lay nearby. She was still trying to get the last paragraph of chapter ten out of her mind from yesterday's reading.

She hesitated a minute and then, unable to help herself, flipped the book open to find out what had happened to the main character, a man named Donnelly.

All he could think in those last seconds was that it wasn't right for a creature of such evil to appear in such innocent guise. A monster should look like a monster. A man should be able to tell the difference between good and evil at a glance.

But he had been too blind to see the truth and now the truth would kill him. Slowly, horribly, unmercifully, it would kill him.

Diana shuddered a little and quickly closed the book. She knew better than to read more of Shock Value at this time of night. She looked down at Specter.

"I think Donnelly's going to make it," she told the dog. "But we're all going to get our socks scared off in the process. Where do you suppose a writer of horror novels gets his ideas? I don't think I would want to dream Colby's dreams."

She got up and started to turn out the hall light. Aaron Crown's letter still lay on the small table near the door. Diana remembered Colby's reaction to it.

"The man spends one afternoon making love to me and he figures he's got a right to read my mail, Specter. Something tells me Colby's the possessive type. He's also arrogant, proud and capable of carrying a grudge against an entire town. I wonder why he came back to Fulbrook Corners this summer."

Specter gave her a look that clearly said, who cares? Then he yawned and padded down the hall to the bedroom.

Colby looked up from the screen of the word processor and watched the morning sunlight fill the valley. In the distance Chained Lady Falls poured silver down the cliffs and Colby's body tightened as he remembered the events of the previous afternoon.

Making love to Diana had resulted in exactly the effect he'd half feared. It had deepened his need for her rather than slaked his thirst.

Why had she said no when he'd asked her to move in with him? They were already sleeping together. It seemed ridiculous not to share one house for the summer. He didn't think she was the type who would care what a townful of strangers thought about her living arrangements, but then, maybe she was.

There was a lot he didn't know about her yet. Colby was just beginning to realize how badly he wanted to know more, now that he had established the physical bond.

The compelling curiosity he was experiencing bothered him. In the first place, it wasn't like him. In the second place, she wasn't even his type. Diana was too self-contained, too confident of her own ability to take care of herself, too focused on her career. A regular twentieth-century amazon.

All in all, there was something about her that let him know she didn't really need a man in her life. A man had to work damned hard at convincing her he had his uses, even if only in bed. Diana was certainly different from every other woman he had ever known.

But in some ways he couldn't quite define, Colby sensed she was also a little like him-self-reliant, accustomed to making her own rules in life, opinionated. She would never expect anyone else to step in and clean up any mess in which she happened to find herself. She had obviously been taking care of herself for a long time.

There was an underlying feminine pride in her that he knew was ultimately bound to clash with his own masculine confidence.

But he had discovered to his profound satisfaction that he could make her shiver in his arms.

"Damn it to hell."

He was going to drive himself crazy if he kept thinking about her. He had a chapter to finish today. Colby punched the key that would save the paragraphs on the screen and then got to his feet. He'd been working since six. It was almost time to get the mail. If he got to the post office around ten-fifteen, he would probably run into Diana and they could have coffee together. Then they could make plans for the evening.

Twenty minutes later he grinned briefly to himself as he pulled into the small post office parking lot. Diana was already there. His smile faded as he remembered the letter she had collected yesterday. He hoped there wouldn't be another one from her boss. Colby had read enough in Crown's letter to know he didn't like the guy.

He didn't like any man who thought he could write to Diana in such friendly, familiar terms. The jerk had been pleading for Diana to come back to her old job, and there had been something in the tone of that plea that had really annoyed Colby. Aaron Crown had made it sound as if he had a claim on Diana, as if he had rights over her.

Colby vaulted from the Jeep and walked past Diana's sedate four-door Buick. Specter glared at him from the front seat.

"Forget it, you big ugly mutt, there's nothing you can do about it. I'm here to stay."

Specter growled just loud enough for Colby to hear.

"Hey, Savagar!"

Colby turned at the familiar voice. Eddy Spooner was hailing him from across the street. Colby waved a hand in acknowledgment. "Morning, Eddy. How's it going?"

Eddy glanced casually up and down the quiet street and then trotted across it. He was wearing his usual outfit, a faded pair of combat fatigues and heavy boots. He had a billed cap on his head and he was wiping his hands on an oily cloth. There was a hopeful smile on his face as he joined Colby.

"Can't complain," Eddy said. "Been waitin' for you to come into town this morning. How 'bout havin' that beer you and I talked about?"

Colby sighed inwardly but told himself he really couldn't put it off any longer. Twenty years was a long time but he couldn't ever forget that Spooner had once been the closest thing to a friend he'd ever had in Fulbrook Corners.

"Sure, Eddy. Sounds good."

"Come on out to the house this evening. I get off work at five."

The last thing Colby wanted to do was waste an evening drinking with Eddy Spooner. He had far more interesting plans for tonight. "Uh, I'm busy this evening, Eddy."

"That Prentice broad, huh? Can't say I blame you. She looks real slick. Real cool in those fancy clothes, but I bet she's probably a real hot piece of"

"Don't say it, Spooner."

Spooner blinked at the blunt warning. Then his grin widened and he held up both hands in a placating gesture. "Okay, okay, I get the picture. No offense. So, when do you want to get together for the beer? We got a lot to talk about, old buddy. Tomorrow's my day off."

He'd better set a time and get it over with, Colby decided. "Right. Let's make it tomorrow. I work in the mornings. I'll come out to your place in the afternoon. I'll bring the beer. That work for you?"

"Sure, Colby. That'll work just fine," Spooner agreed happily. "See ya."

"Sure." Colby watched Spooner make his way back across the street. Everyone in town had said Eddy Spooner wouldn't amount to much. They'd said the same thing about Colby Savagar.

They'd been wrong about Colby, and it looked like Eddy was at least managing to hold down a full-time job so maybe they'd been wrong about him, too. It was obvious Spooner wasn't drawing an executive salary, but he wasn't on welfare, either. Good for him.

Served the bastards right to be proven wrong. Neither Colby nor Spooner had wound up in jail or living on the streets despite all the predictions.

That kind of shared past produced a bond of sorts. He'd have that beer with Eddy Spooner. Maybe a couple of beers.

Diana was waiting for him inside the post office. She was just dropping a handful of letters into her big leather shoulder bag. Colby tried to see some of the return addresses, but he couldn't get a close enough look.

"Hi, honey," he said walking straight up to her and kissing her full on the mouth in front of Bernice and a cluster of post office patrons. "We've got to stop meeting like this."

Diana's cheeks turned a soft pink. She knew what he was doing. He was establishing a very obvious claim on her. If there was anyone left in town who wasn't aware that Colby Savagar was probably sleeping with that Portland woman who'd taken the Martin place for the summer, he would certainly know it by this afternoon. Colby was satisfied with the faint blush that bloomed in his victim's cheeks. He grinned.

"Hello, Colby," Diana said with deceptively bland politeness. "How are you this morning?"

"Take a guess," he invited, deliberately lacing the words with sensual satisfaction as he walked to the counter. "Hi, Bernice. Anything for me?"

"Right here, Colby." Bernice hastened to hand him a long white envelope that bore his agent's return address.

A check. Colby wondered if he'd ever get over the sense of amazed exhilaration he experienced when someone actually paid him real money for a book.

"You're in luck, Diana." Colby waved the envelope at her. "I think I can afford to feed you tonight." He started toward her with a wide grin and then halted abruptly as the post office doors swung inward, admitting two newcomers.

"Hi, Dad."

"Brandon." Colby stared at the lean, dark-haired, brown-eyed young man in the doorway. His son was the last person he'd expected to see this morning. "What the hell are you doing here? You're supposed to be working in Portland."

Brandon Savagar moved a few steps into the room, his arm wrapped protectively around the shoulders of a strikingly pretty little blue-eyed redhead who looked about nineteen.

"Surprise," Brandon said with an almost aggressive cheerfulness. "There was a grease fire at the restaurant where I was working. Place is closed for two weeks. So I decided to come visit you. When I asked the guy at the station across the street for directions to the house, he said you were in here."

"Yeah. Sure. Good to see you." Colby realized Diana was looking at him with obvious interest. He recovered quickly and made the introductions. "Diana, this is my son, Brandon. Brandon, this is Diana Prentice. She's a, uh, friend of mine."

"How do you do, Miss Prentice?" Brandon said, exhibiting the manners Colby had drummed into him after reading a book on the importance of children learning proper social skills.

"It's a pleasure to meet you, Brandon," Diana responded gently

Brandon glanced at his father. "Dad, this is a, uh, friend of mine. Robyn Lambert. Robyn, I'd like you to meet my father."

"I'm so excited to meet you, Mr. Savagar," Robyn said in a soft, shy voice. Her blue eyes were riveted on Colby. "I've read all your books. They're fabulous."

Colby looked at her, aware of the peculiar expression of determination in his son's eyes. His heart sank. A terrible premonition began to take shape. He fought it down. No need for panic. This was just another one of Brandon's girlfriends. At least the kid had good taste in literature.

"Hello, Robyn. I'm glad you like my books." He glanced at Diana and saw the laughter in her eyes.

"Congratulations, Robyn, you said exactly the right thing," Diana remarked. "I'm afraid that when I first met Colby, I didn't have the faintest idea who he was. I'd never read a horror novel in my life."

"She still hasn't," Colby put in. "She can't seem to get more than halfway through Shock Value."

Robyn looked astonished. "But that's one of his best."

"That's right," Brandon said seriously, his pride in his father very obvious. " Shock Value hit all the major bestseller lists. It was Dad's big breakthrough book."

"Enough," Diana cried. "I surrender. I admit I'm culturally illiterate when it comes to horror tales. I swear I'll finish the book, even if it scares me to death."

"Come on," Colby instructed, taking Diana's arm. "Let's get out of here. Brandon, you and Robyn can follow me out to Aunt Jesse's place. I'll be with you in a few minutes. I want to talk to Diana."

"Okay, Dad. We'll be in the car." Brandon nodded toward the sleek little two-seater Mazda Colby had bought for him when he'd gone off to college.

Colby frowned at Robyn Lambert's dancing red ponytail as the girl walked toward the car with Brandon.

"Only a nineteen-year-old looks that good in a pair of jeans," Diana said laconically. "But don't get any ideas. She's too young for you."

"You can say that again," Colby muttered. "Too young for Brandon, too. Or else he's too young for her. I'm not sure which."

"They both look about the same age."

"That's the whole problem. They're just kids." He leaned against the door on the driver's side of the Buick and wrapped his fingers lightly around Diana's forearms. "Now about tonight."

Specter immediately began to grumble menacingly. The dog leaned over to stick his nose through the open window, which put his teeth very close to Colby's thigh. Colby straightened quickly and stepped away from the car.

"Stupid dog."

Specter growled again, pleased at having made Colby move.

"Now don't you two start calling each other names," Diana admonished.

"Tell him that," Colby advised. "Listen, I wanted to invite myself over for dinner again tonight, but it looks like I've got company."

"Brandon looks a lot like you. Except for his eyes."

"He's got his mother's eyes," Colby said impatiently.

Diana snapped her fingers. "I knew they looked familiar. Margaret Fulbrook has those eyes."

"Probably. Honey, I don't want to talk about Brandon's eyes. As I said, I was going to invite myself to your place for dinner"

"As usual?"

"Right. As usual. But now we'll have to change our plans."

"I wasn't aware we had plans."

"Diana, don't give me that wide-eyed, fuzz-brained look. It reminds me of your dog." Diana grinned and, exasperated, Colby bent his head to kiss the amusement from her soft mouth. "Now, then," he said a moment later. "As I was saying, we'll have to alter our plans. Come over to my place tonight. Brandon and I will fix dinner."

"Brandon knows how to cook?"

"Sure. I taught him how to read a cookbook."

Diana smiled quizzically. "You know something, Colby-I think you must have been a very good father."

"Sometimes the best thing you can say about being a father is that you survived and so did the kid. How about dinner tonight?"

"How can I resist letting you cook for me again?" She kissed him lightly. "I was very impressed last night. You were right about the Caesar salad. Best in the world."

"Told you so. See you at five. Leave the dog at home."

Diana did as ordered and left Specter at the cottage. He had not been thrilled with the arrangement, and shortly after arriving at Colby's place, Diana, herself, had begun to question the wisdom of leaving the dog behind.

Specter made a great conversation piece, if nothing else, and it was obvious to Diana that the small party needed something to distract it. A definite tension was building between Colby and his son. Robyn Lambert seemed nervous.

"Perfect tacos," Diana said midway through the meal as conversation came to a halt. She tried a woman-to-woman smile on Robyn. "Men are so well suited to the kitchen, don't you think?"

Robyn blinked, her gaze uncertain as she looked at Brandon. "I don't know," she mumbled, nibbling on a tortilla chip.

Diana tried again. "Brandon, this salsa is just right. Hotter than a sidewalk in August. Did you make it, or did Colby?"

"Dad made it." Brandon gave her a small, uneasy smile and gallantly tried to follow her lead. "He likes it hot enough to set fire to the bowl."

"Brandon made the meat filling," Colby said quietly as he built another taco for himself. He took his time arranging layers of meat, cheese, lettuce, tomato and salsa. The words were his first in several long minutes.

"It's wonderful," Diana said quickly. "Some lucky woman is going to get a terrific husband. Imagine finding one who can cook."

Instantly she realized she had made a terrible faux pas. If the silence had weighed heavily on the table before, it was now crushing everything in sight. Robyn stared at her plate, her lower lip trembling. Brandon's expression was unaccountably grim. And Colby just sat at the head of the table taking savage chunks out of his taco.

Diana thought about getting up and leaving then and there. She wanted no part of a Savagar family quarrel. But something about Robyn Lambert's wounded blue eyes made her decide to stay. It wouldn't be fair to leave the poor girl alone here with Colby and his son if real trouble was brewing.

Without warning, Brandon set his glass of cola down hard on the table. "It's funny you should mention marriage, Miss Prentice," he said tightly. "The main reason Robyn and I are here is because we wanted to tell Dad we're thinking of getting married before going back to school in the fall."

No wonder Colby was sitting there looking as though he were about to explode. "I see," Diana said brightly. "How, uh, interesting." She could not think of anything else to say next.

"Dad doesn't think so," Brandon said.

Colby dropped the last of his unfinished taco onto his plate and fixed his son with a forbidding glare. "I think the idea is goddamned stupid, that's what I think."

Tears trembled in Robyn's eyes. Brandon's face hardened.

Diana winced. The gloves were off. She knew she and poor Robyn were about to witness a full-blown quarrel between the two men. "Excuse me," she said, rising swiftly. "I don't think I want to hear this. Robyn, would you like to come with me? Neither one of us needs to listen to these two do battle."

"Sit down," Colby said through his teeth.

"Give me one good reason," Diana invited.

Colby drew a deep breath, clearly making a superhuman effort to control himself. "Brandon and I will discuss the matter later. This isn't the time or the place."

"True." Diana sat down cautiously. "But I wasn't sure you realized it."

Brandon looked at her with respect. Apparently he wasn't accustomed to hearing his father handled in that manner. He hesitated nervously for a moment and then came up with what he undoubtedly assumed would be a safe topic of conversation.

"Dad said you were just here for the summer, Miss Prentice. How did you happen to pick Fulbrook Corners? From what Dad's told me and from what I've seen, this isn't exactly the vacation spot of the western hemisphere."

Diana took pity on him. She smiled slightly. "I'm not sure why I picked this little town. I took a leave of absence from my job in Portland, and I felt I had to get away from the city for a while. I wanted a complete change of scene. As I told Colby, I just got out a map and Fulbrook Corners caught my eye. It turned out there were a few cottages available, so I took one for the summer."

Brandon nodded. "How come you took a leave from your job?"

"Well, it's a complicated story. I was in line for a promotion at the manufacturing firm where I had been working for the past four years. I felt I deserved the promotion. I'd worked extremely hard for it and, to be honest, I thought it was in the bag."

"What kind of work do you do?" Brandon asked.

"I have a degree in accounting and one in business administration. I was working as second-in-command in the office of a division controller at Carruthers and Yale."

"So you did financial forecasting and things like that?"

Diana nodded, delighted by his interest. "That's right. I helped work up the forecasts and also did a lot of accounting administration work. It's all computerized these days, you know."

"So what happened to the big promotion?"

"As I said, I didn't get it. When it didn't come through, I was forced to reconsider my situation. It became apparent that women could advance to the ranks of middle management but no higher at Carruthers and Yale. The men at the top had drawn the line at the divisional level."

Robyn looked up, showing faint interest in the conversation. "You think you were denied the job because of sexual discrimination?"

"I have to assume that was the reason. There was no one else as qualified for the job as I was and everyone knew it."

"But that's illegal," Robyn said with a puzzled frown.

"I've got news for you, Robyn. Just because there are now laws in place to protect women from discrimination on the job doesn't mean it's always easy to get employers to obey them. In my case, I could never prove discrimination and there was no real way to fight it."

"So you took a leave to think things over." Brandon nodded understandingly. "Going to go back?"

"No. I've done a lot of thinking, and I'm sure I'll end up resigning my position. You have to know when to cut your losses in the corporate world," Diana explained calmly.

"But didn't the whole situation make you mad?" Brandon persisted.

Diana looked up from her taco and for an instant all the helpless fury she had experienced at the time was mirrored in her eyes. "Oh, yes," she whispered tightly, "it made me angry. More angry than I've ever been in my entire life. Nor have I ever felt so frustrated and helpless. I had worked hard for that promotion. I'd put in countless hours of unpaid overtime. I had put out one fire after another for my boss. When I first started to work in the division, it was losing a half a million a year. Within a year we were breaking even, and six months later we were clearing a profit. That division of Carruthers and Yale now makes a million and a half a year. And I had a lot to do with the turnaround, damn it."

"Oh, wow," Brandon said, looking rather awed. Colby and Robyn were staring at her as if they hadn't noticed her sitting there at the table until now.

"But where I really went wrong," Diana continued with barely suppressed violence, "was believing the upper management of Carruthers and Yale when it claimed it would treat women equally on the job. I put my faith in a bunch of male executives who lied through their teeth. They used me, but when it came time to promote me, they ignored me. Yes, Brandon, it made me angry."

Another taut silence descended on the table as the last of Diana's fury evaporated. She had her temper in hand almost immediately, but Colby was still looking at her with a stunned expression.

"Christ, Diana, I hadn't realized it had been like that for you," Colby said bluntly. "Why didn't you tell me how bad it was?"

She shrugged. "You never asked."

"No," he admitted slowly. "I didn't, did I?"

Robyn looked genuinely puzzled. "But I thought it was different for women now."

"Sometimes it is. Sometimes it isn't. Mostly it isn't. Not at the higher corporate levels."

Brandon spoke up. "How will you know if it's going to be any better at your next job?"

"Good question," Diana said, trying to lighten her voice. "It's one of the risks women face in the business world. The only way to know for sure it might be better would be to start my own business, I suppose." She looked at Robyn. "What type of career are you thinking of for yourself, Robyn?"

Robyn chewed her lip nervously and looked quickly at Brandon. "I'm not sure yet. I mean I haven't thought too much about it. It'll probably depend on what Brandon does. That is, I mean if we, uh;md" She broke off abruptly.

"Surely you're not basing your career decisions on what Brandon does, or whether you get married," Diana said in genuine amazement. "Every woman has a responsibility to be able to take care of herself."

"You sound like one of those hard-line feminists we have to study in college," Robyn muttered.

"No," Diana said easily. "I'm just practical. I've seen enough of life and the world to know that when the chips are down the only one you can really count on is yourself. Right, Colby?"

Colby studied her intently. "Yeah. Right. Do you want another taco, Diana?"

She laughed and got up. "No thanks, I'm stuffed. That was a delicious meal. Seeing as how you and Brandon fixed the dinner, I think Robyn and I can handle the dishes. Okay with you, Robyn?"

Robyn nodded reluctantly. Diana got the impression she didn't want to be separated from Brandon by even a few feet. But she got up and began collecting dishes.

"This is a creepy old house, isn't it?" Robyn said as she followed Diana into the kitchen.

Diana looked around at the old two-story structure. The house was in decent repair, but there was an undeniable air of shabby gloom about it. The floorboards squeaked. The walls were bare. The appliances were old. The halls were dark. The furniture was ancient and worn-out, and the drapes were so faded that it was difficult to detect any sign of their original flower print.

There was something quietly, eerily sad about Aunt Jesse's old house, as if the woman's unfulfilled dreams still hovered there.

"Yes, it is a little creepy. Sort of fits the image of the kind of house a horror writer should live in, though," Diana said briskly.

Robyn gnawed on her lip again. "Mr. Savagar hates me."

"Don't be silly. He can't possibly hate you. He hardly knows you. It's the idea of you and Brandon getting married that he doesn't like. He feels you're both too young."

"Brandon said his father was married at nineteen."

"Which is precisely why he's bound to be opposed to Brandon marrying at the same age. He knows nineteen is too young to make that kind of commitment."

"You're on Mr. Savagar's side, aren't you?"

"Not exactly. I do have my own opinions on some things, though, and I'll admit I don't think a woman should consider marriage until she's established a career of her own. It's just too big a risk."

"You sound just like my parents. They're always telling me what I should do. Always trying to dictate my life. They think I'm still a child and they treat me like one."

"They probably just don't want you to make any serious mistakes at your age," Diana said soothingly, thinking that she was highly unqualified to be lecturing a teenager on how to conduct her life. She'd had absolutely zero experience in child-rearing.

"Brandon and I are adults, you know. We can make our own decisions."

"Part of being an adult is not feeling it's necessary to tell other adults that you are one."

"What's that supposed to mean?" Robyn appeared genuinely bewildered.

"Never mind."

"It's not as if the people who don't want us to get married know what they're talking about," Robyn continued earnestly. "Take yourself, for example. You're a lot older than me, you've got a career and everything and you've never married. Do you think I want to end up like you? And look at Mr. Savagar. He's not married either. My parents may be married, but they're always yelling at each other. Always fighting. The fact is, none of you know what real love is."

Diana saw the incipient tears in Robyn's eyes. She gave her a wry smile. "You may have a point, Robyn."

5

"Couldn't wait to get out of there, could you?" Colby demanded roughly as he followed Diana into her cottage an hour later. He tossed her car keys down on the hall table. He had insisted on driving her home and intended to walk back to his place. "Can't blame you. I wish I could walk away from that mess myself."

"It's a common enough situation, Colby. Just a couple of young people in the throes of first love."

"A couple of young fools, you mean. Easy enough for you to sound calm. You're not the one who has to deal with it." He shoved his fingers through his hair. "Marriage. I can't believe it. After all I taught that kid. After all the lectures I gave him on not tying himself down to the first pretty face who comes along. Damn it, Diana, what the hell am I going to do?"

"I don't know," Diana said gently, pouring him a glass of brandy. Specter watched broodingly. She tossed him a dog biscuit.

"I can't let him do it. He'll ruin his whole life. He's got a great future waiting for him. The last thing he needs is to be saddled with a wife and maybe a couple of kids. I've got to make him see that. I can't let him make the same damned fool mistake I made."

"Stop pacing, Colby, you're making Specter nervous."

Colby swore under his breath and swallowed half the brandy in his glass. He looked at Diana mutely for a long moment. "I hadn't realized how upset you were about your situation at Carruthers and Yale."

She sipped her own brandy reflectively. "I'll find another job. I've got contacts in the business world. I've got a good track record. Something will turn up."

"You're cool enough about it now, but when Brandon brought up the subject at dinner, it was clear you'd been through hell. It really got to you. It was a major career disaster for you, wasn't it?"

"These things happen in business."

"Did that boss of yours-Aaron Crown-did he go to bat for you?"

"Aaron said he did everything he could for me. Gave me the highest possible recommendation. Tried to talk the powers that be into making good on their promise to deal fairly with a woman in management. But upper management was inflexible."

"And I'll bet you were as cool as a cucumber right through it all. No tears. No rage. No big emotional scenes and no recriminations."

"One of the first things a woman learns in business is that men do not respect, let alone understand, what they think of as typical female emotions. It's very important for a woman's business image that she never cry or lose her self-control around the men she works with or for."

"Maybe the management at Carruthers and Yale would have a little respect for someone's hands wrapped around their collective throats. I'd like to try it. Maybe I could convince them to be a little more flexible. They had no right to do that to you."

Specter growled, responding to the trace of genuine savagery in Colby's words.

"Thanks for the sympathy, guys," Diana said with a smile.

"Why didn't you explain just what had happened at Carruthers and Yale before?" Colby held up one palm before she could answer. "Never mind. You've already told me why. My own fault. I didn't ask."

"It's my problem. No reason you should be burdened with it."

He eyed her closely. "You're the most self-contained woman I've ever met, Diana."

"I don't think I'm any more self-contained than you are."

He considered that. "We've got a few things in common, I guess. He resumed his pacing. "Damn, I wish I could spend the night with you."

"Going back to your place to play chaperon?"

"Don't laugh at me. That's exactly what I'm going to do." Colby braced one hand against the wall and gulped the rest of the brandy. He stared out into the darkness. "Think he's sleeping with her?"

Diana was taken aback. "How would I know? You're his father and you're a man. What do you think?"

"I can't tell for sure. Maybe I don't want to know for certain. Hell, Diana, if he gets her pregnant, if he's as stupid about that kind of thing as I was at nineteen"

"I assume that along with teaching Brandon how to cook and how to use good manners, you also taught him the facts of life and how to protect himself and a woman?"

"Are you kidding? I wasn't going to have him grow up believing the usual garbled batch of rumors, misconceptions and mythical nonsense a boy picks up from his buddies. I drilled the facts into him from the time he was old enough to understand that little girls were different."

"What kind of sleeping arrangements did they request?" Diana asked. "One bedroom or two?"

"I didn't give them a chance to make a request. I put them into separate bedrooms as soon as we got back to Aunt Jesse's."

Diana couldn't restrain a burst of delighted laughter. "Poor Colby. I'm sorry," she managed when he scowled at her. "I guess it's not really very funny from your point of view."

Colby came away from the wall in a smooth, lithe movement, set down his glass and reached out to draw her quickly to her feet. "You're right. It's not funny. Brandon is a kid of nineteen. He hasn't got a glimmer of what he's getting into." Colby paused thoughtfully. "Maybe I should try to talk him into living with her for a while before they make a decision on marriage. I have a hunch the charm of the idea would fade quickly once they started playing house."

"Easy for you to suggest. You're the father of the young man involved. The parents of the young woman involved may not like the idea of their daughter living with a man at all."

"Damn."

Diana smiled up into his thoroughly frustrated eyes. "I suppose you should be getting back to your place. The duties of a chaperon are quite demanding, I understand."

Colby swore again. Then he kissed her heavily. "Later," he promised in a husky voice as he reluctantly released her. "We'll finish this later."

Specter grinned a wide doggy grin as Colby stalked out the front door.

"So, what's she like?" Eddy Spooner asked after the second beer. "She any good in bed?"

"Get stuffed, Spooner. I didn't come here to talk about Diana. She's none of your business." Colby leaned back against the front porch steps and took a swallow of beer. He was already regretting his decision to drive out here this afternoon. The bonds of past friendship were looking weaker and less meaningful by the minute.

"Okay, okay, I was just askin'." Spooner concentrated on his beer for a while. "Maybe I'm just feeling a little envious, you know? Been a long time since I had me a woman. That Miss Prentice of yours is about the first really interesting female we've had in town in ten years. She looks classy but kind of chilly. Can't blame a guy for wonderin' what she's really like."

Colby didn't respond to that. Diana was anything but cold when she lay in his arms, but he sure as hell wasn't going to share that information with Eddy Spooner or anyone else. Colby considered everything about Diana his own personal turf. He was beginning to realize he didn't want any other man even coming close to her.

He rolled the cold beer can between his palms and stared out at the swaying fir trees that surrounded the old, ramshackle house. The Spooner place looked almost the same as it had twenty years ago, he reflected. A general air of neglect still enveloped every inch of it. The front porch still sagged, and one window was boarded up. There wasn't a scrap of paint left on the wood. Eddy's father had always been too drunk most of the time to tend to home repairs.

Both front and back yards were still filled with weeds and the skeletal remains of old automobiles. Eddy's old Camaro was parked in front. The paint job on the car matched the design on Eddy's fatigues, but Colby knew the engine would be in perfect condition. Eddy's one great passion in life had been cars, Colby remembered.

"You ever marry, Eddy?"

Eddy closed his eyes and rested his head against a post. "Yeah. Girl I met right after I got out of the army. Her name was Angie. Lasted about a year. Then the bitch ran off with some dude from Seattle."

Colby nodded in silent commiseration. "Never tried it again, huh?"

"There was another one. A sexy little redhead. I thought she'd be okay. Had the wedding all set and everything. I was gonna move down to Portland and find a good job, you know. But just before the big day, I found out she was still sleepin' with an old boyfriend of hers. Figured there was no point tryin' again after that. Bitches are all the same."

"You like working at the gas station in town?"

Spooner shrugged. "It's a job. Nothin' else has ever worked out for me, not the way things worked out for you. Came close a time or two, but things fell apart."

"Close to what?" Colby glanced at him curiously.

"Close to gettin' a real break." Spooner stared at Colby through narrowed eyes. "Once, just after the army, I met a guy who had a line on something real hot. Something he'd set up during his tour in the Philippines. He was gonna cut me in on a piece of the action. But things folded."

"Tough." Colby wondered what the action had been, and decided it would be better not to ask.

"Then, another time, I thought I had something set with some dude who owned a string of massage parlors. I was gonna manage a couple of them for him. Sort of be a bouncer, you know? Except I was gonna get a piece of the business. But that didn't work out either. There were one or two other things but, like I said, nothin' ever worked out. Everything always went wrong."

"So you came back here. Never thought you'd wind up in Fulbrook Corners, Eddy. I thought you hated this town as much as I did."

"I still hate it," Spooner muttered. "But after Pa died, I owned this place free and clear, and Clark gave me that job down at the station. What was I supposed to do?"

"I don't know," Colby said honestly, hating the whine in Eddy's voice and simultaneously feeling guilty for his reaction. Eddy's life had been a hard one.

"Hell, you wouldn't understand. You got lucky. You weren't trapped here the way I was."

"No." Luck came in a variety of guises, Colby decided.

"You always came out on top." Eddy was silent for a moment. "Saw your kid in town today. Knew who he was the minute he drove into the station. He looks like you, but he's got those Fulbrook eyes, don't he?"

"Yeah. He's got Cynthia's eyes."

"You gonna introduce him to old lady Fulbrook?"

Colby's mouth twisted slightly. "Are you kidding? She met him once when he was a baby and told me she never wanted to see him again."

"Dumb question, I guess." Spooner paused to open another can of beer. "I read one of those books you wrote. Shock something or other."

Colby felt a flicker of surprise. "Did you? I didn't think you liked to read, Eddy."

"TV's more interestin' than books, usually, especially now that Sam's renting movies down at the grocery store. Got me a VCR and old Sam's got a few of them X-rated flicks he keeps behind the counter."

"I see. Old Sam sounds like he's decided to move with the times. What made you read Shock Value?"

"Dunno. Guess I was kind of curious about what you'd been up to. Everybody in town was talkin' about that Shock book when it came out. Reckon they couldn't believe it was you who wrote it. Bessie must have sold a hundred copies the first week it came into her shop. She said everyone in town wanted to read it. Maybe they was worried you'd put a couple of local folks in the story."

Colby couldn't suppress a certain grim satisfaction. "It was the first book of mine to hit some of the major bestseller lists."

"Make you rich?"

Colby grinned. "Not exactly, but I'll admit it sure changed a few things for me and Brandon."

"I always figured that of the two of us, you'd probably be the one who'd make out okay."

The bitter resignation in Spooner's voice bothered Colby. "It's not too late for you, Eddy. You've got no obligations. No wife and kids to tie you down. You're only forty-one. Why not get out of this town and try someplace else?"

"Sure. Doin' what, for instance?"

"You're a first-class mechanic. You always had a way with cars. You could get a job in Seattle or Portland or maybe somewhere in California. Good mechanics are always in demand, especially by people who own those foreign jobs. Hell, some of those folks would probably put you on a retainer just to keep their BMW or Mercedes running."

"I told you, Colby. I already tried to get out of here. Things always fall through. I never had the magic touch like you did."

"There was no magic touch, Eddy."

"Who are you trying to kid? You always got the breaks. I couldn't believe it when you actually talked Cynthia Fulbrook into marrying you. Richest, prettiest girl in town. Nobody could believe it. People talked about it for months after you and she left. Old Lady Fulbrook and her old man ranted and raved and cursed you up one side and down the other. Then old man Fulbrook croaked and we heard about Cynthia dying in that car crash. Old lady Fulbrook hasn't been quite the same since. Serves her right, the old bat. Always thinkin' Fulbrooks was so much better than everyone else."

Colby concentrated on an old tire that was lying in the front yard. He didn't want to think about Margaret Fulbrook. "When did your father die?"

"The year I finished my hitch in the army. Drunk as a skunk, as usual. Went out huntin' and fell off the top of Chained Lady Falls. No loss. To tell you the truth, I was kind of surprised he bothered to leave me this place. Course, who else did he have to leave it to?"

"That's a fact. You were his only kin." Colby remembered the bastard who had been Eddy's father. The man had been violent when he drank. Eddy had suffered from that violence frequently when he was younger.

However erratic life had been with Aunt Jesse, however emotionally neglected Colby had been while Jesse pursued her poetry, at least he'd never been subjected to physical violence the way Spooner had.

Eddy finished his beer. "You still hate this town as much as you used to?"

"Yeah," said Colby. "I still hate it."

"Why'd you come back?"

"I needed a place to finish the book I'm working on. And I decided it was time to get rid of Aunt Jesse's place. Too much trouble keeping it rented to summer tourists."

"Larry Brockton down at the real estate office said once that you'd given him instructions to keep the place fixed up and rented out during the summer."

"I didn't know what else to do with it after Aunt Jesse died."

"So you're here to take care of that old business and finish another one of them horror books, huh?"

"Right. I thought Fulbrook Corners might offer some inspiration for my writing," Colby explained dryly.

"Inspiration! Here? That's a laugh."

"It is, isn't it?"

"Come to think of it, Chained Lady Falls might be sort of inspirational for a horror writer," Spooner remarked slowly. "Remember that night we were gonna spend there?"

"I remember it."

"You never told anyone I didn't stay with you in that damned cave."

"No point."

"Guess I never thanked you for keepin' your mouth shut about that."

"Forget it, Eddy. That was a long time ago. It doesn't matter now."

"That's kind of what I figured. It doesn't matter much now. Nothing does."

* * *

Diana stood staring up at Chained Lady Falls. The billowing mist dampened her hair as well as the oxford cloth shirt she was wearing with her khaki trousers. The rocks at the base of the falls were slippery. She'd almost fallen once or twice, trying to get close enough to see the hidden entrance to the cave. She still couldn't spot it through the thundering water.

And she still wasn't sure why she had driven out here to take another look at the falls this afternoon. Something about the place had drawn her back for another look. She peered upward, trying to envision a path behind the white veil. The cliff behind the falls looked sheer, offering no obvious footholds.

But Colby had said he and Eddy Spooner had climbed up to the cave the time they had dared each other to spend the night in it. There must be a path. She just couldn't see it.

The legend of Chained Lady Cave had begun to fascinate her. She'd awakened this morning thinking about it, and now she couldn't seem to stop.

At her side, Specter whined softly. Absently, Diana reached down to pat his mist-dampened coat. "What's the matter? Don't like getting wet, do you? You've never been real big on taking baths. Well, come along, then. I think we've seen enough."

Diana made her way carefully over the wet rocks toward the car. "I wonder if Colby would agree to show me the inside of that cave?"

She pondered her own curiosity all the way back to her cottage. It wasn't until Specter gave a sharp, warning bark as they pulled into the drive that she realized someone was sitting patiently on her front porch.

"Hello, Brandon. I didn't expect to see you here. How are you today?"

Brandon got to his feet and smiled tentatively. "Hi, Miss Prentice. I walked over to see you. Dad's gone to see an old buddy of his. Didn't know if you were gone for the day or what."

"I just went for a drive. Come on inside. I think I've got some beer in the refrigerator. And please call me Diana."

"Thanks. I could use a drink. It's hot today." He followed her into the house, idly patting Specter who was tolerant of the caress.

"My dog seems to like you. You should be flattered." In the kitchen Diana opened the refrigerator and found a can of beer. "He doesn't think much of your father, you know."

"Is that right?" Brandon looked surprised. "Dad's usually pretty good with animals. We always had pets around when I was growing up."

"For some reason Specter and Colby have agreed to disagree. They have their own private war going. I try to remain neutral." She handed Brandon the beer and poured herself a glass of iced tea. "Have a seat."

Brandon dropped into a kitchen chair, his casual sprawl reminiscent of his father's easy masculine grace. His young face was set in serious lines as he spent a few seconds groping for the right words. "I came by to ask a favor, Miss...I mean Diana. A big favor."

Diana's heart sank. "If this has anything to do with family matters, Brandon, I would prefer to stay out of it. After all, I'm just a friend of your father's."

Brandon's eyes widened. "You're more than a friend. I can tell by the way Dad looks at you." A dull red tinged his cheeks. He looked away. "Sorry. I didn't mean to be rude. It's just that I know he likes you. A lot. And, well, I thought maybe you could talk to him. God knows I can't."

"Have you tried?"

Brandon nodded wearily. "I tried again last night after Robyn went to bed. It was a disaster. We ended up yelling at each other. I've always been able to talk to him until now. But his mind is absolutely closed on the subject."

"He's got his reasons, Brandon."

Brandon grimaced. "He thinks history is going to repeat itself. He won't even listen to me. Heck, all I want to do is talk to him about it, you know? I want to explain about Robyn and her folks."

"What about Robyn and her folks?" Diana asked.

"They're always on her back. Always telling her what to do. They scream at each other, and then they scream at her. They won't let her do anything on her own."

"How did she get permission to come up here with you?"

Brandon's mouth tightened. "They think she's with a girlfriend on the coast."

"Oh, brother."

Brandon stared at her helplessly. "You see what I mean? I've got to talk to Dad. And fast. I want to ask him some questions. If I could just get him to be reasonable, maybe I could decide what to do."

"Brandon, I don't think anyone could get your father to be reasonable about something unless he wanted to be reasonable about it. And in this case, where he feels he's right, I suspect the chances of me being able to influence him are absolutely zero. I think your best bet is to just back off for a while. You and Robyn are going to be together at school next year, aren't you?"

"Yes."

"Well? It's not as if someone is going to pry the two of you apart. Why rush into marriage? Give it some time. Let your father see the relationship is solid and for real, if indeed it is solid and real."

Brandon looked down at the can in his hand. "Robyn doesn't want to wait. She wants to get married so that she can get away from her parents."

"What about you? What do you want to do?" Diana asked gently.

"I...care for her. A lot. I kind of feel sorry for her. If she wants to get married right away, then I guess that's okay with me."

"Are you sure, Brandon?"

He looked up, dark eyes almost fierce. "I'm sure!"

"All right. Calm down. I was just asking. The decision to marry is a very big one. Look at me, I was never able to make it," Diana quipped.

Brandon looked puzzled. "You've never married?"

"No."

"No kids?"

"No kids."

"Don't you want any?"

Diana laughed. "Even if I did, it's a little late to start having them now."

"That's not true. You're not that old," Brandon said with awkward gallantry. "You hear about those famous movie stars putting off having babies for years."

Diana grinned. "Thanks. Unfortunately, I'm not a famous movie star."

Brandon turned brick red. "I'm sorry, I didn't mean—"

"Forget it. I know what you meant, and it's very kind of you. Another beer?"

"No thanks." He paused. "Getting married wasn't the only thing Dad and I argued about last night."

"Oh?"

"I asked him about my grandmother. She lives here in Fulbrook Corners."

"Yes, I know. I saw her briefly in the post office the other day."

Brandon's head snapped up, his eyes alive with deep interest. "You did? You know her?"

Diana hesitated, beginning to realize she might have said too much. "No, not really. She was just, uh, pointed out to me."

"It's weird to have a grandmother you've never even met," Brandon said slowly. "I don't remember Aunt Jesse too well. She came to see us a couple of times when I was a kid. But then she died. All my life it's mostly just been me and Dad. Do you think my grandmother really hates me?"

"Is that what your father said?" Diana asked carefully.

"He said she doesn't want anything to do with me or him. She blames him for what happened to my mother."

Brandon stared at Diana with an intensity that reminded her of his father. When he reached forty, she reflected, this young man was going to be every bit as formidable as Colby Savagar.

"And you want to meet her? Is that it, Brandon?" Diana asked quietly.

He fiddled with the beer can. "I'd like to get a look at her. Find out what she's like. I guess I'm curious, that's all."

"I can understand that. Why not tell your father just that?"

"I tried last night. He was already mad because of Robyn. When I brought up the subject of my grandmother, he really went through the roof. Said he wasn't going to let the old bitch get near me."

Diana groaned. "Your father can be extremely opinionated."

Brandon's mouth curved wryly. "Yeah, I've told him that on several occasions. Once he makes up his mind, getting him to change it is like trying to move a mountain."

"I know what you mean." Diana thought of the intent way Colby had been pursuing her for the past few weeks. He had been unswerving. And she had eventually succumbed to the inevitable.

"I'm just curious. What's wrong with that?"

"Nothing. I'm sure your father thinks he's protecting you from what might be an unpleasant scene, that's all."

"I can handle it. He's taught me to handle things like unpleasant scenes. Heck, he even signed us both up for karate lessons when I was a kid. We practice together a lot. He ought to know I can handle meeting my grandmother."

"Maybe he's right about Margaret Fulbrook not wanting to meet you. I hate to point that out, Brandon, but it's something to consider. The woman is old and apparently very bitter. She might not be rational about the whole thing." Remembering Margaret Fulbrook's reaction to Colby in the post office, Diana was fairly certain the woman wasn't entirely rational about her son-in-law and grandson.

The growl of a Jeep engine cut off whatever Brandon might have said in reply. Specter surged to his feet with an answering growl.

"Must be your father," Diana said, half-amused. "Specter makes that particular noise only when Colby's in the vicinity."

"Damn." Brandon got hastily to his feet. "Excuse me-but I was hoping Dad wouldn't find out I'd been here. You won't tell him what I asked you to do, will you? He'll be furious if he thinks I dragged you into this and he's mad enough already."

Diana saw the anxious look in Brandon's eyes and took pity on him. "Don't worry," she assured him as she listened to Colby take the front steps two at a time, "I'll consider our conversation confidential."

"Thanks." Brandon looked enormously relieved. "Geez, your dog really doesn't like Dad at all, does he? Look at him."

Specter was bounding forward, toenails scrabbling on the wooden floor as he rounded the corner at a dead run and headed for the hall. He reached the front door just as it opened.

"Damned dog." Colby's irritation carried into the kitchen. "When in hell are you going to learn that I've got as much right to be here as you do? Out of my way, you mangy mutt. Diana."

"In here, Colby."

She looked up with a smile as he strode into the kitchen, ignoring Specter who was making menacing sounds at his heels. Colby's eyes went instantly to hers, but then he caught sight of his son.

"What the devil are you doing here, Brandon?"

"He just came by to say hello," Diana said easily. "That's enough, Specter. You've made your point. Take it easy, boy. Go lie down. I can handle this."

Specter uttered one last final woof of disapproval before flopping down under the kitchen table. From his self-appointed den he kept a wary eye on Colby.

"One of these days that dog and I are going to have it out. Where's Robyn?" Colby opened the refrigerator with easy familiarity and helped himself to the iced tea.

"She's back at the house reading one of your books. She really loves your stuff, Dad." Brandon's voice was almost painfully eager.

Colby grunted and leaned back against the sink, his eyes on Diana. "Where did you go this afternoon?"

She flashed him a look of surprise. "How did you know I'd gone anywhere?"

"The hood of your car is warm. Engine's still hot." He tossed back the iced tea.

"Well, aren't you observant," Diana murmured. "Maybe you should be writing crime fiction instead of horror. As a matter of fact, I drove out to Chained Lady Falls."

"What for?"

She lifted one shoulder. "I don't know. I just wanted to get out for a while, and that seemed like an interesting place to drive to."

"Is that the falls you can see in the distance when you're driving into town?" Brandon asked.

Colby nodded. "You and Robyn can fix your own dinner tonight. Or go into town and eat at one of the cafés. Diana and I are going to be busy."

"Sure, Dad." Brandon got to his feet and dropped his empty can into the trash. "See you later, Diana. It was nice talking to you."

"Goodbye, Brandon. Thanks for stopping by."

Specter walked him to the door, tail wagging in a friendly fashion. Colby watched his son leave. When the front door slammed shut he turned to Diana.

"Let's have it. What was he doing here?"

Diana frowned. "I told you, Colby. He just dropped in to visit."

"Without the precious girlfriend in tow? Doesn't make sense. He must have wanted something. Did he want you to exercise the sweet voice of reason over me? Get me to see what a jewel sweet Robyn is and what a good idea it would be if the two of them got married?"

Colby obviously knew his son all too well. But Diana remembered her promise to Brandon. "Never mind what Brandon wanted. I want something."

He arched his brows. "What's that?"

She leaned one elbow on the table and rested her chin on her hand. "Colby, I'd like to see that cave behind Chained Lady Falls."

He was startled. "You want to go into the cave? Why?"

"I don't know. Curiosity, I suppose. Maybe I'm just getting bored sitting around here working on my résumé day after day. It seems to be one of the local sights, and I'm playing tourist this summer. Will you show it to me?"

6

"How the hell did you talk me into this? I should be working on my book this afternoon. I'm not even sure I can still find the path. Watch your step and stay right behind me." Colby mixed commands with a great deal of mild complaining as he prepared to lead Diana behind the roaring water.

"Yes, oh great leader. I hear and obey. And to be honest, I don't know how I did manage to talk you into this. Guess I must have caught you in a weak moment." Diana grinned up at him through the thick mist. A splash of water drenched the front of her shirt.

Colby's eyes gleamed. His gaze lingered on her damp shirt. The cotton cloth clung to her, outlining the soft swell of her breasts and their thrusting nipples.

"You forgot to wear a bra," he announced. "You look like an en trant in a wet T-shirt contest."

"You've attended a lot of wet T-shirt contests?" Diana asked with grave interest.

"You'd be surprised at the variety of programming available these days on the sports channel."

"I can imagine." She had assumed it would be easier to scramble over rocks without the binding encumbrance of a bra, but she had forgotten the predictable effect of the perpetual mist that surrounded Chained Lady Falls. "Are you sure there's really a path behind the water?"

"There was twenty years ago. A wide granite ledge. It should still be there. Put on your rain slicker. It's going to be wet on the other side of the waterfall." He shrugged into the waterproof windbreaker he'd brought along for himself. "At least we don't have to deal with that idiot dog of yours today."

"He didn't like being left behind at the cottage."

"He'll survive," Colby declared harshly. "And we sure don't need him underfoot on that ledge."

Diana unfastened her yellow slicker and adjusted the hood. After that there was almost no conversation except for an occasional shouted instruction from Colby. The roar of the water made it impossible to speak in normal tones.

Colby found the trail after a few minutes of trial and error. It was a surprisingly easy, if steep, climb to the cave halfway up the side of the cliff. Being behind the falls was an odd experience, however. Diana felt as if she'd stepped into another world.

The torrent created a great, impenetrable shield of noise and power and cut off the view of the valley and town below. The force of the pouring water was awesome. The rocky ledge seemed safe enough, but it occurred to her that if someone slipped and went over the side there would be little chance of surviving the fall.

They reached the yawning mouth of Chained Lady Cave about ten minutes later. Diana stepped through the entrance with a sense of relief. The climb up hadn't been too precarious, but the constant rush of water only inches away was disconcerting.

The cave was heavily shadowed but far from completely dark. Some of the bright sunlight outside managed to pass through the wall of water, illuminating the interior with a faint glow.

Colby switched on the flashlight he had slung on his belt and led the way several feet into the cavern. The farther they moved from the entrance, the darker the shadows grew. The noise of the falls faded somewhat, making conversation possible again.

Diana reached for the flashlight on her own belt, and stared at the damp cave walls. "So this is where he kept her chained. How ghastly."

Colby glanced at her. "Take it easy, honey. It's just a legend, remember?"

"In another hour the sun will be going down. I wonder what the water looks like from this side when it turns red."

"It looks like several tons of blood pouring straight down in front of your eyes."

"Your imagination is sometimes a little too vivid."

"Occupational hazard for a writer of horror fiction."

Diana glanced around. "Is this where you spent the night? On this wet floor?"

"No." Colby was walking toward the back of the cave.

"Where are you going?"

"Since I'm here, I thought I'd check and see if the place where I did spend the night still looks the same."

She followed curiously. "You mean there's more to the cave than just this one big room?"

"Uh-huh. Stay close. Remember I told you I was scared right down to my toes that night?"

"I remember."

"Well, I stumbled around, trying to find a reasonably dry place to sleep, and I eventually wandered into a really weird little grotto. The entrance is hidden way in the back of the main chamber. I only found it by accident. Wait until you see it."

"Colby, I don't know if I want to go any farther into this place."

"Stay out here in the main lobby, then. I'll just be a few minutes." He was edging along the cave wall, heading deeper into the inky darkness.

"Oh, no, you don't. I can do anything you can do."

"Atta girl."

Diana's chin lifted. "Don't be condescending."

"Sometimes you're too damn touchy, honey. Lighten up." Colby and the comforting beam of his flashlight vanished.

"Damn you, Colby Savagar." Diana hastened forward and flashed her own light into the deep shadows where he had disappeared. She could see nothing for a moment, and then she saw a section of darkness that was blacker than the shadows around it. Cautiously she stepped toward it. A moment later she found herself in a small, rocky antechamber.

"Take a look," Colby invited, as if showing off the Taj Mahal. "It's really something, isn't it?"

Her first impression was of warmth. A rocky pool filled a large portion of the room and the water in it was obviously very warm. Diana shone the beam of her light down into the depths of the pool and realized she couldn't see the bottom.

"This is where I spent the night," Colby said quietly. "And I never told Eddy Spooner or anyone else about this hidden room. As far as I know, no one else has ever found it."

"I think that warrior in the legend knew about it," Diana said with sudden conviction. "This is where he kept his poor wife. Not in the outer cavern."

Colby gave her an odd glance. "Know something? The night I spent in here, I was convinced that this was where she stabbed him. Somehow I just knew it."

"Why did you stay in here instead of in the main chamber?"

Colby played his flashlight beam on the walls. "Damned if I know. I just wandered in here and decided it was as good a place as any to spend the night. It was warm in here."

"But it's a lot creepier in here than it is out in the front part of the cave. If I had to choose, I'd sleep out there. Then again," Diana added wryly, "I doubt that I'd get any sleeping done at all if I had to spend the night in this place."

He was watching her through narrowed eyes, the harsh planes and angles of his face thrown into sharp relief by the back glow of the flashlight. "Do caves make you nervous?"

She started to shake her head, then stopped. "I suppose so. I've never spent much time in them. But it's more than that." She broke off.

"Go on," Colby urged softly.

"I don't know how to explain it," Diana admitted. "There's just something very strange about this particular grotto. A feeling."

"What kind of feeling?" he persisted.

Exasperated, she stepped back toward the entrance. "Stop it, Colby. Are you deliberately trying to frighten me?"

"No. I just want you to tell me exactly how you feel about this place."

He moved toward her, making no sound in his soft-soled shoes. He kept the flashlight pointed at her feet. His face was in shadow but his eyes seemed to gleam implacably in the darkness. He loomed over her-large, powerful, wholly male. She was suddenly aware of how vulnerable she was, here alone with him. If she screamed, no one would hear her.

Without any warning, Diana's imagination slipped into high gear. She no longer saw a reasonably civilized twentieth-century male, but a bronzed warrior. The muscles of his broad shoulders were sleek and contoured from years of violence. She shuddered at the fierce strength in him and the utter determination that blazed in his eyes.

He was a great leader, a skilled fighter, a lord among his people, and she belonged to him as completely as his war-horse or the lethal blade he wore at his belt.

He would take her. He thought he had the right to do so. He had been raised from birth to think he was entitled to anything he wanted. And now he wanted a son.

If he had come to her with gentleness, if he had treated her with the respect that was her due, if he had acknowledged her value as an equal, then perhaps, just perhaps, she would have given him willingly what he took by force.

But the warrior knew only the ways of male violence and she would never surrender to such ways. She would never give him a child to be raised in those ways.

There was no hope for either of them in this life. No chance to learn each other's hidden secrets, calm each other's private fears, trust in each other's strengths. No hope for love and gentleness and comfort.

There was no hope in this time and place.

But there would be other lifetimes.

"Diana? Are you all right?"

Diana blinked quickly, taking a frantic grasp on her wayward imagination and thoroughly ruffled nerves. Abruptly, she wanted nothing more than to get out of the grotto.

"What is it, honey?"

"Never mind how I feel about this place. I don't want to talk about it." She whirled to slip back through the opening in the wall, stumbling with relief into the main chamber.

Colby was right behind her. "Diana, what the hell's the matter with you? Are you sure you're okay?"

"Of course I'm okay. I just don't like that little grotto. Maybe your overactive imagination is rubbing off on me."

"Take it easy, honey." He came up behind her, putting a casually comforting arm around her shoulders.

She looked at him, seeing the affectionate amusement in his eyes and the slight curve of his hard mouth. The last traces of her conjured-up image of a warrior vanished. Colby was tough but he wasn't cold-blooded or violent. Smiling wryly, she leaned against him for a moment, seeking comfort from his lean, strong body. He nuzzled the spot behind her ear.

"I'm all right," she mumbled. "But I don't think I was cut out for this. I can't imagine how people can take this kind of thing up as a lifelong hobby. What do you think they get out of it?"

"The chance to comfort terrified lady friends?" He bit her earlobe gently.

"Colby, why is it so dark in here? Is the sun setting already?"

He lifted his head abruptly, glancing toward the cave entrance. It was far darker here in the outer chamber than it had been a few minutes ago when they had first entered. The faint rays of sunlight that had shone through the veil of water no longer filtered into the room.

"No, the sun isn't setting yet. Too early." Colby released her and walked toward the entrance with a frown. "The only thing that could make it get this dark so fast is a storm," he called back above the roar of water.

"A storm? But nothing like that was forecast, not even rain." She followed him to the cavern entrance and peered out. The wall of water falling in front of them had turned a deep steel gray.

"Stay here a minute," Colby shouted. "I want to see how bad it is out there." He stepped out onto the ledge and moved along the path to a point where he could see through the mist. Diana saw how the wind whipped his hair and the water drenched his windbreaker. He returned with a set expression on his face.

"What's wrong?" Diana demanded.

"It's storming out there, all right. Must have come up out of nowhere. A real mean summer thunderbuster. The water's coming down so hard, you can't tell where the waterfall ends and the rain begins. Wind's really howling, too. We'll have to wait until it lightens up before we try to go down that ledge."

"But the ledge is already wet from the mist of the falls. What harm will a little more water do?"

"It's not just the rain, it's the way the wind is driving it. If it caught you just right, it would be strong enough to make you lose your balance. Even if we got down the path in one piece, I'm not anxious to be walking behind that water when the lightning strikes."

As if to confirm his opinion, thunder crashed outside, louder than the falls, and an instant later a flash of light glittered on the other side of the cascade. The lightning faded instantly, leaving the pouring water darker than ever.

"You may have a point," Diana said reluctantly. She backed away from the entrance. "How long do you think it will last?"

"Shouldn't last too long. These summer storms are wicked but short-lived," Colby said easily. "Come on, let's find a place to sit down and wait it out." He guided her toward the back of the main chamber where it was easier to talk.

Colby seated himself on a convenient outcropping and arranged the flashlights so that they provided illumination without having to be held. Diana sank down beside him, aware of a chill from her damp feet.

"Since we're going to have to entertain each other for the next few minutes," Colby said smoothly, "why don't you tell me the real reason my son came to visit you today?"

She threw him a disgusted glance. "I hate nagging men."

Colby's gaze hardened. "He's my son, remember? I've got a right to know what's going on."

"Nothing's going on, as you put it." Diana shifted a little on the hard rock, trying to get comfortable. She stared out at the barrier of roaring black water.

"Now, listen, Diana—"

"Do you want some free, unsolicited advice, Colby?"

"No, damn it, I don't." He hesitated and then flung a handful of pebbles across the floor of the cave. "What advice?"

"If I were you, I wouldn't push Brandon very hard right now. You may force him into a decision he doesn't really want to make."

"He's already made a decision. Or thinks he has. I'm going to change his mind if it's the last thing I do." Colby hurled another fistful of pebbles.

"I don't think he's talked himself completely into marriage," Diana said thoughtfully. "I think he's being pushed into it by Robyn. He obviously cares for her. He's worried about her because of her relationship with her parents. And he's attracted to her. He wants to please her, but I don't think he really wants to marry her. At least, not at this stage."

Colby gave her a sharp look. "I agree little Robyn is probably pushing, but what makes you think Brandon's not eager?"

"He's a lot like you," Diana said simply.

"Too much like me, apparently. He's dead set on making the same mistakes I made at nineteen. But what the hell's that got to do with it?"

"Colby, that's not what I meant," she said patiently. "When Brandon showed up a couple of days ago, all he said was that he and Robyn were thinking of getting married."

"So?"

"So, is that the way you would have handled the announcement if you were determined to get married? Even at the tender age of nineteen, I'll bet once you'd made up your mind to marry Cynthia, you didn't announce it in such a wishy-washy fashion. My guess is that you just came right out and told everyone you were going to get married, like it or lump it. You wouldn't have stood around arguing about it, and you certainly wouldn't have worried too much about getting parental approval."

Colby stilled. His eyes gleamed reflectively. "You're right."

"As I said, I think your son is a lot like you. If he had been hell-bent on marriage, he would have announced the fact that he was going to marry, not that he was thinking about it and if he got any grief from you, he wouldn't have stuck around to argue. He and Robyn would be on their way to Reno by now."

Colby stared at her in silence for a few seconds. "So why is he sticking around trying to convince me he's ready for marriage?"

"Possibly because he's looking for a way to get out of the situation and doesn't know how to do it without hurting the woman he cares so much about. He feels trapped. His instincts undoubtedly sent him to you because he's hoping you'll help him figure a way out. You're his father and he's learned a lot from you over the years. He respects you. But yelling at him that he can't possibly marry Robyn won't work. It's the wrong approach."

"Why not? If he wants an out, let him tell her his father won't approve the marriage."

Diana sighed, "And be forced to admit to himself and to Robyn that at the grown-up age of nineteen he can't do anything without his father's permission? Come on, Colby. You know what a male ego is. You've got one yourself."

Colby swore softly. He leaned back against the damp cavern wall, drew up one leg and draped his arm over his knee. He glowered at Diana.

"This is getting complicated," he said.

She gave him a tiny smile. "Not really. Just think it through logically. I have a hunch your son has gotten himself in an awkward bind. He likes Robyn but he isn't ready to marry anyone, and deep down he knows it."

"What's he want from me?"

"What he came up here to do was talk to you. He wants the benefit of your wisdom, logic and experience so he can use it to pick a path through the brambles that surround him. But he doesn't want to be yelled at. He doesn't want to be forced to admit that you can still tell him what to do. Push him into a corner, and he'll dig in and show you just how independent he is."

"You mean, keep yelling at him and he'll marry Robyn just to show me he can make his own decisions."

"That's the way it looks to me," Diana said softly. "I may be wrong. You certainly know him better than I do. But I definitely get the feeling he isn't all that enthusiastic about marriage."

"And if I calm down and stop yelling at him, I might be able to help him figure out how to get out of the situation? You may be right, Diana. It makes a certain kind of sense. The trouble is, I'm not sure I can stay cool and rational about this. Every time I look at him, I see myself about to make the same damned fool mistake a second time and all I can think about is doing whatever I have to do to prevent it."

"If he's determined to make that mistake, there's really not much you can do about it, Colby. Like it or not, at nineteen, he's a man."

"There ought to be a law against nineteen-year-olds being men."

Diana laughed. "I can imagine how you would respond to that statement if you were nineteen again."

"You've made your point." He ran a hand through his damp hair. "What a mess." Colby got to his feet and walked restlessly to the front of the cavern. Hands on hips, he studied the situation.

"It's not getting any lighter out there, is it?" Diana called from the back of the cave.

"No." He turned around and returned to his place on the rocks. "It's worse than ever. Diana, if we don't get out of here by nightfall, we may have to spend the night in here. I don't want to take you down that ledge path after dark, even with flashlights."

"What?"

"Don't sound so horrified. It'll be a little cold and a little damp, not to mention a little uncomfortable, but we'll survive."

But Diana was genuinely horrified. The thought of spending the night in Chained Lady Cave shook her to the core. "We can't stay here, Colby. We don't have any food...or blankets, or matches."

"Don't worry about it until we have to make the decision."

"I'm worrying about it!" she yelped.

"Well, don't."

"Easy for you to say. Colby, I will not stay the night here and that's final."

"Honey, I'm trying to explain that you may not have a choice in the matter."

"I'll have a choice," she informed him grimly. "I've got a flashlight, and I'll find my way down that path alone if need be."

"The hell you will," he said far too quietly.

She slid him an uneasy, speculative glance.

"And turn off the flashlights. We may need them later. No sense wearing the batteries down now."

An hour later, night descended with no letup in the storm. If anything the gale was wilder than ever.

At least there was no fading sunlight to turn the waterfall into blood this evening, Diana told herself morosely. One had to be thankful for small mercies.

"Looks like the decision just got made for us," Colby said mildly. He reached out and switched on one of the flashlights. "We'll leave the other light off until this one burns out."

Diana jumped to her feet and hurried to the front of the cave. She was greeted by impenetrable blackness and a spray of water. Just beyond the entrance she could hear the relentless roar of the falls. Colby was right. No one in his or her right mind would attempt to negotiate the waterfall path tonight.

She sighed, resigned to a night in Chained Lady Cave, and turned to troop unhappily back to the damp rocks. She ran straight into Colby who had come up behind her. His arms went around her waist, and he bent his head to drop a reassuring kiss on her hair.

"It's going to be all right, honey."

"I'm cold already."

"We'll spread your slicker and my windbreaker out on the floor. They'll keep us reasonably dry. No fire, but never let it be said I don't know how to take care of my woman." He reached into his windbreaker pocket and produced two plastic packets of cheese and crackers.

Diana instantly felt better. "Where did you get those?"

"I just stuck them in at the last minute thinking we might want to have a snack up here before we hiked down."

"My hero!" she exclaimed admiringly. "I have a contribution to make to the effort, too." She reached into her trouser pocket, and pulled out a few sheets of facial tissue.

"What are we going to use that for? To wipe our hands after we eat?"

"Not exactly. It occurred to me it might come in handy for other reasons."

"You're planning on catching cold?"

"No, I am not planning on catching cold. Really, Colby. Use that vivid imagination of yours. Do you see any sanitary facilities around here?"

Understanding dawned. "Ah, I get it."

"Finally."

They ate the crackers and cheese snacks in less than three minutes.

"What we really need is a bottle of good wine to complement this fine cuisine," Colby remarked as he swallowed the last cracker crumb.

"At least neither of us has to cook tonight," Diana pointed out, trying to look on the positive side. "Specter will be okay, I think."

"Assuming he has sense enough to get in out of the rain."

"He knows where the back porch is. He can sleep there. Brandon and Robyn will be worried about us, though."

"They'll probably assume I got caught at your place in the storm and decided to spend the night." Colby paused and swore under his breath. "Which will leave them perfectly free to entertain themselves this evening, won't it?"

Diana read his mind. It wasn't hard to tell the direction of his thoughts. "Stop worrying about it," she advised gently. "If they're sleeping together, they're sleeping together. There's not much you can do about it."

"I know. I'll just have to keep my fingers crossed that Brandon was paying attention during all those lectures on birth control I gave him."

"Yup. Keeping your fingers crossed is about all you can do. Now stop fretting, and let's figure out where we're going to spread this rain gear." Diana jumped to her feet.

Colby looked at her, his eyes watchful in the faint glow of the flashlight beam. "I hate to point this out, but the fact is, it's dryer in the inner cavern. Also warmer. That's why I spent the night in there the last time."

"I don't like it in there," Diana said instantly. "I don't exactly love it out here, but I prefer this chamber to that grotto." She peered at the floor of the main cave, trying to find a spot that wasn't soaking wet. It was useless. "Maybe it will be more comfortable to sit up all night."

"I doubt it."

"Then you think of something, damn it!"

His brows rose. "You're really on edge, aren't you? Here, let me see that slicker of yours."

Wordlessly she handed it to him. A few minutes later he had it spread across a fairly smooth stretch of stone. He used his windbreaker to add some width to the sleeping surface, and then he sat down on top of the slicker and began removing his damp shoes. When he looked up to see what was keeping her from following suit, he smiled and held out his hand.

"Honey, this is as good as it's going to get tonight. Come on down here, and we'll try to get some sleep."

"I won't be able to sleep a wink tonight."

"Sure you will. Take off your shoes and get your feet dry. That will help."

She let him remove her sport shoes, and he was right. Things did seem more bearable when her feet were dry. When he was finished, he lay down, tangled her legs between his and cradled her, spoon-fashion.

"I don't think I'll ever go into a cave again as long as I live," Diana vowed.

"This wasn't my idea."

"Don't remind me." She turned and gave him a quick kiss. "I'm sorry for having gotten us into this mess."

"It's not so bad and it's not your fault. No one could have predicted that storm."

"It was a surprise, wasn't it?"

"Damn weird, if you want to know the truth."

"Don't say that. I'm nervous enough about this cave. Don't start implying the storm is some sort of supernatural event. I already know I'm not going to be able to sleep a wink."

Five minutes later, Diana was sound asleep.

Colby stirred beside her, trying to get comfortable. He stared into the blackness above, aware of how weak the flashlight beam was becoming. He wouldn't switch on the other one unless Diana awoke. As long as she was sleeping this soundly, she wouldn't miss the artificial illumination.

Never in all the years of growing up in Fulbrook Corners had he ever seen a storm as bad as the one that was blowing tonight. The wind seemed to have intensified in the past half hour. It was blowing with enough force now to send sprays of water off the falls straight into the main cavern. If it got any worse, he and Diana would both be soaked to the skin by morning.

Common sense told him they would both be dryer and far more comfortable in the back of the cave.

Colby sat up and looked down at Diana curled up beside him. Her tawny hair was tumbled around her shoulders and her lashes looked very long lying against her cheek. He was just beginning to realize how very important she had become to him lately. His obsession with her had not ended when he'd finally gotten her into bed. A part of him was starting to wonder if it would ever end.

Just what he needed, he thought wryly-an independent, assertive, opinionated career woman. A woman who'd never had children of her own but who felt qualified to lecture him on how to handle his own son.

But he wanted to know the rest of her secrets. He felt as if he'd only peeled away one thin layer of her complex personality. He needed to learn so much more about her.

First things first, however. His primary task tonight was to shield her from the storm. Another spray of water sailed in through the entrance.

Colby got to his feet and reached down to lift Diana into his arms. He picked up the flashlights and started toward the inner grotto.

Sometimes a man had to ride roughshod over a woman's fears for her own good. With any luck she wouldn't wake up until morning.

7

Diana came partially awake, dimly aware of a dream that was fading rapidly. She couldn't remember any of the details, but she was awash in a gentle sea of wistful longing and deep, aching sensuality. She felt a little sad but did not understand why. She was also aware of a distant glimmer of hope, but she didn't understand that, either.

She waited for the dreamy state to subside, and when it didn't she shifted languidly, wondering why the bed seemed so hard tonight. Then she felt the weight of a man's leg lying across her thigh, and a vague recollection of the day's events surfaced.

She managed to get her eyes open just far enough to see the reassuring beam of the flashlight. It was definitely on its last legs, but she didn't have the energy to reach over and switch on the backup light.

"Colby?" she whispered sleepily.

"It's all right," he murmured drowsily, cradling her closer. "I'm right here." His palm stroked over her breast and he dropped a kiss onto her shoulder.

Diana closed her eyes again, feeling safe and secure in his embrace. The wistful longing within her intensified, melding with the sensual warmth that was spreading through her limbs. She turned toward Colby, instinctively trying to get closer. Her arm went around his lean waist.

"You feel good," she muttered. Her hand moved along his back, savoring the hard, contoured muscles. "Warm and strong."

"You feel good, too. Soft. Very soft. Sweet." He kissed her again, a sleepy caress on her brow and then the tip of her nose. She felt his body growing taut.

"Colby?" She slid her foot between his legs, and he instantly tightened his thighs, chaining her.

"Sweetheart," he breathed just before his mouth found hers.

Diana parted her lips for him, inviting him into her warmth and then there were no more words.

Colby's kiss grew suddenly fierce with a hunger that Diana responded to instantly. She welcomed the fierceness in him, knowing that it would never be used against her, knowing that with this man she was safe.

Passion flared without any warning, sweeping Diana into the heart of a swirling storm that seemed as intense as the one howling outside the cave. Colby's arms tightened around her. He rolled onto his back and pulled her with him. Then his hands locked in her hair.

She felt him lift himself against her, and her hands slid up under his shirt. She loved the feel of him. She couldn't get enough of it. Her whole body was beginning to sing with the joy only his lovemaking could give her.

She wanted to join with him, become one with him, love him.

When he pulled off her shirt and tossed it aside, she reacted in kind. His shirt landed on the cavern floor beside hers. He fumbled with her pants, his hands gliding warmly over her curving buttocks as he swept the last of her garments from her body.

She slid down along the length of him, and he began to breathe heavily as she stopped long enough to drop tiny kisses here and there across his broad chest.

When she unfastened and unzipped his jeans, Colby's hands tightened again in her hair. Wordlessly he lifted his hips against her, letting her know the full extent of his arousal. She reached into the opening of his jeans, cupping him intimately. And then her hair flowed over his thighs as she worshipped him with her mouth.

Colby groaned, enduring the sweet torture for as long as possible. But in the next moment he was lifting her and pushing her onto her back. He rose, looming over her for a long moment as he studied her nude body in the weak gleam of the flashlight. His hand moved along her thigh until he reached the flowing liquid warmth that marked her own desire.

Gently he stroked with his fingers until Diana thought she would
fly apart into a thousand pieces. A moment later, when he touched her
with his tongue, she knew she was lost.

The world spun around her. Her body was an exotic instrument that
only Colby knew how to play. She clutched at him, writhed against
him, sobbed out her feminine demands.

And finally he came to her, burying himself deep within her until
she was filled with him and he was surrounded by her. The white-hot
heat of their mutual passion exploded around them, enveloping them.
They clung together, whirling about in an endless universe that knew
no beginning and no end.

Diana gave herself completely, bestowing herself as only a woman
in love can when she knows she has found the right mate. It was a
total capitulation to her own passion and to her lover's. It was the
kind of surrender that forever chains the conqueror.

This time it was right. This time they were meant to be together.
This time she was free to give that which he could never take from
her by force. And she gave it to him willingly, with all her heart, knowing the time had come at last.

Past, present and future were now linked.

Diana cried out, and Colby drank the sound from her lips.

When it was over, neither spoke. They fell into an exhausted sleep
in each other's arms.

He dressed slowly, watching her come awake in the glow of the re-
maining flashlight. He wondered what she would say about the violent
passion that had taken them both by storm in the middle of the night.

Would she be angry at his carelessness? Or would she retreat into
that self-contained, fiercely independent part of herself and act as if
nothing had happened?

It hadn't been a dream, he was honest enough with himself to
admit that, but there had been an odd, dreamlike quality to the whole
thing. Should he say something first?

No, he decided. Let her bring up the subject if she wants to. Let
her decide to say something about it, if something needs to be said.

What had happened had been an unplanned accident. Neither of them was to blame. Both of them were responsible.

Colby knew he was searching for excuses, and there were none. Neither of them had any excuse except the age old one of ungovern able passion. That passion had descended swiftly, taking them by surprise while they were both half-drugged with sleep. It had swept them both into a shattering conflagration of the senses and then cast them adrift, allowing them to lose themselves once more in sleep.

The passion had dominated him so completely that he hadn't re-membered to use the contents of the little foil packet in his wallet. And she hadn't thought about it, either.

All of which added up to the fact that Diana might even now be pregnant.

Colby wondered why he wasn't more alarmed at the thought. By rights, he should be chewing his fingernails to the quick this morning. He hadn't had this kind of reason to worry since he'd been nineteen.

She would be upset, he knew. A little scared, perhaps. Even at her age she was bound to be nervous about this. Maybe he should say something first.

But what could he say? Sorry, I forgot? I woke up in the middle of the night in a cave and you were in my arms and I had to have you, and nothing in this world could have stopped me from taking you?

Because that's the way it had been for him. At his age, that excuse wasn't worth the breath it took to say it.

Diana stirred and opened her eyes. She focused on the dull glow of the flashlight for a moment, obviously trying to get her bearings.

"Colby?"

"Right here, honey." He leaned over and kissed her bare shoulder. "You as stiff and sore as I am?"

"I may not be able to sit up, let alone walk again."

He smiled, telling himself he was relieved that she wasn't going to start out the morning by berating him, even though he deserved it. But part of him was irritated by her calm attitude. Was she going to ignore the whole thing? Diana could be so strong-minded. A regular amazon.

He eased himself to a sitting position and helped her to sit up beside him. Then he began massaging her shoulders with an easy familiarity. She sighed and leaned into the brisk rubdown.

"Better?" he asked. She looked good in the morning, he thought-even after having spent the night on a stone floor-sweet, vulnerable, relaxed and sexy.

"Much better. Colby, we're in the grotto room. How on earth did we get in here? I don't remember moving." She stared around with a small frown. Then she seemed to notice the clothes that were scattered around them.

Maybe she didn't remember any of it, he thought, jolted. After all, she had been half-asleep. "I carried you in here when the wind started whipping the water into the main chamber. We'd have been drenched by now if we'd stayed out there."

"Oh. Thanks, I guess. But the sooner we get out of here, the better. No offense, but there's something about this place that really gives me the creeps."

"Were you scared last night?" Colby asked quietly as he got to his feet.

She looked at him in surprise. "No, not really. I don't like the place, but I have to admit I didn't suffer any real claustrophobia in here. I slept amazingly well, in fact, all things considered." She got to her feet, dressing quickly. "How about you? Scared to your toes like last time?"

He shook his head. Why wasn't she saying anything about the unplanned and unprotected lovemaking? She was acting as if nothing out of the ordinary had happened even as she put on the clothes that he'd removed last night in the heat of passion. "No. It wasn't the same as last time at all." Nothing had ever felt so right, in fact, as making love to Diana on the floor of the grotto. He was chagrined that she wasn't going to mention it. He felt like asking, Was it good for you, too? just to see what she would say.

"Hope that storm has stopped," Diana was saying in a conversational tone.

"Come on, let's see what's going on out there. You ready to go?"

"Believe me, I have no desire to hang around here." She made to follow him out of the little grotto. "I will say, however, that this is probably the most unusual date I've ever been on in my life."

"As a writer of horror fiction I felt I had a reputation to live up to. A guy like me can't take his lady on plain, ordinary dates. She might begin to think he was a fraud."

"You've got a point."

She was going to handle this with her usual self-contained manner, he realized. So be it. If she didn't want to talk about it, damned if he was going to say anything. But he realized he was now thoroughly irritated. The woman was too independent for her own good. She took on too much responsibility-accepted all the risks. Hell, he was a part of what had happened. She should be talking to him about it, not dealing with it all on her own.

He wondered for the first time if Diana had ever in her life turned to a man in a time of crisis-ever leaned on a male when the going got tough-ever asked one to share responsibility with her.

The more he got to know her, the more he doubted it. He wondered what it would take to get her to turn to him for help and comfort. Probably a full-scale natural disaster-say, an earthquake that registered around eight or nine on the scale.

Colby stepped out into the main cavern and relaxed as he saw the veil of white water roaring past the cave entrance. "We're in luck. Sun's out and the wind has stopped. Shouldn't be any trouble getting down that path now."

"I hope we haven't caused Brandon and Robyn any worry."

"I just hope they haven't caused me any more worry," Colby retorted. "I've got enough problems at the moment."

Diana gave him an odd glance but said nothing as he led her down the ledge path.

Colby dropped Diana off at her cottage, exchanged a few epithets with a disgruntled Specter, who had taken offense at having been left alone all night, and drove back to Aunt Jesse's place. A glance at his watch showed it was only seven o'clock. Brandon was an early riser like his father, but Colby had a hunch Robyn wouldn't have gotten out of bed yet. That suited Colby just fine. It would give him an opportunity to talk calmly to Brandon.

Maybe Diana had a point, he thought as he parked the Jeep and took the porch steps two at a time. Maybe the kid was trapped and had come looking for a way out. At nineteen, it was too damned easy for a man to get himself between the devil and the deep blue sea.

Especially when a woman was involved.

He'd back off, Colby decided resolutely. He'd try Diana's advice. He'd give Brandon a chance to come to him-an opportunity to talk without feeling threatened. He and Brandon had always had a good relationship. Now was the time to fall back on nineteen years of a solid father-son bond.

He walked into the house and heard the door of Robyn's room closing upstairs. A few seconds later, Brandon came ambling down the stairs toward the kitchen, yawning. He was wearing a T-shirt and a pair of jeans. He was barefoot and still busy fastening the snap of his denims.

All Colby's good resolutions went out the window.

"If you haven't got brains enough to keep your pants zipped around her, I hope you've at least got enough brains to be taking precautions."

Brandon halted halfway down the stairs, startled. "Dad... I didn't hear the Jeep. When did you get back? Where were you last night? We wondered what had happened."

"Doesn't look like you spent too much time worrying about my whereabouts." Colby slammed into the kitchen and filled Aunt Jesse's old dented kettle. He set it on the stove and started to shovel instant coffee into a large mug. He was aware of Brandon standing uneasily in the doorway.

"I sort of figured you were at Diana's," Brandon muttered.

Colby tried to get control of his frustrated anger. "I was with her. We got caught in the cave behind Chained Lady Falls. Had to spend the night there." He swung around. "Damn it, Brandon, have you got any idea of the risks you're taking?"

"I'm probably not taking any more risks than you and Diana are taking," Brandon shot back.

Colby winced as memories of the night swamped him. "Are you using something?" he asked roughly. "Or are you relying on Robyn?"

Brandon flushed. "Geez, Dad"

"Just answer me, okay?"

"I've got protection. Don't worry, we're not taking any chances. For crying out loud, after all those books you had me read, and after all those talks you gave me on the subject, how could I forget to use something?"

"Sometimes it's too damn easy to forget. Believe me, I know." The kettle began to shriek. Colby swiped it off the stove and poured boiling water into the mug. Too damn easy.

"You're so afraid I'm going to make the same mistake you made—you can't get past that, can you?" Brandon asked moodily. He trooped over to the table and flung himself down in a chair.

"Yeah, that's exactly what scares me."

"What's so bad about getting married at my age?" Brandon asked.

Colby started to lose his temper all over again. Then it occurred to him that if Diana's theory was right, his son's question might be a legitimate opening for rational discussion, not a challenge. With great effort, he got control of his anger. "You want some coffee?"

Brandon gave him a surprised glance. "Sure."

Colby fixed another mug of instant and carried it over to the table. He sat down across from Brandon and stared out at the bright, sunny morning for a moment. "You really want to know what's so bad about getting married at your age?"

Brandon toyed with his mug, giving the impression he was already regretting the question. "I know it might be a little rough trying to finish school while being married, but"

"Rough?" Colby leaned forward, his elbows on the table. "You want to know what rough is? I'll tell you. Rough is wondering how you're going to pay the rent when you've just lost your job and you can't get another because you don't have any experience or fancy degrees. Rough is having to worry about a young wife who gets bored and restless after the novelty of being married wears off and she has to sit home while her girlfriends are out on dates."

"Dad"

"Rough is wishing you could be going windsurfing with the other guys instead of having to hunt for another job and entertain a wife who by now wishes she'd never married you because marriage isn't nearly as much fun as she had thought it would be. Rough is worrying about diaper rash, fevers in the middle of the night, crying that sometimes goes on and on until you think you're going to go out of your mind."

"But, Dad"

"But do you know what the roughest thing of all is? It's realizing that you married before you really understood what you needed from a woman. It's realizing that sex isn't everything, even though, at nineteen, it seems like the most important thing in the world. It's realizing you made a mistake and that there's no going back."

Brandon looked at him. "Is that the way it was for you?"

Colby took a swallow of coffee. "Yeah, that's the way it was for me."

"And you think that's the way it's going to be for me?"

"I think that's the way it would be for anyone who gets married too young."

There was silence for a moment. "Robyn thinks it will work out."

"Does she? How does she know?"

"I don't know." Brandon hunched over his coffee. "She really wants to get married."

"Do you?" Colby asked bluntly.

Brandon's shoulders moved restlessly. "Sometimes I think it would be all right, you know? I really like her, Dad."

"That's obvious. But do you really like the idea of marriage?"

"Last night I told her maybe we should wait a while." The words came slowly, stiffly. "I said maybe next summer we could talk about it again."

This was probably as much as he could hope for right now, Colby told himself. He could hear Diana telling him not to blow it now. The kid had come more than halfway. "Sounds reasonable," he said cautiously.

"She didn't think so. She doesn't like the idea of waiting. She's got it hard at home, you know?"

Something in Brandon's tone told Colby that Robyn had been more than a little upset. Was that how Brandon had ended up in the girl's bed? Had Robyn tried to give him a graphic demonstration of the wonders of married life?

"It's your life too, Brandon. You don't have to live it the way she wants you to live it. You have a responsibility to do what you think is best, not what anyone else tells you is best. All I ask is that you make your own decision while you've still got all your options open."

"I'm thinking about it," Brandon said stubbornly. "You've got to understand Robyn's parents, though. They try to run her life. Always yelling at her. Always fighting."

"Tell me something, son. If you were having the kind of trouble at home that Robyn is having, would you look for someone else to rescue you or would you rescue yourself?"

Brandon scowled. "I'd get myself out of the house. But that's different."

"Is it? If you did use someone else to rescue you, do you think you would ever really feel free?"

"No, not exactly."

"Do you want to deny Robyn the experience of learning how to get herself free? Do you want her to exchange her dominating parents for a husband she thinks will replace them? She'll expect you to step right into the role of taking care of her. But she figures you won't treat her the way they do. You won't yell at her. I'll tell you something, Brandon. After a few months of taking care of her, you probably would be yelling at her. You'd realize she married you only because she wanted to use you."

Brandon looked up, a faint bewilderment in his fine brown eyes. "Sometimes it's hard to think straight about things like that, isn't it? I mean, when you're with a girl and she starts talking about marriage and stuff while you're thinking about other things, and you want her to be happy but you also want to go to bed with her, and she knows that and sort of uses that to...oh hell. You know what I mean."

For the first time since Brandon had arrived, Colby took genuine pity on his son. He gave him a slow, man-to-man grin. "Brandon, good buddy, allow me to tell you that I know exactly what you mean. Welcome to the club. You're learning the hard way what every man apparently learns the hard way. At the age of forty, I have come to the conclusion there is no easy way to learn it. Women can complicate a man's life no end."

"Does Diana complicate your life?"

Colby drummed his fingers on the tabletop. "Enormously. And the worst of it is, I don't think she even realizes it."

Diana drove into town later that morning with Specter sitting beside her.

"The trouble with men," she informed the dog, "is that they can really complicate a woman's life. They're so damned difficult to understand. They don't think logically or rationally, the way a woman does. They don't know how to analyze their emotions or themselves. They don't communicate well. They just sort of blunder into your life and stumble around trying to get your attention. When they have it, they don't know what to do with it."

Specter whined in sympathy and then stuck his nose out the window to sample the morning smells.

"He never said a word this morning, the bastard. Not one word. I would have sworn he didn't even remember making love to me, except that he obviously had to get dressed, the same as I did. He must have realized why he'd taken off his clothes in the first place. Specter, we went crazy last night. We just woke up and went crazy. I've never taken that kind of risk before. What if something happens? I think I'm getting scared."

Specter pulled his large muzzle back out of the slipstream and gave her a curious glance. Diana sighed and reached out to pat him reassuringly. "If I'm pregnant, I'll let you have Colby, okay? I know you've been looking for an excuse to sink your teeth into his throat."

Specter yipped at the name.

"All we can do is wait and see," Diana said gloomily. "The odds are in my favor, I think, although it couldn't have happened at a worse time of the month. But it was only one night and after all, I am thirty-four. I've heard it's more difficult to get pregnant in your thirties than it is when you're younger." She groaned. "But I have to tell you truthfully, Specter. The man felt very fertile to me last night."

She was still trying to comprehend her own incomprehensible behavior. Her romantic relationships had been few and far between and always conducted with great caution and discretion. She had never in her life awakened in the middle of the night and surrendered to over-whelming passion the way she had last night. She still couldn't be-lieve it had been her in that cave.

There was no sign of Colby's Jeep in the post office lot, but Mar-garet Fulbrook's aging Cadillac was parked there when Diana ar-rived. The woman was not in the car, but her unsmiling, heavyset, odd-job man was sitting in the front seat.

"Just my luck," Diana told Specter as she opened the car door and got out. "Maybe she'll ignore me." She didn't really feel like dealing with Margaret Fulbrook today. The woman's bitterness was enough to chill the soul of anyone who got too close to her.

But Margaret Fulbrook didn't ignore Diana. She came through the glass doors just as Diana was about to open them. Diana held the door for her, reflecting philosophically on the ingrained nature of one's per-sonal manners.

"You're that woman Savagar has taken up with for the summer, aren't you?" Margaret Fulbrook demanded without any preamble. Her dark eyes glittered in her rigidly set face.

"I'm Diana Prentice," Diana said mildly.

"I want to talk to you."

Diana's eyes widened. "You do?"

"Come with me." She brushed past Diana, heading toward the Cadillac. The woman was obviously accustomed to giving orders and having them obeyed.

Diana shrugged and followed warily. She watched as the grim-faced Harry climbed ponderously out of the Cadillac and opened the passenger door for his employer.

"Thank you, Harry." Mrs. Fulbrook settled herself in the seat as if she were assuming her throne. She waited while Harry went back to the driver's side, and then she angled her fierce gaze up through the window. "Have you seen my grandson?"

She should have been expecting that question, Diana realized. But she'd been preoccupied with other things this morning. "I've met him, yes. I had dinner with him and Colby the other night."

"I'm told he has the Fulbrook eyes. Is that true?"

Diana gazed down at Margaret Fulbrook's intelligent brown eyes. "Yes, ma'am. He does. He's a very fine-looking young man."

"Heard he's got a girl with him. Probably takes after his father in that respect."

"He has a girlfriend, yes. Most young men do at that age." Diana braced one palm against the roof of the Cadillac and said casually, "He's just finished his first year in college. Doing very well, I gather. I believe he plans on becoming an engineer."

Margaret Fulbrook snorted. "Maybe he'll amount to more than his father ever did."

Diana couldn't repress a smile. "If you're talking about financial success, Mrs. Fulbrook, I assure you, Colby's done just fine."

"I read one of those terrible books of his. Complete nonsense. Nothing but monsters and blood and gore. The stuff of nightmares."

"Not everybody can write a nightmare. Colby has a real talent."

"That bastard. He hasn't got any talent. Leastways, not any respectable talent." But there was little heat in the words. It was as if Mrs. Fulbrook had called Colby a bastard so many times during the past twenty years that she could no longer summon up much venom.

"I imagine his publisher would disagree with you," Diana said gently.

"Bah. What do I care about his publisher?" The woman was silent for a long moment, staring straight ahead through the windshield. "What's he like?" she asked at last.

"Who, Colby?"

"No! Not Savagar." White lines appeared on either side of the woman's mouth. "I know well enough what he's like. He's a seducer of innocent young girls. He's a shiftless, no-account, sleazy opportunist who tried to take the easy way out by marrying my daughter. But it all backfired on him. I made sure he never got a dime. Not one thin dime, by God."

"Did he ever ask for a dime?"

"That's beside the point! If he never asked, it's because he figured out fast enough I'd never give him anything. I am not interested in

Colby Savagar. I was asking you what my grandson is like. Did Savagar ruin him completely?"

"Brandon is an intelligent, well-educated, well-mannered, well-spoken, surprisingly sensitive young man. I like him very much."

"No doubt you've been brainwashed by Savagar."

"No doubt."

"Nineteen years," Margaret Fulbrook said slowly. "Nineteen years. And I haven't seen Cynthia's son since the funeral."

"Who's fault is that?"

"Savagar's, of course. He never brought the boy to see me."

"I imagine that's because he knew you wanted nothing to do with himself or Brandon. I gather you made your wishes clear at the funeral."

"I still don't want anything to do with Colby Savagar. But when I heard the boy was in town, I...wondered."

Diana drew a deep breath and took the plunge. "Brandon asked me about you yesterday."

The silvered head snapped around. "He did?"

"I think he's curious about you. He has no kin except for his father. It's perfectly natural that since he's here in Fulbrook Corners, he might start wondering about his mother's people."

"Probably wonders how much money he can get out of me. The boy was raised by his father and he'll have turned out just like him."

Diana hid another smile. "I'll admit that Brandon is a lot like his father. But he definitely has his mother's eyes. Goodbye, Mrs. Fulbrook. I'm sure you're busy and I've got to go pick up my mail. See you around." She stepped back from the car.

"One moment, young woman!"

It was nice to be called a young woman, Diana reflected in amusement as she turned back. "Yes, Mrs. Fulbrook?"

"If you had a lick of sense or an ounce of decency and self-respect, you'd stop seeing Savagar. He'll do you no good, and the bastard doesn't deserve to be happy, even for the short time he'll keep you around."

Diana looked down at her, astonished. "I beg your pardon?"

"You heard me." There was a relentless malice in the glittering brown gaze. "I saw the way Savagar looked at you the other day in the post office. He's finding happiness with you, and he has no right to that. He has no right to happiness of any kind. He deserves to be punished for what he did to my daughter. Stop seeing him!"

Margaret Fulbrook rolled up the window to cut off further conversation, and a few seconds later the heavy car lumbered out of the parking lot. Diana stood and watched until it was out of sight.

8

When Diana walked back into the cottage half an hour later, her arms full of groceries and Specter at her heels, she almost didn't notice the flowers in the vase on the hall table.

The bright yellow and white daisies were gone. In their place was a bunch of colorless, decaying weeds.

Diana nearly dropped her packages. "Specter," she whispered.

Instantly he was there, pushing a concerned, inquiring nose against her thigh. Then he pressed forward, sniffing around the base of the hall table. He gave a sharp bark and looked at her.

"Somebody's been in here." Diana glanced around nervously. She knew there was no one else in the house at the moment. Specter would have gone crazy. Slowly, she went on into the kitchen, half-afraid of what she might find.

But there was nothing out of place, nothing missing. She let the grocery sacks slide out of her arms onto the tiled countertop and then made herself walk deliberately from room to room. Specter hovered close, sensing her uneasiness. But he obviously knew there was no immediate threat.

Diana went back out into the hall and stared at the unsightly clump of weeds.

"It's a joke," she told Specter, trying to reassure herself. "Someone's playing a very strange joke." But there was something unsettlingly familiar about this particular prank. It took Diana a minute to remember, and then her memory clicked. "There was an incident like this in Colby's book."

Whirling around, she hurried into the kitchen and picked up Shock Value. Her fingers trembled slightly as she turned the pages, searching for the right scene. "So help me, Specter, if this is his idea of comedy, I'll wring his neck. This is not funny."

She found the scene in the third chapter. Donnelly had just walked into his home and discovered that a beautiful arrangement of gladioli had been replaced with a ragged assortment of dead weeds.

Shock sliced through him slowly, a dull blade inching along the nerve endings of his spine. He stared at the moldering weeds, knowing they were both an offering and a warning. Their stench filled the air. They trailed limply out of the crystal vase, evil doppelgängers of the fresh, lush blooms they had replaced.

An offering and a warning.

They were tribute to the dark being which the local people believed haunted the cove, and they were also meant as a warning to Donnelly who refused to take such legends seriously.

A passionate rage seized him. He reached out and jerked the weeds from the beautiful vase. He tossed the dead things onto the hearth and watched with satisfaction as the fire eagerly consumed them.

It wasn't until the weeds had been reduced to ashes that Donnelly asked himself who could have placed them in the vase. He didn't like any of the possible answers.

Diana slowly closed the door. "I don't like any of the answers, either, Specter."

The sound of Colby's Jeep in her drive brought her out of the kitchen and sent Specter bounding to the front door. The dog growled his usual warning as Colby came up the steps.

"Diana?" Colby let himself into the cottage. The screen door slammed behind him. "Out of my way, Specter. I've got better things to do than trade insults with you today. Some other time, maybe. Diana?"

"I'm right here, Colby," she said quietly. She stood in the kitchen doorway and watched him walk heedlessly past the weeds.

His brows rose. "Something wrong?"

Her eyes went to the table beside him. Automatically he followed her gaze. At first he looked puzzled, and then his eyes narrowed.

"I found them there when I got home a few minutes ago. When I left this morning, there were daisies in that vase. Remind you of anything, Colby?"

"Damn." He looked back at her. "Yeah, it reminds me of something. A scene out of one of my books."

" Shock Value."

"Got that far, did you?" He snatched the weeds out of the vase and strode into the kitchen where he tossed them into the garbage. "So who the hell put them in your vase and why?"

Diana folded her arms, unconsciously withdrawing into herself. She was glad to have the weeds gone but the ramifications of the situation could not be dismissed so easily. "I don't know. I thought you might have some ideas."

"Me?" His expression darkened further. "What is this? You thought I might have done it?"

"It occurred to me that maybe this was some sort of joke to tease me about how long it's taking me to read Shock Value."

Colby swore again, this time more crudely. Specter muttered a warning and edged closer to his mistress. Colby ignored the dog. He opened the refrigerator door and helped himself to a can of beer he had stored in there a few days earlier.

"Just so you'll know in the future," he said roughly as he opened the beer, "I am not into practical jokes."

Diana drew a breath of relief. "I'm sorry," she whispered. "It's just that for a few minutes I was very frightened, and I guess it was easier to think it might have been you staging a stupid prank than to think that some stranger was in here today."

Colby watched her face for a moment and then his eyes softened. "Come here, honey," he said gently and held out his hand.

Diana hesitated, and then with a small, wordless exclamation, she stepped close and let him fold her against his side. She leaned into him, allowing herself to take comfort and reassurance from his strength. He held her with one arm wrapped securely around her and sipped his beer thoughtfully.

"When I figure out who put the weeds in your vase, I'll beat him to a pulp," Colby finally announced. Specter gave a small yip. Colby looked down at the dog. "Okay, pal, you can help me."

"Who would do such a thing, Colby?"

"Damned if I know, but we've got a town full of possible candidates."

"What do you mean by that?" Diana demanded.

"In case it has escaped your notice, sweetheart, I am not exactly the favorite son of Fulbrook Corners. I've got a lot of old enemies."

"After twenty years? I doubt that."

"Some folks around here have long memories, believe me. And not everyone is glad I didn't wind up in jail. The general consensus in Fulbrook Corners was that sooner or later I'd come to a bad end. People don't like to be proven wrong."

She heard the old anger in his voice and slipped an arm around his lean waist. "Colby, even if you're right, you're overlooking something. The prank was played on me, not you."

"I hate to break this to you, Diana, but you're a logical target."

"Why?"

"Because everyone in town knows you belong to me."

"Don't be ridiculous!" Indignantly, Diana started to pull away from him. His arms tightened, drawing her firmly back against his side. "I don't belong to anyone."

But Colby wasn't paying any attention to her protest. His brows were knit together in a frown of concentration. "It would be easy enough for almost any of these turkeys around here to figure out that the surest method of getting back at me would be through you."

"Colby, that is an illogical assumption, but even if we go ahead and assume it for the sake of argument, we're still stuck with the question of who would do such a thing."

"Well, for starters, we know it's someone who read Shock Value."

"Hah. From what I understand, that includes just about everybody around here. Why, even this morning Margaret Fulbrook told me she'd read one of your books..." Diana floundered to a halt as Colby pinned her with a sharp glare.

"You talked to Margaret Fulbrook today?"

"She was just coming out of the post office as I was going in. We exchanged a few words."

"About the weather?"

"No, damn it, not about the weather." Diana sighed. "She wanted to know if I'd met her grandson."

"What did you tell her?"

"The truth, of course. I told her Brandon was a very charming, intelligent young man." Diana paused and then added tentatively, "I think she'd like to meet him, Colby."

"I'll see her in hell before I let her near Brandon."

"Oh, Colby, be reasonable. She's an old woman and she doesn't have much left."

"That's her problem. Don't waste your pity on her, Diana. She doesn't deserve it." Colby swallowed more beer. "But I suppose we could start our list of possible pranksters with her. God knows she thinks she's got reason enough to hate me. And she knows about you."

Diana winced, remembering the woman's warning to her earlier. Stay away from Colby Savagar. He has no right to happiness of any kind. No point mentioning that bit of vindictiveness to Colby. He'd pounce on it as evidence of Margaret Fulbrook's guilt. Diana went for logic.

"She's an old woman, Colby. Whoever did this had to rush out here while I was in town."

"She's got Harry to run her around. Harry always felt honored to run errands for the Fulbrooks. Old man Fulbrook sent him after me when Cynthia said she was pregnant. Harry was real happy with the job."

Diana's eyes widened. "Fulbrook sent Harry after you? Why?"

"Why do you think? To beat some sense into me. Get me to leave town. Harry was twenty years younger then and built like an ox. And he never did like me in the first place."

"What happened?"

"He caught up with me outside the old Rawlins place. I'd been out talking to Eddy Spooner, and I was on my way back to Aunt Jesse's. Harry blocked the road with one of the Fulbrook trucks and when I stopped, he got out and pulled me out of my car. Said he was going to give me what I had coming to me. Then he started swinging a length of pipe at my head."

"My God, Colby."

"Fortunately he missed on the first swing, and I didn't give him a chance to get lucky with the second one. He was big, but he wasn't very fast on his feet. The trick to handling guys like Harry the Ox is to have a sucker punch up your sleeve. I managed to kick him where it would do the most good. He went down yelling. I jumped in the car and got out of there. Nobody could catch me in a car in those days." Colby paused reflectively. "Sucker wrecked my windshield with that first swing of the pipe, though. I never collected from him for the damage."

Diana was shaken. "Maybe we have to add Harry to the list."

"Uh-huh. I'm afraid he's one of many."

"Colby, for pete's sake, what did you do as a kid? Run around getting into fights with everyone in town?"

He flashed her an outrageous grin. "From my point of view, it was the other way around. Everyone was always trying to pick a fight with me."

"And you obliged."

He shrugged. "Sure. Why not?"

Diana lightly punched his shoulder. "You big macho idiot. You enjoyed your reputation, didn't you? You liked being a local legend. No wonder you've got a list of non-friends a mile long. How are we ever going to figure out who put those weeds in my vase?"

"Violence will accomplish nothing. At least, not violence against me." Colby made a production out of rubbing his wounded shoulder. Then his eyes grew thoughtful once more. "That's a hell of a good question. Gossip travels fast in a town like this. Eddy Spooner may have heard something down at the gas station. I'll talk to him. In the meantime, whenever I'm not around, make sure you keep that stupid hound of yours close. He should be capable of defending you against the kind of creep who plays practical jokes."

Specter wrinkled his nose.

"I think you've offended him," Diana said.

"Not a chance. Dog's not smart enough to figure out when he's been insulted. Now, about dinner tonight."

"What about it?"

"I was hoping you'd help me baby-sit. To tell you the truth, things are a little tense over at my place. Dear little Robyn is not happy with me."

"Why not?"

"Probably because she knows what you already figured out. My son isn't all that enthusiastic about marriage. I think you're right, Diana. I think he's gotten himself into a tangle, and he's looking for a polite way out. We had a long talk this morning."

Diana frowned. "If Robyn thinks she's losing Brandon, she's bound to be upset."

"Tell me about it. The kid looks at me as if I were an ogre. She's stopped telling me how fabulous my books are, too."

Diana grinned. "Ah, the fickle public."

"You'll come over for dinner?"

"Why don't the three of you come over here? Maybe a change of scene will relieve the tension. You think Robyn and Brandon will like stir-fry?"

"That's not the problem. Have you ever cooked for teenagers?"

"Well, no. What's the big secret?"

"The big secret is that you have to start by quadrupling the quantities of everything you fix."

"I was going to quadruple everything. After all, there will be four of us. I can count, Colby."

"No," Colby said patiently. "You don't understand. You quadruple the amounts for each teenager."

"Oh. I see. That's a lot of vegetables."

It didn't take long to determine that Colby had been right about the tension between Brandon, Robyn and himself. Halfway through dinner, Diana felt she could cut the atmosphere with a knife. Robyn looked wounded and sullen. Brandon tried to respond to Diana's conversational gambits, but invariably he ran out of things to say.

It was Colby who finally generated some real conversation when he casually told Brandon and Robyn about the weeds in Diana's vase.

"Right out of Shock Value," Brandon said. "Who would do something like that? And why?"

"We're not sure," Colby said calmly. "I talked to Eddy Spooner this afternoon, but he hadn't heard any rumors or gossip. I told him to keep his eyes open, though."

"It's spooky," Robyn said slowly. She looked at Diana. "Were you scared?"

"It was very unnerving," Diana admitted. "Rather like getting an obscene phone call. I recognized the scene out of Colby's book, too, and it upset me."

"No need to worry as long as you've got good old Specter," Brandon said with a smile as he slipped a bite of stir-fried carrot under the table.

Colby scowled. "Are you feeding that dog under the table again? He doesn't deserve any treats. He's spoiled rotten as it is."

Diana smiled. "Maybe Specter would think more highly of you, Colby, if you slipped him a bite now and then."

"Over my dead body."

A low, enthusiastic growl rumbled from beneath the table. Diana looked at Brandon and they both laughed. Robyn pushed her food around on her plate, and Colby muttered something about the likelihood of a dog such as Specter biting the hand that fed it.

"How's the job hunting going?" Brandon asked equably.

"Not as well as it should," Diana responded. "I've got to get going on it if I want to find a good job by September. I really don't want to have to go back to Carruthers and Yale."

"Have you ever been married, Diana?" Robyn asked suddenly, her pretty blue eyes reflecting a touch of malice.

Colby glared at Robyn, but Diana answered patiently. "No, Robyn, I haven't."

"And you've never had any kids, either?"

"No."

"Why not?"

"Geez, Robyn," Brandon muttered. "It's not exactly your business, is it?"

"I just want to know what makes her such an expert on marriage."

Diana was startled. "Who said I was?"

"Brandon was telling me all about how women are putting off marriage these days so that they can get a good start on their careers," Robyn explained a little too sweetly. "He was using you as an example. I said you weren't a very good example because you probably never would marry or have kids. All you're interested in is your career."

"That's enough," Colby said coldly.

Diana felt a funny twinge in the pit of her stomach. For some reason she felt obliged to defend herself. "You can't always have it all, Robyn. I made some choices early on, and I haven't regretted them."

"You chose a career over marriage. I don't think that makes you a very good example for someone like me who wants something different out of life."

Colby leaned forward menacingly. "I said, that's enough, Robyn."

Diana forced a reassuring smile. "It's all right. I know what she means. But I'll defend to the hilt the importance of a young woman getting her education and establishing a career before she marries and has children."

"Lots of women get married before they worry about a career," Robyn insisted.

"No female in her right mind should ever put herself in a position of total economic dependence on a man. She should always be able to take care of herself financially. And if she plans to have children, it's even more important that she be capable of supporting an entire family by herself. Women too often wind up raising children alone these days, in case you haven't noticed."

"That wouldn't happen to me."

"I'm sure every woman who gets pregnant feels that way. But do you know who's filling up the ranks at the poverty line in this country? Single women and their children, that's who. The men who promised to take care of them are long gone."

Diana took a deep breath and realized Brandon was looking at her with something close to admiration. Robyn was obviously furious.

But it was Colby's expression that surprised Diana. He was scowling darkly.

* * *

Diana came awake with a shiver of dread. The dream hadn't been truly a nightmare, but it had been emotionally wrenching, nonetheless. She realized with a start that she was crying.

Specter woofed questioningly. He got to his feet and pushed his muzzle into her hand. Instinctively Diana stroked him, drawing some comfort from the process.

"I'm okay," she told the dog. "It was just a dream."

A dream of a terrible darkness. A horrifying aloneness. Uncounted eons of aloneness. And the feeling of a knife in her hand. Blood welling up under her fingers, trickling out of the cave to mingle with the water and the mist. A man's voice was speaking to her, his dying curse filling the grotto even as he rolled free of her body.

You have fought me to the death. I would not have believed a woman could be so stubborn, nor so valiant. If you had been born male, you would have been a mighty warrior.

But you have not won, woman. I die here now, but so will you. And by all the gods, I tell you this, you wretched female: I curse you. With my dying blood I curse you now. Listen well to your fate, for you cannot escape. Your spirit will remain chained here until you give me the child I seek. You will learn at last what it is to be a woman. The final victory will be mine. Yours, the ultimate surrender.

"I should never have let Colby tell me about the legend of Chained Lady Cave, Specter." Diana tossed back the covers and reached for her robe and slippers. "That man is too good at inducing nightmares."

She padded down the hall, too uneasy to go immediately back to sleep. Specter followed, always willing to indulge in a midnight snack.

"That dream was all I needed on top of finding those dead weeds in my vase today," Diana confided as she rummaged around in the refrigerator. She hadn't been this shaken by a dream in a long while. "What with dreams and weeds and worrying about being pregnant, I'll be lucky to get back to sleep tonight."

The cottage seemed chilled and far too quiet to her disturbed senses. She was very glad Specter was there in the kitchen with her. Diana was used to being alone but there were times when it would be nice to have a man around.

* * *

It was the dream again. More intense than ever. Probably because he'd spent the other night in Chained Lady Cave. Was he going to have this dream off and on for the rest of his life?

He stood at the downstairs window listening to the stillness of the house, and his mind drifted back to all the long nights he had spent here as a child. They were usually nights spent imagining the worst things that could happen to him.

Outside in the darkness, deep shadows pooled among the trees. Colby watched them for a while. Why had he come back here to this town? Why couldn't he shake the feeling that there was something here in Fulbrook Corners that remained unfinished? Maybe he was just realizing the simple psychological fact that the past was always part of the future.

Colby sighed. It was more than that. He had been drawn back here by a vague feeling of incompleteness. There was something here that needed to be done before he could really be free of Fulbrook Corners.

He swore under his breath. He wanted to see Diana. He needed her tonight. The cave dream was getting to him.

Colby turned away from the window, scrawled a brief note on a piece of paper and dropped the paper on the kitchen table. He'd probably be home before dawn.

Then again, he might not.

He decided to walk to Diana's. If he took the Jeep, he'd probably waken Brandon and Robyn.

Ten minutes later, he saw the light glowing from Diana's kitchen window and wondered at it. He quickened his pace and was on the first porch step when Specter's sharp bark sounded from within.

"It's me, Diana," he called reassuringly as he pounded on the door. "Call off your damned dog."

He heard her soothing Specter, and a moment later she unlocked the front door. He looked down at her, thinking she looked warm and familiar and altogether wonderful.

"What are you doing up at this time of night?" he asked, stepping into the hall.

"I was about to ask you the same question. Good grief, Colby, it's nearly two in the morning. What are you doing running around like this in the middle of the night?"

"Couldn't sleep. Thought I'd take a walk and I saw your light on." He shrugged out of the leather jacket he'd slung on before leaving the house. "No, that's not quite accurate. The truth is, I thought I'd take a walk and see if by any chance you'd open your door to me at two in the morning." He dropped the jacket on the hall table, pulled her close and kissed her heavily.

She looked up at him when he lifted his head. Her eyes were wide, her gaze surprisingly vulnerable. "To tell you the truth," Diana said softly, "I'm glad you came by."

He held her tightly for a long moment. "Rough day, huh? Those weeds really upset you, didn't they?"

"Yes."

"I promise you I'll find out who put them there, honey. And when I do, whoever did it will be eating small rocks off the pavement. Come on. Let's go into the kitchen and pour ourselves a medicinal glass of brandy."

"I just made some hot chocolate."

"That sounds even better."

They picked up their mugs and headed for the living room. Diana sat down beside him on the old couch, curling her legs under her. Specter lounged nearby, watchful as always, but apparently resigned to the fact that Colby had exerted his right to be here at this hour.

"Are horror writers subject to a lot of sleepless nights?" Diana asked as she sipped her hot chocolate.

Colby smiled faintly. "No, not really. At least I'm not. Not any more, at any rate. I used to lie awake a lot at night when I was a kid."

"Dreaming up stories?"

"Fighting monsters that hid in the closet. I'd imagine the most horrendous monster I could, and then I wouldn't be able to go to sleep until I'd also imagined how to destroy it."

"Sounds like a way of dealing with the trauma of your childhood."

She made the observation with such sweet, grave seriousness that Colby chuckled. "Don't tell me you're an amateur psychologist as well as a first-rate business executive."

She gave him a fleeting little smile. "Well, whatever the reason for inventing monsters, it's certainly stood you in good stead. When did you first start writing, Colby?"

"When Brandon started school, I went back, too, part time. I enrolled in a local community college and, among other things, I wound up taking some writing classes. One of my teachers encouraged me to submit a couple of short stories, so I did. Nothing sold but I was hooked. I decided I wanted to write a book."

"Did you start off with horror?"

He shook his head, remembering the long, lean years. "No, I did a lot of men's action adventure stuff under a variety of names. Not much money in it, but eventually I worked it up to the point where I was earning almost as much writing as I was working in construction. That's when I quit and started writing full-time. That's also when I branched out into the horror market and started using my own name."

"A long, hard road."

His mouth curved reminiscently. "I was rather nervous the day I told my foreman I was quitting construction. I was sure that as soon as I gave up my real job, I'd stop selling books and then what would I do? After all, I had a responsibility to Brandon. But I took a chance, and I got lucky."

"Sometimes we have to make that kind of decision."

He sprawled back into the corner of the couch, pulling her with him. "Speaking of decisions, I get the impression Brandon is definitely pulling back from marriage. I owe you one for the advice you gave me, honey."

"Forget it. I hope they both come to realize marriage probably isn't the best thing for either of them at this age. From Robyn's point of view, especially, I think it would be a mistake."

"I gathered that." He tightened his arm around her. "You sure are big on women being able to take care of themselves, aren't you?"

"It's important to me."

"So important that you've never taken the risk of marriage or the risk of having kids."

Diana tensed. "Hey, don't you start in on me. Robyn's already given me a lecture on the subject of being an overly ambitious, tough, aggressive businesswoman, remember?"

"So, why are you one?" Colby asked abruptly.

For an instant he thought he'd gone too far. She was utterly rigid beside him. "If that's the way you think of me, why are you here tonight?"

"Because I know that beneath all that ambition, toughness and aggression, you are one sexy lady who has a nifty way of driving me stark raving wild." He grinned unabashedly and kissed her soundly. "And any woman who looks as sweet and soft and tasty when she's wearing a robe and slippers as you do has definitely got other talents besides her business skills. So tell me why you grew up thinking you could never rely on a man."

She lay still, looking up at him in surprise. "You're a little more perceptive than I would have guessed, Savagar."

"Don't look so astonished." He was mildly annoyed. "I'm not totally insensitive, you know. It was obvious from the way you lectured Robyn tonight that something has made you afraid to trust men. Was it just that guy who left you for his ex? Or is it all the lousy male bosses you've had over the years?"

"It's a lot of things, Colby. And it all boils down to a conviction that it's safer to rely on yourself. You can hardly argue with me on that score. You've got the same opinions on the subject."

"Yeah, you're right. Okay, in my case, it's probably because I've always felt that I was out there on my own. Aunt Jesse was hardly an anchor in a storm, and there's never been anyone else I could count on. I got used to taking care of myself. What about you?"

"A similar story. Except that I was lucky enough to have my mother. Dad took off when I was less than a year old. He never sent Mom a dime. Just disappeared. Poor Mom had gotten pregnant in high school and married without graduating. Her parents helped out but they didn't have much to spare. My mother has worked hard all her life, but you can imagine the kind of minimum-wage jobs she's had to take. There were Christmases when the only gift under the tree was the one she talked the Salvation Army into giving me."

"And you swore you were never going to get into that situation. You never wanted to take the risk of being financially dependent on a man."

"That's the long and the short of it."

"Did it occur to you that you may have carried your quest for independence to an extreme?" Colby asked dryly.

"I've been reasonably content. I'm in a position now where I have everything I want and I can afford to make my mother's life a lot easier."

"You told Robyn tonight that you can't always have it all."

"That's just being realistic. Life is often a series of trade-offs."

"Tell me something," Colby ordered softly. "Have you ever really trusted a man? Trusted him to take care of you? Trusted him to be strong for you? To be there for you?"

"Have you ever really trusted a woman that much?" she countered.

"No," he admitted somberly. But I've never met a woman quite like you, before, either, he thought.

"I think you understand me, Colby. We have some things in common, don't we?"

"Yes."

They were quiet together for a long while before they both fell asleep there on the lumpy old sofa.

9

Diana awoke feeling pleasantly crushed. It took her a few minutes to realize she was on the sofa, and that Colby was the crushing force that was being applied along the length of her.

"Beats waking up in a cave," Colby muttered without opening his eyes. At that moment, Specter stepped close to the sofa and put his damp nose against the first available chunk of warm human skin he found. He whined demandingly. Colby swore. "Tell that dog that if he wants to survive until nightfall, he'd better get his wet nose away from my back."

"I think he wants to go outside."

Colby opened one eye. "Then why don't you let him out?"

"Because you're on the outside of the sofa. It would be much easier for you to get up and let him out."

"There will be snow in August before I do that dog any favors. I've got more interesting things to do this morning." He slid a warm palm over the curve of Diana's hip.

"Letting him out first thing in the morning isn't exactly a favor. It's more of a necessity."

Specter emphasized the point with another sharp whine. He moved his cold nose up the length of Colby's spine, pushing the rumpled khaki shirt out of the way as he went.

"All right, all right. I surrender. I can take anything but wet-dog-nose torture." Colby rolled to his feet and stretched hugely. "Come on, you great slobbering beast. Outside. I may use you in a book one of these days, you know that?"

Specter leaped forward enthusiastically. Diana listened to the front door open and close and thought about how nice it was to have the man she loved waking up with her in the mornings. A woman could get addicted to this special kind of luxury. It would be dangerous to indulge herself too much.

She opened her eyes to find Colby standing beside the sofa, shedding the jeans in which he had slept. Dawn light danced on his powerful, naked shoulders. There was a possessive intentness in his gaze that sent small shock waves through her nerve endings.

For an instant, time went still in that strange way that it did sometimes when she was with Colby. She saw the fathomless desire etched in the hard lines of his face and felt the waves of his fierce will lapping at her. He was so strong, a legendary warrior, a man who dominated everything and everyone around him. She was suddenly overwhelmed with the knowledge that she was engaged in a battle.

She was caught, trapped, chained

And then Colby was grinning down at her, gray eyes warm and lazy with early-morning sensuality.

Yes, he was dangerous, she thought. But how could she resist? Diana opened her arms to him, and he came to her at once.

A long time later, Colby again rolled off the couch, this time rubbing his bristly jaw. "Too bad I forgot to bring along a razor. I wouldn't have this problem if you were living with me."

"You can use mine."

"I think I'll just do that. Serve you right for being too stubborn to move in with me. And then we'll fix breakfast, and then I have got to get some work done today. What with one thing and another, I'm not exactly producing pages of manuscript lately. I think I'll kick the kids out of the house for the day, lock all the doors, make a large pot of coffee and spend some time doing what I'm supposed to be doing this summer."

"Colby?"

"Hmm?"

"I'm glad you came by when you did last night. It would have been a very long night, otherwise."

He leaned down and gathered her up into his arms, crushing her very close once more. "I'm glad you needed me a little last night. Because I needed you, too."

She clung to him until Specter scratched at the front door.

Three hours later, Brandon appeared in the Jeep. Specter raced out ferociously at the familiar sound of the engine, but when he saw who was at the wheel he immediately lost interest in the attack.

"Hi, Diana," Brandon said when Diana walked out onto the porch. "Dad won't let anyone into the house. He says Robyn and I are supposed to entertain ourselves for the day. We've already gone hiking, and now Robyn is reading out there under the trees. I'm on my way into town to pick up Dad's mail and some groceries. Dad said you might want to go along. He said you usually go into town about this time, too."

"That sounds great, Brandon. I'll get my bag."

"Specter can come, too," Brandon called after her. "That's why I brought the Jeep. There's room for both of you."

"If only your father were so gracious toward my dog. Specter might take an entirely different attitude toward him."

Brandon laughed, and a few minutes later the Jeep pulled out of the yard with all of them aboard.

"You drive like your father," Diana muttered as Brandon whipped the Jeep neatly into a curve and accelerated confidently on the other side. The sense of speed, power and control was very familiar.

"Probably because he taught me," Brandon said with a casual shrug. "Specter okay back there?"

"He's fine." Diana patted Specter, who had his nose stuck out into the wind.

There were several interested stares as Brandon parked the Jeep in front of the post office. Across the street, Eddy Spooner waved from under the hood of a car. Diana waved back on the way into the gossip center of Fulbrook Corners.

"Groceries next," she announced a few minutes later when they trooped back out of the post office.

"I'll come with you," Brandon said. "Got to get some stuff for dinner. Dad says we're having you over again tonight." He glanced around with interest. "Hard to believe Dad grew up in a place like this. Somehow it just doesn't look like him."

"I don't think he fit in too well here," Diana murmured.

"I wonder why he came back this summer."

"It's an interesting question."

It was then that Diana saw the aging blue Cadillac moving ponderously down the street toward them. She knew in that moment that she faced a major decision. She also knew there weren't many options. The Cadillac was already slowing in front of them. Harry was going to park in front of the grocery store.

"Brandon?"

"Yeah, Diana?"

"That's your grandmother in the Cadillac."

Brandon came to an abrupt halt, staring in fascination as Harry got out of the car and opened the door for the regal woman inside. Margaret Fulbrook stood waiting, her eyes riveted on her grandson.

"Good morning, Mrs. Fulbrook," Diana said quietly as she and Brandon drew close. "Allow me to present Brandon Savagar. Brandon, this is Margaret Fulbrook." She held her breath, but Brandon's innate good manners overcame the traumatic nature of the moment.

"How do you do, Mrs. Fulbrook?" he said with admirable calm.

"You look like him," Margaret Fulbrook snapped accusingly. "Just like he did at your age. Except for the eyes. What they told me about your eyes is true. They're just like Cynthia's."

"That's what Dad always said."

"I'm surprised your father would admit there was any part of you that resembled your mother's side of the family. What did Colby tell you about Cynthia when you were growing up?"

"He said she was very pretty."

Margaret Fulbrook's eyes softened reminiscently. "Yes," she said, "my daughter was very pretty. Very full of life. If it hadn't been for your father"

Brandon didn't wait for her to finish. "Excuse me, Mrs. Fulbrook. We've got some shopping to do." He took Diana's arm with all the cool aplomb Colby would have demonstrated in the situation and started toward the entrance of the grocery store. Diana didn't try to stop him.

"Where do you think you're going, young man?" Margaret Fulbrook shrilled behind them. "You come back here this instant. I'm talking to you. Harry, stop him. Stop him this instant."

Harry lumbered into their path, moving as heavily as the big Cadillac he drove. His small eyes were narrowed in anticipation. "You heard her, kid. She wants to talk to you. Do like she says, or I'll give you what I gave your father one night, back when he was your age."

Brandon released Diana's arm. She could feel him preparing himself.

"Don't worry, Brandon," she said smoothly, "your father says Harry's big, but he's slow. And if he was too slow to take your father twenty years ago, I think it's safe to assume that by now poor Harry's turned into molasses."

Rage creased Harry's heavy face. "Slow, am I? I'll show you who's slow." He raised a meaty fist, glaring at Brandon. "You're just like him, damn you. Just like him. He probably taught you a couple of his sucker punches. But I'll take you. See if I don't."

Brandon stood waiting. He never took his eyes off his opponent.

Diana turned to fix Margaret Fulbrook with a withering glance. "This little performance is certainly guaranteed to make sure Brandon never speaks to you again, isn't it, Mrs. Fulbrook?"

"I want to talk to him. I must talk to him. Now that I've seen him, I must speak to him. Don't you understand?"

"I understand. But the first requirement is that you call off Harry." Diana was aware of the gathering ring of onlookers. "If there's bloodshed, this will be the end of it, Mrs. Fulbrook. You'll never see Brandon again."

"But he was leaving," Mrs. Fulbrook wailed. "I was trying to talk to him and he walked away from me."

"Only because you started to bad-mouth Dad," Brandon said, still not looking away from Harry. "I'm willing to talk to you, ma'am, but I won't let you say anything against my father."

There was an acute silence and then Margaret Fulbrook heaved a deep sigh. "Come away from him, Harry."

"But, Mrs. Fulbrook"

"I said, come away from him."

Harry was clearly vastly disappointed, but he obeyed reluctantly.

"Now come back here and talk to me, boy."

Brandon turned around slowly. "You give me your word you won't criticize Dad?"

"It will be hard not to criticize him," Mrs. Fulbrook said honestly. "I've had twenty years of practice. But I'll do my best. Now come over here and let me look at those eyes again."

Diana smiled slightly as Brandon went back toward his grandmother. "I'll do the grocery shopping while you two go have a cup of coffee," she said.

But neither Brandon nor Margaret Fulbrook were paying her any attention. They were too busy looking at each other's eyes.

An hour later, a thoughtful Brandon dropped Diana and Specter off at the cottage. Brandon had said little on the way back from town, but when Diana started to climb out of the Jeep he spoke.

"What do you think of her, Diana?"

She sat back in the seat and studied Brandon's intent, concerned expression. "She's a bitter old woman who has denied herself her grandson for twenty years. Now she's seen you and she's regretting having let all that time go by. You're all she has left."

"I felt kind of sorry for her. In spite of the way she sicced old Harry on us."

"You were generous and kind to her today, Brandon. You gave her something she could never have bought, or stolen, or taken by force. Deep down she knows that." Impulsively Diana leaned across the seat and kissed him lightly on the cheek. "Only a real man could have handled that situation as well as you did today. I'm proud to know you." She backed out of the Jeep. Specter jumped down beside her and immediately headed for the porch steps.

"Diana, wait." Brandon had turned brick red at her comment on his manliness, but he looked very pleased. "What do you think I should tell Dad?"

"I don't know. The truth, I suppose. He must have known that with you in town the meeting was inevitable. I think his main concern was that Mrs. Fulbrook would try to hurt you somehow. But when he realizes how well you handled the whole thing, he'll relax. And you did handle it well, Brandon. You had her eating out of the palm of your hand."

Brandon grinned. "Not quite, but she's certainly not the tough old bird Dad made her out to be."

"Maybe she was a lot tougher twenty years ago."

Brandon put the Jeep in gear. "Probably. See you later, Diana, and thanks."

Diana watched him wheel the Jeep out of the drive, and then she turned toward the cottage. "Come on, Specter, old buddy, let's get ourselves a snack."

But for once Specter did not come to instant attention at the mention of food. He was sniffing around the front door and making odd snuffling sounds.

Diana felt chilled. "Specter? What is it? What's wrong?" She dug her keys out of her shoulder bag and started to fit them into the front door. Specter scratched at the screen, obviously impatient.

Maybe Colby was inside, Diana thought. But why hadn't he come out when he heard the Jeep? She turned the key slowly and then instinctively stood back to let the dog enter first.

Specter didn't hesitate. He trotted inside and began sniffing around the hall table. Diana followed slowly, trying to figure out what was so wrong in the hallway.

It took her a full three seconds to realize the small table with the empty vase was positioned on the left side of the hall instead of the right.

Someone had moved it. Someone who had studied Shock Value.

"My God, Specter. Someone's deliberately spooking me. Someone's trying to scare the daylights out of me."

Whoever he was, he was succeeding.

Diana stared at the hall table for a few more seconds, aware of her pounding pulse and the cold dampness of her own nervous sweat. She tried to think clearly. The intruder must have long since departed, she assured herself. Specter would not be this calm if there was someone hiding in the cottage.

She made herself walk past the table into the kitchen. This time she didn't have to search through her copy of Shock Value to find the pertinent passage. The book was lying open on the table. Diana gazed down at page fifty-six. For a moment she couldn't seem to focus. Then the words settled into place on the page.

It was such a small thing, this new position of the table, just a minor adjustment in his everyday world. It was the kind of casual re-arrangement of furniture that anyone might try, to see if the space could be better utilized or if eye appeal could be enhanced.

But the effect was devastating. Some minor demon had paused long enough in Donnelly's personal universe to introduce an element of horrific chaos.

Because Donnelly knew that no human hand could have moved the table. There was no way anyone could have entered the house unde-tected. The security system he'd installed was foolproof.

But he refused to believe in demons, minor or otherwise.

Perhaps the time had come to ask himself if he was going insane. It would be interesting to see what the verdict was.

Diana couldn't bring herself to read any further. She closed the book and went slowly into the living room. Specter had lost interest in the table. He followed his mistress and flopped at her feet when she sank down onto the sofa.

Diana was still huddled on the sofa half an hour later when the Jeep roared back into her drive. Specter raised his head and barked ferociously.

Relief flooded through Diana when she realized it had to be Colby. It was a shock to acknowledge to herself how much she needed him in that moment, needed to turn to him for comfort and reassurance, needed him for his strength and the protection he could provide. It was the first time in her life she had ever considered turning to a man for such things. But then, she had never known a man like Colby.

Then she heard the screen door slam with sickening fury and Diana's relief turned to dread. The last thing she needed right now was Colby's anger.

Sensing genuine rage, Specter changed his familiar growl of protest into something much more serious. But Colby ignored the dog. He came down the hall in three long strides, and his glittering eyes went straight to Diana. His face was a mask of hard fury as he came toward her.

For an instant Diana felt as if she had slipped back into an ancient past to face an implacable male. The warrior's anger was fully aroused. He would not tolerate her defiance. He would not rest until he had subdued her.

"You couldn't resist, could you?" Colby stopped in front of her and hauled her to her feet. "You just could not resist. I told you to stay out of it. He's my son, goddamn it. My son. And you knew I didn't want him meeting that old bitch. Damn you, Diana. You had no right to get involved. No right. Who the hell do you think you are?"

It was too much to deal with. Coming on top of the shock she'd had earlier, Colby's fury was too much. This was always the way it was. When the chips were down, you could depend on no one but yourself. A woman could not afford to rely on a man. Only a fool would believe that any man would be there when you needed him.

"Let me go, Colby." Her voice was low and tight. Specter crowded close, teeth showing.

"You deliberately set it up for them to meet, didn't you? You went behind my back and planned the whole thing."

"No, Colby, I didn't plan it. It just happened."

"The hell it did. It wouldn't have happened if I'd been there, you can bet on that. Christ, lady, you introduced them. Brandon told me exactly how it worked. You introduced my son to that old she-devil who has totally ignored him for nearly twenty years. I trusted you, damn it. I thought you were on my side. It never occurred to me you'd go behind my back like this."

Diana strove to keep her face expressionless. His hands were like steel clamps on her arms. She looked up at him and knew that it was hopeless. "I'm sorry, Colby."

"Sure you are," he bit out scathingly. "I'll tell you who's sorry. I'm the one who's sorry. Sorry for trusting you. Sorry for believing you were different from other women. I was a fool, but it was my son who paid the price of my damned idiocy." He released her with an angry gesture and stalked to the window. "I don't know what the hell made me think I could trust you just because you're good in bed."

Diana wrapped her arms around herself, withdrawing from Colby's anger and the insult he'd offered. Specter huddled closer, whining softly. His massive body was a source of comfort in the storm. She could feel the tension in him. It occurred to her that Specter was the one male on earth she could rely upon.

"He bought her a cup of coffee. Can you believe it?" Colby slammed the palm of his hand against the windowsill. "He bought Margaret Fulbrook a cup of coffee and sat there talking to her while you blithely went grocery shopping."

"Colby"

"I heard she sicced that stupid ox, Harry, on the two of you. Tell me, what would you have done if that creep had taken a swing at my son? How would you have felt then?"

"Brandon handled him very well. There was no fight."

"No thanks to you. You must have thought you were being so damned clever." Colby raked his hand through his hair in his characteristic gesture.

"You've said enough, Colby."

Her low, cold, utterly formal tone seemed to get through to him. His head came around swiftly and he gave her a seething look.

"What don't you want to hear?" he asked far too softly. "That you're so accustomed to playing lady executive that you can't resist the opportunity to power-trip in someone else's life? That you think you're smarter than anyone else? That you're better equipped than others to make the kind of decisions that will affect people for years to come?"

"Colby, I said that's enough. I get the point. I think it's time you left." It took every ounce of her self-control to hold herself in check. She wanted to cry-to scream abuse at him for not being there for her when she needed him. But if she had learned anything in the business world, it was how to control her outward emotions around a man.

"I've got a lot more to say to you, lady."

She closed her eyes, clutching herself more tightly, holding herself together as she had always held herself together in front of others. "You probably do, but I'd rather not hear it. Now will you please go away, Colby? You've told me what you thought of me. I swear I won't get involved with you or Brandon again. You have my word of honor."

"What the hell is your word of honor worth?"

Diana opened her eyes and looked straight into his smoky gaze. "Believe me, Colby, in this case, you may rely on it completely. If you like, I'll give you a money-back guarantee that I won't see either you or your son again. Now will you leave?"

Specter reinforced the quiet command with a rumbling growl. He stood braced at Diana's feet.

"Yeah, I'll leave, Diana." Colby started past her toward the door. "You've done enough damage. No point hanging around to see what other tricks you've got up your sleeve."

He slammed the screen door more loudly on the way out than he had on the way in.

"He didn't even notice the hall table," Diana observed to her dog. Then she sank back down onto the sofa and let the pent-up tears flow.

The most frustrating thing had been watching her withdraw into herself. She had reacted to him as if he had been some wild, dangerous force of nature. She had battened down the hatches, erected the barriers that would keep her safe and secure and then stood there and let him rage.

She had handled him the way she probably handled every other male in her life. She had retreated behind that cool, collected, untouchable facade and waited for him to do his worst.

He realized he had wanted her to react somehow. He wished she had cried, or shouted, or pounded on him with her small fists. Anything would have been preferable to that cool retreat.

He'd been angry and she was to blame. Colby had wanted a fight, and she had refused to enter the lists. That riled him as much as the original reason for his anger.

Colby snapped the Jeep around the last hairpin turn in River Road and then slowed the vehicle and turned into the parking area below Chained Lady Falls. He switched off the ignition with a violent twist and then sat, arms braced on the wheel, staring at the foaming water pouring down the cliff.

She'd had no right to introduce Brandon to the old bitch.

Brandon had claimed that Margaret Fulbrook had obviously engineered the meeting, but Colby knew it could have been avoided. All Diana and Brandon had to do was perform a simple hundred and eighty degree turn, get back in the Jeep and drive away. But, no. Diana had calmly made introductions and then sent Brandon off to have a cup of coffee with his grandmother.

His son had shared a cup of coffee with the old bat. Colby still couldn't believe it. And Diana had coolly done the grocery shopping while Brandon dealt with Margaret Fulbrook alone. It was too much. Too damned much.

What if Harry had swung at Brandon? It was true Colby had made certain Brandon was trained to take care of himself, but the boy had never been in a real street fight.

Harry was slow, but vicious and strong. One lucky punch was all it would have taken to down Brandon. What if Diana had gotten caught in the middle of such a fight? Not an unlikely possibility since she probably would have tried to stop it. She would have been seriously injured.

Colby's right hand clenched into a fist. He forced himself to relax the fingers one at a time. There was no excuse for Diana's behavior.

She had known full well that he hadn't wanted Brandon to meet Margaret Fulbrook.

Sure, Brandon had been curious about his grandmother, but the boy wouldn't have engineered the meeting against Colby's direct orders. It was Diana who had taken it upon herself to arrange it.

"Damn it to hell."

He should never have come back here this summer. Everything would have been fine if he hadn't taken it into his head to see Fulbrook Corners again. He must have been out of his mind.

But if he hadn't come back here, he would never have met Diana.

Colby got out of the Jeep and walked to the edge of the water. Mist from the falls enveloped him, dampening his hair and his shirt. He stood looking up toward the hidden cave.

She had been so warm and loving and sweet that night. She had been everything he'd ever wanted in a woman. She had given herself to him in a way he knew instinctively she had never given herself to any other man. She had held back nothing. She had been his.

And the next morning she had acted as though nothing had happened, even though there was a very real chance she might have gotten pregnant.

Today she had given him her personal, money-back guarantee that she wouldn't involve herself in his life ever again. She was going to walk away from him the way she planned to walk away from her job. Probably saw herself as a victim of male chauvinism once more.

Colby turned back to the Jeep and got behind the wheel. He didn't like the idea that she was lumping him in with every other unreliable male in her life-her father, the men she worked for, that bastard when she was twenty-five.

But he had a right to his anger, by God. It was she who had failed him, not the other way around. She had no business going cold and brittle on him the way she had when he'd yelled at her. No business withdrawing into herself like that.

He was half way back to Aunt Jesse's before he began to calm down and think rationally.

The first rational thought that occurred to him was that he couldn't let Diana just walk out of his life.

The second rational thought was that there had been something wrong with the hall table in her cottage.

10

Diana had finished cleaning up the kitchen and was packing unused food into a cooler when Specter snarled a warning. A moment later she heard the Jeep engine and closed her eyes in pain. Colby was back to yell at her again. Diana didn't think she could take any more.

She straightened and went quickly down the hall to the front door. She managed to set the lock just as he vaulted up the steps to the front porch. He must have heard the faint click.

"Diana, let me in." Colby pounded peremptorily on the door.

Specter barked loudly in response, but Diana didn't bother to answer. She went back down the hall to the kitchen, locked the back door and then resumed her packing.

The pounding continued. "Damn it, Diana, let me in. I've got to talk to you."

Diana let Specter answer for her. The dog did so enthusiastically. The ensuing racket of barking and fist-pounding continued unabated for a couple of minutes. The pounding stopped first. Specter gave one last victorious woof and trotted into the kitchen.

"Good dog," Diana murmured. "I can count on you, at least, can't I?"

But there was no sound of the Jeep's engine being switched on, and Specter began to growl again. He stood poised for a moment and then, with a loud yelp, went dashing out of the kitchen toward the bedroom.

"Too late, you fool dog. I'm already inside."

Colby's voice came from the bedroom and Diana remembered the window she had left open in there. She turned slowly around to face him as he strode into the kitchen. Specter growled at his heels but made no move to cause genuine injury.

"What the hell is going on here?" Colby demanded, taking in the array of boxes and cleaning items.

"What does it look like? I'm getting ready to leave." Diana made herself go back to work, methodically putting packaged food items into a box to take with her.

"Going to run out now after causing all the trouble?" he asked, his voice rough.

"I gave you my word I would not interfere in your life again, Colby. That means I have to leave Fulbrook Corners. To use an old western expression, this town isn't big enough for both of us. There's no way we can avoid running into each other here."

"Do you always run away when things don't work out the way you had planned?"

"As I told Brandon the other night at dinner, a smart business-woman has to know when to cut her losses."

"And I'm a loss, is that it?"

She took a firm grasp on her jangled nerves and uncertain temper. "The bottom line is that our relationship is a loss. A complete write-off."

He walked over to a kitchen chair, spun it around and straddled it backward. He crossed his arms along the laddered seat back and watched her with brooding eyes. "Is it comfortable and convenient to be able to talk about our relationship in business jargon? It's a complete write-off? It's time to cut your losses? Let me tell you something, the bottom line as far as I'm concerned is that I don't like being referred to as just another bad business investment."

Diana's hands tightened on a box of cereal until the thin cardboard began to crumple. "You're the creative writer in the crowd. You think of a better way to put it."

"Okay, how's this? You're a coward, Diana. You think that when the going gets tough, tough ladies like you can just walk away from the problem."

Her head came up sharply as anger surged through her. "That's non-sense and you know it. You're the one who ended this so-called relationship, not me. You marched in here a little while ago and told me I was an interfering, manipulative troublemaker."

"You were. And I was madder than hell."

"Is that right? Well, so am I. Why don't you just get out of here, Colby? Go on, get lost. I've got work to do."

"You can't run away from me."

"Who's going to stop me?"

"I am," Colby said bluntly.

"You're not making sense. Less than an hour ago you were telling me to stay out of your life."

"I never said that."

"Well, that's what it sounded like to me."

"I told you, I was angry," Colby said through his teeth. "And with good reason. I did not, however, kick you out of my life."

"Close enough."

"And you decided I was just like every other man you've ever known, didn't you?" he shot back swiftly and softly. "But you're wrong. I'll admit I can see where you got that impression about me, though."

"Is that right?"

"You needed me. You were probably scared to death, and all I did was rage at you and then storm out the door. A lot of sound and fury, but not particularly useful when the crunch came. Is that what all the men in your life have been like, Diana?"

"I was not frightened of you," she said with great dignity. "I have never been frightened of any man."

"Is that right? You were frightened of whoever moved that table in your hall."

She dropped the jar of mustard she had been about to place in the box. For an instant there was silence.

"I didn't think you'd noticed," Diana said at last, not looking at him.

"I was too damned mad to notice it right away. But then I drove out to Chained Lady Falls to think, and after a while I remembered there was something different about the hall table. Something that reminded me of a scene out of one of my books."

"Shock Value. Page fifty-six."

Colby nodded slowly, his eyes never leaving hers. "When did it happen?"

"The table being moved? I don't know. While Brandon and I were in town, I guess. It was like that when I got back."

"It was a shock, wasn't it?"

"That's putting it mildly. Someone around here doesn't like me, Colby. And your theory that it might be Margaret Fulbrook is wrong. She was having coffee with Brandon while my table was being moved."

Colby's eyes narrowed. "Harry could have done it."

"No. Harry sat out in the Cadillac the whole time Brandon and Margaret were in the café."

"That leaves a town full of possibilities," Colby mused.

"Well, whoever did it will have to find a new hobby. I'll be safely back in Portland tonight."

"You'll be safely over at Aunt Jesse's place tonight," Colby said flatly.

Diana eyed him warily. "No, thanks. I've had enough of Fulbrook Corners."

"And enough of me, is that it?"

"To be perfectly frank, dealing with a nasty prankster and a man who thinks I've committed the ultimate act of disloyalty is a bit much to handle. Even for me."

"You didn't commit the ultimate act of disloyalty," Colby muttered. "Just a minor indiscretion. The ultimate act of disloyalty would be for you to sleep with another man."

"I can't tell you how relieved I am to hear that my sin was not a mortal one. Will you please go away and let me pack?"

He didn't move. "Diana, I had a right to be furious with you."

She shrugged, pulling more items out of the cupboard. "Maybe. It's a matter of opinion. Your son wanted to meet his grandmother. He's an adult and he has some rights, too, you know. When I saw her standing there on the street, staring at him, I simply made the introductions. As far as I was concerned, the issue was Brandon's to decide. Not yours and not mine."

Colby drew a deep breath. "Maybe that's why I was so mad," he said slowly. "Maybe I didn't want to admit that the decision was

Brandon's. I told you I've made a lot of mistakes as a father. No reason to think I'm not capable of making a few more."

"Tell Brandon that. I'm sure he'll understand. He's a very sensitive, understanding young man."

"Unlike his father?"

"You're a lot more cynical than he is, but then, you went through a far tougher childhood and adolescence. And don't be too hard on yourself, Colby. You're the one responsible for turning Brandon into the fine young man he is. Now, if you'll excuse me, I want to finish this packing."

"Diana, you're coming over to my place for the night. You'll be safe there."

"I'll be safer in Portland."

There was a loud crash as Colby shot to his feet and sent the chair spinning backward against the wall. "Damn you, you stubborn, thickheaded, self-contained female. You don't think you can even rely on me enough to let me protect you, do you?"

Diana clenched her hands to stop her fingers from trembling. "Why should you want to protect me?"

"Because you belong to me. Haven't you figured that much out yet?"

"You mean because we started a brief summer affair you feel you have some responsibility toward me?" she mocked. "Forget it, Colby. I can take care of myself. I've been doing it a long time now. Besides, the affair is over. Your sense of obligation can take a hike."

He reached her in two long strides and caught her deftly by the nape of the neck. His touch was astonishingly gentle but there was too much strength in his hand for her to successfully resist him. His eyes softened a little as he looked down at her. "The affair is a long way from over and you know it. As for my sense of obligation, we can discuss that later. At Aunt Jesse's place. Don't fight me on this, honey. You know I'll go out of my mind if I have to worry about you staying here alone, and I can't let you drive back to Portland. Not yet. There's too much between us."

"Is there?" She could hardly get the words out. She was ensnared in his glittering, determined gazed.

"Yes," Colby stated. "There is."

The fact that he understood that much was what made Diana keep her mouth shut as she went down the hall to get her overnight things.

"Dad blew up when I told him about meeting Grandmother today," Brandon said an hour later. He and Diana were sitting in two of the decrepit chairs on the porch of Aunt Jesse's old house. Robyn was upstairs sulking, and Colby had gone back to work. "But he's seriously angry about these stupid pranks someone's playing on you."

Diana sipped iced tea and regarded her companion with a skeptical expression. "Seriously angry? You think he's more annoyed because of the pranks than he is because I introduced you to Margaret Fulbrook?"

"Definitely."

"I think you've got that backward. Colby's not happy about the pranks, but I would say that he was definitely, seriously angry about your meeting your grandmother."

"Nah. You don't know Dad as well as I do. When he starts yelling, he's mad, all right. But he cools down after he's let off steam. On the other hand, when he gets quiet, that's when you know you've got a problem."

"I'll try to keep the distinction in mind," Diana said with a wry smile.

"Were you really on your way back to Portland?"

"Yes."

"Dad must have come unglued."

"No," Diana said reflectively. "He just got madder."

"I'm glad you didn't go. He's really hung up on you, you know."

"No, I don't know. I can't always figure your father out, Brandon."

"Most people can't. I know him better than anyone, and I still have problems figuring him out at times. But he's okay when the chips are down, you know what I mean? He takes care of things."

"I think you're a lot like him in that respect, Brandon," Diana said gently. She was about to say something else but Robyn wandered out onto the porch at that moment. The young woman gave Diana a baleful glance and turned to Brandon.

"I'm bored. There's nothing to do around here. You want to take a walk or something, Brandon? I need to talk to you."

"Sure." Brandon got to his feet. "See you later, Diana. Want to come along, Specter?" He slapped his thigh encouragingly.

Specter lumbered to his feet and cast a questioning glance at Diana.

"Go on," she said to the dog. "I'll be fine."

Specter trotted happily along after the pair, his shaggy tail waving cheerfully.

"Look at that fool dog," Colby said through the screen door. "Acts like he and Brandon have been best buddies for years. While I, on the other hand, get treated to bared teeth and salivating jaws."

"I guess something about you just irritates him," Diana said as she poured herself more iced tea and watched Brandon and Robyn disappear into the woods. "Do you want some tea?"

"Thanks." He pushed open the screen door, walked out onto the porch and dropped into the chair Brandon had been using. He took the cold glass from her hand and gazed after Brandon and Robyn. "I get the feeling dear little Robyn has about had it with Fulbrook Corners."

"I can empathize."

"You still mad at me?"

Diana thought about it. "Yes."

"You'll get over it."

"You think so?"

"Sure. I got over being mad at you, didn't I?" Colby pointed out with unarguable masculine logic.

"Did you?"

"Yes, damn it, I did." Colby set down his glass and reached over to snag her arm. He deftly removed the glass from her hand and pulled her out of her chair and across his lap. "Now stop trying to provoke me."

"What is this? You get to be mad as long as you like, but as soon as you're finished everyone else is supposed to go back to normal, too?"

"Works better that way." He cradled her close, his hand on her thigh, his lips in her hair.

"Colby, I want to talk to you."

"Talk fast." His hand traveled up her jean-clad thigh and settled on her hip.

"I don't think you've given this whole situation much thought."

"What situation?" His lips were on her throat.

Diana shivered and touched his shoulder longingly. "Me. Here in the house."

"As long as I'm willing to tolerate that stupid mutt of yours underfoot, where's the problem?"

"Well, the sleeping arrangements for one thing. Do you have a fourth bedroom?"

"Nope. Only got three."

"That's what I thought. So where am I supposed to sleep?"

He drew back for an instant to look down at her with genuine surprise. "You sleep with me, naturally. Where did you think you were going to sleep?"

"But what about the kids? Do you think they ought to see us, uh, going off to bed together?"

"As you and my son have both taken pains to point out to me lately, Brandon is no longer a kid. He already knows I'm sleeping with you and he approves. What more do you want?"

"What about Robyn?" Diana asked anxiously.

"If she's old enough to sleep with Brandon, she's old enough to handle the concept of a couple of genuine, grown-up adults sleeping together. Now stop worrying about it. The decision has already been made."

"By you?"

"Yeah. By me." His hand slid up just under her breast, his thumb sliding into her cleavage. "Now, tell me what you picked up for dinner tonight."

"I can't seem to remember at the moment. All I can think about is dessert." She smiled up at him, her fingertips trailing teasingly down the front of his shirt to the waistband of his jeans.

He grinned. "Does this mean I'm forgiven?"

"It means I'm prepared to let you prove just how remorseful you really are."

"Good idea. I'll start proving it right now."

Diana laughed and caught his exploring hand. "No, you will not. It's almost time to start dinner, and Brandon and Robyn will be back soon."

Colby muttered something under his breath and wrapped her so tightly to him that she squeaked. The sexy laughter faded from his eyes to be replaced with something more intense. "I think we can safely say we got through our first major quarrel today."

"Is that something to celebrate?"

"Yeah," he said. "I think it is. With any luck, you learned a few things today."

She gave him an indignant glare. "I learned a few things? What was I supposed to learn?"

His gaze was brilliant and grimly intent. "That I won't let you walk out of my life just because of a disagreement. Remember that, Diana."

She said nothing, touching his hard jaw with her forefinger in an unconsciously gentle action. Privately she wondered what it would take for him to let her walk out of his life.

Would he let her go if it turned out she was pregnant?

Colby waited until Brandon and Robyn were deeply involved in a board game that night before he took Diana's hand and led her toward the stairs.

"Good night, you two. See you in the morning," he said as he started upstairs with Diana in tow.

Brandon looked up from the board and smiled at Diana. "Good night."

Robyn looked up briefly but said nothing. She had said very little all evening.

At the top of the stairs Diana said softly, "I don't think that girl likes me."

"Don't worry about it. I'm the one who has cause for worry. The thought of having her for a daughter-in-law sends chills down my spine."

"I think Brandon has definitely postponed thoughts of marriage. But I'm not so sure about Robyn. She really wants to get married, and she doesn't like being asked to wait."

"I just hope she doesn't do something really stupid like get pregnant."

Beside him, Diana fell silent. Too late he realized the stupidity of his last remark. Diana, of course, would take it personally. If she were pregnant—

Damn, but women were complicated creatures.

Colby opened the door of his bedroom and urged her inside. A surge of possessiveness and satisfaction went through him as he closed the door and watched her standing in the middle of his very personal domain. He leaned back against the door and drank his fill of her as she wandered curiously to the window, over to the dresser and then to the bed.

"Was this your room as a child?" she asked as she touched a model of a Corvette he had once painstakingly built from a kit.

Colby nodded. "Yeah."

She examined the model car. "It's hard to imagine you as a little kid."

He shrugged. "My big dream, aside from escaping Fulbrook Corners, was to own a 'vette."

"Did you ever get one?"

"Senior year in high school. A used one. Got it for a song because some guy had crashed it. Eddy helped me work on it. By the time we were finished, it was a teenager's dream. Black as midnight and faster than a bat out of hell. I beat everything I ever went up against out on River Road in that car. It was the pride and joy of my life."

"What happened to it?"

"I had a great time with it for a while." He took the model from her hand and studied it with a reminiscent smile. Then he shrugged and put the little 'vette down on a shelf. "Then I got married, and Brandon came along and I needed money for baby food and diapers and all the other things that a baby needs."

"So you sold your pride and joy?"

Colby laughed softly and walked over to sink down beside her. "Don't look so sad. It was a long time ago."

"And now you drive a Jeep?"

"I like to take it off-roading. A man's taste changes as he gets older." Colby leaned over her, easing her back onto the pillows and caging her with his hands. "Take you, for instance. I'm not sure I would have had the brains or the sense to properly appreciate you when I was nineteen. But now" He kissed her slowly, deeply, giving her time to respond.

"And now?" she whispered huskily when he finally freed her mouth.

"Now I'm a lot older and wiser. And boy, do I appreciate you..."

Colby bent his head to kiss her again, and when she opened her mouth for him he slid his knee between her thighs. Diana's hand curved around his buttocks, urging him more tightly against her softness and she lifted her hips against his.

"I love the way you get so hot, so fast for me, honey. You make me crazy."

"I'm the one who goes crazy," she whispered, guiding his head down to her breasts. She was already unbuttoning her shirt for him, freeing herself of her peach-colored bra. "You make me ache all over, do you know that, Colby?"

And then she was offering her breasts to him, demanding and pleading for his intimate attention. Colby felt his already taut body ignite. The knowledge that she needed him, wanted him, would give herself to him whenever he turned to her was almost too much to handle. The growing realization that he had only to touch her to know she was his sent flames roaring through him.

He gently sucked one sweet, tight nipple between his teeth and simultaneously reached down to unfasten his jeans and then hers. Together they slithered out of the restricting clothing and then they were clinging to each other.

When Diana reached down to stroke the hardened length of his manhood, Colby nearly lost his self-control. She had a way of pushing him to the edge, and he loved it.

"Here," he muttered, scrabbling about in the nightstand drawer for the little foil packet. "You put it on."

"Me?"

"Yeah, you. I'll just lie here and go out of my mind."

She laughed softly and knelt beside him. Colby knew he'd made a serious error the minute he realized what a long production she was going to make out of the simple action. But the delicious sensations she created as she worked carefully and gently over him almost made up for the agony of waiting.

Almost.

The instant she was done, Diana sat back and examined her handiwork with satisfaction. "A perfect fit. Not bad, if I do say so myself."

Colby grinned, his teeth set as he struggled for self-control. "Come here and finish the job, you little witch."

She raised her brows mockingly. "I thought the job was finished."

"It's just started." He pulled her across his thighs, his hands clenching luxuriously into her hips. "Now show me just how perfect the fit really is."

Her eyes were bold and sensuous as she grasped him gently and began to ease him into her softness. He saw the glittering excitement in her, and it fed the flames of his own fire.

When she hesitated a little, teasing him unmercifully, Colby gave a soft, warning exclamation and then pulled her down abruptly, sinking himself to the hilt.

Diana bit back a gasp of excitement, and her head tipped back. She moved on him, setting the rhythm. She guided his hands to where she wanted him to touch her and finally her whole body tightened.

When her lips parted, Colby quickly pulled her head down to his and stopped the delicious little screams with his mouth. He loved her beautiful cries of sensual surrender, but he knew she would be embarrassed later if she thought Brandon and Robyn had overheard.

Then he was exploding with her, gritting his teeth to stifle his own shout of satisfaction.

Together they drifted for a timeless moment. Colby kept his arms wrapped tightly around her, listening to her soft breathing and waiting for his body to glide back to normal.

"Now that's how I want every quarrel between us to end," he stated finally.

Diana stretched. "I've always heard you're not supposed to use sex to settle an argument."

"We settled it before we got into bed."

"Settled it?" Diana propped herself up on her elbows and glowered down at him. "That's what you call informing me that you're not mad any longer, and therefore the fight is hereby declared over?"

"Hey, I apologized, didn't I? Sort of?"

"You admitted you might have been a teeny-weeny bit out of line, but that's all."

He touched the tip of her nose with his forefinger. "I'll let you in on a little secret, sweetheart. That kind of admission is more than most people ever get out of me."

"Not used to admitting you might have overreacted, huh?"

"No. Because I generally don't overreact. Fulbrook Corners and Margaret Fulbrook in particular are two of the few things on earth that can make me overreact."

"So why are you here in Fulbrook Corners?"

"I wish to hell you'd stop asking me that question." Brandon's sense of satisfaction and well-being began to fade rapidly. "I've told you a dozen times why I'm here. Let's talk about something else before I get angry all over again."

She crossed her arms, leaning on his broad chest. "What would you like to talk about?"

"The fact that you didn't trust me to protect you from whoever is playing those pranks on you," he said coolly. "I think it's time you learned to trust me, Diana."

"I do trust you," she said seriously. "I wouldn't be sleeping with you if I didn't."

He shook his head. "When we argued earlier today, your immediate reaction was to pack and leave. That's not the kind of trust I had in mind."

"I thought things were over between us," she said stiffly.

"Well, they aren't," he growled.

"Trust works both ways, you know," she said quietly. "If you want me to trust you, I've got a right to expect trust in return."

Colby was silent for a long moment. "Just because I lost my temper with you today doesn't mean I don't trust you."

"Doesn't it?"

"No."

"Colby, I don't want to argue any more today. I've had enough."

He was instantly remorseful. "I know, baby, I know." He stroked her hair soothingly for a moment, but he was far from satisfied.

He knew now just how deeply ingrained her sense of independence and self-control were. When it came to dealing with men, she always went on the assumption that the male of the species could not be relied upon. So she'd learned how to take care of herself.

But it had become overwhelmingly important to get her to admit that he could take care of her.

Colby wondered how he was going to break through the last of her barriers. And he wondered if Diana realized how fast his own barriers were crumbling.

"What are you thinking, Colby?" Diana asked a long time later.

"You're supposed to be asleep." He cuddled her closer as she lay in the curve of his arm.

"So are you. What's keeping you awake?"

"I'm thinking about those damned pranks some idiot played on you."

"Any new ideas?"

"No, but I think I'll go out to Gil Thorp's place tomorrow. Eddy was no help, but Gil might have picked up a rumor or two. He used to be good at getting information." Colby grinned wryly in the darkness, remembering.

"Who's Gil Thorp?"

"He used to be the sheriff around here twenty years ago. He and I had what you might call an adversarial business relationship."

"What does that mean?"

"It means that every time I was conducting a little business out on River Road after midnight, Gil Thorp felt duty-bound to try to put a stop to it. Gil also didn't like the way I drove through town at twice the speed limit, or the way I got into fights, or the way I used to hang out with Eddy Spooner."

Diana shifted against him. "You don't sound as if you particularly dislike him."

"I don't dislike him. I told you, we had an adversarial relationship, but Thorp always played fair, unlike several other folks around here. And sometimes, after he'd interrupted a race and sent everyone home, he'd make me sit in that beat-up old patrol car of his and we'd talk. He had a way of getting me to tell him things I had never told anyone else. It was Gil who suggested I join the army."

"He became the closest thing to a father figure you ever had, is that it?"

"It wasn't exactly a close relationship, but he was there from time to time when I needed someone to tell me I'd gone too far or steer me clear of the kind of trouble that might have landed me in jail. One way or another, I probably owe Gil."

"Have you kept in touch?"

"Some. Christmas cards. A letter once in a while. Like I said, it wasn't really a close relationship. But he wasn't a half-bad cop, all things considered. He had a way of getting information. I'll check with him tomorrow."

"Colby?"

"Hmm?"

"One thing still doesn't make sense about those pranks."

"What?"

"The fact that they've been played against me, not you."

He stroked her arm. "Honey, I've told you, anyone who knows me would be able to figure out in a hurry that one of the fastest ways to get at me would be through you."

"I'm not so sure about that."

She didn't credit herself with enough power, he realized as he bent his head to kiss her. The woman was his weak spot, and she didn't even realize it. Maybe it was just as well. Women could be the very devil when they sensed they had real power over a man.

Colby wondered if he was becoming a weak spot for the self-controlled little amazon he held in his arms.

11

Diana found herself at loose ends the next morning. Colby had taken the Jeep to go out to the Thorp ranch. Brandon and Robyn had gone on another hike, this time leaving Specter behind.

By eleven o'clock, Diana was worrying about the résumés she had planned to get in the mail that week.

"What do you say we walk over to the cottage, pick them up and take them into the post office, Specter?"

Specter was stretched out on the porch enjoying the morning sunlight. He didn't look overly enthusiastic about the prospect of a walk, but he obligingly got to his feet.

Fifteen minutes later Diana opened the door of her cottage with some trepidation. She acknowledged to herself that she was a little afraid of finding that another prank had been played in her absence.

"Colby probably would not approve of us coming back here alone," she informed the dog. "He seems to be very big on playing bodyguard these days."

Specter grunted, obviously unconcerned with Colby's approval. He bounded straight into the house without any sign of concern and headed for the kitchen. Diana walked in behind him and found the dog nosing around the cupboard where his biscuits were kept.

She fed him two crunchy tidbits and then went into the living room to stuff a few résumés and covering letters into envelopes. Half an hour later she was ready.

"Okay, boy, let's run these into town. If I don't find a good job by September, I'll be back at C and Y."

The trip into town was uneventful. Diana sent the résumés off with a silent prayer for good luck and headed her compact car back across the bridge toward Aunt Jesse's place. It was getting close to lunchtime. Brandon and Robyn would be hungry, and Colby might be back from visiting Gil Thorp.

She drove into the yard and parked the car. Specter jumped out and trotted toward Brandon who was sitting alone on the porch.

"I was wondering where you were," Brandon said cheerfully. "Figured you'd probably gone into town."

"You were right. Where are Robyn and Colby?"

"Dad hasn't come back yet. And Robyn took a book and went off into the woods to read again. Said she wanted to be alone for a while." Brandon looked at Diana. "She's not real happy with the idea of waiting a little while longer before we make up our minds about marriage, you know. And she's bored. Said she wants me to take her back to Portland."

"That might be a good idea under the circumstances," Diana said quietly.

Then it hit her that Robyn was gone again, vanished into the woods with a book. Robyn had never been around during the periods when an intruder had been rearranging things in Diana's cottage.

And the angry young woman could conceivably believe she had a motive to get even with Diana.

"Yeah, that's what I thought, too," Brandon was saying. "I told her I'd drive her back tomorrow." He got out of his chair. "You want some lunch?"

"Sounds good, but I think I'll wait," Diana said quickly. "I want to run back to my cottage for a few minutes. Uh, Brandon?"

"Yeah?" He was opening the screen door.

"Do you happen to know if Robyn is still reading Shock Value?" As soon as she had asked the question, Diana would have given a fortune to be able to call back the words. Brandon was as bright as his father at times.

Brandon slowly turned to look at her, wariness and concern in his dark eyes. "That's the book she took with her a little while ago."

Diana tried to pass it off lightly. "One of these days, I'm going to have to finish that book myself. Colby is getting impatient. I keep telling him that it's his fault it scares me to death, but I know he doesn't think that's much of an excuse. I'll be back in a few minutes, Brandon. If you're making tuna, make enough for me."

Brandon walked to the edge of the porch. "Why aren't you taking the car if you're in a hurry, Diana?"

"The walk will do me good." She started down the steps.

"Diana, wait! I'll come with you."

She whirled to face him. "I don't know if that's such a good idea, Brandon."

He gave her a keen glance. "I want to know, too. I have a right to know if Robyn's the one."

Diana stared at him helplessly. "Brandon, I'm just going to pick up a few items I left behind last night. There's no need for you to come along."

"You're going to see if someone's played another prank, aren't you? And you think that someone might be Robyn. She's out there in the woods alone with her copy of Shock Value. This is the second time she's read that book and she knows it very well. She also knows you're reading it."

Diana drew a deep breath. "Brandon, please, listen to me. I'm just going to pick up a few things I need. That's all."

"She could have done it," Brandon said slowly. "On the other two occasions the pranks were staged, she's been off by herself somewhere."

Diana gave up and started walking briskly along the road. Specter trotted close, sensing the change in the atmosphere. "I don't think she would do such things," Diana said after a moment. "I really don't."

"I'm not so sure," Brandon said with a calm that disturbed Diana. "She's got a motive. She really dislikes you. Blames you in some way for having made me think more carefully about getting married."

"Be careful, Brandon. Don't say things you'll regret later." Diana didn't like the new trace of cynicism she heard in his voice. It reminded her too much of his father. But maybe a certain degree of cynicism was inevitable in the growing-up process.

They walked in silence until the cottage came in sight. And then, when they were a few yards up the drive, Specter suddenly came to attention. The dog began barking loudly. He leaped up the steps and nosed the front door.

"There's someone inside," Diana said, feeling a cold sweat break out under her arms.

"Specter's tail is wagging," Brandon observed quickly.

Diana frowned. "That means he must know whoever it is who's in there."

"Maybe it's Dad." Brandon's relief was obvious as he dashed up the steps. "Maybe he stopped by to pick up your things for you."

"There's no sign of the Jeep," Diana said as she put the key into the lock.

The back door slammed just as Specter dashed into the hall. The dog raced into the kitchen, searching for his familiar quarry. Diana ran after him and promptly went sprawling as she tripped over a pile of garbage that had been left just inside the doorway.

"Are you all right?" Brandon demanded, pausing only for a second.

"Yes." Diana heaved herself up out of the mass of old coffee grounds, wet paper towels and vegetable peelings. "Let Specter out the back."

"Right." Brandon was already opening the back door. Specter hurried through, barking excitedly. Brandon followed the dog at a run, and Diana dashed after both of them.

She caught a brief glimpse of a running figure before it disappeared into the trees. The dog was hot on the intruder's heels. Brandon and Diana followed the sound of loud yipping and the equally loud sound of someone crashing through the undergrowth.

It was all over in a matter of minutes. The intruder didn't stand a chance of outrunning the dog and must have known it. Diana and Brandon raced into a small clearing a short time later and saw Specter panting heavily over Robyn Lambert's huddled, weeping figure.

"Robyn." Brandon looked stricken. Gone was his earlier dash of adult cynicism. He walked up to the girl slowly. "Why?"

Robyn lifted her tear-stained face from her arms and glared at Diana with anguish and rage. "It's her fault. You would have married me if it hadn't been for her."

"Oh, Robyn," Diana said softly.

"I know your Dad was against our getting married, Brandon. But we both knew that in the beginning. You were willing to stand up to him, you said. You wouldn't let him tell you what to do, you said. But then he stopped trying to order you around, and he started talking to you and you listened to him. She's the one who told him what to say to you. I know she is. She thinks she's so damn clever."

"Geez, Robyn." Brandon sounded thoroughly disgusted.

"And you listened to her, too, just like he did. You believed all that stuff she said about a woman having a career and being able to take care of herself. You quoted her to me, damn you. She put the words in your mouth. You said it would be best for me if we waited-but I know the truth. She talked you out of marrying me."

"That's enough, Robyn." Brandon reached down to help her to her feet.

Robyn lashed out at him with her hand. "Don't touch me, you bastard. I don't want you to ever touch me again. Who do you think you are, anyway? You're nobody, do you understand? Just the son of an ex-construction worker who writes cheap thrillers. My father is a lot richer than your father. He's got a college degree and he belongs to the right clubs, and he and Mom go to parties with the most important people in Portland. My parents were right. You aren't good enough for me."

Brandon's expression was frozen. "I had a close call, didn't I? The thought of being married to the kind of selfish, vicious little creep who would pull the kind of stunts you've been pulling on Diana is enough to make a man stay single for life." He turned and started walking back toward the cottage. "Come on. Let's get your things together. I'll drive you back to Portland this afternoon."

"Brandon. I love you."

"No you don't," Brandon said with astonishing wisdom. "You're just trying to find some guy who will marry you so you can get out of your parents' house. Any man will do. But if you had any brains, any self-respect, you'd move out by yourself. You'd learn to deal with things on your own. You just want someone to take care of you and make everything easy for you. Find another patsy."

"Brandon." When Brandon didn't respond, Robyn swung around and confronted Diana. "It's all your fault. Brandon was going to marry me until you got involved. You ruined everything."

Diana stepped forward impulsively and put her arms around the young woman. Robyn pushed violently against her and then collapsed, weeping, on Diana's shoulder.

A long time later, when Robyn's tears had finally dried, Diana turned to find Colby standing quietly in the trees behind them. Without a word he led them both toward the cottage.

"Chapter Twelve of Shock Value," Colby explained an hour later as he and Diana sat eating tuna sandwiches alone on the front porch. "Donnelly gets up in the middle of the night and falls into a pile of dirt taken from a freshly dug grave. Guess Robyn couldn't find any freshly dug graves and decided to make do with garbage."

"I hadn't gotten quite that far," Diana admitted. "I'm still on Chapter Ten. That poor girl. She's got some major problems."

"They're her problems, not ours and definitely not Brandon's. She was trying to use him."

"To escape her domineering family."

"Everybody's got something to escape," Colby said coolly. "It takes a while to learn that the only way you can really escape anything is to cut yourself free. You can't use other people to do the dirty work for you."

Diana concentrated on her sandwich. "No, I suppose not. Still, I feel sorry for her."

"After what she did to you? She deliberately tried to terrorize you, honey. In my book that means she's not entitled to any sympathy."

"You can be very hard at times, Colby."

He scowled at her and took a huge bite out of his sandwich. "Don't try to make me feel sorry for that little twit."

Diana decided to let the subject drop. She knew Colby's loyalties were limited but extremely fierce. His son was far more important to him than some neurotic little teenager who thought marriage was the ticket to freedom. Diana wondered exactly where she ranked on Colby's list of loyalties. She needed to know because something told her that very soon she was going to have to make a major decision.

"Is Brandon coming back tonight?"

"He said he was. Two hours to get to Portland, drop off Robyn and two hours to get back. He should be back here around seven."

"How did your visit with Gil Thorp go?"

"Maybe I'll have him and his wife out here for dinner one of these days. Is that okay with you?"

Diana smiled. "Certainly."

Colby was silent for a while, chewing reflectively. "He hadn't heard anything about the pranks."

"That stands to reason, since Robyn was behind them. She doesn't know anyone in town and therefore wouldn't have confided in anyone locally."

"Yeah."

Diana frowned slightly. "Colby, is something wrong?"

He shook his head. "Not any longer. The only thing that's bugging me is that Robyn is getting off damned light for what she did."

"She doesn't see it that way. She wanted marriage in the worst way, and now she's missed her chance with Brandon."

"Thank God."

Brandon walked into the house shortly after seven. Colby took one look at his son's haggard face and headed for the kitchen. He opened the refrigerator, took out a six-pack and returned to the living room.

"You want to go outside and sit on the porch for a while?" he asked his son.

Brandon looked up wearily. He nodded and got to his feet.

Diana settled back against the sofa and picked up Shock Value. "You two go on," she said easily. "I'm going to get through this book if it kills me."

Colby gave her a faint smile. The woman understood things, he thought. They didn't have to be spelled out for her. She knew that right now he needed to talk to Brandon alone.

It was crisp out on the porch but not too cold for a couple of macho males who happened to have a six-pack handy. Colby opened two cans and handed one to his son.

"There are times in a man's life," Colby said, "when the one thing he needs most in the world is a beer."

"Yeah."

"Rough drive back to Portland?"

"Yeah. I hurt her bad."

"And she hurt you just as bad."

"She wasn't the kind of girl I thought she was." Brandon looked perplexed. "I mean, she always seemed so sweet and helpless. I couldn't believe it when I realized it was her running out of Diana's house today. I wonder how Diana guessed about Robyn?"

"Diana's pretty sharp."

"Robyn blamed her for everything going wrong. But it was my fault, wasn't it?"

Colby shook his head. "You changed your mind about rushing into marriage. Everyone's got a right to do that. That's why it's a good idea to take your time about it. That's why you have to leave your options open until you're very sure of what you want."

Brandon grimaced. "Translated, that means you have to be careful about not getting the girl pregnant until you know damned well you want to marry her."

Colby shrugged. "Pregnancy has a way of closing down options, all right."

"Do you ever regret getting stuck with me?"

"Hell, no. Not for a minute. You're the best thing that ever happened to me, Brandon. If it hadn't been for you, I might have wound up in jail or in a gutter somewhere. You're the one who taught me the meaning of responsibility. You're the one who gave me something to work for. No, I don't regret having you. I just wish I'd been a little older and wiser when I did get you. As it was, you had to teach me about fatherhood, too."

"No," said Brandon after a long pull on his beer. "I didn't have to teach you about fatherhood. You're a natural. Too bad you didn't have some more kids somewhere along the line. You're wasting your talent in that department."

Colby felt an unexpected paternal warmth well up inside him. His voice became a little gruff. "Thanks, kid. I guess we both turned out okay, huh?"

"Yeah. I guess so."

"What you went through with Robyn was a very difficult situation. I want you to know I think you handled it damned well."

"I should never have gotten into it in the first place."

Colby grinned faintly. "Son, let me tell you something. Whenever you're talking about women, you're talking about difficult situations. They go together like fleas and dogs. You don't get one without the other."

Brandon smiled for the first time since he had walked in the door. "I'll remember that. By the way, just for the record, there was never any danger of me getting Robyn pregnant."

Colby nodded. "Glad to hear it."

"Not because I wasn't using precautions," Brandon said deliberately. "Although I would have if we'd ever done it. I'm not stupid. But we never did. Do it, that is. She said we had to wait until we were married. She kept telling me how good it was going to be after we were married. She really had me going."

Colby raised his brows inquiringly. "You're telling me I misinterpreted that little scene of you coming out of her bedroom the other morning?"

"I was in there, all right. But it was just the usual heavy make-out session. I was planning on going back to my own room before you, uh, got home, but I fell asleep."

"I apologize for jumping down your throat that morning." Colby shoved his fingers through his hair. "Seems like I've been doing a lot of apologizing lately. First to Diana and now you."

"There's something else I wanted to tell you, Dad."

"What's that?"

"Robyn swore over and over again during the drive back to Portland that the only prank she staged was the last one with the garbage. She claims she got the idea of doing something out of Shock Value after hearing about the other two incidents."

Colby gave Brandon a level look. "Do you believe her?"

Brandon looked thoughtful. "I know there's no reason to believe her, not after what she pulled. But for some reason, I think that this time she may have been telling the truth."

"Difficult situation," Colby mused.

"Do you think we should tell Diana?"

"No, she's got enough on her mind as it is."

"Like what?" Brandon asked curiously.

"I'm waiting for her to tell me."

She couldn't wait any longer. She was sure. It wasn't just that she was several days late-it was that she had a feeling. Somehow she knew for certain she was pregnant. The knowledge existed within her on some deep level that defied rational analysis. She stared down at the calendar in her hand, and the little numbers and days blurred together.

"You're not supposed to count the days when you're on a vacation, honey." Colby walked up behind her and put his arms around her. He deftly removed the calendar from her fingers. "Or is something more important going on here?"

"More important?" She was nervous, she realized. Far more nervous than she would be if she were interviewing for a new position.

"Am I about to overlook your birthday?" He smiled wickedly and nuzzled her neck. "Don't worry, I can come up with a terrific gift on very short notice."

"My birthday isn't until November."

"That's all right, my present can be unzipped early."

"You're supposed to be writing this morning."

He nibbled her ear. "I have already written great things this morning. I could use a break. Then I promise I will go back and write some more great things."

"Colby," Diana said very seriously. "Do you realize I don't even know when your birthday is?"

He stopped nibbling. "September second. Is that a problem?"

"No, of course not. It's just that it only goes to show there are a lot of things we still don't know about each other."

"We're both fast learners." He resumed munching her earlobe.

Diana took a deep breath. It was time to make her decision. "Colby, let's pack a lunch and go eat it on top of Chained Lady Falls."

"You talked me into it. A man can write great things any time. I'll make the sandwiches and pack the other essentials we always seem to need when we go to Chained Lady Falls." He gave her a quick, anticipatory leer and headed for the stairs that led to the bedroom.

Diana watched him go with a feeling of chagrin. She wondered if Colby even remembered the one time they had forgotten those essentials. He still hadn't mentioned what had happened that night they spent in the cave.

What if he denied his part in the whole thing? What if he honestly did not remember making love to her without taking precautions? What if he remembered but didn't want to believe she could have been so unlucky as to get pregnant the one and only time they had been careless?

What if he didn't want to share the responsibility with her?

The what ifs had been going through her mind for days now. They had intensified after Brandon had left to return to Portland. Diana had become increasingly tense as the reality of her pregnancy had begun to establish itself.

She knew Colby had noticed her preoccupation and the anxiety she had tried so hard to quell. Once or twice he had asked her if something was wrong but he'd stopped asking after she'd denied it.

"Don't forget we have Gil and his wife coming over for a late dinner tonight," Colby said as he came back downstairs. "We'll have to pick up some things in town after the picnic. I think you'll like Gil. He's a tough old character. Says what he thinks. Evelyn is his second wife. I don't know her very well, but she seems nice enough" Colby broke off. "You okay, honey?"

Diana nodded quickly and turned toward the kitchen. "I'm fine. Let's get the sandwiches made."

Forty minutes later they reached the top of the falls. Diana immediately gave Specter a handful of his favorite dog biscuits, which he promptly wolfed down. Then he went off to check out the nearby woods while Colby spread the blanket on the ground.

"If you're going to make a habit of seducing me out here in the open, we may have to invest in an air mattress," he remarked as he finally settled the blanket on a patch of grass between two large boulders. "Either that, or you'll have to promise to always be on the bottom. At forty, a man starts to notice the rocks digging into his back."

"I'm crushed." Diana managed a smile as she unpacked the sandwiches. "Where's your sense of romance?"

"Where it always is. Right inside my jeans." He lowered himself into a sitting position beside her and reached for a sandwich. "I take it you want to eat first?"

Her fingers clenched around her sandwich. "To tell you the truth, I'd like to talk to you first."

"You're going to leave dents in that sandwich if you don't relax," Colby said with astonishing gentleness. He reached over and removed the sandwich from her hand. His gaze was intent and watchful. The teasing mood was gone. "So talk, lady. I'm listening."

She looked at him for a long moment and then she looked away, staring unseeingly at the landscape below. Unconsciously she wrapped her arms around her drawn-up knees.

"Colby, we've got a problem."

"We?"

She went cold and closed her eyes. "Maybe it would be more accurate under the circumstances to say I've got a problem. I'm pregnant."

"So that's it." He took a large bite out of his sandwich and chewed with enthusiasm. "I was wondering why you've been acting as if you were walking around in a minefield."

Diana heard the unconcerned tone in his voice and thought she would lose control and burst into tears right there in front of him. He didn't care because he didn't consider her pregnancy his problem.

She had made a huge mistake. She had been wrong, all wrong, to tell him. She should have kept it to herself. She should have handled her problems alone, just as she always did. In the end, a woman could only rely on herself. She'd always known that. Why had she allowed Colby Savagar to make her think there might be a few exceptions to that rule?

"It was that night in the cave, wasn't it?" Colby asked around a mouthful of sandwich.

"Yes. I thought you didn't remember. You never said anything." Diana didn't look at him. She could barely keep her voice steady. A sense of panic was setting in. She wanted to run, but she couldn't seem to move. Her stomach was in a knot. Her palms were damp. She certainly couldn't eat a single bite of her lunch now.

"I never said anything because you never mentioned it. I wasn't sure you remembered. I figured you'd bring it up if you wanted to discuss the situation. We were careless that night."

"Yes." At least he was noble enough to admit the fault had been mutual.

"You almost didn't tell me about the baby," Colby remarked musingly as he polished off the last of his sandwich. "You've been keeping all your fears and concerns to yourself, as usual. Tell me something, Diana. What made you decide to break the news today?"

"There was no point waiting any longer. I'm as sure as I can be without a test. I have to start making some decisions. Before I do that I need to know how you, uh, feel about the situation."

"Nice of you to include me in on the decision-making process, Madam Executive."

The edge that had appeared in his voice jolted her. Diana glanced at him nervously, unable to determine his mood. Colby's gaze was cool and direct. He was staring into her soul. "I'm sorry," she said a little helplessly.

"Yeah, so am I. Sorry it took you this long to tell me. Sorry you tried to shoulder the whole burden alone in your usual Diana-the-Amazon style. Sorry I didn't pin you down and wring the truth out of you earlier. I knew something was wrong. I shouldn't have let things go on this long. Ah, well. Live and learn. And I obviously still have a lot of things to learn about you, Diana."

Anger began to burn within her. Diana was grateful for it. It drove out some of the cold chill that had been creeping through her. "I'm sorry if I didn't handle this in exactly the way you think I should have handled it, but the fact is, I haven't had any experience along this line. I've been going crazy trying to figure out what to do."

His brows rose. "What's so damned hard about figuring out that the first thing you should have done was tell me?"

"Damn you, Colby." Diana brushed her wind-tousled hair back out of her eyes and looked at him with despair and rage. "I wasn't sure you'd want to know. We're involved in an affair that's only scheduled to last for the summer, remember?"

"Oh, Christ. Not that again. You're the one who always talks about our relationship as if it was scheduled only for the summer. I've told you a dozen times there's no need to put a time limit on it."

"Colby, this may come as a shock to you, but I have to make plans. I can't do that when everything's open-ended and casual. I need to know a few basic facts so I can organize my life. I don't know the first thing about having a baby."

"Lucky for you, I do."

She stared at him. Some of the warmth began to return to her mid-section. "What's that supposed to mean?"

"Just what it sounds like." He fished around inside the picnic basket for another sandwich. "I'm an expert on kids, remember? You want cheese or egg salad?"

"Neither. Colby, stop fooling around with the sandwiches and tell me exactly what you mean."

He looked at her. "Just what I said. Trust me, I know what I'm doing."

"I wish I did."

"Relax, honey. We'll take this one step at a time."

Diana searched his face. "What's the first step?"

"Simple. We get married."

Diana couldn't move for an instant. "I knew," she finally whispered. "Deep down inside, I knew you were different. I knew you would never run from something like this. Thank you, Colby. Your offer means more to me than I can possibly say." She dashed the back of her hand across her eyes to wipe away the moisture. Then she sniffed. "But I can't marry you."

"The hell you can't."

She threw herself into his arms, her eyes damp with more unshed tears. "Don't you understand? It wouldn't be right. Listen to me, Colby, I've thought about this a lot."

"Knowing you, honey, you've thought about it too much. You have a tendency to overanalyze things." His arms tightened roughly around her. "This is not a complicated situation, Diana. Don't try to make it complicated."

Her fingers clenched into the fabric of his shirt as she buried her face against his chest. "I can't put you through the same situation you were forced into twenty years ago. You've made it clear that once was enough. I won't let history repeat itself for you. It's not fair. It's just not fair."

"My sweet stubborn little amazon," Colby said into her hair. "History has nothing to do with this. And neither does fairness. We're talking about you and me. We're going to have a baby. That means we get married."

At sunset the last of the sun's rays turned the waterfall first to gold and then to scarlet. Colby privately decided he'd never seen the veil of Chained Lady Falls look more like blood than it did that evening. A curious sense of rightness flowed through him.

For the first time since he had returned to Fulbrook Corners, he had the feeling that he was finally going to complete the unfinished business he sensed had brought him here.

Being an expectant father was playing tricks on his mind, he thought, amused. He had the oddest feeling that he was somehow holding both past and future in his hands, and that the link between the two was Diana.

Dreams

Part Two

1

"Gil, I'd like you to meet Diana Prentice. Diana, this is Gil Thorp and his wife Evelyn."

"How do you do?" Diana murmured politely. Her smile was real but strained. Her hazel eyes were shadowed as she greeted the couple on the doorstep. The Thorps were in their sixties, nicely dressed and smiling affably. "Colby has told me so much about you."

"I'll just bet he has." Gil Thorp chuckled as he took Diana's hand. "Did he remember to explain that twenty years ago I was the good guy in the white hat and he was the town's chief troublemaker, or did he alter the past to make himself look good?"

"He did mention that you were the sheriff here in Fulbrook Corners when he was in high school. I believe he said the two of you had what he described as an adversarial relationship," Diana said.

"An adversarial relationship, Colby?" Gil's bushy gray brows rose. "Now that's an interesting way of putting it." He turned to his wife. "I can't remember how many times I got a phone call in the middle of the night telling me the Savagar kid was staging another drag race out on River Road. I lost more sleep the year he got that black Corvette than I care to think about."

"You had nothing better to do at night in those days," Colby said dryly. "You weren't married to Evelyn then."

"True enough," Gil agreed with a small grin. "But that was twenty years ago, Savagar, and even though I probably looked like an old man to you back then, I wasn't completely past my prime. In fact, I wasn't much older than you are now. You're not married, either, but I'll lay odds you don't spend all your nights alone."

Colby saw the faint red flags in Diana's cheeks, but he ignored her reaction. "Hell, Gil, if I'd had any idea my racing was affecting your love life..."

"You would have set up twice as many races down on River Road," Gil finished for him.

Evelyn smiled at Diana. "If I were you, my dear, I wouldn't pay too much attention to the stories men swap about their pasts. They always exaggerate outrageously."

"I'll keep that in mind," Diana said with another strained smile. "Won't you have a seat, Evelyn?"

If he were a sensitive, empathic, understanding, truly modern male, Colby Savagar decided, he would probably be able to summon up more sympathy for Diana. It was obvious she was nervous. Scared right down to her toes might be a more accurate description. Which was almost amusing because he knew it took a lot to frighten Diana. He frequently thought of her as his personal amazon.

But even though he wasn't overly sympathetic, he knew Diana had good reason to be floundering in a state of anxiety tonight. She was, after all, thirty-four years old, single and devoted to her career. The last thing she had ever expected or planned for at this stage of her life was a baby. But today she had faced the fact that she was pregnant.

Colby was having a hard time mustering sympathy, empathy, understanding and other such modern male attitudes because he was the father. It wasn't that he was saving all his sentiment for himself, rather, he had discovered he was not particularly unhappy about the situation. In fact, he hadn't been surprised when she had told him about the pregnancy. Some sixth sense had told him she had conceived that night in the cave.

Colby figured it must be the irredeemably primitive, possessive, chauvinistic male traits locked in his genes that were causing him to be experiencing an almost euphoric satisfaction about the situation. Diana would strangle him if she realized what he was thinking.

It wasn't that he had set out to get her pregnant. Far from it. Colby already had a nineteen-year-old son and, as he had told Diana often enough, he'd paid his dues when it came to fatherhood.

But now that the unplanned pregnancy was a reality, Colby found himself quite prepared to handle it.

He wasn't at all sure about Diana. She still appeared dazed.

"Yeah, have a seat," Colby said easily to his guests as he waved them to two of the well-worn living room chairs. "Evelyn, what can I get you?"

"A glass of white wine will be fine," the older woman replied with a smile as she sat down beside her husband.

"Whiskey for me," Gil said. "This place doesn't look like it's changed a bit," he added as he lowered himself onto the faded upholstery of a heavy armchair. His eyes moved assessingly over the rustic, shabby interior of the old two-story house.

"I never bothered to do anything to the house after Aunt Jesse died," Colby explained as he fixed drinks for his guests. "I turned it over to Larry Brockton's real estate firm and told him to keep it rented as much as possible. I gave him instructions not to sink any more money into it than absolutely necessary to keep things working."

"And you never came back to Fulbrook Corners to check on the place, did you?" Gil asked shrewdly. "In fact, this summer is the first time you've been back since you left town twenty years ago. Why are you here now, Colby?"

Colby decided he was getting tired of that question. "Lately a lot of people seem to be asking me that." He shot a wry glance at Diana who'd asked it more frequently than anyone else. "The answer is simple. I needed a quiet place to finish the book I'm working on. I also want to make a decision about this house. I think that when the summer is over I'll tell Brockton to put it on the market."

Gil nodded, looking unconvinced. He turned to Diana and smiled. "And you came to this little corner of Oregon this summer for a vacation, is that right?"

Diana flashed Colby an unreadable glance before nodding politely to Gil. "That's right. I'm on leave from my job at Carruthers and Yale in Portland. I hadn't had much time off during the four years I worked for the company, so I thought I'd take the summer off."

"What do you do at Carruthers and Yale?" Evelyn asked.

"I have a background in accounting and business administration. I work in the office of a division controller."

Colby heard the cool precision of Diana's response and knew that it was meant to cover up the underlying anger she felt toward Carruthers and Yale. She had almost resigned her position with the firm when she had realized that her superiors were not about to promote a woman into the rarified air of upper management. Her boss, Aaron Crown, had talked her into taking a leave of absence instead.

For a woman whose main focus in life until now had been her career, the shock of running head-on into such blatant sexual discrimination had been hard to take.

But now that she was pregnant, Colby told himself, Diana had better learn there were other important things to focus on in life besides a career. Twenty years ago, when he'd found himself about to be a father at the age of nineteen, he'd had to learn that lesson the hard way. Babies had a way of reprioritizing one's world.

"Here you go, Evelyn," Colby said as he handed Mrs. Thorp the glass of wine. He gave Diana a glass of mineral water. "Diana was thinking about looking for a new job to start in the fall, but she's recently had to make a few changes in her plans. We're getting married."

Diana's head snapped around in shock. Her beautiful turquoise, gold and green eyes blazed at him.

"Congratulations," Evelyn exclaimed, apparently oblivious to Diana's stunned expression. Oblivious, or perhaps too polite to show she'd noted it. "How exciting."

"Nice going, Savagar," Gil said with an easy grin as he raised his glass of whiskey in a small salute. "I'll say this much for you, you're showing a lot more sense this time around than you did the last time."

"I've had twenty years to figure out how to do it right," Colby said blandly.

"Excuse me, I'd better go check on dinner." Diana shot to her feet with an awkward movement that sent her glass of mineral water flying. "Damn," she muttered and started blotting uselessly with a tiny cocktail napkin.

Specter, her massive brindled dog, lumbered to his feet and wandered over to take a few sample licks of the mineral water.

"Get out of the way, monster," Colby ordered the dog, who ignored him, as usual. "I'll take care of the spilled water, Diana. You go check on the food."

She nodded quickly, managed a weak, apologetic smile for Gil and Evelyn and rushed to the kitchen.

"Is she all right?" Evelyn asked worriedly.

"She's nervous about the marriage," Colby explained in a confidential tone. "Diana's never been married, and I think she'd decided she probably never would tie the knot. I guess I sort of rushed her into a decision this afternoon."

"You always did tend to take charge and do things your way," Gil observed. "What made you decide to try marriage again after nearly twenty years of single parenthood?"

Colby hesitated and then grinned slowly. "Thought it might be interesting to try double parenthood."

Evelyn blinked. "Oh, you're planning on starting another family?"

"As soon as possible," Colby said easily as he finished mopping up the small spill. He heard a clatter from the kitchen. Diana had dropped a pan on the floor. The sound told him she'd overheard his words. "Diana's thirty-four, you know. Biological clock's a factor now. We can't wait around and take our time."

"Well, from the sound of things, you did all right with your first boy," Gil said. "Heard he met Margaret Fulbrook while he was here in town."

"The old bat connived a meeting one day when Brandon went into town with Diana. I was irritated when I found out about it." That was an understatement. "But maybe it was for the best. Like it or not, the old lady is Brandon's grandmother. I guess he's got a right to meet her."

"I heard her tell you at Cynthia's funeral that she never wanted to see you or her grandson again. That you'd never get a dime from her."

Gil sipped his whiskey thoughtfully. "You stood there in the rain beside the grave, as cold and proud as Lucifer himself. I remember you had that little baby in your arms, and you told Margaret Fulbrook to go to hell. You and Brandon were going to make it on your own, you said. Everyone there heard you. Talked about it for months afterward. No one had ever told a Fulbrook to go to hell."

"How terrible," Evelyn whispered, obviously shocked. "To send you away like that with a baby when you were hardly more than a boy yourself."

"It was time I grew up," Colby said, shrugging.

"You know something, Colby?" Gil said quietly. "The day of the funeral was the day I knew for sure you would make it. I'd always thought you had what it took to pull yourself together and make something of yourself, but that day I realized you'd really go out and do it."

"People change," Evelyn mused. "I wouldn't be surprised if Margaret Fulbrook has had a few second thoughts over the years."

"I'll tell you one person who hasn't changed," Colby said. "And that's Harry the Ox."

"Harry Gedge? Mrs. Fulbrook's odd-job man?" Evelyn looked at Colby inquiringly.

"Yeah."

"He's not a very pleasant person, is he? I've often wondered why Margaret Fulbrook keeps him around."

"Because he obeys her unquestioningly," Gil told his wife. "Aren't many people left here in Fulbrook Corners who take orders from a Fulbrook the way Harry does."

"Why does Harry Gedge devote himself to Mrs. Fulbrook?" Evelyn asked with genuine curiosity.

"If you ask me, it's because he figures he's going to come into some cash when Margaret dies." Gil swirled the whiskey in his glass. "No one else left to inherit the Fulbrook fortune, you know, except the Fulbrook Community Hospital Foundation. Cynthia was the last of the line. Margaret's become very dependent on Harry Gedge, and he encourages that dependency."

"What about Brandon?" Evelyn pointed out. "Colby's son is Margaret Fulbrook's grandson."

"She made it very clear long ago that Brandon would never get a penny of her money," Colby explained. "And that's exactly the way I want it. She ignored him for nineteen years. She can damn well go on ignoring him."

"Nothing here in Fulbrook Corners is quite the same as it was twenty years ago, Colby," Gil said. "Not even Margaret Fulbrook."

"Could have fooled me," Colby drawled.

"You've been away a long time, Colby. Like Evelyn said, things change. People change."

"Maybe." He didn't believe anything in Fulbrook Corners ever changed but he didn't want to argue with one of the few friends he had from twenty years ago. "Excuse me a second. I just want to check on Diana. Be right back."

He found her at the counter, her shoulders stiff with tension as she sliced tomatoes. He knew she had overheard the conversation in the living room. Colby went up to her from behind, put his arms around her and gently removed the knife from her fingers.

"Relax, honey. You're going to give yourself a permanent manicure at the rate you're going."

"Colby, I can't go back in there."

"Don't be an idiot," he said affectionately. His arms still around her, he used the knife to finish slicing the tomato. "Of course you can go back in there. What's more, you will go back in there."

"They'll find out the truth," she wailed softly. "Sooner or later everyone will know."

"What will they know?"

"That history is repeating itself, that you're marrying me because I accidentally got pregnant. Everyone in Fulbrook Corners will be gossiping soon. How could you tell Evelyn about wanting to start another family right away? She's bound to guess the truth."

Colby cut off the muddled protest with a quick, hard kiss. "Hush. Now listen to me and listen good. First, you and I will be long gone from here before anyone knows you're pregnant. We're only here for the summer, remember? In another few weeks, we'll be out of here. Second, you are a mature woman, not an eighteen-year-old girl. I would greatly appreciate it if you would start acting like the adult you are. I'm not going to let you cower in the kitchen."

"I am not cowering."

He ignored that. "Third, the Thorps are good people. They won't spread gossip. Fourth, this may come as a shock to you, Diana, but if you were to announce your pregnancy to them tonight, the Thorps would assume it was a planned event based on the fact that we look as if we're old enough to know what we're doing."

She glared at him from beneath her lashes. "You mean at our ages we're not supposed to make that kind of mistake?"

"Exactly."

"But we did make that kind of mistake. We got carried away that night in Chained Lady Cave, and we took a reckless chance. Just like a couple of teenage kids."

Colby put down the knife and spun her around in his arms. He caught her face between his palms. "Stop calling it a mistake. Do you understand me, Diana? From now on I don't want to hear you ever again refer to what happened that night as an accident or a miscalculation or a mistake. You're pregnant, and we're getting married, and that's all there is to it. We're not going to waste time looking back at what might have been. Agreed?"

She closed her eyes and drew a deep breath. "You're right," she said, her husky voice a little unsteady as she made an obvious effort to take hold of herself. "There's no point looking back. What's done is done."

"And you can stop acting so damned melodramatic about the whole thing while you're at it," Colby ordered crisply. "We're not the first couple to find themselves in this kind of situation, and we won't be the last."

"Oh, that's a tremendous comfort," she snapped back, showing a spark of her usual spirit.

Colby grinned wickedly. "I thought you'd appreciate having the situation put in perspective. Just remember you're not in this alone. I keep telling you I know what I'm doing. I'll take care of everything. Just leave it all to me."

She looked at the buttons of his shirt with a thoughtful expression. "I haven't thanked you for asking me to marry you," she said humbly.

"Probably because I didn't ask you. As I recall, I told you we were getting married. I didn't get down on my knees and beg."

She looked at him with misty eyes. "True, but it was still very, well, noble of you and I want you to know I really do appreciate your gallantry. I don't know any other man who would have insisted on seeing this through with me."

Her gratitude annoyed him. "There isn't any other man who would see this through with you because the baby you're carrying doesn't belong to any other man. It's my baby. Our baby. So we'll see it through together. Now stop making a federal case out of the whole matter and start worrying about the rice."

Her eyes opened wide and she sniffed cautiously. "Oh my God, the rice." She freed herself from his arms and raced over to the ancient stove.

"I'll let the Thorps know we're ready to eat." Colby started for the door, satisfied that Diana's attention was now focused on the practical matter of dinner. For a calm, cool and collected businesswoman, she was sure having trouble accepting the inevitable.

As far as he was concerned, the more he thought about the whole thing, the more it all did seem inevitable and right. Besides, Diana was going to look cute pregnant.

This time around it might be fun to have a little girl, Colby decided with a small grin.

Ten minutes later Colby had everyone seated at the battered oak table in the kitchen. The conversation had shifted to more innocuous subjects, and Diana seemed to have herself back in hand again. Colby felt an odd rush of pride as he watched her cope with their guests and the details of the small dinner party.

It was hard to believe that at one time he had thought she was all wrong for him. The last thing he needed, he had told himself, was an arrogant, self-contained, tough-as-nails career woman. But Diana had proven to be very sweet and soft and surprisingly vulnerable beneath her cool, controlled exterior. She had never needed a man in her life, but she was beginning to realize she needed Colby Savagar. Colby intended to make sure she understood that.

It was only fair because lately he had begun to realize just how much he needed her.

"Did you get that business with the pranks settled, Colby?" Gil asked as he helped himself to a heaping plate of the stir-fried vegetables Diana had prepared.

"What pranks?" Evelyn asked curiously.

Colby frowned. "Some creep was playing practical jokes on Diana."

"I hate practical jokers," Evelyn said with a shudder.

"So do I," Diana agreed. "This particular joker was duplicating scenes out of one of Colby's books."

"Which book?" Evelyn demanded.

Diana took a bite of rice. "Shock Value."

"Oh, yes. I read that one." Evelyn's eyes lit up.

"You and everyone else in town, apparently," Diana said with a smile.

"That was the book that made everyone in Fulbrook Corners realize Colby Savagar was going to become famous instead of winding up in prison," Gil explained sardonically. "But like I told Colby, since everyone in town had read the book, it was going to be difficult figuring out who was playing the pranks."

"We discovered the culprit," Colby said.

Gil shot him a quick look. "Who?"

"My son's girlfriend. Ex-girlfriend, that is. She was angry at Diana because Diana had helped me convince Brandon not to get married right away."

"Poor Robyn wanted marriage in the worst way, I'm afraid," Diana explained to Evelyn. "She was trying to escape her domineering, battling parents."

Evelyn nodded in understanding. "And she thought marriage was her ticket to freedom. Poor kid. And poor Brandon if he had, indeed, married her."

"So you think she was the one behind the pranks, hmm?" Gil looked at Colby again.

Colby nodded abruptly. "Yeah. Diana and Brandon caught her in the act of setting up the last prank. That was the end of it." He gave Gil a meaningful glance and then picked up the bottle of wine. "Another glass, Evelyn?"

Gil took the hint. "I hear you've been in touch with your old buddy, Eddy Spooner."

Colby nodded. "He and I shared a couple of beers and talked about old times a few days ago. I see he didn't end up in jail, either. That must have really irked most of the townsfolk. They were so sure he'd come to a bad end, too."

Gil's brows rose again. "I think Spooner came a little closer to ending up behind bars than you did. That boy had some real problems, and he didn't have the inner fortitude to work 'em out the way you did."

For some reason Colby felt obliged to defend his old friend. "Eddy had it rough. That drunken bastard he had for a father was nothing short of a child-abuser."

"I'll grant you that much. No one shed any tears when Dwight Spooner fell from the top of Chained Lady Falls."

Diana looked up in surprise. "Eddy's father died there? But it's not that treacherous around the top of the falls. Colby and I have been up there a couple of times on picnics. As long as you don't get too near the edge, it's safe enough."

"That's true. No one else has ever fallen from up there in all the time I've lived in Fulbrook Corners. But Eddy's father was drunk at the time. As usual. He'd taken a rifle and gone out hunting. He'd also taken along a fifth of that old rotgut he liked so much. They found him and the bottle in the pool beneath the falls."

Something in Gil's voice caught Colby's attention. "What's the matter, Gil? You think it was something besides an accident?"

Gil toyed with his knife. "I'll tell you something I've never told anyone else except Evelyn, and I don't want it going beyond this room. Clear?"

"Don't worry, Gil. Diana and I aren't likely to start gossiping with the locals." Colby knew his disdain for the good people of Fulbrook Corners was reflected in his voice.

"Right. Well, I was still sheriff at the time Dwight Spooner died. I was the one who did the investigation and wrote up the report. It looked like an accident and there was no evidence to the contrary, but I always sort of wondered if Dwight hadn't had a little help going over those falls."

Colby was silent for a moment. "Eddy?" he finally asked softly.

"If it was, I couldn't rightly blame the boy. Lord knows the kid had provocation. But there was no way anyone was ever going to prove anything one way or the other. So I wrote it up as an accident and that was the end of it. Eddy never gave me or Roy Barnes, the man who took my place a couple years ago, any trouble after that so I figured the least I could do was not cause trouble for him."

Colby glanced at Diana and realized she was staring in shock at Gil.

"Can a sheriff just do that? Ignore a suspicion of murder?"

Gil grinned at her, and Colby couldn't help himself. He started to laugh.

Evelyn frowned severely at both men. "Pay no attention to them, my dear. A man's sense of humor is biologically different from a woman's, you know. The male of the species finds humor in the oddest things."

"What is so funny, Colby?" Diana demanded.

"Nothing, I swear it." But he was unable to control his smile.

"Colby, if you don't tell me what is so amusing, I'm going to let you do the dishes alone."

He held up one palm in a placating gesture. "Okay, okay, I'll try and explain. It's just that you looked so naive and innocent when you asked Gil if a sheriff could ignore something like Eddy Spooner's father going over the falls."

"Well?"

Colby looked at Gil. "You tell her. I don't want to be the one to disillusion her."

Gil groaned. "Thanks a lot, Savagar." He turned to Diana. "You have to understand, Diana, that in a lot of ways the sheriff of a rural community like this is not only the enforcer of the law and an investigating officer, he's also judge and jury a lot of the time. There was no evidence to indicate Spooner's death was anything but an accident. So I called it quits with a report stating exactly that. The county coroner agreed with me. What was the point of pursuing a suspicion when the victim was a vicious, drunken fool with a history of child abuse? Sometimes you settle for rough justice. I'll tell you something else, too. It's no different in the big city. Cops are cops."

"I see what you mean."

Gil grinned widely. "Hell, if you only knew how many times I turned a blind eye to the activities of your fiancé when he was a kid, it would curl your hair. Why, if I hadn't been such a nice, understanding guy, I could have"

"Forget it, Gil," Colby broke in quickly. "Diana's had enough disillusionment for one evening. Let's change the subject."

"You sure have gotten straitlaced in your old age, Savagar."

"People change," Colby reminded him smoothly. "Have some more of Diana's stir-fry."

"It's delicious," Evelyn said brightly.

"It's the one company dish she's mastered," Colby explained. "After we're married, I intend to broaden her repertoire."

Two hours later, the Thorps rose reluctantly to take their leave. Evelyn hung back to have a few last words with Diana, and Colby took the opportunity to walk out onto the porch with Gil. Specter padded behind them, yawning mightily.

The big dog stood with his front paws planted on the top step and sampled the night air as Colby drew Gil away from the door.

"About those pranks someone played on Diana," Colby said quietly.

"What about 'em?" Gil leaned against the porch railing and fished a cigar out of his pocket.

"There's no question that my son's ex-girlfriend was behind the last one. But she swears she had nothing to do with the first two little jokes. Brandon believes her. And I've got a few questions, myself."

"That right?"

"I can see Robyn cooking up one prank as an act of childish revenge. She's young and impulsive, and she was furious that Brandon had changed his mind about marriage. But I don't see her as the type to wage a deliberate campaign of terror against Diana. And that's what was going on before I pulled Diana out of that cottage she was renting and moved her in here with me."

"You think Robyn might have set up just one scene from your book after hearing about the other two scenes?" Gil asked shrewdly as he carefully lit the cigar.

Colby braced one hand against the railing. "I think it's a possibility."

"Who started it then?"

"That's the hell of it, Gil. It could be almost anyone from Margaret Fulbrook or Harry to some jerk I beat out on River Road twenty years ago. It wouldn't take much to figure out that one sure way to get back at me would be to frighten Diana. If there is some lunatic running around who thinks he's got a score to settle, he'd better figure out fast that this is a game two can play. When I find him I'm going to teach him that I won't let anyone hurt Diana."

"Not everyone in town is carrying a twenty-year-old grudge, Colby. You caused a lot of trouble when you were a kid but you weren't quite as much of an SOB as you think you were. In fact, you became some kind of local legend the day you left town. People around here never forgot you. And after you started writing those horror novels, they talked about you more than ever."

Colby grinned. "Be careful what you say around Diana. I've got a reputation to protect. And if I did turn out okay, it's because of you, Gil, and you damn well know it. You had a way of pulling me up short whenever I got too close to the line. I owe you for that."

"I couldn't have done it if I hadn't had something to work with. You always had what it took to make it. Not like Eddy Spooner."

"Eddy turned out okay, too. He's holding down a job, isn't he?"

"Eddy's weak. He was weak as a kid, and he turned sour when he grew up. He failed at the army, failed at marriage and failed at everything else he ever tried."

Colby scowled. "I heard his marriage broke up, but that's no big deal in this day and age. What's this about the army?"

"He was discharged early. Didn't you know that?"

"No."

"Something about him being temperamentally unfit for the service."

"That's hardly a crime," Colby muttered. "I wasn't too fond of the army myself."

"Let's face it. For Eddy, pumping gas in Fulbrook Corners is as far as he's going to get and deep down inside he knows it. I feel kind of sorry for him."

Colby stared out into the night, thinking of the bleak resignation he had seen in Eddy's eyes the other day. "Yeah. So do I."

There was silence for a while as Gil puffed on his cigar. Eventually he spoke. "I'll keep my ears open about that other business for you. I can have a word with Roy Barnes, if you like. He's a good man. Done a decent job as sheriff around here."

"Thanks, Gil."

"You're real fond of that little lady in there, aren't you?" Gil's eyes gleamed in the moonlight.

"Yeah."

"Why'd you come back here after all these years, Colby?"

"Why in hell does everyone keep throwing that question at me?"

"Legends inspire curiosity," Gil said dryly. "So what's the answer?"

"I'm not sure," Colby admitted. "Do you believe in fate, Gil?"

"No."

"Neither do I. But sometimes I get the weirdest feeling that maybe I came back here this summer just so I'd find Diana."

"Sounds like a good enough reason to me."

2

She was trapped inside the grotto. She could not leave until her warrior husband came for her. She was a woman of great power who had never needed a male, but now she desperately needed the man who had fathered the child on her even as he died. There was a danger in the outer cavern, a threat to both herself and the babe she carried. Only the warrior could save her from the terror that hovered in the darkness beyond the grotto. For the first time in her life, she needed the help of a man. The knowledge terrified her.

The warm mist from the pool enveloped her, clouding her senses. Soon the pain would start.

"No." Diana sat straight up in bed, her heart pounding, her eyes wide open as she stared into the darkness.

"Diana." Colby was awake beside her, reaching for her. He pulled her tense body into his arms. "What is it, honey? What's wrong? A bad dream?"

Specter arrived at the edge of the bed and thrust his nose against Diana's bare leg. He whined inquiringly.

Diana took a deep breath, patted her dog and then patted Colby. "It's all right. I'm okay. Just another one of those dreams." She made no move to pull free of Colby's embrace. His arms felt good around her—reassuring and strong.

"Another one of what dreams? What are you talking about, Diana?"

She was startled by the sharpness of his voice. "Nothing, really. It's just that ever since you and I spent the night in Chained Lady Cave,

I've had a recurring dream. I don't get it every night, but this is the second or third time. I'm getting tired of them."

"The same dream every time?"

"Not exactly. It's like I'm having different parts of the same dream, though. Fragments. But all the dreams seem to be taking place in the cave. That little grotto, to be exact. It's your fault, Colby," she added with a weak smile. "You should never have told me about the legend of Chained Lady Cave. You're too good a storyteller. My subconscious mind has obviously glommed onto the tale and is having a ball with it while I sleep."

"You're dreaming about the cave?" Colby asked, as his hand stilled in her hair.

"Is that so surprising?" She wondered at the odd tone of his voice. "Colby, what's wrong?"

"I knew you'd had a dream or two that had awakened you since that night, but I never realized..."

"Never realized what?" she demanded.

"Tell me about the dreams, Diana."

"There's not much to tell. I dream I'm in the grotto and there's a sense of menace coming from the outer cavern. Usually I'm waiting for someone to rescue me, and I'm not at all sure he's going to get there in time. Tonight the dream was all mixed up with the fact that I'm pregnant."

"Who is it you're waiting for?"

"I don't know." She paused. "No, that's not true. I'm waiting for that idiot warrior who put the curse on the woman who killed him. In my dream I think I'm the woman." Diana shivered. "In the dream I'm the woman who could not leave until I had conceived and borne a child in that awful place. Colby, do you realize what's happened? Part of the legend has come true. I got pregnant in that cave."

"Take it easy, honey." His hand moved soothingly in her hair. "If your imagination gets more active, I'll have to let you write your own horror fiction."

"It's scary when you think about it."

"Only when you think about it at two in the morning," Colby retorted. "I've got a confession to make, though."

Her head came up so quickly that she nearly collided with his chin. "What kind of confession?"

"Don't look at me like that. I wouldn't dare cheat on an amazon. I was just going to tell you that you're not the only one who's had a few dreams about Chained Lady Cave."

"You've had them, too?" she asked in amazement. "For how long?"

"Since the night I spent there when I was a teenager," he admitted.

"You've had nightmares about that cave for the past twenty-odd years?" Diana peered down at him, trying to read his face in the weak moonlight. His gray eyes gleamed, and he stroked down her spine in a soft, sensual movement.

"They're not exactly nightmares, but they do tend to wake me up out of a sound sleep. Are yours nightmares? Do they terrify you?"

She tried to think. "Not exactly. At least, not yet. I'm not scared to death in them, but there is a sense of urgency about the dreams. As if things were going to get worse. Colby, I've never heard of two people having the same dreams."

"The dreams aren't identical. In my dream, I'm usually struggling to get up the path behind the waterfall and into the cave. I have this feeling that I have to get to the grotto."

"So maybe they're not exactly identical, but you've got to admit it's very strange that we're both having dreams about that cave."

Colby slipped his hand to the curve of her hip. "I don't know if it's all that strange. We both spent the night in that cave, and something very memorable happened in it."

"Colby, this is serious."

"No it's not. They're just dreams. But I'll tell you something. Right now I've got an overwhelming urge to go into another little grotto."

"Really?"

"Really." His palm was warm on her thigh. He squeezed gently. "In fact, I don't think I can resist."

Diana's eyes widened. "You want to go out to Chained Lady Cave tonight?"

His soft laughter was deep and sexy. "I didn't say that. I just said

I'd like to explore a certain hidden grotto." His other hand slid over her stomach and cupped the soft mound between her legs. He bent his head and gently nibbled her shoulder. "You going to let me inside your sweet little grotto tonight?"

Diana blinked as she finally realized what he was talking about. "Honestly, Colby, this is no time for joking."

"Tell me about it, baby." He caught her hand and guided it down to his thighs. "I've never been more serious in my life."

Her fingers closed around the hard, broad shape of his manhood and Diana knew she was about to get sidetracked. She groaned. "I think we should talk about the dreams, Colby."

"There's nothing much to talk about. We're both having them. They can't possibly mean anything, except that we've both got overactive imaginations, which we already know. So let's forget the dreams and get on to more pressing business." His forefinger slipped into her heat.

"You, Colby Savagar, are trying to change the subject."

"And I'm succeeding. The entrance to this tight little grotto is already getting hot and wet." He eased Diana onto her back and lowered himself along the length of her. "Sweet Diana." His voice roughened as he put his knee between her legs. "You always make me feel so wanted. There's never been anyone else like you. There never could be anyone else like you. All I have to do is touch you and I go crazy."

Diana sighed as the passion stole over her. She wrapped her arms around him and pulled him close. There would be time enough later to talk about the dreams. Right now Colby was making love to her and when he made love to her, nothing else mattered.

A long time later Colby stirred beside Diana. "You still awake, honey?"

"Yes. Do you want to talk about the dreams now?" She wasn't nearly so concerned with them as she had been earlier. Colby's lovemaking had soothed the jangling sense of uneasiness the dream had created.

"No, I want to talk about marriage."

"Oh." She didn't know what else to say. "I guess there's no real rush, is there?"

"There damn sure is a rush. You're pregnant. About three weeks along. We're going to get married as soon as possible."

"We are?" She felt as if she were being swept over Chained Lady Falls. Having accepted the inevitability of the marriage, she still hadn't quite accepted the reality of it. Just as she hadn't fully accepted the reality of her pregnancy, she realized. She was half-afraid that when the marriage became a fact, the pregnancy would also become real. "Maybe we should wait until I get tested to find out for certain if I'm pregnant."

"We both know you're pregnant. But we can get the test done here in town tomorrow just to tie up loose ends. We can also apply for the license tomorrow and have the official ceremony on Friday."

Diana felt stunned and breathless. "The end of the week?"

"You want to invite your mother?"

"Oh, my God. My mother. Of course I want to invite her."

"I'll invite Brandon. Anyone else we need to worry about?"

"Well, no, I guess not, but Colby, this is so sudden."

"Relax. I'll take care of everything."

"You keep saying that," she wailed.

"Try believing it." He turned on his side and met her eyes in the shadows. "You know what your problem is?"

"I'm afraid to ask."

"You're still playing the denial game. You figure if you just ignore the pregnancy, it might go away and your nice, neat, conveniently structured life will return to normal. I'm disappointed in you, Diana. You're a businesswoman. You should be able to face facts. You know damn well nothing will ever be the same for you again."

"They won't be the same for you, either," she shot back, goaded.

"I can handle it."

"Terrific. I can't tell you how relieved I am to hear that."

"Diana?"

"Yes?"

"It's going to work out. Wait and see."

"Famous last words." She turned toward him with a little moan and burrowed into his arms. "I'm scared," she confided.

"I know."

Her mouth brushed his shoulder in a soft, humble caress. "I'm very glad you're with me," she added in a barely audible voice.

Colby chuckled in the darkness. "At least you can admit it. There was a time, my sweet little amazon, when you didn't think you needed a man, remember?"

"Don't rub it in." She found his ribs with her finger.

"Hey, no fair tickling me when I'm luxuriating in postcoital afterglow." He caught her fingers.

"Is that what it's called?"

"Something like that. I don't have my thesaurus handy, or else I'd double-check my terminology."

"Shame on you. A writer should never be without his thesaurus."

"Obviously you're a bad influence on me." He kissed her throat.

Diana laughed for the first time in days. "I can't resist. You're so good when you're bad."

Colby joined in her laughter and tumbled her down across his aroused body.

Eddy Spooner paused in the act of drawing the rubber squeegee across the Jeep's windshield. He used a grease-stained hand to push his limp blond hair behind his ear as he peered down at Colby. The old army combat fatigues he wore smelled of gasoline and oil. His glacial blue eyes were narrowed in amazed consternation.

"Is it true what I heard this morning? You really gonna marry that Diana Prentice?"

"I see gossip still travels around this town as fast as it did twenty years ago. Yeah, it's true. Damn it, Specter, quit drooling on me." Colby pushed Specter's heavy muzzle off his shoulder. The dog had been leaning over the front seat, his tongue lolling between his teeth as he watched Spooner clean the windshield.

Specter didn't take offense. He lumbered to the other side of the Jeep and stared across the street at the post office. Diana had disappeared inside to collect the mail a few minutes earlier.

"Jesus, Colby, don't take this personal or nothin', but why in hell you want to marry the woman? You're already livin' with her bold as brass."

"Women like Diana need marriage to settle 'em down," Colby said, feeling a rush of masculine wisdom as he said the words.

"That right?" Eddy's eyes widened with interest. "She kinda wild?"

Only in bed, Colby thought with private satisfaction. "No, she's just used to being independent. You know these modern women. They don't think they need a man to look after them."

"Wish I could find me one of those modern women. Some gal who didn't want marriage but who'd be willin' to keep my place clean, fix my dinner every night and hit the sack with me whenever I felt like havin' a little fun. I'd like to get me some babe who wouldn't give me any lip when I wanted to take off by myself for a while."

"I don't think you're going to find too many women who are that modern," Colby said.

"Not in Fulbrook Corners, I won't," Spooner agreed morosely. "Your son comin' up for the wedding?"

"Brandon will be here on Friday. So will Diana's mother. She's flying in from California."

"You ready to take on another mother-in-law, Colby? The last one you had should have been enough to put you off marriage for life."

"I know. It's taken me twenty years to recover. Speaking of Margaret Fulbrook, here she comes now." Colby removed cash from his wallet, his eye on the aging blue Cadillac pulling into the parking lot across the street. "Let's settle up, Eddy, so I can get over there. I don't want the old bitch cornering Diana alone in the post office."

As she turned away from the service window, Diana glanced thoughtfully at the envelope she had just been handed. Another letter from Aaron Crown. He would no doubt be outlining more reasons why she should return to work for him as soon as possible. Her former boss certainly was being persistent.

Diana unconsciously touched her stomach. It was reassuring to know she had at least one secure job possibility available to her. She didn't want to go back to work for Carruthers and Yale, but she felt awkward about starting a new position with another company knowing she would have to go on maternity leave within a few months.

She shook her head ruefully. Colby was right. Being pregnant changed everything. Nothing would ever again be the same in her life. She couldn't even make career decisions the same way she had in the past. There were new factors to take into consideration.

"I hear Colby Savagar is getting ready for another shotgun wedding." Margaret Fulbrook's loud voice filled the post office, mesmerizing everyone inside.

Diana looked up and saw the matriarch of Fulbrook Corners standing in the doorway. Her gray hair was in its customary regal chignon. Her fine brown eyes were as piercing as ever, and her face was set in its usual rigid lines of disapproval and bitterness.

"Good morning, Mrs. Fulbrook. How are you today?" Diana smiled with cool politeness.

"As well as can be expected. What about you, Miss Prentice? Is it true you're marrying Savagar?"

"Word travels fast around here, doesn't it?"

"Saw Evelyn Thorp at the grocery store," Margaret Fulbrook explained impatiently. "She told me all about it. I couldn't believe it at first. You look like a reasonably bright young woman. Why on earth would you want to marry Savagar? Has he gotten you pregnant the way he did my daughter?"

For some reason the blunt question got to Diana. She had thought she was ready for anything Margaret Fulbrook could dish out, but in spite of herself, she turned pink.

"I don't think that's any of your business, Mrs. Fulbrook. If you'll excuse me, I have a few other errands to run."

Colby appeared on the other side of the glass doors. He strode into the small lobby just as the old woman's sharp eyes widened and then narrowed in open speculation. She studied Diana's blushing face.

"So that's it, is it?" Margaret Fulbrook said with grim satisfaction. "Forty years old and the man still hasn't learned how to keep his jeans zipped up. You have my sympathy, Miss Prentice. But not much of it. I warned you to stay away from that man."

Diana came close to losing her temper. She had always felt sorry for the bitter woman who had denied herself her own grandson for nearly twenty years, but this was going too far. Colby was already moving forward, a dangerous expression on his face. In another moment there would be fireworks.

Diana smiled serenely at Margaret Fulbrook. "The wonderful thing about being my age is that one gets to make one's own decisions. One needn't listen to the warnings of others."

"Diana?" Colby came to a halt, no longer certain he had an adversary. "What the hell is going on here?"

"There you are, Colby." She went to him and stood on tiptoe to kiss him lightly. "I've got the mail. Shall we leave?"

Colby scowled at Margaret Fulbrook. "Yeah, let's get out of here."

"Just a moment, you two," Mrs. Fulbrook snapped. "I hear you're getting married here. Is my grandson going to be coming up from Portland for the wedding?"

"Not that it's any business of yours, but, yes, Brandon will be here on Friday," Colby growled as he shouldered open the glass doors. He let them swing shut on the older woman's next remark. "What was that all about?" he demanded.

"Margaret Fulbrook was speculating on the reason behind our hasty marriage plans."

"Yeah, that figures. The old witch." Colby came to a halt beside the Jeep and captured her face between rough palms. "Are you okay, honey?"

"I still feel a little dazed whenever I think about being pregnant," she answered truthfully.

"You're going to make a good mother once you settle down and get your priorities straight. You're still panicky, but once you're past that part, you'll be fine."

"How do you know?"

"Because I've been there, remember?"

Diana clasped his wrists and looked up at him with anxious eyes.

"Oh, Colby, I know you have and it's not fair for you to have to go through this again."

"If you bring up the subject of fairness again, I'm going to get really angry. There's no going back for either of us, so we don't talk about it. I thought I made that clear?"

She nodded, her smile tremulous. "You did. And you're right. I won't bring up the subject again."

"Good. Let's go pick up those groceries." Colby glanced into the Jeep. "Stay put, you idiot dog. We'll be right back."

Specter gave him a bored look.

"You and my dog have made some headway toward détente," Diana observed. "At least the two of you don't growl openly at each other any longer."

"I wouldn't trust that mutt as far as I could throw him, and what with the way you overfeed him, that's not far. If he's behaving himself around me these days, it's only because he knows he's living under my roof and he'll get kicked out if he tries anything really nasty. This isn't détente, it's a power struggle. Specter's gone underground for the time being."

"I think you credit him with a little too much deviousness. He's only a dog, Colby."

"Hah. He's jealous of me. Before I came along, he was the only male in your life." Colby glanced down at the letter in her hand. "Except for that damn boss of yours. What's he writing to you about this time?"

Diana opened the envelope as they walked toward the grocery store. Quickly she scanned the contents of the letter. "He says my position is still waiting, work is piling up, and they could really use me. He thinks he could wangle a raise for me if I return from my leave soon."

"Forget it."

"I'm not so sure, Colby. I was thinking that going back to work for Carruthers and Yale might be the perfect solution until the baby arrives. I'd feel strange about starting a brand-new job with another company and then having to take maternity leave within the first year. But I've worked for Carruthers and Yale for several years now, and as far as I'm concerned they owe me."

"They do owe you after the way they refused to promote you because of the fact that you're a woman."

"Don't you see? I could use my old position as the perfect fill-in job until the baby arrives, and then I could quit. It would serve those old fogies right, and it would give me a well-paying job for the next few months. After the baby gets here, I can start hunting for a permanent position with another firm."

"You don't have to work at all until the baby arrives," Colby said irritably. "There's not much point. I can support you, and you can spend the time getting ready to become a mother. You've got a lot to learn on that subject."

Diana slid him an uneasy glance. She did not want to start a quarrel but she also wanted Colby to understand. "You know how I feel about working."

"I know you've got this thing about not becoming financially dependent on a man, but that's hogwash in this situation. You know damned well I'm not going to run off and leave you stranded."

"I know that, but..."

"But you still don't quite believe it, do you? Forget finding another job for the next few months. Trust me, Diana. I'll take care of you. After you've settled down and gotten comfortable with motherhood, you'll have plenty of time to find another job."

He didn't understand, and she didn't want to argue about it just then. Diana said nothing as they walked into the small grocery store.

"Hey there, Savagar, I hear congratulations are in order."

"'Morning, Brian." Colby smiled wryly at the man behind the checkout counter. "You heard right."

"Well, that's great. Just great. Good luck to both of you." The dark-haired, slightly plump man behind the counter was close to Colby's age, perhaps a few years younger. He wore glasses and his hair was thinning. He had an open, cheerful expression. His name was Brian McDonald, and although he seemed cautious around Colby, as if uncertain of his welcome, he was one of the handful of people in town who treated Colby like an old friend.

"This time you're going to stick around and have the wedding in town instead of running off to Reno, huh?" Brian grinned. Then he began to look nervous at the small joke he had just attempted.

Colby shot him a quelling glance, reinforcing Brian's anxious expression. "I didn't have much choice last time."

"That's true. There wasn't a justice of the peace or a minister in the whole county who would have married you and Cynthia over the Fulbrooks' objections. But that was a long time ago and times change, don't they? Congratulations, Miss Prentice."

"Thank you, Brian."

"You two going to have a party or something to celebrate?" Brian asked.

"No." Colby spoke over his shoulder as he headed down the narrow aisle, hunting for tuna.

"Too bad," Brian said wistfully. "Might be kind of fun. We haven't had anything to celebrate around Fulbrook Corners since the Renley girl got married. That was three years ago. Not many weddings in this town these days. All the young people head for Portland as soon as they get out of high school."

"I can't imagine anyone in Fulbrook Corners wanting to celebrate my wedding," Colby said as he came back with the tuna and a few other items.

"You might be surprised," Brian said. "You're a legend around here, Colby. And not just because you used to cause so much trouble. Folks in town are real proud of all that horror stuff you've been writing. Do you realize you're the only person from Fulbrook Corners who ever got himself famous? Caused quite a stir when Larry Brockton down at the real estate office spread the word you were planning to come back for the summer."

Colby shook his head. "The only stir it caused was one of amazement that I wasn't in prison. Do we need anything else, Diana?" He waved a hand at the items he'd put on the checkout counter.

"Dog food. Specter won't be pleased if we return without his rations."

"Damn. I almost forgot," Colby said, looking innocent.

* * *

"Well, it's about time," Angela Prentice announced in ringing tones as her daughter introduced her to her future son-in-law on the steps of the courthouse. "I was beginning to think this child of mine was never going to find herself a man. I hope you two don't waste any time getting started on my grandkid. Lord knows, I've waited long enough."

Diana was getting tired of blushing lately. She glared at her attractive, petite mother, aware that Colby was grinning broadly. "Honestly, Mom. The least you can do is refrain from embarrassing me at my own wedding."

Angela's hazel eyes gleamed with amusement. "Don't pay any attention to her, Colby. She can be a real stick-in-the-mud. Spent too many years being a hot-shot lady executive, if you ask me. Look at the result. Thirty-four years old, and never been married. It's a wonder you weren't put off by all those chilly corporate manners of hers. Most men are scared to death of her."

"I had my moments of doubt," Colby said gravely as he shook hands with Angela. "But I persevered. There's more to Diana than meets the eye at first. And we writers are good at looking below the surface, you know."

"Any money in this writing business?"

"Mother!"

Colby's grin widened. "Don't yell at your mother, Diana. She's got a right to know if I can support you in the style in which you've been supporting yourself for the past few years." He turned back to Angela's bright, inquisitive face. "Yes, Angela, there is some money in the writing business. Nowadays, at any rate. There didn't used to be, and one never knows about the future, but I've always been able to take care of my son one way or another. I'm sure I'll be able to take care of Diana and the baby."

"Colby!" Diana was turning from pink to red. She could have strangled him. One look at her mother's face told her the damage was done.

"What baby?" Angela swung around gleefully to confront her daughter. "Don't tell me you're pregnant already? Good grief, Diana. When you decided to go, you went all the way, didn't you? Congratulations, honey, I didn't think you had it in you to finally cut loose and live a little."

"Mother, let me explain..."

"No explanations needed. You're thirty-four years old, not eighteen. I'm thrilled. Positively thrilled." Angela threw her arms around her daughter, and then she hugged Colby. "This is the happiest moment of my life. I'm going to sign up for a knitting class as soon as I get home. I can't wait to get started on some cute little booties."

Colby's eyes gleamed with laughter as he regarded Diana over the top of her mother's curly blond head. "Who would have guessed," he asked gently, "that mother-in-laws came in so many varieties?"

Diana didn't know whether to laugh or cry. She was saved from having to do either when she spotted Brandon trotting down the steps.

"Hey, Dad, they're ready inside," Brandon called. "You two better get in there."

"We're on our way." Colby put his arm around Diana and pulled her close against his side.

She leaned into his strength, aware that her knees suddenly felt weak. "Colby, are you absolutely sure you want to do this?"

"Are you kidding? Your mother would kill me if I backed out now."

Half an hour later Colby kissed Diana and bundled her into the front seat of the Jeep. He touched the ring on her left hand. "You look terrific, Mrs. Savagar. Sexy as hell. Can't wait to get you into bed."

"You're going to have to demonstrate a little patience, Mr. Savagar. Brandon told me earlier there would be a few people waiting at the house."

"A few... what?" Colby was dumbfounded. He swung around to search out Brandon who was starting toward a small, red two-seater Mazda. He had Angela Prentice in tow. "Brandon."

"Yeah, Dad?" Brandon glanced back over his shoulder.

"Who's waiting at the house?"

"I don't know for sure. I was just told that a few people wanted to congratulate you and Diana. That's all I know, honest." He ushered

Angela into the front seat of the racy little car. "Probably the Thorps and maybe that man who owns the grocery store. No big deal."

"No big deal," Colby grumbled as he got into the Jeep beside Diana. "I had other plans for this afternoon. The last thing I want to do is share a few drinks with the Thorps and McDonald."

As it turned out, Colby didn't have to share a few drinks with the Thorps and Brian McDonald.

He had to share wedding punch and cake with the entire population of Fulbrook Corners. Everyone in town, including Margaret Fulbrook, showed up for the reception honoring Colby Savagar's second hasty marriage.

3

"What the hell is going on here?" Colby raked his fingers through his hair and stared at the crowd of approximately two hundred people milling around the front yard of Aunt Jesse's old house.

"I'll take a wild guess and say that you have more friends in town than you thought you did," Diana murmured as she slid out of the front seat. "Don't sit there grumbling to yourself. Come and enjoy your party."

A cheer went up as people realized the wedding couple had arrived. A group of men swarmed around Colby when he climbed slowly out of the Jeep. Most of the women hastened forward to offer congratulations to Diana as she stood smiling beside the vehicle.

Specter was barking furiously from the back porch where he had been confined during the wedding.

"That dog of yours has been going wild," Evelyn Thorp said with a laugh as she came forward to greet Diana. "If he hadn't been locked up we'd never have been able to pull this off. Now that you're here, maybe he'll calm down."

"Specter's not accustomed to so many people being around. He tends to be protective and possessive," Diana explained as she started toward the rear of the house to soothe her irate dog.

"Not unlike someone else I know," Evelyn remarked. She glanced over her shoulder to where Colby was the center of a throng of males. "I hope Colby doesn't take offense at all this. It was a spur-of-the-moment decision on my part. But once I put the word out that I was going to have a small reception for you two, everyone in town wanted to come."

"It was very thoughtful of you." Diana opened the screen door and steadied herself as Specter leaped forward. He checked her out quickly to make certain she was all right, and then he perked up his huge, floppy ears and surveyed the crowd.

"Colby's kept to himself so much in the few weeks since he arrived in town that most people are afraid to approach him. I think everyone is rather intimidated by him, if you want to know the truth. But they're all equally fascinated. From what Gil told me, your husband was a real hellion when he was a kid, and when he left town with Cynthia Fulbrook he was instantly elevated to the status of a local legend. Then he went on to become a successful author. Now he's back twenty years later—Fulbrook Corners' one and only celebrity. I don't think he quite realizes how excited people are to have him here."

"Maybe this will break down a few of the barriers between him and the town," Diana said. "Let's just hope Margaret Fulbrook doesn't make a scene."

"She's unpredictable, but I think she'll behave herself. She's enthralled with her grandson, you know. She's told everyone how he's got the Fulbrook eyes. She won't want to embarrass herself in front of Brandon or do anything to jeopardize her fragile relationship with him."

Diana nodded, watching as Brandon led Angela over to introduce her to his grandmother. "Brandon's a wonderful young man. Mrs. Fulbrook should be proud of him."

"Colby did all right with his son," Evelyn agreed. "Margaret can't bring herself to admit it yet, but she's secretly very impressed with Brandon. And she knows in her heart that Colby's responsible for the boy turning out so well. One of these days maybe she'll be able to say as much to Colby."

Diana laughed. "I doubt she can go that far. But I agree with you. She is excited about establishing contact with Brandon after all these years."

"I doubt they would have managed to get together if it hadn't been for you. I heard about the day you introduced the two of them."

"Colby was furious when he found out," Diana admitted.

"The fact that he got over his anger is a tribute to you, my dear. Obviously you have the power to make the man see reason. Gil says that is an uncommon talent. One of Colby's biggest problems as a kid was his arrogant pride, according to my husband. It was all he had. Come along and introduce me to your mother. I'm anxious to meet her. How did she take the news of your sudden marriage?"

Diana grinned. "She's thrilled with Colby, and she let him know it. More or less told him she'll be everlastingly grateful to him for marrying me. She'd figured I was going to spend the rest of my life on the shelf."

Evelyn chuckled. "She sounds delightful. Nice change in mothers in-law for Colby."

In the end, there were no embarrassing scenes. Margaret Fulbrook nodded stiffly to Colby when they encountered each other in the crowd. Colby nodded back, and that was the end of it. Neither spoke to the other. Diana decided that was probably just as well.

Harry Gedge, Margaret Fulbrook's beefy odd-job man, hung around at the fringes of the crowd. He stayed out of Colby's way, which was also just as well, Diana thought. The grudge between Harry and Colby wasn't going to disappear just because of a wedding party.

Somewhere in the middle of the affair, Eddy Spooner drifted over to where Diana was standing alone. In honor of the event he had evidently polished his old army boots and washed the camouflage shirt and pants he favored. He shoved a handful of long, thin blond hair out of his eyes and gave Diana a quizzical twist of a smile.

"It's just like I was telling Harry a while back. Colby Savagar always did have all the luck. I been workin' at that gas station for years. Put gas in damn near every car in town. Clean the windows, check the oil and fix problems every damn day of the week. But no one here even knows I exist. Colby, though, he leaves town with everyone around callin' him every name they can think of, and he comes back twenty years later like some kind of hero."

"I don't think they consider him a hero," Diana said gently. "They're just curious about him because of his past and the fact that he wrote some popular books."

Eddy shook his head. "It ain't that. People always talked about

Colby. They were always curious about him. Whenever he got into trouble, everyone in town gossiped about it. I was with him a lot of the times he got picked up by Sheriff Thorp, but no one said much about me. They just talked about Colby."

"I gather that when they did talk about him, they didn't have much good to say," Diana reminded Eddy.

Eddy nodded. "They all claimed he'd come to a bad end, all right. But as usual, Colby made out like a bandit. Some guys get all the breaks."

Half an hour later Diana caught sight of Colby making his way toward her through the crowd. His eyes narrowed briefly as he saw the kindly-faced older woman to whom his wife was talking. Then he smiled faintly.

"Hello, Mrs. Grimley," he drawled as he drew close. "Giving my wife a quick rundown on what an outstanding student I was in high school English classes?"

Ada Grimley smiled with the air of superiority only a veteran high school teacher can muster. "As a matter of fact, I was just telling Diana that I always knew you had the ability. It was just a matter of your settling down and getting to work, which you obviously eventually did. Congratulations, Colby. I've read all your books, and I like to think I can take some personal credit for having pounded the basics of English into you. Lord knows it was tough going at times."

Colby grinned, surprising not only Diana, but Mrs. Grimley. "Yes, ma'am. I know it was. But I couldn't have written any of those books if it hadn't been for you. I never thought I'd say it, but here goes: thanks for all the hours you spent beating English Lit. and grammar into my head."

Ada Grimley beamed. "You're quite welcome, Colby. I shall look forward to your next book."

"There you are, Dad. I've been looking for you." Brandon wove his way through the crowd. He was carrying a small package, and he had Specter at his heels. The dog was licking wedding cake frosting off his muzzle as he trotted along in Brandon's wake.

"What's that?" Colby asked, eyeing the package in his son's hand.

"A present." Brandon waited until Ada Grimley moved away to speak to a neighbor. Then he glanced at Diana and flashed her a brief, almost apologetic smile. He turned to his father with a very serious expression.

"Dad, before I give you your wedding gift, it occurs to me we need to have a little father-son chat."

"Is that right?" Colby's brows rose ironically.

"I'm afraid so." Brandon cleared his throat portentously. "It has come to my attention that, in spite of all those talks we had about the male reproductive system, in spite of all those lectures on the merits of a man learning how to say no, in spite of all those warnings about how hard it is for a man to stop once he gets started and how it's better to finish the job by hand, so to speak, on certain occasions..."

"Brandon, you are my one and only son and heir, but if you want to live to see the ripe old age of twenty, you'd better cut this short."

"Don't rush me, Dad. This is for your own good. As I was saying, in spite of all those conversations we had on birth control and how to keep the zipper of one's jeans in an upright and locked position, it seems something, uh, fell through the crack, as it were."

"Brandon..."

"I'm sure you can just imagine my surprise when Diana informed me I was about to get a baby brother or sister."

"Son, I'm warning you, you can be replaced." Colby was going a slow, dull red.

Brandon ignored him, his fine brown eyes alight with mischief. "Now, while I am absolutely thrilled at the prospect of being a big brother," he continued, "I nevertheless feel it's my duty as your son to fill in certain gaps in your education which have recently become glaringly apparent." He presented the brightly wrapped package to his father with a flourish. "Here you go. A wedding present from your son purchased with your educational advancement in mind."

Diana managed a smile as she watched Colby unwrap the package. She knew Brandon was only teasing, and the last thing she wanted to do was spoil the humor of the situation. But it was hard for her to see anything amusing about her pregnancy yet. She was learning to accept it, and she thought that with Colby by her side she just might be able to handle it, but she hadn't gotten to the point where she could joke about it.

Colby ripped off the wrapping paper and gazed down at the book he found himself holding. "Geez, Brandon, this was real thoughtful of you. Remind me to flatten you later when there are no witnesses around." He grinned and playfully cuffed his son.

Brandon laughed and dodged. "I knew you'd appreciate it, Dad. You've always been real big on learning things from books."

"Let me see." Diana moved closer to peer over Colby's shoulder. She read the title aloud. "The Responsible Man's Complete Guide to Modern Sex."

"Don't worry," Brandon said cheerfully. "It's got lots of pictures."

"It's a good thing I've got another kid on the way," Colby said to Diana, "because Brandon's chances of surviving until next week are real shaky."

"Alone at last. I thought all those people would never leave," Colby declared several hours later as he began unbuttoning his shirt.

"What's that?" Diana called from the other side of the closed bathroom door. "I didn't hear what you said."

"I said I thought that damn wedding reception would never end."

"It was very sweet of Evelyn Thorp to organize it for us. Were you surprised that so many people showed up?"

"'Stunned' would be a better description. It must have been the promise of free booze and cake that brought them out of the woodwork."

"They came to see you, Colby. They wanted to congratulate you. You're the town's local celebrity, in case you don't know it. How does it feel to breeze back into Fulbrook Corners twenty years later and find out you're a legend?"

"Damn weird, if you want to know the truth. And don't be taken in by all the big smiles and hearty handshakes today. Some of those people who were offering lots of good wishes this afternoon were the same ones who wouldn't let me date their daughters and who couldn't wait to see if I'd wind up in jail twenty years ago."

"Well, you didn't wind up in jail. You showed 'em all, Colby. And now they're proud of you."

"I wouldn't bet on it. They all showed up today out of sheer curiosity," he muttered. But he didn't sound particularly annoyed.

"Don't be such a grouch. This is our wedding night. I hope you're planning something romantic out there."

"I'm planning to jump on top of you just as soon as you get your little tush out of the bathroom."

"Be still, my beating heart." Inside the bathroom Diana shimmied into the peach-colored negligee her mother had given her and surveyed herself in the old, cracked mirror. It was definitely the sexiest nightgown she'd ever worn.

"Diana?"

"Yes, Colby?"

"I liked your mother."

"She liked you. It was nice of Brandon to pick her up in Portland and drive her back to the airport this evening."

"She's different from what I expected."

"What did you expect?"

"Oh, I don't know. From what you'd told me about your past, your father deserting her after he got her pregnant and all, I guess I expected her to be more bitter toward men in general and her daughter's husband in particular."

"Mom's not like that."

"So I found out. She's really happy about the baby. She told me she'd been afraid her own experiences raising you alone had warped your attitude toward men forever. You were so determined not to trust men that she was afraid you'd never let yourself fall in..." Colby broke off abruptly. "Afraid you'd never take the risk of marrying anyone, let alone the risk of having a kid. She actually thanked me for barging into your life and rearranging things for you."

"That sounds like Mom," Diana said with a barely stifled groan. She was as ready as she would ever be. "Colby?"

"Yeah, honey?"

"I'm coming out. Don't jump on top of me right away, okay? I want you to see this nightgown. It's beautiful."

"I don't care how pretty it is. It'll look better off."

Diana cautiously opened the door. Colby was on the far side of the small bedroom. His back was turned toward her, and he was doing something at the dresser. He had the light turned down low, and she could see that he was naked except for his sexy briefs. His broad shoulders gleamed in the faint light. She saw the traces of silver in his dark hair and her heart quickened. She was lost every time she looked at him.

Diana wondered if he realized even vaguely how much she loved him. She hadn't found the courage to tell him. She was just beginning to acknowledge it fully to herself.

"Colby?"

He swung around at the sound of her voice, and she saw that he was holding a small vase full of wildflowers in his fist. His gray gaze moved over her slowly.

"I can't believe it," he finally said.

Diana looked at him uncomprehendingly. "Can't believe what?"

"That you really do belong to me at last." He became aware of the flowers he was clutching. "Here, these are for you. I picked them this morning and put them in water to keep while we drove over to the courthouse. Not much of a wedding gift, but Fulbrook Corners' general store didn't have much to offer. I'll get you something nice when we get to Portland."

"Oh, Colby, they're beautiful. The most beautiful flowers in the whole world. Thank you." Diana was afraid she was very close to tears. She had never been more touched by a gift in her life.

Colby was no grand romantic, as she had informed him often enough. But the vase of delicate blooms held so carefully in his strong hand had to constitute the most romantic present she'd ever received.

"You like 'em, huh?" He looked down at the flowers with a small, lopsided grin.

"I love them." Almost as much as I love you, she added silently. She went forward to take the flowers. Her hand came around from behind her back, and she handed him his wedding gift.

"What's that? A stone? From the river?" He took the small, polished rock from her palm, examining it as if it were a gemstone.

"As you said, the shopping available around here is a little limited." Diana was suddenly nervous. Maybe this hadn't been such a great idea after all. "But I got this idea of going out to Chained Lady Falls yesterday, and I found that stone at the base of the falls. It looked so beautiful shining there in the water, almost as if it had been professionally polished. I guess all that water pounding over it all those years did the polishing job."

Colby looked up from the stone in his palm, his eyes burning with an intensity that took her breath away. "You went out to Chained Lady Falls to get this?"

She nodded quickly, uncertain of his reaction. "I know you said we weren't to talk about what happened between us that night in the cave, about how we were reckless, and I got pregnant, and why we had to get married and all, but..." Her voice trailed off.

"But?"

She couldn't look away from the gray fire in his eyes. Diana swallowed and sought an explanation. She'd never felt this tongue-tied in her whole life. "But I wanted to tell you somehow that I don't think that what happened that night was so terrible after all. In fact, the more I get used to the idea, the more I think it's going to be all right. This baby I'm carrying feels as if it was meant to be. Do you know what I mean?"

"Diana..." he began gently.

She interrupted him, the rest of the words tumbling out in a rush, "If it had happened to me with any other man, it would have been a disaster. But it happened with you and you're different, and I want you to know I appreciate that and I...I won't be looking back on that night as an awful mistake for which I'm now having to pay a high price."

"I picked those flowers up by the falls," Colby said quietly. "I went there for the same reason you did. I wanted to give you something from Chained Lady Falls so you'd know that I won't be looking back on that night and thinking it was a mistake, either."

Diana smiled at him, her relief and happiness making her eyes glow. She took the stone from his palm and gently set it down beside the vase full of wildflowers. Then she went into his waiting arms.

"My sweet, sexy Diana," Colby breathed as he held her close for a long moment. "We've got a hell of a lot going for us. We'll make this marriage work."

"I'll do my best, Colby," she vowed earnestly. She leaned against him, inhaling the scent of his body and absorbing his strength.

He chuckled softly. "You sound as if you were accepting a new job."

"Well, it is sort of like starting a second career, isn't it?"

"I guess you could look at it that way." He lifted her chin to gaze down into her eyes. "So long as you understand that this is the most important job in your life, and that you can't resign if the benefits don't suit you."

She wasn't sure she cared for the wary, searching intensity of his gaze. Diana smiled. "I think some of the benefits are going to be very satisfactory," she murmured. Her palms glided over his shoulders, savoring the strength of him.

Colby studied her for a long moment, and then he smiled back with lazy sensuality. The expression in his eyes took on a new and different gleam, one Diana was familiar with. It was the kind of look that made her think she was going to melt. Colby's hands snagged in her hair and he bent his head to kiss her parted lips.

"You want to talk benefit packages, Madam Executive? I'll show you benefit packages." His mouth closed over hers.

Diana moaned as the heat of his kiss scorched through her. She tightened her arms around his neck and shivered as she felt his palm sweep down her spine.

Her mind whirled, and then the room spun, too, as Colby lifted and carried her over to the bed. When she felt the pillow beneath her head, she opened her eyes to watch as Colby stripped off his briefs.

His strong, lean body was heavy with arousal. She looked up at him, and a fantasy flickered in and out of her head. It was a fantasy she'd had once or twice before when Colby made love to her.

He reached over to turn out the bedside light and Diana's fantasy grew stronger. She watched him move about in the darkness, preparing to come to her, and it seemed that he was someone she had known before in another time or in her dreams.

He had been fierce and primitive in that other dimension—a dangerous, arrogant, warrior male who had accepted no restraint, no feminine bonds. He had refused to grant her the respect and honor that were her rights. He had used her and abused her, and she had fought back with the only weapons she had at her disposal, for she had been as fierce and proud as he.

She had refused to give him the child he had demanded, and in the end she had used his own knife to kill him.

But she had known to her sorrow and anguish, even as the blood welled between her fingers, that it could have been different. In some other lifetime it would be different.

"Diana?" Colby came down beside her, reaching for her. "What's wrong?"

"Nothing." She shook her head quickly. "It's just that sometimes fragments of those dreams flash through my head. It can be disconcerting."

"I know what you mean." He loomed over her, his legs anchoring hers. His eyes glittered in the shadows. "Sometimes when we're like this, very close, about to make love, I get images in my head, too. Like scenes out of those damned dreams."

"You never told me."

"I didn't know how to explain it. But now that I know you've had similar dreams, maybe you can understand." He hesitated and then asked urgently, "What's it like for you?"

"I see you as you are now," she began slowly, hunting for the right words, "but also as someone you once were. The warrior who chained the lady in the cave. It's as if the dream image of you, the warrior image, is superimposed onto the real you. Does that make sense?"

"Unfortunately, yes. Sometimes I see you that way, too."

"As a warrior?"

Colby gave her a gentle shake. "No, not as a warrior." He drew a breath. "As the lady who got chained in the cave—proud, powerful huntress who refused to bend to any man's will."

A frisson of fear, laced with excitement, went through Diana. "What's she like, this other woman you sometimes see in me?"

"She's not another woman," Colby said slowly. "She is you. But a slightly different version of you. A more primitive you, I guess. She's some kind of amazon. Fierce, arrogant, untamable. And I handled you all wrong last time. I didn't understand..."

"What?" Diana looked up at him as he broke off. She was bewildered and desperately curious. "What do you mean, you handled me all wrong?"

Colby shook his head, as if to clear it. He scowled in the shadows. "Honey, those images are just fragments of our dreams."

"I know, but it's so strange that we're both dreaming about the legend of Chained Lady Cave." Diana was very serious now.

Colby grinned slowly in the darkness, showing his teeth. "Does it get you excited?"

"I didn't say that!"

He bent his head and kissed the base of her throat. "I think it does."

"Colby, stop it. I want to talk about this dream business. There's something going on here, and we ought to discuss it."

"It will be more fun to act it out. What's the point of having a vivid imagination if you don't get some use out of it in your fantasy life?" His eyes were glittering with sensual intent as he slowly and deliberately lowered his weight along the length of her.

"Colby?" Diana wriggled experimentally and discovered her legs were trapped beneath his. She suddenly realized just how much more he weighed than she did.

"Are you getting hot yet, honey?" He tugged off the peach-colored nightgown in one swift, efficient move.

"Don't be ridiculous. Honestly, Colby, I'm trying to have a serious discussion with you, and you're playing games."

"A man's got a right to play a few games on his wedding night." He used his foot to part her legs.

Diana shivered as his hair-roughened thigh slid between her knees. She sucked in her breath, and her fingertips splayed across his chest. He slid one finger into her, testing her readiness and groaned with satisfaction as she began to dampen his hand. Her eyes widened as she looked up at him.

Colby was suddenly very big, very male and very much in charge of the situation. When he gazed down into her face, Diana knew he was well aware of her quickening response.

Holding her captive with his eyes as well as his weight, Colby gently caught her wrists and pinned them to the pillow on either side of her head.

"This primitive enough for you?" he asked, his voice sexy and excitingly rough as he arched his lower body against her softness. Again and again, he moved against her, seducing her into the ancient rhythm. His hard, blunt manhood pressed against her but he didn't enter her. "Remind you of a professional warrior you used to know?"

Diana moaned as he began to sink into her with slow deliberation. "What do they feed professional warriors these days to make them grow this big?"

"A lot of raw meat."

"Oh." She closed her eyes and cried out softly as Colby thrust deeply into her.

She waited for him to resume the mesmerizing pattern he had used to tease her a moment before. She knew the pattern well—knew that it would bring them both to a glorious release, but Colby didn't move. He stayed where he was, locked within her softness. Keeping her wrists chained to the pillow, he lowered his head to trail a string of hot, damp kisses down her throat to the peaks of her breasts.

"Colby?"

"Hmm?" His attention was on the valley between her breasts now.

"You're driving me crazy."

"Good. I like it when you go crazy. I like to hear you scream."

"I do not scream."

"What do you call it?"

"Little cries of sensual completion," Diana stated loftily. She wished he would start moving within her. She could hardly stand the tight, full feeling of having him lodged within her pulsating body.

"Little cries of sensual completion, my foot," Colby muttered. "You're a screamer. You go wild in my arms and you scream. There's no other word for it. I'm going to make you scream for me tonight."

"Are you?" Diana gave up trying to dissuade him. The feel of him inside her and all along the outside of her was overwhelming her with excitement. A savage warmth was pouring through her. She was suddenly hot and restless and full of fire. Deliberately she tightened herself around him.

Colby groaned. "Oh, yeah, honey. That's what I want." He released her wrists and began to thrust slowly in and out. The muscles bunched in his shoulders as he held himself in check while he waited for her to reach the heights.

Diana wrapped her arms around him, and then she wrapped her legs around his driving thighs. And when he had finally summoned them forth, Colby drank the feminine screams of release from her lips. An instant later he shouted his own satisfaction into the darkness.

Floating on the edge of dreamy contentment, Diana smiled to herself as a stray thought drifted through her mind. This time around everything was different. This time around everything was right.

A long while later Colby stirred in the shadows. "I've been thinking. Making some plans."

"Have you?" Diana yawned.

"It's time we made a doctor's appointment for you. You heard what they said at the clinic when they gave us the results of your test the other day. We need to get started on a prenatal care program."

Diana, who had been on the verge of sleep, came awake in a hurry. "I have a gynecologist in Portland. I can make an appointment with her." Diana stared up at the ceiling, feeling rather flustered. So many new things to think about. So many changes to make in her normal routine.

Colby's palm settled warmly on Diana's still flat stomach. "Set it up, and we'll drive down to Portland to see her. It'll give us a nice break."

"What about your writing? I can drive to Portland by myself."

"I'll handle the writing. And I'll drive you to Portland."

Diana tried to decide how it felt to have someone else making the decisions. On the one hand, it was an enormous relief to share the responsibility. But on the other hand, it frightened her to have a man assuming that responsibility for her. She wasn't accustomed to having anyone look after her, least of all a man.

"Stop worrying about it, honey," Colby said. He sounded amused. "You'll get used to it."

"Have you taken up mind reading?" she demanded.

"No. But at times like this, it's not hard to figure out what you're thinking."

She decided to ignore that. "Maybe it would be a good idea to spend a couple of days in Portland. I could check with Aaron Crown and talk about going back to work for Carruthers and Yale for a few months."

"You don't need to go back to work. You can wait until after the baby arrives."

"No," Diana said firmly. "I want to go back to work while I wait for the baby."

"Just so long as you remember that you've got other priorities in your life now."

She heard the determination in his voice and decided to try to defuse his new mood with a little teasing. She rolled onto her side and propped herself up on her elbow to gaze down at him.

"Other priorities?" Deliberately she drew her nails across his thigh.

It startled her sometimes to see just how quickly Colby could move when he wished. He caught her wrist and tumbled Diana back down onto her back. Then his strong, hard body was looming over her, blocking out the pale moonlight. His thumb rubbed the gold ring on her left hand.

"Two other priorities to be precise, Madam Executive. Me and the baby. And I'm not going to let you forget either of us."

"How could I?" she asked softly just before his mouth captured hers.

4

"The next thing we do, now that we've gotten married and seen your doctor, is start thinking up names for the kid." Colby forked up a large slice of salmon and regarded Diana across the small restaurant table. "How do you feel about Bertha Maud if it's a girl, and Horace if it's a boy?"

"You can't be serious." Diana was still dwelling on the conversation she'd had with her doctor the previous afternoon. The pregnancy was becoming more and more real by the day. And Colby seemed determined to make sure she faced it. Every time she turned around, he was bringing up some subject that had to do with babies. Tonight they were eating at one of the best restaurants in town, but she could hardly concentrate on the excellent food she had been served. Now Colby wanted to talk names. "I wouldn't stick any kid with a name like Bertha Maud or Horace. Besides, it's too early to start thinking of names for the baby."

"No, it's not. You just want to put it off because you'd rather worry about your career."

"I understand my career better than I understand babies." The hum of conversation at nearby tables and the clatter of dishes made the words almost inaudible. But not quite. Colby had heard her.

"You'll learn." Colby swallowed another bite of fish. "You about ready to head back to Fulbrook Corners? We've spent enough time here in Portland this week. I've still got a book to finish this summer."

"I haven't even contacted my boss yet. I was going to call Aaron tomorrow."

"You can wait until the end of the summer. That's what you were planning to do, anyway."

Diana was getting accustomed to Colby's efforts to sidetrack her every time she began to fret about her career. "I'd rather settle things as soon as possible now that I know I'm pregnant. I need to know if going back to Carruthers and Yale is even a viable possibility."

"You know it is. That Crown character has been pestering you all summer to come back to work for him."

"Yes," she admitted. "You know, I think I'm going to do it, Colby. It's the perfect solution."

"The perfect solution is for you to stop worrying about your career until you've settled into marriage and motherhood."

"Do we have to go through this again? You know how I feel about being financially dependent on a man. I made a vow a long time ago that I would never expect someone else to pay my way in life."

"You mean you promised yourself you'd never take the risk of trusting a man to support you either financially or emotionally. That's a bit different than saying you don't want someone else to pay your way in this world. Yeah, I know how you feel about it." Colby pointed his fork at her, scowling. "You've made it damned clear you don't like the idea of trusting me to take care of you. But I think it's time you realized that you've carried that particular phobia to extremes."

"Why are you so opposed to my career plans? Don't you understand how important that part of my life is to me? I didn't think you were a chauvinist in that regard, Colby. You know how you feel about your writing. Surely you can empathize with me."

"It's not a question of being chauvinistic," he exploded, trying to keep his voice low. "My writing is every bit as important to me as your career is to you, but I learned the hard way that there are other things in life. It's time you learned the same lesson. You've been too self-contained, too focused on your job and your narrow little world for too long. It's time to learn what it means to be a woman who's also a wife and, soon, a mother. You're going to broaden your horizons, lady. The amazon bit wears after a while."

"I'll bet you never gave up a paying job while you learned about the little joys of fatherhood."

"All right, I had to do it the hard way. That doesn't make it the right way. Raising Brandon alone and working full-time to support him and myself was not the ideal way to handle things. I had no choice, but you do."

An old fear twisted into life inside Diana. "Do you know what I think? I think you're being difficult about this because deep down you aren't sure you like the idea that I can take care of myself."

"That's not true, Diana."

"It bothers you, doesn't it? You're just old-fashioned enough to want me to be dependent on you. It's some kind of power trip for you, isn't it? In this society the one who controls the money controls everything else. That's the way it works in business, and that's the way it works in a marriage."

"Your ability to take care of yourself doesn't bother me, Diana." Colby spoke through set teeth. "I admire it. Most of the time. What bothers me is that you're too damned scared about what will happen to your precious independence now that you're a wife and a mother-to-be. I've told you before, you've got new priorities now. You're going to have to learn how to balance all of them. And you can start learning that by giving up your cast-iron bra and spear."

"Diana." The masculine voice that interrupted Colby's lecture was the carrying kind—the voice of a man who likes to draw attention to himself and knows how to do it. "I thought it was you when I saw you a few minutes ago, but I told myself no way. You're supposed to be tucked away for the summer in some little backwater mountain town. What are you doing back in Portland?"

Diana looked up at Aaron Crown. She would have been grateful for almost anything that managed to interrupt the argument that had developed between herself and Colby, but she wasn't prepared to see her boss standing by the table. She took refuge in the formalities.

"Hello, Aaron. Good to see you again."

"It's good to see you. We've missed you, friend." Aaron gave her his most engaging smile. He was a blandly attractive man who had the sleek, corporate look down to an art. His suit had been made to measure, his tie was vaguely reminiscent of an old school that he had never attended and his shirt was definitely not a polyester-cotton blend. Aaron Crown believed in dressing for the role he wanted to play in the organization, and that role was at or near the top.

Diana realized a pause had developed in the conversation. Colby was regarding Aaron with a cold ex-pression, and Aaron was waiting politely for introductions. Flustered, Diana hurried to make them.

"Uh, Aaron, this is Colby Savagar. Colby, this is Aaron Crown, my boss from Carruthers and Yale."

"Her boss, huh?" Colby shook hands perfunctorily with Aaron. "I'm her husband."

Diana went bright pink. She cleared her throat quickly as Aaron turned to her with a look of shock on his face. "Oh, yes, right. Colby's my husband. I forgot to mention I just got married." She knew from the expression in Colby's eyes that she was going to hear about her lapse later.

"Your husband!" Aaron managed a belated smile. "Well, congratulations are in order, then, aren't they? I had no idea you were even seeing anyone on a regular basis, Diana, let alone that you were contemplating marriage. Where have you been keeping Colby here?"

"In the freezer," Colby said.

Diana glared furiously at him. "We've only been married a few days," she explained to Aaron. "We're both still busy adjusting to the whole idea, aren't we, Colby?"

"I've already adjusted," Colby announced grimly. "You're the slow one in the crowd."

Aaron summoned up a polite chuckle, but he looked vaguely dazed. "I can't believe it. Where did you two meet?"

"We met in Fulbrook Corners," Diana explained crisply, hoping to put an end to the awkward conversation.

"You mean you've only known each other a few weeks?" Aaron shook his blond, well-groomed head in astonishment. "And you're married? I don't believe it."

"Believe it," Colby advised.

Aaron ignored him, turning to frown at Diana with deep concern.

"That's not like you, Diana. It's hard to imagine you, of all people, rushing into marriage. You're just not the type. You always think things through so carefully before you act. Wait until your co-workers hear about this. We'll have to arrange a little party at the office to celebrate."

"Don't plan anything in the near future," Colby said. "She's still thinking about whether she wants to return to a job where there's no career potential for women."

Aaron blinked and then his eyes narrowed slightly in consternation. He switched his troubled gaze to Diana. "All of us in business have to go through the experience of being passed over for promotion at one time or another. It's tough, but it's part of corporate life. And there's always a next time. I feel sure that after another year or two with me, management will look more favorably on an upward move for Diana. In the meantime I was hoping you'd had a few thoughts about cutting short your leave of absence, Diana. You were always such a levelheaded type. Being away from your job this long is not good careerwise."

"As a matter of fact, I wanted to talk to you about that, Aaron."

Aaron beamed with satisfaction. "Terrific. There's nothing I'd like more than to talk about getting you back into the fold ASAP. As I said, we've missed you in the office. When can you start?"

"Not until the first of September at the earliest," Colby said coolly. His stern gaze defied Diana to contradict him.

"That's another month away." Aaron looked gravely disappointed.

"Colby has to finish a book he's working on," Diana explained, annoyed with the way Colby had answered for her. She brightened. "But I suppose I could return to Portland a little earlier than I'd planned," she began, thinking it through.

"No, you will not be returning to Portland earlier than planned." Colby's voice had an edge in it that could have sliced ice.

Diana was furious, but she kept her mouth shut. The last thing she wanted to do was provoke an argument that would only succeed in embarrassing her in front of Aaron Crown. Image was everything in business. She had to maintain hers as a cool, calm, competent woman who was in charge of her marriage as well as her career. She forced a polite smile.

"I'll let you know when I have my plans nailed down," she said to Aaron. No point letting him think she was too eager, she told herself.

"I'll hold you to that," Aaron said swiftly. He patted Diana on the shoulder again. "I'll be looking forward to working with you again as soon as possible, Diana. You're good. Damned good. And I'm sure that with a little more experience under your belt you'll go right to the top. You take care now and enjoy your honeymoon. Contact me as soon as you know your plans." He gave Colby a superior smile and walked off to join his party across the room.

Colby turned a simmering gaze on Diana. "You know what you need?"

She moistened her lower lip, uncertain of his mood. "What?" she asked warily.

"Practice."

She looked at him blankly. "Practice at what?"

"Being a wife. It's a wonder you didn't forget my name along with the fact that you're married to me."

Diana struggled to suppress a flash of humor. "I'm sorry," she murmured, using her napkin to hide her smile. "I was caught off guard." She shouldn't have been, though, she thought. This restaurant was one that was popular with the staff of Carruthers and Yale. She had suggested it to Colby out of habit. It really wasn't such a surprise to run into Aaron here tonight.

Colby glowered at her. "How long did you say you worked for that turkey?"

"About four years." She didn't bother to contradict Colby's opinion of Aaron Crown.

"How could you stand it? He's a complete phony."

"Phonies and turkeys are very common in the corporate world." Diana shrugged unconcernedly. "You learn to deal with them. Are you going to tell me either species is unknown in the publishing world?"

Colby sighed. "No. We've got our share. But at least I don't have to take orders from them from nine to five, day in and day out. I only deal with them occasionally. The rest of the time they leave me alone so that I can write."

"Unfortunately, in my world they're a little harder to avoid."

"You can avoid that particular turkey easily enough. Don't go back to work for him. How did he happen to show up here tonight, anyway?"

Diana shrugged. "This is one of his favorite restaurants."

"I see." Colby's gray gaze was chillier than ever. "Did you two come here a lot in the old days?"

Diana's head came up in surprise as she caught the blatant male jealousy in his voice. "We had a few business meals here, but that's all. I've told you that Aaron and I are professional colleagues, not...not anything else."

"Why aren't you anything more than professional colleagues?" Colby was clearly spoiling for another fight. "He looks like the type who'd sleep with one of his women managers if he got the chance."

Diana grinned slowly. "I don't date turkeys."

Colby relaxed. His mouth twitched at the corner. "You just work for them, huh?"

"As I said, sometimes it's unavoidable."

Spencer was waiting when Diana turned the key in the lock of her downtown apartment door. The dog's heavy tail wagged affectionately as he greeted her. He leaned heavily against her leg while he gave Colby a half-hearted glare.

"He's losing his cutting edge," Colby said as he stripped off his jacket. "Doesn't even show his teeth to me anymore."

"I told you he's beginning to like you."

"Sure he is." Colby slung his jacket on a hanger in the closet. "And if you believe that, I've got a nice bridge..."

Whatever he was going to say next was cut off by the ringing of the red phone on the black lacquer table near the window.

Diana walked across the gleaming hardwood floor and picked up the receiver. She stood in front of the full-length windows, admiring her precious view of the Willamette River as she spoke into the phone. "Hello?"

"Diana? This is Brandon. I'm at Dad's apartment. Sorry to bother you two at this time of night, but I've been trying to get hold of Dad. Is he there?"

"He's here. He's busy insulting my dog, as usual. I'll get him for you. By the way, how are things going at the restaurant where you're working?"

"Fine. I don't think I'd want to wait tables the rest of my life, but it's not bad for a summer job." There was a pause. "I saw Robyn yesterday."

"Did you?" Diana's eyes flicked to Colby's face, and then she looked away. "Is she all right?"

"Yeah. Guess I didn't exactly break her heart after all. She's dating some preppy type she met at her parents' country club."

"What about you?"

"Me? I've sworn off women for at least another week."

Diana laughed. "I'll get your father." She held out the phone to Colby who took it with a raised eyebrow.

"Yeah, Brandon?"

Diana listened to the one-sided conversation as she slipped out of her high heels and went into the kitchen to find a snack for Specter.

"Okay, I guess that'll work. Put one scratch on the Jeep, though, and I'll nail your hide to an outhouse door. Right. We'll see you in the morning." Colby tossed the receiver back into the cradle.

"What was that all about?" Diana asked from the kitchen.

"Brandon wants to borrow the Jeep for a few days. He and some buddies from the restaurant want to take it over to the coast and do some off-roading. We're getting the Mazda for the week. He'll drive the Jeep up to Fulbrook Corners on his next day off and switch back."

"Sounds complicated."

"Teenagers and cars are always complicated." Colby wandered into the kitchen in time to see Specter wolfing down the last of his snack. "What's he eating?"

"A dog biscuit. Want one?"

"No thanks. I'd rather nibble on you." He put his arms around her waist from behind and kissed the nape of her neck. "I'm sorry about that argument at the restaurant."

Diana was startled by the quiet apology. She turned in his arms and hugged him. "This is a time of adjustment for both of us. After all, you may know something about raising kids, but you don't know much more about marriage than I do. You were only married for less than a year and that was twenty years ago."

"That's true. I may not be the world's leading authority on the subject. But I'm way ahead of you. You've never been married in your life."

"All you wanted this summer was an affair."

"I wanted you," he corrected harshly. "I didn't much care how I got you."

"And I wanted you," she admitted. More than she'd wanted anything or anyone in her life.

"Looks like we both got what we wanted." His hands tightened around her waist.

"But not quite the way we had planned."

"So we got a baby thrown in for good measure. We'll manage." His hands slid to her buttocks, and he drew her more tightly against his lean, taut body. "You know, when we come back to Portland at the end of the summer, I think I'll give up my apartment and move in with you. Your place is nicer than mine. More style. It suits you better than my apartment would. You're used to being around nice things, aren't you?"

"Only in recent years when I finally got to the point where I could afford them."

"I can afford them, too, honey," he said meaningfully. Then he smiled. "The doctor said something today about getting plenty of rest. You ready to hop into bed? I've got some interesting ideas on how to spend the rest of the night."

Specter growled.

Diana lifted her head and smiled. "Just as soon as you take Specter out for his evening walk."

Colby groaned and released her. "Any objections if I accidentally lose him during our little tour around the block?"

"Shame on you. He's just an innocent dog."

"The hell he is." Colby picked up Specter's leather lead. "If he returns without me, call the police and tell them to suspect foul play."

Specter grinned his wolfish grin. Colby grinned back, showing just as many teeth.

Diana watched them go out the door and then she walked over to the windows to gaze out into the night.

She was in love with Colby Savagar. She had known it for some time now. But she wished desperately he had not felt obliged to marry her because of the baby. Now she would never know for certain how long their affair would have lasted, or whether it would ultimately have ended in marriage.

There was no way she would ever know for certain if Colby would have eventually fallen in love with her.

It felt good to be behind the wheel of Brandon's sexy little two-seater. Colby took pleasure in the firm, sure glide of the gears and the responsive steering. The narrow mountain road was a challenge that both he and the car accepted eagerly.

"If you don't slow down, my dog's going to get carsick," Diana announced from the other seat. The sunroof was open and the big dog, who was scrunched into the small space behind the bucket seats, had his head stuck out through the opening.

"There's nothing wrong with my driving," Colby said with a grin. "But I'll tell you one thing, if that dog gets sick in this car, you're going to have to explain it to Brandon."

"I wouldn't dare. Brandon loves this car."

"Yeah. The kid's a good driver. I wanted him to have a good, responsive car."

"I don't think I approve of fast cars and drag-race-style driving. I'll stay with my Buick."

"Like your mother said, sometimes you're a real stick-in-the-mud, honey. Lucky for you I came along, or you would have spent the rest of your life with your nose to the grindstone and stuck behind the wheel of a dull four-door. By the time you were forty, you would have been so bored with yourself you'd have gone nuts. About time you learned to live a little."

She slid him a speculative, mischievous glance. "You're going to teach me, I gather?"

Colby's grin widened. "I consider it my privilege as your husband.

Now that you're married to me, life's never going to be the same for you again, honey."

Or for him, Colby added silently. He used one hand to shove Specter to the side so he could check the rearview mirror. Satisfied that everything was clear, he returned his concentration to the winding road ahead.

Life had definitely taken a surprising twist, but Colby was satisfied. He wondered how long it would take Diana to accept her fate as willingly as he had. She was still struggling with her emotions and the vast changes that had taken place in her life this summer. Deep down he knew she was still frightened.

So was he, but for different reasons. Colby realized he wasn't going to be able to relax until he knew Diana had settled down and truly accepted the drastic upheaval in her life.

And while he was waiting for her to adjust to having a husband and a baby, he sure as hell did not want Aaron Crown subverting her with promises of a glowing career at Carruthers and Yale.

"Colby? Is something wrong?"

"No, honey. I was thinking about some plot problems I'm having."

"Thinking up some horrific twists for Blood Mist?"

"Not exactly. I've already got the horrific parts worked out. I was thinking up ways for the hero to save the fair lady."

"What kind of a jam is she in?"

"She's trapped."

"Aha. And the hero has to free her?"

"Something like that." He was going to do his best, Colby decided, even if the fair lady didn't want to be freed.

They reached Fulbrook Corners later that evening, and the next day Colby got back to work on Blood Mist. There had been so many distractions lately that he was getting impatient with the slow progress of his writing.

He wasn't completely insensitive to Diana's feelings about her career, he told himself as he called up the third chapter of Blood Mist on his word processor. He knew how he'd feel if someone tried to tell him he would have to give up writing—homicidal.

But he wasn't asking her to give up her career. He just wanted her to trust him enough to take some time away from it while she reset her priorities.

Amazons were a hardheaded, stubborn, feisty bunch. Obviously they all needed a strong man to take them in hand and show them what it meant to be a truly well-rounded woman.

Colby grinned wickedly to himself as Chapter Three appeared on the computer screen. Diana would throttle him if she knew what he was thinking. It wasn't his fault that she sometimes brought out his primitive side.

He stared for a minute at the last paragraphs he'd written before leaving for Portland.

Banner crouched at the top of the falls and watched the water turn bloodred in the light of the setting sun. He knew that some day he would have to return to the cave hidden behind the veil of thundering water. The forces that had been set in motion last night while he had slept in the grotto would one day pull him back here to this place.

But he sensed that day was still far off in his future. He was only seventeen. There was much to learn before he returned to uncover the ancient secrets behind the falls. He knew the first thing he must do was become a man. Banner wondered how long that would take and did not realize that simply by asking the question he had begun the process.

It wasn't hard to tell where the inspiration for this story had sprung from, Colby thought wryly as he went to work. He had never forgotten the night he had spent in Chained Lady Cave when he was a teenager. He had been dreaming about it ever since.

Diana seemed to understand about his writing. She left him to it with no complaint. She went into town in her sedate Buick to pick up the mail and groceries, and she stayed out of Colby's way the rest of the day.

One thing about being married to a strong-minded career woman, he told himself when he took a quick break for coffee, was that she didn't hassle a man about his work. She was perfectly capable of entertaining herself without masculine assistance.

When he finally turned off the small computer later that evening, he realized it was nearly time for dinner. Colby stood up, stretched and sniffed the aroma that was coming from the kitchen. Rice and stir-fried vegetables. One of these days, he was going to have to sit down with Diana and show her how to read a cookbook.

There were a lot of things he wanted to teach Diana.

He glanced out the window at Brandon's dashing little red sports car and decided to give Diana a lesson in how to have a little fun. From what she'd told him, she'd had a seriously deprived adolescence.

"You want to drive out to Chained Lady Falls and make out tonight?" Colby asked as he strolled into the kitchen.

Diana's head came around in startled surprise. "Do I want to do what?"

"You heard me." He helped himself to a cracker and cream cheese. "You said you never dated in high school. I'll bet you never had the thrilling teenage experience of making out in the back seat of a car."

Diana raised her eyes heavenward. "I'll admit I missed that particular ritual of youth."

"Don't worry, it's not too late." He settled back against the counter and munched his cracker. He grinned, aware that she was intrigued by the idea. "We'll take the Mazda."

"Brandon's car doesn't have a back seat," she pointed out demurely as she sliced green peppers. "Aren't you supposed to use a back seat?"

"We're not going to take your car, that's for sure. It's too dull. Brandon's car has some style. Besides, it works just as well in the front seat as it does in the back seat."

"You had a lot of experience in that Corvette you owned back when you were a senior in high school, I take it?"

Colby gave her a thoughtful look. "It's hard to remember. It's been over twenty years. But I think it will come back to me once I get the car parked."

Diana giggled. It was a delightful sound. Colby stared at her, realizing he'd never heard her laugh quite like that.

"I'll just bet it will all come back to you in a hurry."

"Hey, are you complaining? You told me you never had an opportunity to date a bad boy from the wrong side of the tracks. You always wondered what you'd missed, you said. Well, I'm going to fill in the gap in your education."

"How can I resist such a magnanimous offer?"

"Hurry up and get dinner on the table. I'm getting all worked up just thinking about that gear shift in Brandon's car."

"Christ, that damned gearshift is going to emasculate me before we finish this," Colby growled two hours later. "I must have been out of my mind to come up with this idea."

"Maybe you're just out of practice." Diana was lying across his lap, wedged between him and the steering wheel. She looked up at him with teasing eyes as he tried to angle himself more comfortably across the seats.

"I think the problem is that they've shrunk the front seats of modern cars." And by so doing, had definitely increased the frustration factor, he decided. He could feel Diana's sweetly rounded rear pressed tantalizingly against the bulge in his jeans. The sensation was inflaming him, but he could hardly move.

"Aren't we supposed to have the radio on?" Diana asked. "I had a girlfriend once who dated guys like you, and she said they always had the radio on."

"I can't reach the ignition or the buttons on the radio."

"I can." Diana twisted in his lap.

"Ouch! For crying out loud, woman, be careful." Colby swore as she ground her tailbone into his sensitized groin. "I have future plans for that portion of my anatomy."

"Sorry." An instant later, music from a distant rock station filled the little car with a pagan beat. "There, that's better. Now, shouldn't you have a cigarette in one hand?"

"I don't smoke," he said, inhaling sharply as she readjusted herself across his thighs. "Never did."

"Oh. Well, what about a black leather motorcycle jacket? Shouldn't you be wearing one?"

"I haven't owned one in twenty years."

"Darn." Diana brightened. "Well, at least you've got jeans on. Now you're supposed to feed me some clever line about how we won't really go all the way, and how you just want to touch me, and how you'll still respect me in the morning if we do happen to go all the way."

"For a woman who never got to experience this kind of thing first-hand, you sure know a hell of a lot about it."

"I told you, I had this girlfriend who used to give me a blow-by-blow account of all her dates."

"What happened to her?"

"She came to a bad end. Wound up pregnant and had to drop out of high school. I never saw her again."

"Well, at least we don't have to worry about that happening to you, do we? You're already pregnant and you're a long time out of high school. Geez, lady, I guess that makes you the perfect date for a guy like me." Colby held his breath as he teased her. The one thing Diana had not been able to laugh about thus far was her pregnancy.

"I guess it does," Diana said softly. Her eyes danced with wicked amusement. She reached down to unzip his jeans.

Colby was enchanted. The humor in her was real. He felt an exhilarating sense of relief, as if some major hurdle had been crossed. He grinned and slid his hand up under the hem of her blouse.

"Wouldn't it be easier to unbutton it?"

"Too obvious. You have to sneak up on a girl's, uh, frontal area. If you just start unbuttoning her blouse, she'll feel obligated to protest."

"I get it. This way she can pretend not to know what's happening until it's too late to slap his hand away, right?"

"Right." He groaned with pleasure as he found the snap of her bra and freed it. "Oh, baby," he muttered as he cupped her breast. "This is good. Very, very, good."

"Should I tell you to stop now?" Diana asked innocently.

"If you do, I'll go crazy." He shifted his right leg to get better leverage and sucked in his breath as the gearshift caught him again. "Damn."

"Colby, are you all right?"

"Fine," he gasped, unwilling to call a halt when he was this aroused. "Could you, uh, lift up a little?"

"Like this?"

"Yeah. Easy, honey. Take it easy. My zipper..."

"Oh, sorry. Here, let me finish getting it down."

" No. Wait a second. Not like that. Things are kind of jammed up inside. Let me do it." Colby found the zipper tag and started to ease it down cautiously.

"The windows are getting steamed up."

"They're supposed to get steamed up," Colby informed her as he tried to find a more comfortable position on the seat. "Steamed up windows are crucial to the essential ambience of the situation."

"But it's such a beautiful night." Diana reached over the front seat to wipe her hand across the slanting rear windshield.

"Diana. You're going to ruin me for life."

"Oops. Oh, now I see why you keep the windshields fogged up."

"Yeah? Why?" he grumbled as she settled back down into his lap.

"So the other make-out artists can't see you."

"What the hell? What other make-out artists? Don't tell me someone else is parked here? I didn't hear another car." Colby snapped his head around to stare out the rear window. "I don't see another car."

"Over there. He's just pulling into the parking area now, see? You can't hear the engine yet. The noise of the falls is too loud."

"He's got his lights off," Colby said slowly as he studied the faint gleam of moonlight on a sleek fender. The shape of that fender brought back old memories.

"Probably doesn't want to disturb us."

"Let's get out of here," Colby said abruptly. He lifted Diana off his lap. "Come on, honey. Slide on over."

"Ouch. My head." Diana rubbed the top of her head where she had struck it on the roof. "Don't tell me you're embarrassed that someone might recognize us. It's probably just a couple of teenagers who are here for the same reason we are."

"Everyone in town knows this car. They saw it a lot when Brandon was visiting a while back." He twisted the key in the ignition.

"Then they'll think it's Brandon sitting here."

"Tomorrow when they realize I'm driving his car, they'll know it was you and me sitting here tonight. Forget it. This town has enough to talk about as it is. I'm not going to have everyone saying Savagar hasn't changed one bit in twenty years. They'll laugh themselves to death down at the post office."

Jayne Anne Krentz

Colby spun the wheel as the engine caught. He sent the little Mazda rocketing out of the parking area and onto River Road. He didn't switch on the lights until he was a hundred feet away from the parking lot near the falls.

Then he glanced in his rearview mirror and realized the other car was following. The black Corvette was right on his bumper.

5

"Colby, what's wrong? What are you doing? Why are we slowing down?" Diana turned in her seat to stare at the dark shape of the car that was following closely behind them. She could see nothing beyond the glare of its headlights.

"I'm trying to tell whoever that is behind us that I'm not in the mood for a race."

"You think it's some kid who's trying to goad you into a drag race?"

"Some things don't change, especially in small towns like Fulbrook Corners."

"Does it bring back old memories?" Diana asked lightly.

"It makes me goddamned mad, is what it does."

"He's not going around us." Diana drew a startled breath. "Colby, he's coming closer. He's right on top of us. He's going to hit us if he's not careful."

"I see him." Colby's voice was suddenly very cold. "Turn around and tighten your seat belt."

"But, Colby, I think..."

"Do it," he snapped, his eyes on the side mirror. His foot eased down on the accelerator. The Mazda pulled quickly away from the heavy monster behind it.

Diana didn't argue. Something was very wrong, and Colby had decided they were in real trouble. She wanted to ask him what he intended to do, but it occurred to her that this was not a good time to distract him.

The Mazda was moving very swiftly down the lonely, narrow

road now. But the car behind it was picking up speed with the eagerness of a hawk swooping down on its prey.

"Whoever it is, he's spoiling for either a race or a fight," Colby observed dispassionately.

"I take it we're going to give him the race?" Diana held her breath as Colby downshifted for a tight turn.

"I'm not about to stop and invite the alternative. Not when I have no way of knowing how many people are in that car, or if the driver's carrying a gun. Lots of crazies around these days."

Diana closed her eyes as the Mazda whipped out of the turn in a controlled skid and accelerated rapidly. She opened them again as she heard the engine growl in preparation for another curve.

"How well do you remember this road, Colby?" she asked, trying to sound calm and collected.

"Like the back of my hand."

"That's very reassuring." She gripped the dash with both hands as Colby sent the responsive car plunging into another curve. They came roaring out of the turn a few seconds later with the monster still on their heels.

"He had a little trouble with the last curve," Colby observed, his gaze flicking briefly to the side mirror. "He's got a lot under the hood but he isn't in complete control of it."

"I see." Diana carefully kept all inflection out of her voice. She was getting scared, very scared. She thought about all the times Colby had raced down this road for wild thrills and hard cash, and then she reflected on the number of times she herself had ever driven even five miles over the speed limit. She could count them on one hand.

She really had led a sheltered life.

"Remember I told you I could usually lose the competition on the turn near the bridge?" Colby asked.

"I remember."

"I'm going to try it now. It's a little tricky, though. Hang on tight and don't panic."

"Right." She couldn't possibly panic. She was beyond panic. The hairpin turn near the bridge was coming up swiftly in the headlights and Colby was taking it with what seemed far too much speed.

They were going to wind up in the river. Diana knew it as surely as she knew her own name. She closed her eyes and wrapped her arms around her stomach. In that moment all she could think about was the baby. It was the first time she had ever visualized the growing being within her as a distinct and viable entity. But suddenly it was very real and her overwhelming urge was to protect it.

There was a sharp squeal of tires, and the shriek of rubber on blacktop seemed to go on forever. Diana waited for the inevitable impact but nothing happened. The Mazda slammed out of the hairpin turn unscathed. From behind them came the nerve-shattering sound of brakes being frantically applied.

"Lost 'em," Colby said with calm satisfaction as he checked the rearview mirror. "Or he lost his nerve, to be more precise. Thought he could take that 'vette into the turn the same way I took the Mazda and realized at the last second he couldn't. Just as well. If he'd gone into the turn fast enough to catch us, he'd have gone into the river."

"Is it over?"

"Yeah. He's not following us." Gradually Colby eased off the pedal.

Diana took several deep breaths. She looked over at Colby's grim profile. He flashed her a quick, reassuring grin and she closed her eyes again.

"You enjoyed that. I was scared to death and you enjoyed it," she accused softly.

"No I didn't. I'm just glad it's over. What's wrong with your stomach?"

"Nothing." She realized she still had her arms folded around herself protectively. "I was just...when we started into that last turn, all I could think about was...was..." She floundered.

"The baby?" he asked gently. "Is that what you were thinking about?"

"For the first time it seemed real, somehow. I was frightened something would happen."

"I was, too," Colby said grimly. "Scared something might happen to you and the baby. That's why I decided to try outrunning whoever was in that car. Twenty years ago it wouldn't have been a problem. I'd have known who was in the car and the worst thing that might have happened would have been a fistfight with the other driver. You would have been safe enough. But these days you never know what kind of weirdos are out playing tricks in the middle of the night. It was safer to outrun the 'vette than stop and risk finding ourselves facing a psycho."

Diana swallowed. "You're right. Colby, we should report this."

"I'll check into it tomorrow. I'll talk to Gil and maybe the new man, Roy Barnes, who took his place."

"Good idea." Diana clasped her hands between her knees to stop them from shaking.

"Wish we'd gotten a better look at that car."

"You said it was a Corvette?"

"An old one. A classic."

"Like the one you used to drive on this road?"

Colby didn't answer that. Instead he said thoughtfully, "Eddy Spooner would remember working on a car like that. I'll talk to him tomorrow, too. Are you sure you're okay, honey?"

"I'm fine. Honest."

"The adrenaline dies down after a while. Take a few deep breaths."

"I already did that. Maybe it's just as well I led a sheltered existence as a high school student. I don't think I'm cut out for walking on the wild side."

"Don't kid yourself. You've got guts, lady. You didn't scream once. Real cool."

"Thank you, Mr. Savagar. I can't tell you what that means to me." But she was smiling, Diana realized. Colby was right. The adrenaline was dying down quickly. "And may I compliment you on your driving prowess? Very impressive. Even if you did forget to bring along a leather jacket."

"Thank you."

"What's so funny?" Diana demanded.

"I was just thinking. That's the first time I've ever raced with a female in the car."

"I'm glad we're doing some things differently this time around than you did them the first time here in Fulbrook Corners."

"Everything's different with you, Diana. Remember that."

She wondered at the sudden intensity in his voice. She was silent for a moment as Colby turned onto the narrow bridge that crossed the river.

"Colby?"

"Yeah, honey?" He sounded preoccupied, his mind elsewhere.

"You are one hell of a driver."

He slid her a surprised, sidelong glance. "Thanks."

"I'm glad it was you behind the wheel tonight rather than me or even Brandon."

Something in her voice must have caught his attention. "What makes you say that?"

"Because I think the person in that other car was out for blood, not just a race. I think whoever it was would have cheerfully sent us into the river if he'd gotten the chance."

"Honey, calm down. Your imagination is running at high rev. It was just some teenager who was looking for action on River Road. Like I said, some things never change."

"The guy was a real terrorist, Eddy. It wasn't just some kid trying to get a race going. He was out for blood. Even Diana sensed it, although I told her that what was happening was just standard operating procedure for drag racing on River Road. But it wasn't, at least not the way we used to do it twenty years ago. Have things changed around here that much?"

Eddy Spooner rolled his beer can between his hands and studied the uninspiring view of his moonlit backyard.

Colby leaned back against the sagging step and followed Eddy's gaze. The weed-choked space behind Eddy's tumbledown house was a graveyard for dead automobiles. Moonlight gleamed on the skeletons of an old Chevrolet and a Ford. At the edge of the porch was a pile of rusting auto parts. A dark pyramid of old tires loomed in the shadows near a large shed.

"There isn't much racing down on River Road these days," Eddy finally said slowly. "Leastways, not that I hear about. Some of the local kids have some hot stuff under their hoods, and once in a while one will challenge the other, just like in the old days, but not too often. You think the guy that jerked your chain last night was driving a Corvette?"

Colby nodded. "A black one. Older model."

"Twenty years old?" Spooner asked meaningfully.

"No, not quite that old. Old enough to bring back a few memories, though."

"The guy nearly took you, huh?"

"He nearly took me by surprise," Colby clarified roughly. "But I suckered him into that turn by the bridge. He realized too late he was going into it too fast. Lost his nerve. By the time he recovered, Diana and I were long gone."

"You always had a good sucker punch up your sleeve. Good thing it wasn't your son driving last night, huh?"

Colby set his back teeth and lifted the beer can to his lips. "Brandon's a good driver. I taught him. But he's never raced on River Road. He could have been in big trouble last night. Whoever was driving that 'vette did know the road. That's what made me think he was out for blood. He knew that road, and he tried to push me into the river."

"Maybe he figured you'd forgotten that road. It's been twenty years."

"That would be assuming whoever was driving the 'vette knew I was behind the wheel in the other car."

Eddy flicked him a glance. "You don't think he did?"

"I don't know what to think, Eddy. I just know I don't want some hotshot thinking he can put Diana at risk the way he did last night. I want to make it real clear to him, in fact, that it will be worth his life if he tries anything like that again."

"Before you can tell him that, you got to find him," Eddy pointed out.

"That's why I drove over to see you this evening. I figured you'd know if there was anything as hot as that Corvette around here."

Eddy frowned intently. "Hasn't been anything that hot around here since you drove off in that black 'vette twenty years ago. Most of the kids around here who are into cars drive Camaros like mine or four-by-fours. Could have been an outsider. Someone from, say, Vickston, who'd heard there might be a little action on River Road. I'll ask around, if you like."

"I'd appreciate it, Eddy." Colby got to his feet. "Thanks for the beer. I'd better be getting home. I told Diana I'd just be gone for an hour or so."

"Wives are kinda nosy, huh? Like to keep tabs on a guy."

Colby shrugged. "I don't mind." As he said the words, he realized they were the truth. He didn't mind Diana's interest in his where-abouts when he wasn't with her. He damned sure wanted to know where she was when she wasn't with him.

"You've changed," Eddy observed as he ambled around the side of the old house beside Colby.

"We all do, Eddy."

"Think you're as tough as you used to be?"

Colby grinned. "I wasn't all that tough twenty years ago, Eddy. I was just a lot younger. Didn't know what I wanted out of life. Now I do."

"Does knowing what you want make a difference?"

Colby glanced at him. Eddy wasn't usually given to philosophical questions. "It makes a hell of a difference."

"How? You think you're tougher now because you know what you want?"

"Put it this way, Eddy. When a man finally gets his priorities straight, he knows what's worth fighting for and what isn't. He can conserve his energy for the important stuff."

Eddy walked in silence for a long moment. As they approached the Mazda parked in the front drive, he resettled his camouflage cap on his thin blond hair. "I got me some new priorities these days."

"Glad to hear it." Colby opened the car door and slid behind the wheel.

Eddy braced his arm on the car roof. "I got a line on something real good this time, Colby. Real good."

Colby looked up as he switched on the ignition. "That's great, Eddy."

Eddy leaned closer, excitement simmering in his voice. "It's some-thing hot, Colby. I mean really hot. It could be the big one. The break I've been waiting for."

"Good luck." Colby meant it but he knew Eddy Spooner would be looking for his big break until the day he died. Eddy's big breaks always had a way of falling to pieces before he could get his hands on them.

"You'll see," Eddy said with soft intensity. "You and everyone else in this hick town." He stepped back from the car. "I'll keep an eye out for the black 'vette."

"Thanks, Eddy. See you later." Colby slipped the Mazda into gear and picked his way through the ruts and potholes of Eddy's front drive. He realized he was eager to be away from the moonlit cemetery. It wasn't just old cars that were buried here. A lot of impotent dreams had also been buried in Eddy Spooner's yard.

Colby drove down the lonely country road and thought about fate and luck and priorities.

It was a while before he noticed the altered feel of the road, but when he finally did he groaned and reluctantly pulled over to the side. Why did flat tires always happen at night five miles from the nearest gas station?

Colby turned off the engine and reached for the flashlight he had instructed Brandon to always keep in the glove compartment. Then he climbed out of the car and morosely surveyed the shrinking rear tire.

"Damn."

He was going to be late getting home to Diana. He hoped she wouldn't be unduly alarmed. She had been a little nervous following last night's idiocy out on River Road. But at least she had Specter with her. Whatever else you could say about the stupid dog, he was highly protective of Diana.

Colby hauled out the tools he would need to change the tire.

He was removing the last of the lug nuts when Margaret Fulbrook's heavy old Cadillac pulled off the road and cruised to a halt behind him. Its headlights illuminated the Mazda in a harsh glare. Harry Gedge opened the door and got ponderously out of the driver's seat. He was alone.

Colby stayed crouched near the tire, but he kept the wrench in his hand as he watched Harry come toward him. It had been twenty years, but he knew Harry could carry a mean grudge.

"Well, well, well," Harry drawled as he stopped a few feet away. "Got yourself a little project there, I see."

"It'll keep me busy for a while." Colby went back to work on the lug nuts, but he watched Harry out of the corner of his eye.

"I'll leave the Caddy parked where it is while you change the tire," Harry volunteered. "The headlights will make it a little easier to see what you're doin'."

"Thanks," Colby muttered, dropping the last of the lug nuts into the hub cap.

"Don't thank me. Thank old lady Fulbrook. She gave me strict instructions about how I wasn't to cause any trouble with you." Harry leaned against the fender of the Cadillac, a dark, bulky shape behind the glare of the headlights.

Colby said nothing. He hesitated and then put down the wrench in order to grasp the flat tire and pull it off the wheel.

"You hear me, Savagar? I said old lady Fulbrook doesn't want me causing any trouble with you."

"I hear you."

"You know why she doesn't want no trouble?" Harry asked conversationally.

"No."

"She's afraid you'll keep her from seeing that boy of yours. Weird, huh? Twenty years go by, and she pays no attention to that kid at all. Then one day he shows up in town and she's fascinated with him. It's probably those eyes of his. Just like little Cynthia's eyes. Remember those eyes, Savagar?"

Colby didn't respond. He wished he could pick up the wrench again but it took both hands to fit the spare tire onto the axle. He told himself that if Margaret Fulbrook had given her gofer instructions not to start a fight with him, Harry the Ox would follow orders. Harry had always followed Fulbrook orders.

"Old lady Fulbrook's gettin' on, you know?" Harry continued. "One of these days she's gonna kick the bucket. Been having a few chest pains lately. Doctor can't find nothin' wrong, but you know what chest pains mean."

Colby hoisted the spare tire and started to slide it into place.

It was then Harry moved, charging out of the shadows and into the glare of the Cadillac's headlights with a speed that was astonishing in a man his size.

Colby dropped the tire and spun to one side, trying to get to his feet. He didn't move fast enough. Harry's arm came down in a vicious arc. There was a length of pipe in his fist.

Just like old times, Colby thought. His spinning movement ensured that the pipe missed his skull but he took the blow in his ribs. Pain shot through him. He went sprawling on the pavement, forcing himself to roll quickly to the side.

"Now that's a sucker punch, you son of a bitch," Harry roared and swung the pipe again. "I've been waitin' twenty years to do that."

The second swing narrowly missed Colby's shoulder. He staggered to his feet as the pipe clanged on the pavement and he stepped quickly back out of Harry's range. The big man charged again.

This time Colby went in under the swing but he was still off balance. He managed to sink a fist into Harry's huge belly, but Harry fell on top of him, using his massive weight to carry Colby toward the ground.

Colby barely escaped the full weight of the other man. He threw himself to one side as they both hit the hard pavement. Harry lashed out with his fist because the hand holding the length of pipe was trapped momentarily under his body. Lights danced in Colby's head as the huge, meaty hand caught the side of his face.

But Harry lost his advantage on the ground. He lay like a beached whale for a few seconds, breathing noisily as Colby got to his knees.

Colby wasted no time taking advantage of the situation. He used the heel of his hand in a chopping action that was designed to numb Harry's shoulder. Harry yelled as his fingers went into a spasm, and the pipe clattered on the pavement.

Colby kicked the pipe well out of the way and then stepped back out of reach. He sucked in air and watched Harry sit up slowly.

"Let's call it even," Colby said, aware of the pain in his side.

Harry said nothing. He got awkwardly to his feet, edged around Colby, who never took his eyes off him, and moved heavily toward the Cadillac. He lowered his bulk slowly into the driver's seat and yanked the door shut.

With a protesting groan from its overworked engine, the big car shot out onto the road. Colby had to jump out of the way. An instant later he was staring at the big car's taillights.

Some things would never change in Fulbrook Corners.

Specter raised his head from his huge paws and yawned inquiringly as Diana paced back across the length of the living room. She eyed the dog.

"Am I disturbing you?"

Specter blinked sleepily and put his head back down onto his paws. He knew when to keep his mouth shut. His eyes stayed open, however, as he watched Diana pace.

"He should have been home by now. If he's out getting drunk with that Eddy Spooner, I swear I'll give him a piece of my mind when he shows up." She glared at the dog. "Do you realize I don't even know if he does things like stay out with the boys half the night? He's my husband, and I still don't know nearly as much about him as I should. I must have been crazy to marry him on such short notice."

Specter's tail flopped once or twice in general agreement.

"Oh, you're biased. You didn't like Colby the minute you saw him."

Specter's ears rose and fell briefly. He lifted his muzzle in anticipation and turned his head toward the front door.

Diana followed his gaze. A few seconds later she heard what the dog had heard, the sound of the Mazda's engine. Relief flooded her veins with such intensity she felt weak. She hurried over to the front door, jerked it open and dashed out onto the front porch.

"It's about time you got home, Colby Savagar," she declared in ringing tones as the car door opened. "Where have you been? Do you have any idea of the time? It's nearly midnight. I've been worried sick. You said you'd only be gone for an hour."

"Always nice to know I've been missed," Colby said as he got slowly out of the car. He stood for a minute, steadying himself with one hand on the door. "It's not anywhere near midnight, by the way. It's only about ten."

"Well, it seems a lot later than that. What did you do? Hit the local tavern with Eddy and a few old buddies?"

"I ran into an old acquaintance after I left Eddy's. But he didn't offer to buy me a beer." Colby slammed the car door and started toward the porch.

Diana's eyes narrowed. "What's wrong with you? Are you drunk?"

"No, ma'am." Colby was holding his side with one hand. His eyes were shadowed in the dim porch light. "Are you going to conduct an inquisition every time I come home late?"

"I don't know," Diana retorted. "I'm not accustomed to dealing with the situation. Isn't this what wives are supposed to do?"

"Damned if I know. It's been twenty years since I had one." He put one foot on the bottom step. He winced.

"Colby, this is ridiculous. Where have you been?"

"Out," he stated laconically as he started up the steps.

"What have you been doing?"

"Nothing."

"So help me, Colby, I..." She broke off in shock as she finally got a good look at his face. "What happened to you?"

"I told you, I ran into an old acquaintance." Colby managed a weak grin. "Or maybe I should say he ran into me."

Diana stared at him in shock. "Who?"

"Harry the Ox."

"Oh, my God." She broke free of her momentary paralysis and leaped forward to take Colby's arm.

Colby sucked in air. "Careful, honey. I'm finding out the hard way that this kind of thing hurts more than it used to."

"Oh, my poor Colby. What did that bastard do to you? How dare he hurt you like this! I'll get a lawyer. I'll call the cops. I'll have him sent to prison for the rest of his life. Here, let me help you. Lean on me, Colby."

His mouth curved sardonically. "If I did, we'd both wind up flat on the porch. Relax. I can make it inside the house. I managed to finish changing the tire and drive home, didn't I?"

"You had to change a tire in this condition?" Diana was outraged. "What happened? Where were you?"

"On the way back from Eddy Spooner's. Had to stop to change a flat. Harry cruised by and saw I was having a little problem, so he felt obliged to stop and add to my worries."

"That man should be horsewhipped. Look what he's done to you. You're bleeding."

"I got a little scraped up when I hit the pavement."

"He knocked you to the pavement? Colby, I won't stand for this. I will not tolerate anyone doing this to you."

"You won't?" Colby looked down at her with a speculative glance as he allowed her to guide him through the door.

"I certainly will not. I will call a lawyer in the morning and sue the fat off that big ox. How dare he do this to you!"

"He was carrying an old grudge, you know. I told you about the time he and I tangled twenty years ago."

"That doesn't give him the right to beat you up like this. Oh, Colby, just look at you," she said in despair. "You're bleeding and you can hardly walk."

"He got me in the ribs with a length of pipe."

"A pipe?" Diana was horrified. "We've got to get you to a doctor."

"I don't think anything's broken," Colby said quickly. "I just need a little rest."

"You need to get to a doctor," Diana stated firmly. "I'll drive you."

"Honey, I don't think I could stand any more jostling in the car," Colby said gently. "In fact, I don't even know if I can make it up those stairs to bed. Would you help me?"

Diana glanced worriedly at the old staircase. "Maybe you should stay down here on the couch. I'll get some stuff from the bathroom to disinfect those cuts. I've got some tablets I use for cramps. They might help with the pain."

"Uh, are you sure? The last thing I'm worrying about at the moment is menstrual cramps."

"They're pretty effective on things like headaches, too," she assured him. "I'll get you a couple of tablets. You sit right down here. I don't want you trying the stairs."

Colby allowed her to lower him gingerly to the sofa. He clutched his ribs and looked up at her with an expression of noble suffering. "I really appreciate this, honey."

Diana fussed with the pillows, trying to make him more comfortable. "I just cannot believe someone would do this. What a creep that Harry is."

"My feelings exactly." He lay cautiously down on the sofa, groaning softly.

"Don't move. I'll be right back."

"Don't worry. I'm not going anywhere."

"Are you sure you couldn't tolerate the ride into town to see a doctor in emergency?"

"Believe me, it would be the death of me."

"Maybe I could get a doctor to come out here."

"Not a chance. Fulbrook Corners may be a bit behind the times, but you can bet the local physicians have adopted all the latest medical practices. They won't make house calls."

"I can call an ambulance."

"No, you will not call an ambulance."

Diana dithered anxiously for another few seconds, wishing she could get some medical advice. Then she dashed up the stairs to the bathroom to find some basic first-aid supplies.

She spent the next hour devoting herself to making Colby more comfortable and swearing vengeance on Harry Gedge. Colby bore up gallantly but it was obvious he was in a lot of pain.

"I'm sorry I yelled at you when you drove in earlier," she apologized humbly as she prepared a pot of tea for him.

"Don't worry about it," Colby said magnanimously. He levered himself up carefully to take the tea mug from her hand. "Sorry I worried you by getting home late."

"I guess I'm a bit jumpy after what happened out on River Road."

"So am I, if you want to know the truth. In fact, I think we're going to cut short our summer vacation in scenic Fulbrook Corners."

She stared at him in surprise. "We are? Why? You seemed determined to spend the whole summer here."

"I can finish Blood Mist back in Portland."

"Colby, I don't understand. What made you decide all of a sudden to leave? Was it because of Harry's assault on you tonight?"

"Not exactly. I finally started asking myself the question everyone else has been asking me."

"Which question?"

"Why in hell did I come back to Fulbrook Corners after all this time?"

"Did you come up with an answer?" Diana asked gently.

"I told Gil the other night that I must have come back to meet you. Well, I've met you and I've married you. So we're leaving just as soon as I'm able to move without feeling like I'm going to fall into a million pieces."

"Colby, it makes me so angry to see you hurt like this. Do you want some more tea?"

"No, thanks, honey."

"Are the pain pills helping any?"

"Well, I haven't got cramps."

6

Colby was still ensconced on the sofa at noon the next day when Gil Thorp arrived. He looked up from some notes on Blood Mist that he was making on a yellow pad and grinned ironically behind Diana's back as she opened the door. Gil saw the grin and his bushy gray brows rose. But he said nothing.

"I'm so glad you could stop by," Diana said as she ushered Gil into the room. "When I saw your wife at the post office this morning, I told her I felt very strongly that something should be done about this. Colby gave me strict orders not to say anything to anyone about it, but I just couldn't keep silent when I saw Evelyn. Here, have a seat. I'll go fix some coffee." She looked over at Colby. "Would you like another cup, Colby?"

"Thanks, honey. That would be nice. Maybe another one of those cookies you picked up at the store?"

"I'll be right back." She scurried toward the kitchen.

Gil patted Specter and sprawled in the armchair across from the sofa. He gave Colby an appraising look.

"So," Gil said dryly, "I understand you're suffering nobly after being the victim of a savage, unprovoked beating."

"You know me, Gil. I'm nothing if not noble."

"Uh-huh." He surveyed the depleted tray of snacks that had been placed within easy reach of the sofa, the pile of books and magazines arranged conveniently on the table, the carefully plumped pillows and the remains of an earlier cup of coffee. "You know what I think?"

"What's that?"

"I think you've just discovered one of the little joys of married life, and you're wallowing in it. Ever had a woman fuss over you before, Colby?"

"Not that I can remember," Colby responded with total honesty. He grinned back. "A man could get used to it."

"It appears you're taking to it like a duck to water. From the report I got, I assumed you were at death's door, but you don't look like you're going to croak on us any time soon. What's the real story?"

"The bruises you can see and a few more on my ribs. Nothing's broken. I'm a little sore but Diana's keeping me dosed with female medicine. It works fairly well."

"Female medicine? What's that?"

"Take a guess."

Gil's expression cleared. "I get it. That kind of medicine."

"Yeah, that kind of medicine."

"Is it working?" Gil asked with interest.

"Like I told Diana, I don't have cramps."

"That must be a great relief to you. You want to tell me what happened last night?"

"Didn't Diana fill Evelyn in? I understood they had a real heart-to-heart chat at the post office this morning."

"I hope you didn't chew Diana out when she told you she'd talked to Evelyn. She's really upset, Colby."

"I know. That's why I didn't yell at her when she admitted she'd run into Evelyn and spilled the whole story." Colby chuckled. "You should have heard her yelling at me last night, though, when I finally got back here. She thought I'd been out drinking with some old buddies. She really started to let me have it with both barrels until she realized what had happened."

Gil regarded him with amusement. "Wives tend to do those things. When they stop fussing over things like that, you got cause to worry. What did happen last night?"

Colby shrugged, and winced when his ribs protested. "It was all pretty straightforward. Harry caught me alone on the way back from Spooner's. I was changing a tire."

"Not the best position to be in when Harry's around."

"Yeah. That's what I found out. Harry took the opportunity to try to get even for an old grudge. It was like an instant replay of twenty years ago."

"Who won this time?"

"It was a draw. I encouraged Harry to be satisfied with that."

"I doubt if he will be. Kind of convenient, him finding you out in the middle of nowhere fixing a flat tire."

Colby looked at Gil for a long moment. "Yeah, that occurred to me, too. He might have followed me to Spooner's, I guess. He could have put a knife into one of the tires while I was out back having a few beers with Eddy and then followed me until I finally realized I had a flat."

"Want me to have a talk with Roy Barnes?"

"No, because I'm not going to do anything about it, and you know it. What happened was between Harry and me and goes back twenty years. It's got nothing to do with Barnes or anyone else."

"Kinda thought you'd feel that way. You might have a tough time convincing Diana to let it drop, though. She's mad."

"I can handle Diana."

"Who says you can handle Diana?" Diana glowered at him from the kitchen doorway, a tray of cups in her hand. "Colby, this is not a matter of machismo. This is a matter for the law. I will not have that big ox thinking he can beat you to a pulp and get away with it."

"Now, honey," Colby said soothingly, "there's no need to get any more upset about this. It's over."

"It's a long way from over."

Gil interrupted. "If it's any consolation, Diana, Harry didn't exactly get off unscathed last night. Someone saw him when he drove Margaret Fulbrook into town this morning and he looks kind of skinned up from bouncing off the pavement. I hear the match ended in a draw."

"This is not a professional prize fight we're talking about," Diana fumed. "This was a clear case of unprovoked assault."

"Diana, I think I need another one of those tablets," Colby said quickly. "Would you mind getting me one along with a glass of water?"

Instantly her attention was riveted on his physical condition. "Of course. Here, Gil. Help yourself to the coffee. I'll be back in a few minutes." She set down the tray and hurried toward the stairs.

Gil watched her dash up the stairs and then he gave Colby a quick grin. "You can't play the wounded hero forever, you know. Sooner or later the bruises will fade."

"I'm going to milk it for all it's worth in the meantime. By the way, Gil, Diana and I are leaving in a day or two."

"I thought you were here for the summer."

"I've changed my mind."

"Because of Harry?"

"Hell, no, not because of Harry." Colby picked up his coffee mug. "Because of something else." He gave Gil a brief description of what had happened out on River Road.

"A black Corvette, huh? I can't think of anyone who's driving one around here," Gil said thoughtfully.

"Neither can Eddy Spooner."

"He'd know if there was a car like that around."

Colby nodded. "Yeah. But the fact that he doesn't know anything about it is what worries me. It's too much like no one knowing anything about those pranks that were played on Diana when she was living in the cottage."

"You still think someone besides your son's girlfriend was responsible for those incidents?"

"I don't know, Gil. I just know that those pranks coupled with that damned fool who tried to take us on River Road add up to too many incidents. Someone besides Harry Gedge may be carrying an old grudge, but if that's the case he's not coming after me directly the way Harry did. He's threatening Diana. I have to get her out of here."

"I don't blame you. None of it makes any sense, but I'd do the same in your situation."

"You'll keep an eye out in case anything new crops up?"

Gil nodded, his face grim. "You bet. I'll give you a call if I hear anything."

"Thanks."

The sudden silence from upstairs made Colby glance over his shoulder. Diana stood on the landing, the bottle of pills in her hand. She was staring down at him, and he wondered how much she'd overheard.

"Colby?"

Colby smiled reassuringly and said the first thing he could think of that might distract her. "Relax, honey. You wanted to go back to work at Carruthers and Yale, didn't you?"

The pleading call from the grotto was stronger than ever. She had to stay. Torn between the desperate, silent demand and the need to escape, she hovered at the edge of the hot spring. She could do nothing until the warrior came for her. She was helpless.

Her feet were damp. She looked down and saw that a thin ribbon of fluid was trickling along the cave floor, angling toward the entrance. The fluid was tinged bloodred and it came from between her thighs.

Soon the pain would start. She was so afraid of the pain.

Diana's eyes snapped open. She lay still for a moment, trying to bring herself back to the reality of her Portland bedroom. It had been two weeks since Colby had hustled her and Specter back to the city. She had been back at work at Carruthers and Yale for over a week.

She waited a few seconds longer and then she couldn't resist.

"Colby?" she asked softly. "Are you awake?"

He groaned. "You, too, huh?"

"This is getting ridiculous. Nobody shares dreams like this. It's spooky."

He turned on his side, yawned and gathered her close. His hand stroked her with a familiar, sleepy sensuality. "Relax, honey. It's a little unusual, but it's not anything to get nervous about. I told you, I've been having dreams about that damned cave for twenty years."

"But have you ever known anyone else who's had them?"

"No." He leaned over to nuzzle the curve of her neck. His leg angled across her thighs. "But, then, I've never spent the night there with anyone else except you. I also am not in the habit of discussing my dreams with other people. How would I know if someone else was having the cave dream unless he or she volunteered the information?"

"It's not normal, Colby."

"Maybe all married couples share their dreams."

"If the phenomenon was common, we'd have heard about it by now," Diana retorted.

"Maybe we're unique." His hand slid down over her hip, and his mouth followed the line of cleavage that disappeared beneath the low bodice of her nightgown.

"Colby, I'm trying to have a serious discussion."

"Could we have it in the morning? I'm sort of busy at the moment."

Diana laughed softly, the uneasy spell of the dream broken by his unabashed lust. "It's nearly two o'clock. We should go back to sleep."

"I'll make this fast." His hand slipped between her thighs.

"No, you will not make it fast." Diana pushed at his shoulders. He went over onto his back, his eyes gleaming in the shadows.

"I won't?" he asked.

"No. You will make this nice and slow." She let her breasts brush his naked chest as she leaned over him and found his mouth with her own.

"Anything you say, honey."

But everything was not quite as she said, Diana reflected the next morning as she dressed for work, not by a long shot. Colby was accommodating enough in bed, but he could be intransigent out of it. She was learning the hard way that marriage required a great deal of adjustment. As far as she could tell, she was the one doing most of the adjusting.

Colby had never really given her a reasonable explanation as to why he wanted to leave Fulbrook Corners before the summer ended. She knew he was uneasy about the pranks that had been played on her, and she thought he had been more concerned about that late-night race on River Road than he had admitted to her, but he'd refused to say much about it.

"Just kids playing dangerous games," he'd explained briefly when she'd grilled him. "What's the problem, anyway? You wanted to go back to work as soon as possible. Here's your chance."

She'd been happy to head for Portland, but not for the reasons he'd assumed. It was true she wanted to start back to work as soon as possible now that she'd made her decision, but as they'd driven out of Fulbrook Corners, Diana's main feeling had been a sense of relief that they were going to be beyond the reach of Harry the Ox.

She'd abandoned the attempt to get Colby to sue, but she wasn't happy about it.

Diana sighed and examined herself closely in the mirror. She could still fit into most of her expensive business suits, but it wouldn't be long before she would have to go shopping for maternity clothes. The first signs of changes in her body were starting to manifest themselves.

Colby seemed to take great satisfaction in watching for them, but Diana found the changes disconcerting. She had always kept her figure firmly under control by dint of exercise and diet. But now her body seemed hell-bent on following its own path. Just one more example of how her life had begun to slip out of control since she'd met Colby Savagar.

Nothing would ever be the same again.

She walked into the kitchen a few minutes later and found Colby stacking the breakfast dishes in the dishwasher. He glanced up and surveyed her from head to foot, taking in the neat sophistication of her tawny brown hair, the small gold earrings, the cream-colored suit and silk blouse and the matching cream-colored heels. He grinned possessively.

"I wonder if you have any idea how intimidatingly professional you look when you're dressed for work," he said as he closed the dishwasher and leaned back against the counter. "A twentieth-century amazon warrior."

"Are you intimidated?"

His grin widened wolfishly and he folded his arms across his chest. "Do I look like the kind of man who'd let himself be intimidated by an amazon? Especially when I know I'm responsible for getting this particular amazon pregnant?"

Diana walked toward him, letting her hips sway with just enough emphasis to get his attention. She stopped very close to him and tapped her enameled nail against the side of his mouth. "Mr. Macho, hmm?"

He shrugged with fine modesty. "What can I say? When a man's got it, he might as well flaunt it."

"If I see you flaunting it in front of any other females, I'll show you just how much of an amazon I can be." Diana drew a quick little breath as the teasing threat left her lips. She was still new to the kind of games lovers play.

Colby's eyes narrowed swiftly. He made no attempt to hide the flare of masculine pleasure in his gaze. His voice lowered to a rough, sexy growl. "I love it when you go all primitive and jealous."

"Do you?"

"Yeah. Gets me hot." He unfolded his arms and put his hands around her waist. "What do you say we get in a quickie before you leave for work?"

"You've got a book to finish and I'm late." She kissed him briefly and stepped back. Her lashes lowered mischievously when she said, "Save it for me, tough guy. I'll see you later. Try not to get into an argument with Specter." She swung around and started to sashay out of the kitchen.

"Specter's not as dumb as I once thought. Ever since it dawned on him that I've now got control of his dog biscuits all day long, he's been negotiating for a truce."

"Don't abuse your power, Colby. Nobody likes a tyrant." Diana leaned down to scratch Specter's ears as he padded over to say goodbye.

Colby's voice stopped her just as she reached the door. His tone was no longer teasing or sexy.

"Diana, try leaving work on time this afternoon. You've been getting home later and later all week. Crown's sucking you back into the overtime routine. I don't like it."

Diana glanced back, her hand on the doorknob. "There's a major project on," she explained. "We're putting together semiannual financial forecasts."

"You mean Crown's using you to put it together."

"Colby, this sort of thing is what I do. It's my job."

"You already gave Carruthers and Yale enough overtime during the years you worked for them. Look how they rewarded you."

"I know, but this is important."

"I doubt it. Crown's trying to get his hooks back into you. He knows what buttons to push with you and he's doing it."

Irritation washed over Diana. "Don't be ridiculous. He needs everyone he's got on this project."

"He doesn't need you after four-thirty. Leave on time tonight, Diana. If you don't, he's just going to ask for more and more overtime."

"How do you know?" But deep down she was afraid Colby was right.

"I've got him figured and I don't like him. He's a user. He's got a notion he can use you. I want to make sure he gets the message that he can't. Not anymore."

"But, Colby..."

"You're a pregnant lady and you've got a husband. You've got other priorities now, Diana. Be home on time tonight."

Her chin came up angrily. "Let's get something straight, Colby. Just because you're my husband, that doesn't give you the right to tell me how to run my professional life."

"Someone has to. You don't seem to be able to run it on your own."

She wrenched open the door and walked out into the hall, fuming. If she hadn't been afraid of disturbing the neighbors, she would have slammed the door shut behind her. Instead she closed it far too softly. Then she strode angrily down the hall to the elevator and stabbed the call button.

This business of being married was proving complicated. Colby was getting much too dictatorial; that was all there was to it. He was arrogant, demanding and possessive. And he had taken a strong dislike to Aaron Crown.

What made matters so difficult was that Diana didn't completely disagree with him about her boss. Crown was sliding quickly back into the familiar groove of using her skills and talents as much as he wished.

In the past she'd been cooperative because she had believed she was working for her own future at Carruthers and Yale. Diana knew now that she was not, but her sense of professionalism was ingrained. She had always been a hard worker, ever since school. It was difficult to tell the boss that she could not put in the overtime he had come to expect from her.

But it was proving even more difficult to call Colby each afternoon and tell him she would be a little late.

On the one hand, she had to admit Colby was right. But on the other hand Diana was not about to admit it. She had been running her own life too long to just casually turn over the reins to someone else, especially a man.

The situation was shaping up into a confrontation she badly wanted to avoid.

It was a twenty-minute drive from her apartment complex to the downtown high rise where Carruthers and Yale had its corporate offices. As she parked her Buick in the garage and stepped into the elevator, Diana thought about how easily she had slipped back into the routine of her old job.

It was as if everything had been on hold, waiting for her to return. The fact that a great many projects were almost two months behind was odd, to say the least. It was also one of the reasons she had been working late all week. The professional side of her nature hated to get behind in her work.

At noon, Diana glanced up from her desk to see a familiar face.

"Want to go to lunch, or are you going to work right through the lunch hour again today?" Milly Sweeney asked.

Diana smiled regretfully. She had worked with Milly for nearly two years and liked her. The two women were about the same age and shared many of the same interests.

"I wish I could, Milly, but I've got to get through this summary today."

"I don't know why," Milly said bluntly. "It's been sitting around since the day you left on your leave of absence."

Diana sat back in her swivel chair and eyed her friend speculatively. "I know. Any idea why?"

"Sure. Come to lunch and I'll tell you," Milly advised cheerfully.

Diana hesitated and then got to her feet. "It's a deal."

Fifteen minutes later when they were both seated in a crowded downtown restaurant that catered to the business crowd, Diana put her menu down on the table.

"Okay, Milly, let's have it. Why are things in such a mess at the office?"

"Simple. I'll give you three guesses and the first two don't count."

"I don't want to play guessing games, Milly."

"All right, I'll give it to you straight. Things ground to a halt the day you left, and they've been barely squeaking along since then. Crown has been barely holding it together waiting for you to return. He let most of the really crucial stuff slide, hoping you'd return quickly. He never expected you to stay away as long as you did. He didn't realize you'd be so upset about not getting that promotion. It came as a great shock to him."

Diana frowned. "But he must have known how I'd feel after I didn't get that new position."

Milly smiled pityingly. "You don't understand the corporate male psyche, my friend. I'll admit I don't always comprehend it myself, but after you left a couple of the finer nuances of Crown's mind-set became very clear."

"Such as?"

"Such as the fact that he honestly thought you'd stick around after you got turned down for the promotion. After all, your present job is a good one. You've already risen higher than most of the other female employees of C and Y, and he figures you ought to be damned grateful. You've always shown every sign of corporate loyalty. You've always been more than willing to make the boss look good. You have, to be blunt, been the perfect corporate female. How was he to know you would take deep offense when you were turned down for a promotion?"

"What in the world did he expect me to do?" Diana demanded forcefully.

"He expected you to go on playing the role of hardworking, faithful employee and be grateful to have gotten as far as you had," Milly said.

Diana stared at her and then, in spite of herself, a tiny, rueful smile curved her mouth. "It does sound a bit like playing the classic role of being a good, faithful wife while I thank my lucky stars I've got a ring on my finger, doesn't it?"

Milly grinned. "That's exactly how men expect women to behave in the corporate world—as wives. We're supposed to dress nicely, be deferential to males, work hard and not make too many demands. And in some cases, the male bosses even get upset if you don't agree to sleep with them. But above all, we're supposed to know our place and stay in it. Come on, Diana, you know all this as well as I do. You're not naive."

"I know. But I had thought things would be different with Aaron Crown. He always seemed so supportive."

"The reason Aaron has risen so fast during the past four years and has taken you with him is because you've made him look fabulous. The truth is, he's just another pretty face. Very good at playing the corporate game, but no real solid ability to back it up. He feeds on people like you who can make him look good."

"I realize that, but I still thought I could get what I wanted out of the deal."

"Not likely. He's taken all the credit for the financial turnaround in our division. You know as well as I do that he's not the kind to share the glory. Why should management promote you when they believed it was all Crown's doing? Besides, who would believe that it was a woman who was responsible for the changes that had taken place?"

"I'll admit a part of me was curious to see how Aaron would get on without me, but to tell you the truth I assumed he'd find someone else to take my place."

"He hasn't been looking for anyone else," Milly said.

"He was that sure I'd return?"

"Yup. He was that sure. And he was right, wasn't he?"

Diana smiled slowly. "In a way."

"What's that sneaky smile supposed to mean?"

"There have been a few changes in my life since I left C and Y, Milly."

"I know. You're married. That came as a real shock to the Crown Prince, let me tell you. He was stunned when he found out."

"That's not the only change. I'm pregnant."

Milly's jaw dropped. "You're what?"

"You heard me. I only came back to good old C and Y because I wanted to work until the baby arrives. Then I'll be quitting for good."

Milly's eyes lit up with laughter. "Does Crown know?"

"Nope. But I'm sure he'll figure it out when I start wearing maternity clothes into the office."

"And you won't be coming back to work at Carruthers and Yale after the baby is born?"

Diana shook her head. "Not a chance. I hadn't intended to come back at all after my leave of absence. I was job-hunting. Why should I want to work there permanently? There's no future for a woman at C and Y."

Milly grinned. "You realize, of course, that this is the perfect feminine revenge. It's going to drive Crown insane when he realizes you're only using your job as temporary fill-in work until you have the baby. He'll start working on you right away to get you to change your mind."

"About having the baby? It's a little late for that."

"No, Diana," Milly said patiently, "not about having the baby. About coming back to work for him just as soon as your maternity leave is over."

"No way," Diana said calmly.

Milly studied her for a minute and then picked up her salad fork. "How's married life?"

"You should know. You've been married twice."

"True, but I'm still curious. Somehow I always assumed you'd manage to avoid the fate altogether. You never seemed particularly interested in getting married."

"Things change," Diana murmured.

"And getting pregnant so quickly. That surprises me, too. I didn't think you were the maternal type."

"I didn't think I was, either," Diana admitted dryly. "I assure you, I was as shocked as everyone else is going to be."

Something in her tone must have cued Milly. Her friend looked at her, a slow grin shaping her lips.

"No," said Milly. "Don't tell me it was an accident? At your age? And you decided to marry because of it? Nobody does that these days."

"I've got news for you, Milly. There are still a few men around who insist on doing the right thing."

"And the one who got you pregnant was one of that rare breed?"

"Uh-huh."

"I wonder if there are any more where he came from," Milly said wistfully.

At four-fifteen that afternoon, Aaron Crown paused in the doorway of Diana's office. The fluorescent light gleamed on his gilded head and bounced off his very white teeth as he smiled.

"Looks like another long day, doesn't it, Diana? Hope you don't mind staying over for a couple of hours. That report is already several weeks late. I'd like to have it on Rensley's desk Wednesday morning."

Diana took a breath. She had known this was coming. She also knew she could not pick up the phone and tell Colby she would be late again tonight. "I'm sorry, Aaron, I won't be able to work late this evening." She tried a friendly smile. "The demands of married life, you know."

Aaron looked troubled. "That report is crucial, Diana. You know that."

"I'll get back to it first thing in the morning," she assured him. "I can have it done by Friday."

"Rensley will be a lot more impressed with this department if we get it in by Wednesday."

Diana looked at him, and for the first time she was conscious of a curious sense of freedom. This job was not the most important thing in the world. She'd walked away from it once, and she was planning to walk away from it again in a few months. She didn't have to put up with Aaron Crown's quiet coercion.

"Tell me something, Aaron. Which of us will he be impressed with, if this report reaches his desk by Wednesday? You or me?"

Anger flashed briefly in Crown's expression. "What's that supposed to mean? You know I've always shared credit with my staff."

"Apparently sharing the credit wasn't enough to get me that last promotion. Let's face it, Aaron. There's nothing in this for me. Why should I bother to work overtime just so you can get this report to Rensley by Wednesday?"

Aaron was completely taken aback. "I thought you were a professional, Diana."

"I am. And my professional opinion of this job is that it's a dead end. Therefore, I will only work the hours for which I'm paid. No more overtime. I've got other things to do with my life."

"What's the matter with you?" he snapped. "This isn't like you. You've never had this kind of attitude before."

"I guess marriage has corrupted me," she said, amused by his anger. She glanced at her watch. "I've got ten minutes left. Do you want me to spend them working on this report or chatting with you?"

"Who the hell do you think you are?" Aaron stormed furiously.

"I'm the same person I always was, but there have been a few changes in my life. I've had to reorganize my priorities."

"What's the matter? You can't wait to get home to hop into bed with that new husband of yours? Is that it?" Aaron took two steps into the office, his face a mask of fury. "You should have told me months ago that you weren't getting what you needed in bed. I could have handled that end of things for you. It's just that you always seemed so damned frigid—I got the impression you weren't interested in sex."

"Stop it, Aaron," she said crisply, getting to her feet to collect her coat and purse. "You're totally out of line."

"Damn you, I need that report by Wednesday."

"Then you'll have to stay late and work on it yourself." She started to slip into her coat.

"You can't do this to me, you little bitch." He reached for her.

Diana was so startled by his hand on her shoulder that she yelped, more in surprise than real pain. It was when she swung around with an angry protest that she saw Colby materialize in the doorway behind Aaron.

"Get your hands off of her, you bastard," Colby snarled. He was already moving through the doorway, leaping toward Aaron Crown.

7

"Colby. No! Don't hit him. I don't want you hurt again." Diana grabbed Colby's arm. He shook her off as if she were nothing more than a kitten.

"You stupid son of a..." Aaron lashed out blindly as Colby spun him around. His clenched fist caught Colby on the shoulder.

Colby didn't seem to notice the blow. He used his grip on Crown to send him spinning up against the wall. Crown hit it with a thud and sank to his knees.

"Get your things," Colby said to Diana. "Take everything you need. You're not coming back." He looked at her as if he expected an argument.

Diana said nothing. She finished putting on her coat, collected a few personal items from the drawers of her desk and picked up her purse. Then she picked up a red pen and scrawled her resignation across the face of the report she had been working on for Aaron.

Crown inched his way to his feet, using the wall for support. He glared at Colby with baleful eyes. "You'll pay for this," he hissed.

"Not likely," Colby said carelessly. "If you do decide to go to the cops, tell them you were manhandling my woman before I ever laid a hand on you. If you don't explain that part, I will. Come on, Diana, let's get out of here."

"You can't leave, Diana," Aaron hissed. "If you do, I guarantee you'll never work here or anywhere else in this town again."

Diana looked at him. "This is some kind of macho power play, isn't it? But you don't have the power to keep me from getting a job outside of C and Y and I don't like macho power plays, Aaron. They bore me." She started toward the door, conscious of Colby close behind her.

"I was right about you," Aaron yelled at her. "You didn't deserve that promotion. It's a good thing for this company that I talked management out of giving it to you two months ago. I told them you weren't ready for it. I told them you were just another flighty woman who wasn't really interested in a long-range career, that you were perfectly content where you were."

Diana whirled around. "You told management I wasn't ready for that promotion? That's why I didn't get the position?"

"And I was right to do it, wasn't I? You've proved me right. You ran out and got married to the first man who'd have you, and now all you can think about is getting home early every night to screw your new husband. You're not management material. You're just a thirty-four-year-old spinster who's finally discovered regular sex. Obviously you can't get enough of it."

Colby started to swing back toward Aaron. Diana stopped him with a hand on his arm. This time he hesitated, glancing down at her.

"I'll handle this," she said firmly. She could feel the muscles bunched in his shoulders, but he didn't argue. He stood waiting as she stepped around him and went to stand a couple of feet from Aaron.

"I've got news for you," she said smoothly, her eyes brilliant with anger, "I am not only going home to be with my husband, I am going home to prepare for my baby. And you're quite right. Both of them are far more important than my job here at C and Y."

He stared at her, openmouthed. "You're pregnant? Pregnant?"

"That's right, Aaron. I only came back to Carruthers and Yale because I needed a short-term, fill-in job. A little work to fill in the time until I was ready to resign permanently. Come on, Aaron. What did you expect? You didn't really think I'd come back here to work on a full-time basis for you, did you? After what happened a couple of months ago? I knew then there was no future for me here. I never intended to come back at all until I got pregnant."

"Why you little..."

"Say it and I'll rip your tongue out and feed it to you." Colby's voice was very even.

"Get out of here," Aaron snarled. "Both of you. Go on. Get out of here."

"We're on our way," Colby said agreeably. He took Diana's arm and steered her toward the door.

Diana didn't resist. She was suddenly very eager to leave. But when she saw the ring of curious faces out in the hall, she couldn't hold back a cheeky grin.

"I leave him to you with my compliments. Just don't trust him any farther than you can throw him."

"We heard," Milly said. "So he was the one who kept you from getting that promotion. That fits when you think about it. He can't afford to lose you, Diana. He's just barely smart enough to know that."

Behind Diana, the door to her office slammed shut.

"The Crown Prince is not amused," Milly observed. She grinned at her friend. "Good luck, Diana. We'll miss you around here."

"You mean Aaron Crown will miss her," muttered another man. "Crown got used to relying on Diana to save his bacon. I'll bet he doesn't last six months without her. Especially when none of us is going to go out of our way to cooperate with him."

"Sounds like a good idea for an office pool," someone said. "I think I'll start a Guess the Date Aaron Crown is Forced Out Due to Incompetence Pool. Who wants in?"

As Colby walked Diana down the hall, she heard the concerted rush of her former co-workers surging forward to get into the newest office game.

Colby said nothing until they were outside the building. It wasn't until they reached her car in the garage that he spoke. "I know you're upset because returning to Carruthers and Yale didn't work out," he began gruffly as he took the key from her hand and slid in beside her. "But it's for the best. You heard that jerk—he deliberately sabotaged your promotion."

"What made you come by the office today, Colby?" she interrupted quietly. She was so tense her fingers were shaking.

"You know why I'm here." He guided the Buick out of the garage and into the traffic.

"You were going to make certain I followed orders and got home on time tonight. It may interest you to know I was preparing to leave at exactly four-thirty today." She clenched her fingers, trying to control their trembling.

Colby grunted. "I believe you probably intended to leave on time, but I'm not so sure you would have made it."

"I'd have made it. The reason Aaron was manhandling me, as you put it, was that I had just told him very firmly there would be no more overtime."

"It's finished. I don't want to argue about it any more."

"And that's the end of it?" she asked coolly. "You don't want to discuss it further, so we just dismiss the whole subject?"

"What's to talk about? You're not going back to Carruthers and Yale. You wrote that resignation out yourself. I didn't make you do it."

"I know." She lapsed into silence.

"Diana?"

"Yes?"

"Are you going to give me the silent treatment because of what happened today?" He sounded only mildly interested in her answer.

"You're the one who said you didn't want to talk about it."

"But that won't stop you from thinking about it and analyzing it and fretting over it, will it?"

"It's my career that's at stake here, Colby."

"And that's all you can think about?"

Anger shot through her. The last of her precious self-control snapped. She whipped around in the seat, her eyes blazing.

"It's not all I think about." She fought to keep her voice from rising. "I also spend a lot of time thinking about being married to a man who doesn't seem to understand how important it is to me to be able to support myself. When I've analyzed that to death, I spend hours thinking about this baby I'm carrying and trying to plan for a future I never expected."

"Take it easy, honey. You've been under a lot of stress lately."

" Stress? Is that what you call it? That's a wimpy term for what I've been feeling lately. Let me tell you what I've been going through. I can hardly get into my clothes anymore, Colby. I've been a size eight for fifteen years, and in another couple of weeks I won't be able to button my skirts or jeans. I've been browsing through the pregnancy section of the bookstores and realizing that I don't handle pain very well. I break out in a cold sweat while getting a shot of Novocain at the dentist's, for heaven's sake."

"You're scared, aren't you?" he said with sudden, unexpected insight. "One of the reasons you were so determined on going back to work until the baby arrives is that you thought it would help keep your mind off what's happening to you."

She closed her eyes and drew a steadying breath. "Yes, I'm scared. And yes, a job would have helped me cope. But the fear isn't the worst of it. What's really getting to me is this awful sensation of being totally out of control."

"I know."

"No, you don't. Because you're totally in control. You always are. But look at me, Colby. I've lost control of my career, my body, my future and even my dreams."

"Honey, I've told you, I've had those cave dreams for years, and they're meaningless."

"Well, they're not meaningless to me. They're beginning to frighten me. It's not natural to share a recurring dream with someone else. I'm getting a horrible feeling that those dreams of ours are somehow linked to the fact that I'm pregnant."

"That's just your imagination," Colby said soothingly.

Tears burned in her eyes. She dashed them away with the back of her hand. "On top of everything else, I've even lost control of my emotions. Look at these stupid tears."

Colby threw her a concerned glance as he eased the Buick into the apartment garage. "Pregnancy makes women very emotional. Don't worry about it."

"Don't worry about it,' he says." Diana shoved open the car door and leaped out. She wiped away more tears as she hurried toward the elevator. " Don't worry about it. My whole life is coming apart and he tells me not to worry about it."

Colby caught up with her. He put an arm around her shoulders and pulled her against his side as he punched the call button. "As I said, it's just stress that's getting to you. You've been through a lot of changes in the past couple of months."

"So have you," she snapped. "I don't see you falling apart."

"You're not falling apart. You're just a little tense."

She glared up at him, her eyes brimming with tears. "Do you want some advice, Colby? Don't say another word."

He ignored her, squeezing her gently as he urged her into the elevator. "What you need is to take a nice hot shower, get into a robe and have a cup of tea or something while I get dinner on the table. You've had a hard day and you need to relax."

"Colby, I'm warning you. If you say anything else, I may scream. Don't treat me as if I were some silly, emotional, bubble-headed idiot."

He smiled. "I've never claimed you were an idiot. And you're never silly. You are, however, feeling a little emotional at the moment and it's perfectly understandable."

"Is it?" she asked with a dangerous expression.

"Sure." He moved a hand expansively. "Look at what you've been through this summer. "You've lost a job. You've gotten pregnant. You've been forced to marry a man you hardly know..."

"I wasn't forced to marry you," she interrupted fiercely.

He gave her a small, admonishing shake. "Come on, honey. We both know you felt you had to marry me because of the baby."

"I didn't marry you because of the baby," she said, surprising herself with the steel in her voice.

"Yes you did," he contradicted easily. "I didn't give you any option and you wisely realized marriage was the only reasonable solution under the circumstances."

"Will you kindly shut up, Colby? I did not marry you because of the baby. I'm not saying I wouldn't have married you solely because of the baby. I mean, you were willing and you're a good man and you are the father and babies deserve the advantage of having both parents whenever possible, and I might have married you because of all those things. But those don't happen to be the reasons I did marry you."

"No?" He tugged her through the elevator doors as they opened and dug his keys out of his back pocket. "So why did you marry me?"

Diana could tell by the light tone of his voice that he was humoring her. It was the last straw. She dug in her heels and fixed him with a furious gaze. "I married you because I'm in love with you, you big dumb macho idiot. Now get out of my way. I want a hot shower and then I want my robe and slippers and then I want dinner. I've had a very hard day."

As soon as he'd opened the apartment door she rushed past him, dodging Specter's eager greeting, and fled down the hall to the sanctuary of the bathroom.

Colby stood staring after her for nearly a minute before he became aware of Specter's anxious whine. He switched his attention to the dog.

"I think," Colby announced, "that this calls for a beer and a dog biscuit. You want to join me?"

Specter followed him into the kitchen without protest.

Colby came awake hours later with the last few pages of *Blood Mist* as clear as crystal in his mind. It wasn't the first time he'd awakened with a sure knowledge of where he wanted to go next in a book, but it was rare to have it this detailed.

He lay still for a moment, conscious of Diana's sleek, soft warmth beside him. He didn't really want to leave the bed, but the need to get the ending of the book nailed down while it was fresh in his mind was too strong to ignore.

He waited for a little while longer, going over the details of the scene, and then slid quietly out of bed. He reached for his jeans. He hesitated, gazing down at the sleeping woman in the bed and trying not to think about what she had said earlier while she had been in the grip of an emotional storm.

A man could drive himself crazy dwelling on the real meaning behind a woman's emotional outbursts.

Specter heaved himself to his feet and padded silently after Colby as he went down the hall to the front room.

A few minutes later Colby was staring at the glowing computer screen, his fingers moving quickly over the keys.

The roar of the water was a never ending crescendo of sound. It filled the whole world, cutting off everything that was normal, reasonable, rational. He was in another universe, another time and place and he had to play by the new rules if he and the woman and the unborn child were to survive.

The granite was slippery. In the omnipresent darkness the water that flowed over every surface looked as black as moonlit blood and was just as treacherous. Banner scrabbled for purchase as he fought his way up the narrow, sloping ledge toward the cave entrance. He could hear nothing except the thundering water, see nothing except the hulking shadow of the slick rock wall that concealed the cave.

He could not risk a flashlight. He could not risk warning the evil that waited in the cave.

A gust of wind drove water into his face, blinding him even more effectively than the darkness. He wiped his eyes on the sleeve of his sodden shirt and moved forward another few feet.

Then, without any warning, his groping fingers touched empty space and he froze. He was standing at the great yawning mouth of the cave. He stared into the dark pit, aware of the silent summons from the hidden grotto. She was waiting for him there. He had to get to her. But first he had to get past whatever it was that threatened her.

After all these years he would finally learn the truth. He was no longer certain he wanted to know the answer.

"Colby?"

He was startled by the sound of Diana's voice. He turned around and found her standing near his desk, wrapped in her robe. Her face reflected the faint, eerie glow of the computer screen and he could read the concern in her eyes.

"Hi, honey. Didn't mean to wake you. I got a couple of ideas for finishing the book and thought I'd better get them down while they were fresh in my mind."

"I suppose a professional writer has to take advantage of a burst of inspiration when it strikes." She came closer.

"Bursts of inspiration are damned rare in this business." He smiled faintly. "You make use of them when you're lucky enough to get them."

"Don't you have them all the time? Isn't that how the creative process works?"

He shook his head. "Unfortunately, no. A book gets written through sheer, unadulterated hard work, sweat and perseverance. Anyone who sat around waiting for inspiration to strike would probably take ten years to finish a book, if he finished it at all."

She smiled slightly. "Sounds a little like real work."

"Yeah. That's exactly what it is."

"Well, that certainly ruins the image, doesn't it? Can I read what you've written?"

"If you like."

She stepped closer and peered down at the screen. He felt her tension as she recognized the setting.

"That's our cave dream you're writing," she whispered.

"Not quite. It's a modern story. Our dreams seem to involve that old legend about the Chained Lady. But I'll admit there are some similarities. I told you soon after I met you that I got the idea for this story from my dreams and from memories of the first night I spent in Chained Lady Cave."

"You said that the experience terrified you as nothing else ever had," Diana said musingly. "You also told me once that you knew the writing was going well when your fantasies scared even you."

Colby shrugged. "That's right."

"Colby, how is it going to end?" she asked tensely. "Have you dreamed the ending?"

"No." He grinned briefly. "That would be too easy. Writers never get off that easily. But I've got a feeling about it, and I can structure the last part of the plot based on it."

"Banner has to rescue the heroine, right? She's trapped in the grotto?"

"Right."

"Have you decided what it is that's menacing her?" Diana asked.

"Just a standard, run-of-the-mill cave monster."

"Colby, please. Tell me the truth."

He caught the thread of fear in her voice and was instantly contrite. "Hey, take it easy, honey. The villain is something of my own creation, not something from our dreams. I told you, all I got from the dream was an idea, a feeling of fear that I can translate into a fantasy and a setting."

"You're sure you haven't seen something in our dreams? A real monster? Colby, if you have, you've got to tell me."

"No. If I had, I wouldn't have to work so hard to think one up."

But he didn't want to tell her the rest. He didn't want to explain how the sense of menace from the cave was stronger in his dreams these days. The desperate, pleading longing from the hidden grotto was still present but the danger in the outer cave was becoming the main component of his dreams. If that overwhelming feeling of threat got much more intense, Colby knew the dreams would cross the boundary from disturbing to nightmarish.

"I should let you get back to work." Diana took a step back. "I didn't mean to interrupt you."

"Don't worry about it. Want some hot chocolate?" He got to his feet.

"If you're going to have some." She traipsed after him as he headed for the kitchen. "When I woke up and found you gone, I got a little nervous, I guess."

He stopped and dropped a quick kiss on her forehead. "That just shows how well you're adjusting."

"Adjusting to what?"

"Married life. You're getting used to sleeping with me on a regular basis. You're getting so accustomed to it that now you feel strange when you're alone in bed." He opened the refrigerator. Specter trotted over and stood perusing the contents with him.

"Colby?" Diana sat down at the kitchen table and tucked her feet into the warmth of her robe.

"Yeah?"

"I'm sorry I embarrassed you earlier when I told you I loved you."

He went still for a second and then forced himself to continue preparing the hot chocolate. He reached for the milk. "Don't worry about it. You didn't embarrass me. You were, what's the old-fashioned term? Overwrought. As I said, pregnant ladies tend to be emotional. Remember that last book I brought home from the library? The one that talked about mood swings in the early months of pregnancy?"

"You think that's what happened to me today? I went through a mood swing and got overly emotional?"

She sounded as though she might get angry again. Colby tried to soothe her. "You've been through a lot lately."

"Not enough to addle my wits completely," she said tartly. "Besides, I knew I was in love with you weeks ago. Why in hell do you think I went to bed with you the first time or all the times after that, including that night in the cave?"

Colby stopped stirring the hot milk. "Diana, you never said anything about love."

"Of course I didn't. I wouldn't have said anything today, either, if I'd been in control of myself. Colby, I really hate this feeling of being out of control. You don't know how hard it is for me to accept that my whole life is running wild and that there's not much I can do about it."

Colby turned around, his own emotions suddenly precarious. Diana was staring out the window at the city lights, her chin cradled on her palm. She was idly stroking Specter with her other hand. Her tawny hair was tumbled around her shoulders and her bare feet gave her an air of sweet vulnerability. She looked like a very forlorn little amazon tonight, he thought. He wondered if she had any idea of how far he would go to protect her.

"Diana, you don't have to tell yourself you're in love."

"Why not? We're married." Her head came around, her eyes searching his face. "And we're going to stay married, aren't we? At least for the foreseeable future?"

"You're damned right we're going to stay married." He heard the harsh certainty in his own voice.

"Then where's the harm in my telling you I love you?"

"The harm lies in the fact that you might wind up fooling yourself and me as well."

Her eyes widened. "You don't believe me, do you?"

He ran his hand through his hair. "Diana, listen to me. You've been under too much stress lately. I've explained to you that at this stage of your pregnancy you're going to go through a whole range of emotions. It's all right. You're not responsible for them. I just don't want you to say things you'll regret later."

"The milk's burning."

"We're both adults, Diana," he went on seriously. "We don't need to feed each other the kind of silly romantic fiction teenagers need in order to justify having sex. We've got all we need for a solid marriage. There's no point in inventing a fantasy to romanticize our physical attraction."

"You'd better do something about the milk. It's burning."

"What?" He stared at her, feeling acutely stupid.

"I said the milk's burning." She got to her feet. "Never mind. I don't want any hot chocolate now, anyway. I'm going back to bed. Good luck with your book."

She yawned and padded out of the kitchen. Specter trailed after her.

Colby whirled around as the smell of burned milk finally got through to him.

"Damn it to hell." He dropped the sizzling pan into the sink and stood glowering at the black, gooey mass of burned milk. He realized he had a violent urge to put his fist through the nearest wall.

Diana wasn't the only one whose emotions were running too close to the surface these days.

Half an hour later, he realized he wasn't going to get any more done on Blood Mist that night. He knew where he wanted to go with the story, but his mood had been shattered. All he could think about was Diana lying alone in her bed.

With a small, disgusted exclamation, he turned off the computer and headed back down the hall to the bedroom. Specter raised his big head from his paws briefly as Colby walked silently into the room. Then the dog went back to sleep.

Colby stepped out of his jeans and walked over to the bed. Summer moonlight mixed with the background glow of a city at night played over Diana's sheet-covered body. He could see the lush sweep of her hip and the gentle curve of her breasts.

Her breasts had become tender lately, Colby reminded himself. He was very careful now when he caressed her there or took one of her nipples into his mouth.

He pulled back the sheet and eased into bed beside Diana. She turned toward him, seeking his warmth. Colby gathered her close,

aware of the deep pleasure and satisfaction he experienced in knowing she sought him instinctively in her sleep.

He was old enough to know that love between a man and a woman
was a fancy word designed for arrogant, self-indulgent teenagers who
were driven by their hormones. He'd learned everything he needed to
know about love at the age of nineteen. At forty, he was finally figuring out what he really needed and wanted in a woman. Diana could
give those things to him and he would do his best to make her happy
in return. If they both worked at it, they could make the marriage
work. They didn't need to play word games.

But as his hand stroked slowly over her thigh, Colby wondered if
perhaps she had a point. Where was the harm in letting her tell him
that she loved him?

Perhaps it reassured her to say it. Women, even intelligent, mature
women, sometimes liked the emotional trappings of romance. If she
wanted to believe she was in love with him, if it helped her justify the
situation into which she had been dropped and which clearly terrified
her, who was he to deny her that simple relief?

"I thought you were going to write the rest of Blood Mist tonight?"
Diana murmured, her voice husky with sleep.

"I'll finish it tomorrow." He drew the sheet slowly down to her waist
and bent his head to kiss the peak of one breast. He was exquisitely
careful with his teeth and his tongue, and his reward was the way
Diana sighed and shifted in his arms.

"What is this? Am I a substitute for burned hot chocolate?" she
asked with sleepy amusement.

"You're not a substitute for anything, sweetheart. You're you. And
when I want you, nothing else will do." He brushed his fingertips
through the silky fur below her softly curving belly.

She stretched slowly and languorously, her leg sliding between his.
Her fingertips traveled down his chest to the hard shape of his waiting
manhood. Colby sucked in his breath as she stroked him gently. He lifted
his head to capture her mouth. She parted her lips for him as she always
did, assuring him once more of his welcome. She never failed to make
him feel wanted, more wanted than he'd ever felt in his whole life.

"Diana?"

"Hmm?"

"Tell me you love me."

She stilled in his arms. Her eyes opened and she looked up at him through her lashes. "Why?"

"Because you're right. We're married. There's no harm in the words and I think I like hearing them."

"Do you think you'll ever be able to say the words back to me?" she asked.

He hesitated and then made his decision. "I'll say them, if you want me to. If it makes you happy."

"I'd like that," she whispered. "I'd like that very much. I love you, Colby."

"I love you." The words felt very rusty in his mouth.

"I think you need practice."

"I haven't said those words for twenty years, and I was wrong then."

"Practice makes perfect."

"If you say so."

8

Three months later Diana walked into the apartment with the basket of clean laundry she had just finished doing in the basement laundry room. She could barely get the door open, her hands were trembling so badly.

Colby came out of the kitchen, a mug of coffee in his hand, and stopped abruptly. "Diana. What the hell's the matter, honey? You're as white as a sheet. Here, sit down. Do you feel faint?" He put down the mug and came quickly across the room to take the basket of laundry. "I told you to wait until I could help you with the laundry."

"I'm supposed to be playing housewife, remember? Colby, I'm fine. Really."

"Sure you are. And I'm at the top of the New York Times bestseller list. Sit down. Are you dizzy? Want me to call your doctor?"

"No, please, I'm okay. Just a little traumatized."

"What happened?" His eyes narrowed. "Did someone harass you in the basement?"

"Of course not. There's never been any trouble in the laundry facility in this building. Stop worrying, Colby. I'm okay. Honest."

"Then what made you turn pale like this?" he demanded.

"I just had a lovely chat with Jennifer Landsdown from 301."

He frowned. "Is that the young woman who had her baby last month?"

"Right. First time I've seen her since she got home from the hospital. She was doing her laundry alongside me this afternoon. Couldn't wait to share her experience with me."

Colby groaned. "I think I'm beginning to get the drift. What did that chatty little twerp tell you?"

"The chatty little twerp gave me a blow-by-blow description of her entire delivery from the onset of labor straight through to the gory end. You should have been there, Colby. You could have used her descriptions somewhere in your next book."

"Wait until I get my hands on her."

"Why? I'm sure she only told me the truth." Diana took a deep breath and sank down onto the sofa. She looked down at her rounded stomach and thought about what Jennifer had just finished explaining to her in graphic detail. "I got it all, Colby, from ruptured membranes and uncontrollable shaking to a detailed account of torn flesh, heavy bleeding and afterpains."

Colby's mouth crooked wryly. "Sounds like little Jennifer had a field day terrorizing you."

"Her final words of advice had to do with all those pregnancy books you've been bringing home from the library."

"What's wrong with them?" Colby was incensed. "They were recommended by your doctor."

"Jennifer read them, too. You know all those parts that use descriptions such as `discomfort' and `intense' to describe labor?"

"What about them?"

"Apparently words like discomfort and intense are euphemisms for unbelievable, unrelenting, extreme agony. I have to tell you, Colby, I am not good at handling unbelievable, unrelenting, extreme agony."

"That's why they invented anesthetics," Colby said hardily.

"They aren't very free with the anesthetics, according to Jennifer. Too little and too late, she says. They're afraid of the effects on the baby. Mostly you just have to tough it out."

"Come on, honey," Colby coaxed. "You've talked to your doctor about your fears. She told you what to expect."

"Jennifer says the doctors lie because they don't want to scare off all their patients. She says all her women friends who'd had babies deliberately lied to her about what to expect, too. Jennifer says that's because there's some sort of unspoken agreement among mothers not to frighten the women who have yet to go through the process. I gather it's like a rite of passage. Once you're through it, you don't tell the uninitiated the whole truth. You just give them a little song and dance about how the pain of childbirth is quickly forgotten."

"But Jennifer the Twerp has decided to set the record straight?"

Diana grimaced. "She's vowed to tell the truth to others who are about to follow in her footsteps so that we won't all go into it as naive and unsuspecting as she was."

"Jennifer looks as if she's about twenty-four years old, if that. Are you going to let yourself be traumatized by a woman who's ten years younger than you?"

"That's another thing. Jennifer says she's heard that labor is a lot harder on older women." Diana glared at Colby as she saw his mouth twitch. "What's so funny?"

"You are. For a businesswoman, you certainly have a vivid imagination. I can't believe you stood there and let that kid scare you half to death like this."

"Thanks for the sympathy."

"Honey, you know I'm sympathetic. You also know I'll be right beside you when the time comes. And so will your doctor and a whole bunch of nurses and trained medical personnel. You'll have all the facilities of a first-class hospital. Babies get born every day in that hospital. You're going to do just fine."

Diana touched her stomach. "I don't have much choice, do I?" She grabbed his hand and kissed his palm quickly. "Thanks. You always seem to know the right things to say to me. And you're quite right. I should never have listened to Jennifer. I don't know how I'd get through this without you, Colby."

"You wouldn't be going through it in the first place, if it wasn't for me."

There was a short, taut silence.

"It was a mutual endeavor, as I recall." She did not like it when the reality of the reason behind their marriage was brought out into the open. Most of the time it stayed discreetly out of sight these days. Colby was as careful as she was not to bring it up. But once in a while it slipped out, usually as a joke that fell flat.

"Diana?"

"I'd better get to that laundry. Got to earn my keep around here." She started to struggle out of the thick-cushioned sofa. It was getting harder and harder to move about easily. Gone was the old familiar sense of energetic flexibility and womanly grace she had always taken for granted. She wondered sadly if it would ever return.

Colby reached down to assist her to her feet. "You do more than earn your keep and you know it. Is being a wife and expectant mother all that bad?"

"Heavens, no," she said lightly as she picked up the laundry basket. "Why, if I'd known what a cushy job this housewife business was, I'd have thought about enlisting ages ago." She started down the hall.

"You won't be calling it a cushy job after the baby gets here," Colby warned behind her.

"So I've been told. Jennifer filled me in on that part, too. Apparently I will turn into a walking zombie, what with night feedings, postpartum depression and colic."

Colby swore softly. "I really am going to shake the stuffing out of that little bubble-brain the next time I see her. By the way, Brandon called. He and some friends came up from Eugene for the weekend. He invited himself over for dinner and a night on the sofa. Is that okay with you?"

"Certainly." Diana smiled suddenly. "But I'll have to go shopping. I don't think we have enough food in the house to feed more than half a dozen or so people. We'll need provisions for a battalion if Brandon's going to be here. Did you get any more ideas for your next book proposal?"

"Yeah. While you were letting Jennifer terrify you, I got a couple of ideas I think I can use."

"Do you realize it's nearly Christmas?"

"What about it?"

"I was just thinking how quickly time flies," Diana said.

"When you're having fun, you mean?" There was a soft, goading edge in Colby's voice.

"Something like that," she agreed wryly.

"Diana?"

"Yes, Colby?"

"Has it been so bad, these past few months?"

She turned at the end of the corridor and saw him standing at the other end, his legs braced, hands on his hips. There were times when he seemed to challenge her, as if he wanted a clean, hot battle. He was good at winning battles.

Her face softened. "No, Colby, it hasn't been so bad. Thanks to you. You've made it all a lot easier than it would have been if I'd had to face it on my own. I won't ever forget that." She hurried into the bedroom, dumped the laundry onto the bed and began sorting socks.

She had discovered an odd thing about men's socks. They almost never matched.

Several hours later Brandon dropped into a chair at the dining-room table and eyed the huge pan of spinach and feta cheese lasagna sitting in the center with keen anticipation.

"Who made it, Diana?" he demanded with a grin as he helped himself to a large slice. "You or Dad?"

"I did." Diana glanced at Colby. "Colby washed the spinach, though."

"I remember the days when the only dish you could make was stir-fried vegetables," Brandon said. "You've come a long way, if you don't mind my saying so."

"Thank you."

"Not that your stir-fried vegetables and rice weren't terrific," Brandon added quickly. "But a man needs something that will stick to the ribs once in a while, you know?"

"I'm learning," Diana agreed. "Under your father's expert tutelage, I have become a whiz at reading cookbooks, clipping coupons and shopping for something besides vegetables."

"I'm going to turn her into a wife yet," Colby said with a grin. "She's getting very good at catering to a man's needs."

There was nothing like actually living with a man to teach a woman about male needs, Diana reflected. When she caught Colby looking at her with a sardonic expression, she knew he was reading her mind. Lately he'd gotten better and better at that kind of silent communication. So had she.

"So how's the apartment-hunting going?" Brandon asked conversationally.

Colby cut himself a chunk of lasagna. "We made a decision. Signed the lease last week. We'll move in on the first of January. It's a house, though, not an apartment. Three bedrooms and a den."

"A darling little yellow and white Victorian that's been completely remodeled," Diana explained eagerly. "Colby can have his own space for writing and there will be a room for the baby and a spare for you. Even Specter will like it. He'll have a real yard to dig up."

"Diana took one look at it and fell in love," Colby explained dryly. But it was obvious he was pleased by her show of enthusiasm.

"Took you guys long enough. You've been looking for months."

"House-hunting is hard work," Colby said. "And the next few months are also going to be busy. There are a lot of things to do to the place before the baby arrives."

"Well, at least you haven't had a chance to get bored with the housewife routine, huh, Diana?" Brandon gave her a curious glance. "Between house-hunting, learning how to cook something besides stir-fried vegetables and getting ready for the baby, I'll bet you've hardly missed your old job."

"You're right," Colby answered for her. "She's hardly had time to miss it. Have some salad, Brandon."

"Huh?" Brandon blinked at the huge bowl that was being held out to him. Automatically he took it. "Oh, sure. Thanks." His gaze swung back to Diana. "Given any thought to what you'll do after the baby is born?"

"As a matter of fact, I have," Diana said, aware that Colby was eyeing her warily. She hadn't talked to him about her plans because he rarely seemed inclined to discuss her working future. "Remember that conversation we had one evening back in Fulbrook Corners, Brandon? The one where you asked me how I could ever get away from the problem of sexual discrimination in the business world?"

Brandon nodded. "I remember. You said the only answer might be to open your own business." He glanced up suddenly. "Is that what you're going to do?"

"I'm thinking about it. I have all the skills I need to set myself up as a financial consultant to small businesses. Maybe I could specialize in helping women-owned businesses. There's an office complex near our new house where I could rent space. I'd be able to get home early every day as well as at lunchtime. There's a woman I used to work with at C and Y, Milly Sweeney, who might like to go into partnership with me."

"Sounds great," Brandon said with a genuine show of enthusiasm.

Colby looked at Diana. "Why haven't you bothered to mention all these great ideas to me until now?"

"Because you never want to talk about my future," she responded with a small shrug. "Whenever I try to bring it up, you change the topic."

"We talk about your future, our future, all the time. We've talked about where we're going to live, what we'll need for the baby, whether you're going to breast-feed, all kinds of things, damn it."

Brandon glanced at his father's set face, and then he grinned at Diana. "Don't mind him, Diana. Dad doesn't know much about having a wife, least of all a modern sort of wife. But he's learning fast."

Colby turned a scowl on his son. "Since when are you an expert?"

Brandon held up both hands, at shoulder height, in a mocking gesture of surrender. "Hey...no offense intended. It's just that you're not quite as forward-thinking as you like to believe you are, Dad. I hate to be the one to tell you this, but you're real old-fashioned in a lot of ways."

"Is that right?" Colby's brows rose ominously.

"Afraid so. It's obvious to anyone who knows either of you that there was bound to be a, uh, difficult period of adjustment, after you got married. But I'm pleased to say you both seem to be doing very well."

"Listen to him." Colby helped himself to another thick chunk of lasagna. "My son, the twenty-year-old marriage counselor."

Diana smiled conspiratorially at Brandon. "I agree with you, he is adjusting fairly well, all things considered."

"Thank you, Madam Wife."

The humor left Brandon's face a few minutes later. "I wanted to talk to you about Christmas, Dad."

"What about it?"

"Well, I was wondering if you'd mind if I didn't spend it with you and Diana."

"You and some of your friends have found something more interesting to do this year than spend Christmas with your families, hmm?" Colby didn't seem concerned. "Where are you going? Mexico?"

Brandon cleared his throat. "Not exactly. I was thinking about going to Fulbrook Corners."

Colby's forkful of lasagna stopped halfway to his mouth. He lowered it slowly, his eyes suddenly very cold. "What the hell for?"

Brandon shifted uneasily in his chair. He glanced at Diana for support. "Well, I got this call from Grandmother yesterday. She, uh, sort of invited me to spend Christmas with her."

"The hell she did."

"Dad, I'm not all that keen on driving up to Fulbrook Corners to spend the day with her, but I got the feeling she'll be real lonely. There's no one else for her to be with. There hasn't been anyone for her to spend Christmas with in years. You'll have Diana and Diana's mom. I could drive up and back on Christmas Day. In fact, I could probably be back here by early evening."

"Forget it. You're not going." Colby's voice was utterly lacking in inflection. He picked up the loaf of sourdough bread and tore off a slice.

Brandon looked down at his plate. "Would it really be such a big deal?"

"That old witch is laying a guilt trip on you, Brandon. You owe her nothing. She's the one who ignored your existence for nineteen years."

"I think she's changed."

"I don't care if she sprouts wings, a halo and learns how to fly. You're not driving up to Fulbrook Corners for Christmas."

"But, Dad..."

"I said no. That's the end of it. You can go to Mexico with your friends, or Hawaii, or Taos if you don't want to spend the holidays here, but you're not going to Fulbrook Corners."

Diana heard the intractable tone and recognized it instantly. Five months of living with the man had taught her what it meant. When Colby was in this mood, there was no point pushing or cajoling or trying to reason with him.

She met Brandon's eyes across the table. His mouth tightened but he said nothing. Brandon knew his father even better than she did.

With a wifely skill she didn't even realize she had developed, Diana deftly changed the subject. Both men followed her lead but the mood had changed. Brandon left shortly before nine o'clock, saying he was going to a film with his friends. He took a key with him. Diana did not bring up the subject of Fulbrook Corners again.

At one-thirty that morning, her subconscious mind brought it up for her. She found herself in the middle of the dream.

It was pitch-black and the pain was coming in endless tidal waves. She would be safe here in the grotto only as long as she stayed silent. She had to fight to keep from screaming in agony. If she cried out, the night terror that hunted her would find her. She and the baby would both die.

She must hold on until the warrior reached her....

"Colby. Colby?" Diana came awake, aware that she was damp with perspiration.

"Right here, honey." His arms moved around her, gathering her close against him. He stroked his fingers through her hair, brushing it gently back from her face. "It's okay. Just that goddamned dream again."

She shivered and clung to him. "It was different this time. There was more urgency. I was very aware of the baby. In fact, I was in pain. There was blood."

"Sounds like Jennifer's conversation in the laundry room managed to affect your dreams."

"I guess so." She relaxed slowly as Colby's palm soothed her. Instinctively she began stroking him with a similar calming motion. They were getting in the habit of comforting each other after waking up from the dreams. "How was yours?"

"The same. I was still climbing the path to the cave. There was a little more urgency involved than last time but other than that, things were about the same."

He was lying. She could feel the rigidity of his muscles. "Colby, they're turning into nightmares, aren't they? And they're getting more frequent. What are we going to do? Maybe we should get counseling or something."

"We don't need a shrink. They're just dreams. Besides, what shrink would believe we're having the same dreams at the same times?"

It wasn't the first time they'd had this conversation. It never got beyond this point. Diana knew Colby's dreams were getting worse, just as hers were.

"Maybe it's just stress," Diana offered. "Maybe they'll let up after the baby arrives."

"Yeah. Maybe."

Diana waited a few more minutes until she felt him unwinding under her touch. Then she asked the question she hadn't dared ask earlier.

"Why did you jump down Brandon's throat tonight when he asked if he could go to Fulbrook Corners for Christmas? I thought you'd accepted the fact that he was forming a relationship with his grandmother."

"I don't want him driving alone to Fulbrook Corners, and I sure as hell don't want to go with him. So he doesn't go."

"Why don't you want him going up to the mountains alone? He's driven that road often enough. You've never worried about it before."

Colby grew tight again. He folded his arm behind his head and stared at the ceiling. "The subject is closed, Diana."

"I see. By your edict, it's closed. Just like that. With no reasonable explanation to any of the other parties involved."

"You got it."

She winced at the edge in his words. "Right. I got it." Her hand fell away from him and she turned onto her side, her back toward him. Specter came over to the bed and nuzzled her inquiringly. She scratched his ears, aware of Colby's tension. "Colby?"

"Yeah?"

"I don't know how to say this, but..."

"But what?"

"I've been thinking about going back to Fulbrook Corners, too. In fact, I think about it a lot."

"What is this? You fell in love with that dump of a town or something?" Colby demanded, exasperated.

"No. It's not that. But lately I've been thinking I would like to visit it again. Soon, Colby."

"That's crazy. It's the dream."

Diana blinked. "Yes, I think you're right. The feeling about Fulbrook Corners is connected to the dream. Have you had the same feeling? That maybe we ought to go back?"

"I've had it. I'm ignoring it." Colby's voice was grim. "And so will you, is that clear? We're not going to let that damned dream dictate our actions."

Diana sighed. "Whatever you say."

"How long are you going to hold this stupid argument against me?" Colby asked after an endless moment.

"I'm not holding anything against you. Whatever your reasons, I know you think that what you're doing is right. I just don't understand why you won't let Brandon go see his grandmother, that's all. And neither does Brandon."

He sighed. "I've been wrong before. I might be wrong this time."

"Always a possibility," Diana agreed promptly. "You could try discussing the matter with me instead of staying locked behind your wall of outdated, patriarchal machismo."

"Patriarchal machismo?"

"Brandon was right this evening. In some ways you're very old-fashioned, Colby."

He moved, catching her by the shoulder and turning her onto her back so that she lay gazing up at him. "And you're so damned modern, aren't you?"

She touched his face. "No, not really. I don't think of myself as old-fashioned or modern or anything else. I'm just me."

He stared down at her for a long time. "Still think you love me?"

Time flickered for an instant, the darkness of the past merging with the shadows of the present. Diana saw the warrior looking out at her from Colby's eyes; she felt the challenge from him and the urgent need that underlined that challenge, and she smiled faintly. She was getting accustomed to this strange melding of an ancient legend with a modern one. Colby would always be part warrior to her.

"Yes, Colby. I still think I love you."

"Show me."

The longing in his voice caught at her emotions. "All right." She

put her hands on either side of his hard face and brought his mouth
down to hers.

"Diana."

She opened her mouth for him, and he groaned deep in his chest as he
took the offering. When she slid her palms down his back and sank her
fingers into the deep, strong muscles of his buttocks, Colby shuddered.

His hand rested possessively on her rounded belly, and he was very
gentle as he took one of her nipples into his mouth.

"You're always so careful with me," she whispered. "So tender."

"I'll always take care of you," he vowed. "You can trust me, Diana."

"I know. One of these days I hope you'll learn to trust me, too."

His head came up sharply. "I do trust you."

She shook her head. "No, you don't. Every time I talk about my
career, you think I'm getting ready to turn my back on my responsibilities to the baby and to you. I would never do that, Colby. One of
these days you'll realize that."

"Part of me knows that. Part of me is still afraid to believe it." His
voice was raw.

"There was a time when part of me was afraid to believe you'd stick
around, too. But I don't have any doubts now. That's why I can tell
you that I love you."

"Say it again." His hand tightened on her thigh.

"I love you." She smiled in the shadows. "Your turn to practice, Colby."

"I love you, too."

He eased into her, filling her gently, completely. His fingertips slipped
down to the delicate little nubbin of sensation hidden in the tawny curls
between her thighs, and when she went taut in his arms and started to
cry out, he kissed the soft, sensual screams from her lips so that Brandon would not hear them. He held her while she convulsed, and then he
thrust forward one last time, his entire body rigid with his release.

Diana clung to him, knowing he'd given her the words of love because she asked for them, not because he fully understood them or
his own emotions. Colby always needed prompting before he told
her that he loved her. It was hardly ideal, but she had decided to take
what she could get. She was going on the theory that if Colby said

the words often enough, they might get to be a habit and he might discover he was addicted to the habit.

A long while later as they lay side by side, hands clasped, Colby spoke again.

"There's something I want to talk about," Colby said.

"Yes?"

"Your plans for opening your own consulting business after the baby gets here."

"Oh." She shut her eyes. "Do we have to talk about them now? I don't want another argument, Colby. I'm too tired."

"That's why you never mentioned them to me, isn't it? You assumed I'd give you a lot of static."

"The thought had crossed my mind," she admitted.

"Maybe I would have a few weeks ago," he said slowly. "But when I heard you telling Brandon about your ideas this evening, I realized I wasn't upset about them, only about the fact that you hadn't felt free to discuss them with me."

"I would have. Sooner or later."

"I don't want you to feel you can't talk to me about things like that, Diana. I know you think I've got a thing about your working, but that's not true. I just want you to keep your work in balance with all the other things that are going to be happening in our lives."

"I'm learning."

"I know. You're changing, aren't you? I realized tonight it didn't make me nervous now to hear you talk about going into business for yourself. I just want you to know that I think your ideas are terrific, and you'll have my full support when the time comes."

Diana studied him in silence for a moment, and then she leaned over and kissed him softly. "That's one of the reasons I love you, you know. When push comes to shove, I can count on you."

There was another long silence and then Colby said, "Speaking of feeling free to communicate..."

"Yes?"

"It's the car," he said.

Diana pulled herself back from the edge of sleep. "What car?"

"Brandon's Mazda. It was his car we were driving when that fool in the 'vette tried to take us that night on River Road."

"Oh, my God." Colby's logic was suddenly clear to her. "You think it might have been deliberate? That someone thought Brandon was in the car that night?"

"It's a possibility I can't ignore. That jerk who tried to run us down wasn't just looking for a one-mile run. He was trying to send us into the river, Diana. He could have been after us or he could have been after Brandon. Coming on top of those pranks that were played on you, I can't take any chances. I don't want either of you in the vicinity of Fulbrook Corners unless I'm around."

Diana was silent for a long while, assimilating the facts. "I guess I've known deep down how worried you were but I haven't thought much about what happened in Fulbrook Corners since we've been back in Portland."

"No reason to think about those incidents. No one's bothered you or Brandon since we left town."

Diana sat up abruptly. "You've got a perfectly valid reason for not wanting Brandon to go back there alone."

"Thanks. Does this mean I'm no longer viewed as just another example of outdated patriarchal machismo?" Colby smiled faintly in the darkness.

"Oh, no, you're not excused from that accusation. But you can redeem yourself."

"Yeah? How?"

"First of all, you can explain your concerns to Brandon."

"And second?"

"You can offer him an alternative."

"What alternative? Like I said, I am not driving up to Fulbrook Corners for Christmas. We're going to have our first Christmas together right here."

"You can suggest he invite his grandmother down to Portland for the holiday."

Colby shot straight up in bed. "Pregnancy has rotted your brain, woman. Are you crazy? Have that witch here under my roof for Christmas?"

"She could stay at a hotel, just as my mother is going to do," Diana said, thinking quickly. "We'll open presents here and then we could all go out to Christmas dinner afterward."

"Diana..."

"It'll work out just fine, Colby, you'll see."

"Now listen, Diana..."

"Brandon will be pleased. Don't worry, I'll make certain you and Margaret Fulbrook don't come to blows. You've met my mother. She's very good at keeping the conversation going. If things get awkward, she'll come to the rescue."

"Diana, will you listen to me..."

"I'd better make reservations for dinner tomorrow. The few restaurants that will be open Christmas Day will be filling up quickly."

"Damn it, Diana, if you don't close that mouth of yours by the time I count to five, I will close it for you. One, two, three..."

She smiled brilliantly and didn't say another word.

"That's better," Colby said. "Silence at last. You know, there's a lot to be said for outdated patriarchal machismo."

Diana leaned over and kissed him. "Shall I give Brandon the good news in the morning, or do you want to tell him yourself that you've changed your mind?"

"I'll tell him," Colby muttered. "I want to make damn sure he makes certain Margaret Fulbrook knows that this invitation definitely does not extend to Harry the Ox."

"I agree with you one hundred percent." Diana batted her lashes. "I think you've made a very wise decision, Colby."

He ran his palm up her bare arm. "And I think you're picking up the finer nuances of being a wife faster than I'd ever imagined you would. How the hell did I wind up agreeing to spend Christmas with Margaret Fulbrook?"

"How the hell did I wind up pregnant and unemployed and financially dependent on a man for the first time in my life?"

"You forgot barefoot," he said with satisfaction. "At the moment you're barefoot, pregnant and unemployed."

She started to tickle him in the ribs. A few minutes later Colby's sexy laughter aroused Specter. The dog sighed heavily, got up and padded down the hall to find some peace and quiet in the living room.

9

Three weeks until he became a father for the second time. Colby finished bolting the headboard of the crib onto the sturdy little frame and stepped back to admire his handiwork. One thing his background in construction had given him was a certain skill in taking care of the little things that a husband and father was always being called upon to do. Diana admired his ability in the home improvement department, and Colby knew he occasionally gave in to the urge to show off.

She would be pleased with the way the white crib had gone together. It looked good in the cheerful yellow and white room. Brightly colored mobiles hung above the bed, and there was a small mountain of plush animals sitting on a nearby shelf. All the necessities of modern baby-raising from a top-of-the-line padded car seat to a chrome-wheeled stroller were neatly arranged around the nursery.

Things were going to be a lot different for this baby than they had been for Brandon, Colby reflected as he angled the crib into position. Everything in this room was brand-new. Not one stick of furniture had come from a thrift shop. That had been his idea, not Diana's. She had casually mentioned the possibility of picking up a few used items, and he had vetoed the suggestion so vehemently she hadn't raised the notion again.

He could afford to do things right this time around, and he didn't intend to settle for anything less. Colby knew he wasn't doing it for the baby, who wouldn't know the difference between a shiny new crib and a cardboard box. He was doing it for Diana. He wanted her to take pleasure in everything that had to do with the baby. She was a woman who appreciated nice things, and he was determined that she would be surrounded by them while she cared for their child.

Colby finished adjusting the position of the crib and took one last look around the room. All was in order.

This time he was ready.

And so was Diana, he had decided. She'd settled down during the past few months. She'd begun to get genuinely excited about the baby. Colby knew there was still a certain amount of apprehension mixed with her anticipation, but she seemed to be taking everything in stride these days.

At Colby's insistence, they'd taken a tour of the maternity ward at the hospital where Diana would be giving birth and she'd seemed satisfied that she would be in good hands. She'd asked questions about all the fetal monitoring techniques, anesthesia procedures and the equipment that would be available in the delivery room. She'd had several long conversations with the staff on the subjects of pain control and emergency intervention measures.

And then they'd stood outside the nursery window and looked at babies for a long time. Colby had been pleased with the results. Diana had gotten a distinctly maternal gleam in her eye as she'd gazed at the tiny packages of newborn humanity. They'd gone right out and bought the crib and several small yellow blankets that afternoon.

Diana had kept busy since January decorating the little Victorian house. She'd spent hours poring over wallpaper designs and the latest in Italian lamps while Colby had started work on a new novel.

Diana seemed content with her role of wife, too. Colby congratulated himself. He'd chosen well the second time around, even if he had chosen in haste again. He'd learned a lot about Diana in the past few months. She was a mature adult just as he was, and when she made a commitment, she kept it.

Colby realized that somewhere along the line he had gradually begun to relax. When Diana had gone to view office space for her prospective consulting business, he'd gone with her and even offered suggestions. He knew now she wasn't going anywhere without him and the baby.

She was a competent woman who could handle a career and a family. She was not an immature young girl who'd run home to her mother when she got bored or frustrated or angry with the hand she'd been dealt by fate.

Colby was just now beginning to acknowledge to himself that he had been a little hard on Diana for the first few months. She'd had a lot of old fears about the basic unreliability of men to contend with, as well as the shock of finding herself unexpectedly pregnant and married.

Colby had instinctively fought to tear down all the barriers Diana had relied upon to protect herself and to reinforce her inner fortitude. She'd never really needed or wanted a man.

Colby realized that from the beginning he had seen her self-contained strength not so much as a challenge but as a genuine threat. Deep down he'd been afraid she would use that considerable feminine independence and willpower of hers to lock him out of her life.

Even back at the start of their relationship, when he had told himself she was the wrong kind of woman for him, he had wanted nothing more than to prove to her and to himself that she wanted him. When he had accomplished that task, he realized he had dug himself into a deep hole.

Because then he'd had to prove that she needed him.

Was that why he had made love to her without any protection in the cave last summer? Had he, on some primitive, subconscious level, wanted to get her pregnant so that he would have a hold on her?

Colby tossed aside the screwdriver he had been using. He didn't mind exploring some of life's fuzzier questions in his books, but he wasn't particularly fond of analyzing himself in reality. No point in it, he decided. A man dealt with life as it came. He did what had to be done and made the best of it. Sometimes he got lucky.

The phone rang in the den. He started down the hall and reached the sunny, bay-windowed room just as Diana picked up the receiver.

"Hello, Brandon. How are you?"

Colby leaned in the doorway, his gaze moving possessively over Diana's ripe figure. She was wearing a blue denim maternity jumper with a striped shirt. Her rich, tawny-gold hair was tied back in a ponytail and her face was bare of makeup. She looked very lovely and sweet and vulnerable. All his protective instincts hummed just beneath the surface of his awareness whenever he looked at her.

"Oh, no, I'm so sorry to hear that. When did you find out? Just now? The hospital called you?" Diana turned worried eyes to Colby. "What's her condition? I see. Hang on a minute. I'll get Colby."

Colby took the receiver. "What's up?" he mouthed to Diana, his hand over the mouthpiece.

"It's Margaret Fulbrook," Diana whispered. "Brandon says she's in the hospital. Possible heart attack."

Colby spoke into the phone. "Brandon? What's this about the old... I mean, what's this about Margaret being ill?"

"I just had a call from the Fulbrook Community Hospital. Apparently she put me down as next of kin on the admitting forms. She's suffering severe chest pains. Has trouble breathing. All the symptoms of a heart attack. They're doing tests now." Brandon paused and then said quietly, "She's asked to see us, Dad."

"Us?"

"You and me both."

Colby closed his eyes in brief resignation. He knew there was no way out of this one. "She probably wants to tell me one last time what a lousy son-in-law I've been for the past twenty years. All right, Diana and I can take a day and drive up there with you. When do you want to leave?"

"It's only eight o'clock now. If we leave by nine we can be there before eleven."

"That's what you think." Colby's sense of humor kicked in briefly as he looked at his wife. "Diana's three weeks away from her due date. She makes a lot of trips to the ladies' room these days. She'll insist we hit every rest stop between here and Fulbrook Corners. Better count on it taking us three hours to get there." He hung up the phone.

"We're going to Fulbrook Corners, I take it?" Diana asked gently.

"I gather Margaret thinks she's dying. Knowing her, she'll make a production out of it."

"She might very well be dying, Colby. She's nearly seventy and from the sounds of things she's having a heart attack."

Colby held up his hand. "I know, I know. Look at me. I'm not arguing against the trip, am I? I told Brandon we'd go with him to see her. The old lady has asked to see both of us. Can you believe it?"

"Perhaps she wants to say her goodbyes."

"More likely she wants to put a curse on me with her farewell breath," Colby muttered. He eyed Diana thoughtfully. "You don't have to come unless you feel like it. If Brandon and I go alone, we can be back tonight."

"I want to come with you." Specter padded forward and looked up at Diana with beseeching eyes. "And so does my dog." She grinned and stroked Specter's huge shaggy head.

"It's going to be a full car," Colby said. "We'd better take your Buick. It's got the most room. Brandon and the mutt can sit in the back."

Diana patted her tummy. "Yes, baby and I need our space these days."

"And pack some clothes. If you're coming along, I don't want to do the drive up and back in one day. It will be too tiring for you. We'll spend the night at the cottage and return tomorrow."

"Yes, dear."

Colby grinned. "Whenever you say `yes, dear' in that tone of voice, I know exactly what you're thinking."

"What's that?" She stepped closer and lifted her face for his kiss.

"That I'm slipping into my heavy-handed husband routine again." He brushed her mouth with his own and then paused to deepen the kiss.

"You're so good at it," Diana said finally as he freed her mouth.

"Good at what? Kissing you?"

"No, the heavy-handed husband routine." Her eyes were wide with teasing admiration. "But as a matter of fact, you're also good at kissing me." She started to say something else but stopped, a tiny catch in her breath. She touched her stomach.

Colby put his hands on her full belly. "Baby kicking again?"

"Uh-huh. Feels a little different this time, though."

"This little one's going to be a handful," Colby announced, quite satisfied at the prospect.

"Good thing there will be two of us to cope with this baby," Diana said softly.

Colby laughed and kissed her again. "You said it."

"I love you, Colby."

"I love you, sweetheart." It occurred to him that he didn't even have to stop and think now before he repeated the words back to her. They just came naturally lately. He had no real desire to break the habit.

Margaret Fulbrook occupied the hospital room with the air of a queen on her deathbed. The tubes, machines and monitors that surrounded her did not detract from her royal air. She wore an old-fashioned satin bed jacket. Her hair was in its usual regal bun, and her makeup had been carefully applied in an effort to conceal the pallor of her skin. Nurses, doctors and assorted attendants moved in and out of the private room with deferential respect.

Diana hung back a little as Colby and Brandon went through the door. This was between the three of them, she thought. It had little to do with her. She stayed near the back of the room and absently massaged her lower back.

She'd been plagued with lower-back pain on and off for weeks but the discomfort seemed different today. The long drive in the car had probably aggravated it. She wouldn't mention the problem to Colby, Diana decided in silent amusement. He'd just get worked up about the fact that the trip had made her uncomfortable. He'd probably blame himself for allowing her to come along.

Colby certainly took his role of husband and father seriously and as Diana had learned to trust him in that role, she had also learned to enjoy the cosseting and concern. The sensation of being fussed over by a protective male was entirely new to her, and she was discovering that she liked it.

The backache wasn't the only thing that was bothering her today. Something she'd eaten earlier apparently wasn't agreeing with her. She was also experiencing a strange restlessness.

"There you are," Margaret Fulbrook announced in tones that carried out into the hall as she caught sight of her visitors. "About time you got here. I could have been dead for hours. What did you do? Stop and have lunch along the way?"

Colby raised his eyes to the ceiling, but he managed to keep his mouth shut.

"Hello, Grandmother," Brandon said, going toward the bed. He leaned down to kiss her pale cheek. "How are you feeling?"

"Terrible. How did you expect I'd be feeling?" Her sharp brown eyes went over her grandson. "How's Diana?"

"I'm fine, Mrs. Fulbrook." Diana came forward a few steps. "Do you need anything from home? We could stop by and pick up some clothes or books for you."

Margaret's eyes softened a fraction. "No, thanks. I've got Harry to fetch and carry for me. How's everything going with the baby?"

"Just fine."

Margaret frowned. "Looks better than fine to me. You look like you're about to go into labor any minute."

Diana laughed. "The doctor says three more weeks."

"Humph. Doctors. What do they know? Bunch of fools. Women have been having babies for thousands of years without doctors."

"True," Diana agreed equably. "But a lot of women suffered terribly and frequently died in the process, and so did a lot of babies. I'll stick to the modern method. I want lots of professionals around me who know what they're doing when the time comes."

"Hah. Look at me. I've got dozens of medical professionals running around here and hardly any of them know what they're doing."

Colby wandered over to the window. "If you've got incompetents here, it's your own fault, Margaret. Fulbrook money built this hospital, and you sit on the board of directors. If you haven't got good doctors, it just means you're not paying decent salaries."

"Listen to the expert," Margaret scoffed. "What would you know about running a hospital?" But there was no real heat in her voice. Her eyes tracked Colby as he came to a halt and stood looking out over the panorama of mountains, river and town. The white veil of Chained Lady Falls could just barely be discerned in the distance.

"Why did you demand to see us, Margaret?" Colby asked after a long moment of silence.

"I'm dying." Margaret Fulbrook's voice was stark. "There are a few things I want to get cleared up before I go."

"Don't talk that way, Grandmother. You're not dying." Brandon's voice was vehement.

She patted his hand almost absently, her brown eyes still on Colby's back. "It's all right, Brandon. You'll understand some day that we all have to deal with death sooner or later. There's no point in denying the reality of it. There's not much we can do about it, except get through it with as much dignity as possible. Colby?"

"Yeah, Margaret?"

"I want you to keep that business about dignity in mind, do you understand? No telling what these fools around here might try to do if they're left to their own devices. Doctors don't always understand about dignity, and they do so love to play with their stupid machines. I want someone strong-minded in charge of making the decisions that might have to be made. I don't know anyone more strong-minded than you. I also don't know anyone who understands pride better than you do."

Colby glanced back over his shoulder. His eyes met hers in a level look of mutual understanding. He hesitated and then nodded once. "I'll handle it, Margaret."

Margaret Fulbrook seemed to relax a bit. Her mouth twitched at the corners as she looked over at Diana. "Do me a favor, my dear. Don't let him get carried away and pull the plug too quickly."

The macabre humor got to Diana. She found herself smiling in spite of the situation. "I'll make sure he doesn't get too enthusiastic about his responsibilities, Margaret."

Brandon's brows were knit with anxious concern. "What are you guys talking about? What's going on?"

"Never mind, Brandon." Margaret patted his arm again reassuringly. "Just some minor business I wanted to get out of the way before I go on to more important matters."

Brandon looked bewildered. "What important matters?"

She studied him intently for a long moment. "I want to tell you that the greatest joy I have experienced in the last twenty years was meeting you, my boy. It will be easier to say goodbye to this world now that I know some part of me will go on through you. You're a fine young man, and I know who to thank for the way you turned out. Colby?"

"Yes?" He didn't turn from his contemplation of the scene outside the window. Diana could see the tension in his shoulders.

"It's time for me to say that my poor, confused Cynthia made a mistake when she abandoned you and Brandon to run home to her parents. You would have made a good husband for her. You did a fine job of raising my grandson. I owe you for that, Colby."

"You owe me nothing."

"That's not true. I owe you an apology for twenty-odd years of foolish pride, and I owe you my thanks for ensuring that Cynthia's son turned into a man any grandmother could be proud of."

There was a long moment of silence before Colby said quietly, "Forget it, Margaret."

"No, we will not forget it, damn it. You will accept my apology and my thanks, do you hear me?"

Colby swung around slowly, the faintest trace of a smile edging his mouth. "I hear you, Margaret. You always could issue orders in a loud, clear voice. I'll accept your apology if you'll accept mine."

"That won't be necessary. Perhaps you're right. We'd best forget the whole thing. Let's leave the regrets and the pride and the mistakes in the past where they belong. Agreed?"

Colby inclined his head. "Agreed."

Satisfied, Margaret turned to Diana. "And you, my dear. I also owe you my thanks. You are the one who made it possible for me to meet Brandon and to get to know him. I also want to thank you for last Christmas. It was the happiest Christmas I have known since my daughter died. It was good to feel like part of a family again. I shall carry that pleasure with me to my grave."

"You'll be here next Christmas, too," Brandon declared roughly. He looked around at the others in the room, challenging all of them. "Isn't that true?"

Colby suddenly chuckled. "Hell, it wouldn't surprise me. Like I've always said, Brandon, your grandmother is one tough old broad."

The nurse who came through the door at that moment was startled by the sound of the laughter that filled the somber hospital room.

"Heard you was back in town, Colby. Bet the old lady wanted to see her grandson before she died, right?" Eddy Spooner wiped his hands on a grease-stained rag and reached for the gas hose.

"That's about it." Colby climbed out of Diana's Buick and leaned against the front fender as Eddy began filling the vehicle's tank. "We're staying over tonight. We'll head back to Portland in the morning."

"Where're Brandon and Diana?"

"Visiting with Margaret Fulbrook. I took a break to come into town and see how you were doing."

Specter put his head over the front seat and surveyed Eddy with a calm, unreadable gaze.

"I'm doin' okay, Colby. Okay. I see you still got that big dog of Diana's."

"Yeah, Specter's a born mooch. He won't be moving out anytime soon. I've given up trying to encourage him to leave." Colby idly reached over to scratch the dog behind one shaggy ear. "But he and I have come to a gentlemen's agreement."

Eddy eyed the dog with respect. "He always looked like a mean one to me."

Colby glanced down at Specter. "I think he could be, under the right circumstances. How are your plans coming, Eddy?"

Eddy looked up quickly, peering at Colby from under the brim of his beat-up fatigue cap. His glacial blue eyes were narrowed to slits. "Plans?"

"Yeah, you know. The plans you told me about last summer, remember? The last time you and I had a few beers at your house, you said something about being onto something big."

"Oh, yeah. My plans." Eddy concentrated on putting gas into the car. His shrug said it all. "You know how my plans always work out, Colby. They don't go nowhere."

"That's too bad." Colby wished he'd kept his mouth shut. He should have known that whatever Eddy had going last summer had fallen through. But he honestly hadn't been able to think of any other topic of conversation, and some part of him felt compelled to try to touch base with his old boyhood companion.

"Is it true that old lady Fulbrook's probably going to die?" Eddy kept his attention on the nozzle of the hose.

"I don't know, Eddy. The doctors said she's holding her own, but they still haven't pinned down the exact nature of her chest pains. Margaret thinks she's going to die, though."

"Reckon she left you and Brandon all her money, huh? Now that she's talkin' to you again? Got to hand it to you, Colby. You sure played your cards right. Skip town for twenty years, and then come back just in time to inherit the Fulbrook fortune."

"Brandon and I don't need or want her money and she knows it," Colby said harshly.

"That don't mean she won't leave it to you."

Colby glanced down the main street of his old hometown, thinking that no matter what had happened earlier in the hospital room, he'd never be able to spend a dime of Margaret Fulbrook's money. "She'll probably leave whatever's left of the Fulbrook fortune to Fulbrook Community Hospital. The place could use it," he said carelessly. In fact, he added to himself, he'd have a little chat with Margaret this afternoon and make sure she did exactly that.

"Harry says she started talkin' last summer about changing her will. She went to see a lawyer about it a few months back," Eddy said slowly.

"Did she?" Colby asked vaguely, losing interest in the topic. "Hey, Eddy, you ever find out anything about that black 'vette that tried to run Diana and me off the road last summer?"

Eddy pulled the nozzle out of the tank. "Some."

Colby watched him intently. "Come on, Eddy. Give. What did you find out?"

"Not much. That's why I never called you. Figured it wouldn't do you much good."

"Well?" It was like pulling teeth, Colby decided.

"The 'vette's been seen again a few times at night on River Road. Some of the local hotshots have tried out their wimpy little Camaros against it. No one's ever beaten the 'vette, though."

"Anyone ever end up in the river? I told you that car was out for blood."

"Nah. No one's gone over the bank. Just a few close shaves on some of the curves. Same routine as twenty years ago. You remember how it works, Colby? You should, you're the one who set it up. The black 'vette picks up any takers down at the old turnout under the cliff. Same place you used when you were running things out there at night. The parking area at the base of Chained Lady Falls is the finishing line."

"Who's driving the 'vette, Eddy?" Colby kept his voice casual as he slid his wallet out of his jeans pocket. He didn't want to let Eddy see just how interested he was in the answer.

"Nobody knows who's drivin'."

"Nobody's seen the driver?" Colby was astounded.

"Nope." Eddy shook his head as he made change. "The dude's not racing for money, I guess. Just for the hell of it. He hangs around the cliff turnout until some local yokel comes looking for action. The 'vette and the challenger line up and take off. The 'vette wins and just keeps going on into the night. Never comes back to collect any money or gloat or nothin'. He's just gone. Like a ghost."

"Think he's from around here or out of town?"

Eddy shrugged. "The kids I've talked to who have seen the 'vette don't know. They say there aren't even any tags on the car."

"That new sheriff, Barnes, has he tried to stop the races?"

"Hah. Sheriff Barnes ain't like old Gil Thorp. Barnes has got more important things to do than come all the way over from Vickston in the middle of the night to break up occasional drag races on River Road. I'll tell you something, Colby. That black 'vette is becoming a legend, just like you were twenty years ago."

"If I ever get my hands on the new legend of River Road, I'm going to shorten his career real quick. I owe him for what he did last summer. He could have killed Diana." Colby opened the car door and dropped onto the front seat. "You tell him I'm lookin' for him if you ever meet him, Eddy."

"What happened to you and Diana took place last summer, Colby."

"Doesn't matter. I've got a long memory."

Eddy pulled the brim of his cap down lower to shield his eyes. "I'll spread the word, Colby."

"Do you really think she's going to die, Dad?" Brandon sat on the edge of the lumpy armchair in Aunt Jessie's house and looked at his father, who was seated on the sofa beside Diana.

"I don't know. As far as I can figure out, no one knows at this point."

"I thought her color was much better tonight." Diana stirred and shifted slightly, trying to find a more comfortable position. There were very few such positions these days, she'd discovered. And today she couldn't seem to find a single one. Colby was massaging her lower back with an automatic motion. He always knew when she was hurting. She leaned into his warm palm, savoring the small comfort.

"You okay, honey?" Colby asked with concern.

"I'm fine. Just the usual aches and pains. I'll be so glad when this baby gets here."

Colby grinned. "This from the woman who's been worrying about surviving labor pains for nearly nine months?"

"I've reached the point where I just want to get it all over. Even if it hurts to get it over," Diana admitted wryly.

"You two settled on the names?" Brandon asked. "You're still going to call the baby Josh if it's a boy, and Tabitha if it's a girl?"

"Tabitha Jane," Diana said, drawing out each word with loving care. Do you like it, Brandon?"

"Josh sounds old-fashioned, but it's okay. You do realize that if it's a girl everyone's going to call her Tabby?" Brandon pointed out. "Like a cat?"

Colby was about to respond when they all heard the sound of a car in the drive. Specter's ears snapped forward and he got up to prowl toward the front door.

"Who is it?" Diana asked.

"Might be Gil Thorp. He's probably heard we're in town and decided to stop by and say hello." Colby stood up and went to join Specter at the door.

A moment later there was the sound of a man's heavy boot on the front porch and Colby pushed open the door.

"Eddy," he said. "What's up?"

Eddy Spooner appeared on the threshold. He was turning his camouflage cap in his hand and he had a concerned expression on his face.

"'Evenin' Diana. Brandon."

"Hi, Eddy." Brandon got to his feet.

"Hello, Eddy. Won't you come in?" Diana smiled at him.

"Can't. Thanks, anyway. I just came by to see Colby about somethin'."

"What's this all about?" Colby opened the door wider. "You'd better come inside. It's cold out there."

"Thanks. Yeah, it's plenty cold out there. Supposed to get snow in a couple of days." Eddy looked at Colby. "You said you wanted to know if I ever heard any more about that black 'vette on River Road."

Diana frowned as she saw Colby's quiet, keen attention. "Eddy? What's this all about?"

"Never mind, Diana. I'll explain it later." Colby watched Eddy closely. "You've got something?"

Eddy nodded quickly. "One of the kids came by the station just as I was closing. Said he'd heard the 'vette would be out looking for action tonight. The kid's been workin' on his car for six months, and he's been itchin' to try it out against the 'vette."

"He's going to have to wait a while longer. I get first crack at that bastard in the 'vette."

"Figured that's what you'd say. Well, good luck, Colby. But, then, you always did get all the breaks." Eddy turned and walked out of the door to where his multicolored old Camaro sat in the drive.

Colby opened the closet door.

"Colby? What are you doing?" Genuinely alarmed, Diana struggled to get out of the deep sofa.

"Don't worry, Diana. I'll be back as soon as I get this settled." Colby was hauling his jacket out of the closet as he spoke.

"Where are you going?" she demanded, seizing the arm of the sofa to lever herself to her feet.

"River Road."

"You can't. Don't be ridiculous. You can't go after that 'vette by yourself. What do you think you're going to do? Have some sort of macho showdown? Colby, you said that whoever was driving that car last summer was probably a little crazy."

"Don't worry, Diana," Brandon said soothingly as he reached for his own jacket. "I'll go with Dad."

Colby swung around to confront his son. He started to argue but something he saw in Brandon's set expression must have changed his mind. Perhaps it reminded him of himself. Colby nodded brusquely. "Let's go."

"Colby, please, listen to me. At least check with Gil Thorp or contact the sheriff's department. This is police business."

"No, it's not," Colby said as he dug out his keys. "It's personal. You'll be fine here with Specter, honey. Just sit tight."

He and Brandon were gone before Diana could think of any way to make them see reason. She was left standing at the door with Specter, listening to the sound of her Buick roaring out of the drive.

"When I drive that car the tires never squeal like that. Bunch of idiot, macho males. What am I going to do with them, Specter?"

Specter leaned against her, offering silent comfort, but his muzzle was pointed in the same direction Colby and Brandon had just taken. The dog looked faintly wistful at being left behind.

10

River Road was a twisting ribbon of darkness that paralleled the snaking black band of water that curved alongside it. The night was cold, ebony dark and eerily still. Chained Lady Falls was over a mile away from this point, hidden behind the bends and turns of the gorge walls.

Colby eased his foot off the accelerator as he guided the Buick into the empty turnout under the cliff.

"You think we'll find him?" Brandon asked.

"Who knows? From what Eddy told me he's been getting bolder lately. He said the kids have been coming down here to race more frequently and the black 'vette has been showing up fairly often. With any luck, we'll snag him tonight."

"I know this probably isn't the time to ask but, what exactly are we going to do with him if we do catch him?"

"First, I'm going to beat the crap out of him for what he tried to do last summer. Then I think I'll hunt up Gil Thorp. Gil always had a way of seeing that justice got done, even if it was a little off the record."

"You think we'll have to run down the 'vette first?"

"We can't. Not in this tin can. One of these days I'm going to have to get Diana something with some zip under the hood." Colby slid the Buick into the shadow of the looming granite cliff and switched off the engine. He sat contemplating the night for a moment. "Feels like old times."

Brandon's teeth flashed in a brief, knowing grin. "Hard to believe you're an old married man with one grown son and another baby on the way, huh?"

"You're wrong," Colby said. "I don't have any trouble believing it at all. The reminders are all around me. And I'll tell you something, kid. I wouldn't go back. Not for anything."

"Things are a lot better now?"

"Things are infinitely better now." Colby's mouth curved faintly. "The best they've ever been, in fact."

"I can tell. I'm glad you found Diana."

"Not half as glad as I am."

Brandon nodded. "What do we do now?"

"We wait."

"Where's Eddy? Why did he take off and let us come out here alone?"

"This isn't his fight. Eddy tries to keep a low profile. He always has, poor bastard. He's probably home by now."

Brandon nodded and unfastened his seat belt. "I know how you feel about wanting to get this dude. Thanks for letting me come along."

Colby reached up to unsnap the cover of the dome light. "I'm not completely stupid," he informed his son as he unscrewed the tiny bulb, "in spite of Diana's probable opinion to the contrary this evening. I know enough not to turn down reliable help when I can get it. There isn't anyone else I'd rather have watching my back than you, Brandon."

"The feeling is mutual."

"Good. You want to flip a coin to see who gets out of the car to fetch the lug nut wrench?"

"Geez, Dad," Brandon's voice was laced with mocking innocence. "They didn't teach us how to use a lug nut wrench in that karate class you signed us up for a few years ago."

"The beauty of a lug nut wrench is that just about any fool can figure out how to use it in a pinch. No special training required."

The waiting lasted another two hours. It got very cold in the car. Once or twice Colby started the engine and turned on the heater. But mostly he and Brandon just sat talking quietly and waiting. Nothing moved out on River Road.

Colby had about given up when he saw a pair of headlights in the distance. They arced around a curve, disappeared briefly and reappeared much closer.

Brandon stirred in the seat. "Anybody we know?"

"Can't tell yet. Could be just a kid looking to put his car up against the 'vette."

The car cruised slowly toward the falls, skimming along the ribbon of blacktop, its identity hidden behind the glare of its headlights.

And suddenly Colby had a premonition. He'd seen those headlights before. "Get down, Brandon. I don't want him to catch sight of you in his lights."

Brandon wedged himself down under the edge of the dash. The approaching lights angled off to the left as the vehicle eased into the parking area. Cold starlight gleamed off a familiar large shape.

Colby draped his arms over the Buick's steering wheel and watched intently. "Well, hell," he finally said. He could feel the surge of adrenaline through his veins.

"Who is it?" Brandon asked.

"It's Margaret Fulbrook's Cadillac."

"Not the 'vette? What's going on, Dad?"

"That's what I intend to find out. I wonder when Harry the Ox started cruising River Road. When I get out of the car, you slide out on your side. He won't see your door open because I removed the dome light. But stay out of sight on the far side of the Buick for a while until I see what's going on."

"What the hell for?" Brandon whispered, an angry young male animal spoiling for battle. "You brought me along to back you up."

"I told you once the only intelligent way to go up against someone like Harry is with a good sucker punch. This time around you're it. When you get out of the car, take the wrench with you."

Colby opened the door on his side and got out. Brandon followed suit on the opposite side, staying below the level of the windows. In the darkness, with no dome light to illuminate the small action, Brandon's movements on the far side of the car were virtually invisible.

Just to make certain Harry's attention was focused where Colby wanted it to be focused, Colby made himself very obvious. He walked straight up to the window on the driver's side of the Cadillac. He could see the vague outline of Harry's beefy shoulders and broad face. Small, mean eyes glittered at him from the shadows. They made Colby think of a rat.

The driver's window slowly lowered. Colby looked down into the car.

"Things get so boring waiting around for your employer to die that you had to come out here and look for trouble, Harry? What kind of game are you playing these days?"

"One I can win, Savagar." Without any warning the barrel of a revolver appeared in the open window. Harry's vicious smile was just barely visible in the glow of the dashboard lights.

Colby stood unmoving. Now he knew how a highway patrolman felt when he stopped a car for speeding and got a gun in the face instead of a lot of excuses.

"I think I'm beginning to get the picture," Colby said softly. He stepped back.

"Are you, Savagar? About time. Sure taken you long enough. Too bad it's gonna be the last picture you ever see." Harry opened the Cadillac's door and climbed out. The revolver never wavered. The gun gleamed in the icy starlight.

Colby took another step backward. "You want to tell me what this is all about, Harry, old pal?"

"Don't move, you bastard. You always thought you were real slick, didn't you? Thought you could keep just out of range and get away with anything. Twenty years ago you almost walked off with the brass ring. But you blew it. You got into Cynthia Fulbrook's hot little pants long enough to get her pregnant, but you didn't get anything out of it except the baby she left you holding. You didn't get one thin dime out of the Fulbrooks, did you? I told Eddy you weren't nearly as smart as he always said you were. I told him last summer that things were gonna be different next time."

"That was a long time ago, Harry."

"I'm not likely to forget. I wanted her, Savagar. I wanted her real bad.

I'd watched her all those years I'd worked for the Fulbrooks. All those years I spent fetchin' and carryin' like some slave. I had plans for her. She liked me, you know. Flirted with me. Used to wiggle that little rear of hers whenever she walked past me. She wanted me bad, I could tell."

"Harry, get real."

"I was gonna make sure it was me she had to marry. Her folks liked me. I always did everything they told me to do. They would have let me marry her if I'd gotten her pregnant. They might not have liked it at first, but they'd have tolerated it. Eventually they'd have made me a real member of the family."

"Christ, Harry, you're crazy, you know that?"

"Shut up. I had it all planned. I was gonna become a real Fulbrook. I'd have been in line for all that money. But then you breezed into Cynthia's life, and she couldn't resist adding your scalp to all the others on her belt. You were a real prize. The town's one and only legend. Only this time she made a mistake and got knocked up. The Fulbrooks were gonna take care of that mistake. They had a doctor all lined up. But you talked Cynthia into marrying you, instead."

"Harry, that was twenty years ago. It's over. It's been over for a long time. The Fulbrooks wouldn't have tolerated you marrying her any more than they tolerated my marrying her."

"I'd have made them put up with me," Harry exploded. "I did everything they told me to do. I did all their dirty work."

"That doesn't mean they would have let you marry their one and only daughter." Colby almost felt sorry for the man. "As far as they were concerned neither of us would have been good enough for her. And I'll tell you something else, they weren't the only ones who felt that way. Cynthia herself didn't think either of us was good enough for her."

"She married you."

"Only because she was confused and scared. When she finally came to her senses and realized what a mess she was in, she jumped in the car and headed back to Mom and Dad. She had no intention of staying married to a guy from the wrong side of the falls."

"I could have made her stay with me. I wouldn't have screwed up the way you did. But you're right. It's over. I've got other plans now, though, and I'll be damned if I'm going to let you ruin everything for me a second time, Savagar."

"What plans, Harry?" Out of the corner of his eye, Colby saw the shadow moving among deeper shadows. Brandon was slipping through the darkness, leaving the cover of Diana's Buick to slide behind the Cadillac on the passenger side.

"Don't you see?" Harry raised the barrel of the gun. "There was no one left after Cynthia got killed. No one left to inherit all that money, except me. The old lady changed her will after Cynthia died. She said she planned to leave a lot of money to me because I'd stayed loyal all these years. She said she owed me something. She wasn't going to leave you or that kid of yours a cent. She hated you. But last summer you came back with your son and wrecked everything. She started changing her mind the day she met Brandon and saw those goddamned eyes of his."

Colby stared at him. "You think Margaret Fulbrook was going to leave you all her money? Harry, you're a bigger fool than I thought."

"She told me she'd put me in the will, damn you! Oh, she was gonna leave a chunk to the hospital, but I was also going to get some dough. A lot of it. She was grateful to me, you see. I was the only one left. I was the only one who'd take her orders—did what she said, no questions asked. Then she met that boy of yours and all of a sudden she couldn't talk about nothin' except her grandson. She went to see a lawyer, and that's when I knew I had to do something."

"There's nothing you can do, Harry. Margaret's got a mind of her own. You ought to know that by now."

"You're wrong, Savagar. There is something I can do. I can get rid of you and the boy. Then there won't be anyone left again except me. I've been thinkin' about this for months. Ever since last summer, in fact. I started makin' plans then. I was just gettin' some ideas together when you suddenly left town and I had to wait. But when old lady Fulbrook went into the hospital with the heart attack night before last, I knew it wouldn't be long before she sent for you."

"And you figured this would be your big chance?"

"Damn right. So I got you out here alone. I decided to take care of you first, you see. You're the one I got to watch, you and your damned sneaky sucker punches. I can handle your kid later."

"You really think you can kill me and Brandon and get away with it, Harry? Come on. Gil Thorp will be around asking questions before you can blink. And he'll go straight to that new sheriff."

Harry's grin was wide in the darkness. "Won't be no questions to ask, Colby. Got to have bodies before you can ask questions. You know these mountains as well as I do. You know there's places up here where I can dump you and that kid of yours, and you won't be found for years, if ever. As far as everyone around here is concerned, you'll just disappear for another twenty years or so, same as last time you left town."

Colby's stomach tightened. "Harry, you're going to risk a murder charge for no good reason. I'm not going to take a dime of Margaret Fulbrook's money. I never have and I never will. She knows that. I made it clear to her this afternoon."

"So maybe she'll leave it all to Brandon. Who knows? That's why I have to get rid of both of you."

"Are you going to pull that trigger right here? There'll be blood, Harry. Lots of it." Colby called on all the creative writing talent he could muster on such short notice. He'd written scenes like this one. He knew how they went. "You've never killed a man, have you, Harry? You don't know what's it's like to see someone die. It's hard to believe how much blood there is in the human body. It'll just pour out all over. It'll get on your hands when you try to move me. It'll get all over the trunk of the Cadillac when you shove me inside."

"Stop it. I won't kill you here unless I have to. I'll take you up high into the mountains."

"That won't make it any cleaner, Harry. You'll still end up covered in my blood. Dead bodies are real messy, Harry. It isn't just blood that gets all over everything. The body lets go of other stuff as well. All the muscles just suddenly relax. Can you imagine what that means, Harry? You're going to have to get real dirty before this is all over..."

"Shut your mouth, damn you. I've done enough hunting in my time. If I can gut a deer, I can handle your body."

"You think so? Can you handle two dead bodies? Because you'll have to go through it all again when you pick up Brandon. You'll have all that blood to deal with a second time. You're going to have nightmares about that blood, Harry. You're going to wake up screaming in the middle of the night. You'll look across the room and you'll see me looking back at you from the shadows. The blood will never go away. Every time you go to sleep, you'll wonder if this is another night you'll have to relive the murders. Pretty soon you won't be able to sleep at all..."

"I won't have any nightmares, damn you. If I do, I'll just think about all the money. That will give me sweet dreams. Now just shut up and get down on the ground. I'm going to tie your hands behind you."

The crash of splintering glass shattered the tension. Harry flinched, shouted incoherently and whirled around to confront the noise.

Colby launched himself at Harry's back as Brandon quickly dropped to the ground on the other side of the Cadillac.

Colby slammed the heel of his palm into Harry's neck. The big man staggered and fell to his knees. Colby tried a second blow and this time Harry toppled slowly onto his back. The revolver fell from his hand.

Brandon appeared from around the hood of the car. He had the lug nut wrench raised and ready for action.

"I don't think we'll need that," Colby said, rubbing his aching hand. "But keep it handy while I find something to tie his hands." He ended up using the rope in the trunk of the Cadillac that Harry had undoubtedly intended to use on him.

Five minutes later the job was done. Colby stood up and studied Harry's half-conscious form lying on the ground.

"Now what?" Brandon asked.

He stared at his father, his voice still tense with the unfamiliar adrenaline that Colby knew must still be rocketing through him. Colby experienced a flash of pride at his son's coolness in the bizarre situation.

"We'll contact Gil. He'll be able to handle it from here."

"Should we put him into the Cadillac?" Brandon asked worriedly.

"Too much trouble."

"It's really cold out here, Dad. If we leave him on the ground, he might die."

Colby groaned and reached down to grab Harry's ankles. "You're right. We don't need the extra complications. You get his shoulders."

It took a lot of doing but they finally managed to wedge Harry into the back seat of the Cadillac. Their victim groaned but he didn't fully regain consciousness.

Colby opened the front door and reached toward the dash to switch off the lights. His hand paused for a moment as a tiny flicker of memory jogged through him. For a minute he gazed through the heavily starred windshield, studying the kaleidoscopic pattern of fragmented headlight beams that still cut a swath through the night.

"You worried about the windshield, Dad?"

"No," Colby said absently, struggling to pin down the elusive sense of wrongness. "I owed Harry a broken windshield. What do you want to bet that if she lives, your grandmother makes me pay for it, though?"

"Breaking the windshield was the only thing I could think of to distract him."

"It worked. Like I said, Brandon, this time around you were my sucker punch."

"That was some spiel you gave him about blood and bodies. It even made me a little queasy. It was getting to him. I wonder if he would really have been able to pull that trigger. If you'd kept talking long enough..."

"Brandon, keep quiet a minute. I'm trying to think."

There was silence for thirty seconds and then Brandon couldn't resist. "About what?"

"Did you overhear our whole conversation?" Colby straightened up from his contemplation of light through a ruined windshield. He looked at his son.

"Yeah, I guess so, why?"

"He said something about telling Eddy last summer that things would be different this time around."

Brandon nodded. "I heard him."

"Just before Diana and I left town last summer, I had a talk with Eddy. He told me he was onto something big, that he was finally going to get his big break. That was the night I had the flat tire and nearly got my skull caved in by Harry."

"Dad," Brandon said softly, "it was Eddy who told us the 'vette would be out here on River Road tonight. Instead of the mystery car, we get Harry in an old Cadillac. You think maybe your good buddy set you up both times?"

Colby swore. " Diana. If anything happened to us, she wouldn't rest until she turned this whole town upside down. She'd go straight to Gil Thorp and he'd help her shake out the answers. Harry must have known that. He couldn't let her live, either."

Brandon's eyes widened. "She's alone at the cottage."

"And Eddy's still running around out there somewhere." Colby opened the rear door of the Cadillac again and reached inside to pull Harry to a sitting position. Harry blinked groggily.

"What are you going to do, Dad?"

Colby didn't answer. He gave Harry a single shake. Harry's eyes widened as he saw the cold expression on Colby's face.

"Tell me what the plan was, Harry. What's Eddy supposed to do with Diana?"

"I'm not gonna tell you a damned thing, Savagar. You're so smart, you figure it out for yourself."

Brandon leaned into the car. "You want the wrench, Dad?"

Colby held out his hand without a word. Brandon slapped the lug nut wrench into his palm.

Harry's mouth fell open as he stared from one implacable face to the other. "You're crazy, Savagar. You're both crazy. You can't do this. You're crazy."

"Probably comes from writing too much horror fiction. You going to argue with a crazy man, Harry?"

Harry chose not to accept the challenge. He closed his eyes and leaned his head back against the seat. "Chained Lady Falls. She's supposed to have an accident. Same kind of accident Eddy's old man had. It's all over by now, Savagar. The Legend of River Road has finally lost a race. Eddy and me are going to have the last laugh."

Colby shut the door and ran for the Buick. Brandon was hard on his heels.

Diana clutched her stomach and bent forward as the next contraction went through her. She breathed through it, trying to remember all the instructions Colby had drilled into her. When the discomfort passed, she resumed walking. She had been pacing the living room for nearly two hours.

Beside her, Specter whined again. Her anxiety had put him on battle alert, but he could find no enemy.

"It's okay," she muttered to the dog, trying to comfort herself as much as Specter. "I've got time. Probably hours and hours of time. This is only the first stage of labor, I think. Women stay home and clean the silver during this stage. No need to even call the hospital yet." Which was just as well since there was no phone in the cottage.

She couldn't even drive herself to the hospital, she thought despairingly. Colby and Brandon had taken the car.

"It wasn't supposed to be like this," she told Specter. "I'm supposed to be at home in Portland, packing my bags and preparing to check into a modern, state-of-the-art hospital. Colby's supposed to be here timing contractions and giving breathing instructions. He said he would be here with me when the time came. He promised he'd be here."

Specter paced silently beside her.

"He should have been back by now." She felt herself tensing through another contraction and tried desperately to relax. Fear lanced through her, not just for herself and the baby but for Colby and Brandon. "What if something happened out there on River Road tonight, Specter? What if that terrible car showed up and there was a fight? What if Colby and Brandon are hurt?"

Panic gripped her. It was an amorphous sensation that seemed to well up out of nowhere and roll over her in a crushing wave. Or maybe that was just the pain of another contraction.

The pain wasn't too bad yet. She could handle this. But it would get worse, much worse, before it got better. What was it Jennifer from apartment 301 had said? Unrelenting agony. Yes, she still had unrelenting agony ahead of her.

Diana experienced another overpowering urge to go to the bathroom. This would be the third time during the last hour. At first she thought she was just having problems from something she had eaten at dinner. But she had finally realized what was happening. Her body was flushing itself clean in preparation for birth.

When she emerged from the small room a few minutes later, she started downstairs and saw Specter at the front door, whining softly. He looked up at her, and then his attention fixed on the door again. Relief flowed through her. Colby and Brandon were home. She hurried on down the stairs, pausing on the last step to let another contraction pass.

"Is it them? What do you hear, Specter? My car?" Diana went to the window and pushed aside the faded curtain. Headlights swiveled and pointed straight at the house as a car pulled into the drive. She closed her eyes in mindless relief. The amorphous feeling of panic receded. Colby was here. He would take care of everything.

"It's okay now, Specter. He's back. We're all going to be fine."

She dropped the curtain and opened the front door. Specter growled softly, his body rigid. It was then Diana realized that the car in the drive was not her trusty Buick. The vehicle stopped just beyond the limited range of the porch light.

Cold night air flowed through the screen as Diana stood waiting to see who her visitor was. Maybe it would be Gil Thorp, she thought. Gil was an old-time county sheriff. He would know what to do. He'd probably rushed lots of women to the hospital in his time.

"Gil?" she called out as a car door thumped shut.

"Hello, Diana. It's me again." Eddy Spooner came up onto the porch, his once-handsome face set in the familiar lines of lifelong bitterness and regret. His glacial blue eyes were almost colorless in the weak light. "Sorry to bother you, but I got to tell you there's been an accident out on River Road."

Diana felt a vast darkness closing in on her. She clutched the knob of the screen door, clinging to it for support. She could handle anything but this.

"Colby," she whispered bleakly.

"They got him down at the hospital, ma'am. Car crash out on River Road. Nearly went into the water. Colby's askin' for you. I said I'd come pick you and Brandon up and take you down there."

Diana rallied. "He's alive?"

"Yes, ma'am, he's alive. But he's hurt bad."

Diana opened the screen door and stepped out onto the porch. The cold chilled her to the bone.

Eddy frowned down at her, looking concerned. "Uh, you'll need a coat, ma'am."

"Yes, of course, I will." Dazed, Diana automatically turned to go back into the cottage. Eddy followed.

"Where's Brandon? He'll want to come, too, won't he?"

"Brandon? Oh, my God, Brandon. He's with Colby. He would have been in the car. Eddy, did you hear anything about him? Is he all right or was he hurt, too?"

"Brandon?" Eddy looked confused. "No ma'am, no one mentioned him. I don't know if he...never mind. We got to get going."

"I'm ready. Hurry, Eddy. Please hurry. I have to get to Colby." Specter slipped through the door beside her, staying close to her ankle.

"Don't you want to leave the dog behind? The hospital staff sure won't want him hanging around."

Diana looked out into the darkness and saw the dark shape waiting beyond the glaring headlights. It had a vaguely familiar look to it, but she couldn't be certain.

Another contraction seized her and she couldn't think clearly. She responded to Eddy's question on gut instinct.

"The dog comes with me," she said flatly.

"But, Diana..."

She didn't bother to answer him. She had to get to the hospital. One way or another, she had to get there and Eddy Spooner was the only source of transportation.

She walked over to the large dark car and opened the door. Specter brushed heavily past as he vaulted over the front seat into the small space behind it. He kept his head at her shoulder.

Eddy Spooner climbed slowly into the car and turned the key in the ignition. A big, heavy engine exploded into life, the kind of engine seldom heard in modern automobiles.

"What kind of car is this, Eddy?" Diana asked quietly.

"It's a Corvette, ma'am. Hottest car in the county."

11

"Where did you get the car, Eddy? I thought you drove a Camaro." Diana watched the darkness flow past the window. Eddy was driving too fast, and she sensed immediately he didn't have the control over his vehicle that Colby always had. Eddy's driving added to the panic she was battling. She put up her hand and touched Specter. The dog touched her ear with his nose.

"The 'vette's mine." Eddy's voice was infused with pride. "Found her in a junkyard a while back. I've worked on her on and off for the past couple of years. Keep her in a shed I got out back of my place. No one's ever seen her in the daylight."

"Is that right?" Maybe if she could just keep him talking, she could figure out what was going on.

"Started takin' her over to the next county on weekends. Wanted to test her out, you know? She beat everything that she went up against. Just like that black 'vette of Colby's. Nothing could touch her. This here car's going to be more of a legend than that 'vette ever was."

Diana swallowed, her fingers tightening on Specter's collar. "You told Colby that the black Corvette was going to be down on River Road tonight."

There was silence beside her. "Yeah," Eddy said finally, "I did, didn't I? You know somethin'? I'd kinda liked to have gotten another chance to go up against Colby on River Road. This time I could have taken him. I know I could have. He wouldn't have lost me on that turn near the bridge the way he did last summer."

Diana shivered. "Eddy, this isn't the way to the hospital."

"I know."

She fought to keep calm. "Where are Colby and Brandon?"

"Don't know." Eddy sounded vague. "Somewhere up in the mountains, I guess. That's where Harry was going to take them. Except he was only supposed to take Colby first. We were gonna get Brandon when we got you."

" Harry? What does Harry have to do with this?"

"Harry and me, we're in on this together," Eddy explained. "He's my partner. This is it, you see. Our big break. We're gonna cash in on this one together, and then we're both gonna blow this town for good."

"Cash in on what, Eddy?"

"The Fulbrook money." He glanced at her as if surprised she hadn't figured it all out. "Old lady Fulbrook was plannin' on leaving Harry a lot of cash, you know? But she cut way back on his share when she met that boy of Colby's. She went to see a lawyer and changed her will. Harry says he's pretty sure she put Brandon in it and maybe Colby, too. Harry says that if we get rid of Colby and Brandon, he'll get their shares, just like he was supposed to originally. He told me that if I help him, he'll split the money with me."

"Eddy, you know it won't be that simple. That kind of thing never is."

"Harry says this will work and he ought to know. He's been planning it for months now. We got lucky when the old lady had the heart attack. That was a real lucky break, all right."

"Why?" She breathed through another contraction. Her eyes watered with the effort.

"Don't you understand nothin'? We had to get Colby and Brandon back up here into the mountains, you see? Thought the three of you might come at Christmas, but instead the old lady got a phone call from Brandon invitin' her down there. That wrecked everything. But we figured you'd all come up next summer. Then the old lady got sick a couple days ago and Harry said this would be our chance."

"He knew we'd come up to see her?"

"Right. And it's just what you did. Harry's real smart. Colby and

me used to figure him for a fool, the way he kowtowed to the Fulbrooks and all. But it turns out he's just played it real cool all these
years. Now it's gonna pay off."

It was taking more concentration now to handle the contractions.
Diana felt as if her mind was being strained to the breaking point. She
was panicky about Colby's fate and equally panicky about the immi-
nence of birth. It was too much to deal with at the same time.

"Colby," she whispered. "You haven't seen him since you came by
the house to tell us about the 'vette, have you?"

"No."

"So you really don't know what's happened to him."

"Harry's got him by now. That's why I picked you up. I was supposed to wait a couple of hours and then come tell you there'd been
an accident."

"But there was no accident." She clung to that. "Of course there
wasn't an accident. Colby's too good a driver."

"He ain't the best," Eddy muttered. "He just thinks he is."

Diana seized on that. "Oh, he's good, Eddy. He left this Corvette
in the dust that night on River Road. You had more power than he did,
but you didn't have his driving skill, did you?"

"It was another sucker punch, the way he went into that curve."
Eddy was clearly outraged. "Made me think I could take it faster, made
me go into it too quick. Faked me out. But he knew I couldn't take it
that fast. He knew I'd lose it. He tricked me. Harry says Colby always
has a sucker punch up his sleeve. That's why we had to get him first."

"But you don't know for certain Harry's got him, do you?"

"He'll have him by now."

"I wouldn't be too sure of that. Harry was expecting only Colby,
but instead he'll have had to deal with Brandon as well. Brandon's a
lot like Colby, you know. Colby taught him everything he knows.
Brandon even drives like his father. Think your friend Harry could handle two Savagar men?"

"Shut your mouth, you little bitch," Eddy shouted. He took his eyes
off the road to glare at her.

"Watch out!"

The Corvette swerved sharply as Eddy quickly brought it back in line. "Don't say nothin' more about how Colby might have taken out Harry. It didn't happen that way. Couldn't happen that way."

"Why not?"

"Harry has a gun. He knows what he's doin' with it. Harry and me been huntin'. I've seen him handle a gun."

Diana sucked in her breath and wrapped her arms around herself as the next contraction hit her. "Oh, my God." She tried not to think of Harry's gun, but the image kept getting mixed up in her mind with the rapidly escalating pain of her contractions.

No, not pain, she reminded herself with grim humor. Discomfort. Intense discomfort.

The real pain was yet to come.

Colby, where are you? I need you. You promised you'd be here with me. It's happening too fast, Colby. It's not supposed to happen this fast.

"What the hell's wrong with you?" Eddy asked. "Is it the baby? You're not having it now, are you?"

"Yes, it's the baby. I'm in labor, Eddy."

"Damn. Goddamn it to hell. I got to get this done. Harry didn't say nothin' about what to do if this happened. I got to hurry up and get it over."

"Get what done, Eddy? Are you going to kill me?" She was surprised at how calm the question sounded. It was probably because she had too many other things to think about. It was hard to get worked up over a mere murder threat when you were in labor and you were trying to deal with the fear that the man you loved might be dead.

No. Colby wasn't dead. She'd know if he were dead. A light would have gone out somewhere in her mind. He was still alive and as long as he was alive, he would be there when she needed him. He would move heaven and earth to get to her. She just had to keep going until her warrior found her.

"Don't say nothin' else, okay? I don't want to talk."

Diana kept her fingers wrapped around Specter's collar. He waited, tense and expectant, making no sound.

Somehow Diana wasn't surprised when Eddy pulled into a familiar parking area. She sat staring out at the starlit veil of water and knew that this was the way it had been meant to be.

"Chained Lady Falls," she said quietly. "What are we going to do here, Eddy?"

"You're gonna have an accident from the top of the falls." He opened the car door and as the overhead light came on, he showed her the small handgun in his fist. His eyes were glittering.

"The same kind of accident your father had?"

"He deserved to go over those falls. Everyone in town said so at the funeral. I heard 'em."

"Do I deserve to go over the falls, Eddy?"

"You got to. No other way. I'm sorry, if you want to know the truth. You're a real classy lady. But you belong to Colby Savagar and everything of his has to be destroyed. Don't you see? Everything of his has to go."

"Including my baby?"

"Don't say nothin' more, you hear me? Now get out of the car."

Specter's lips peeled back, revealing his teeth, but he made no sound. He followed Diana out of the car. She had never seen him quite like this. There were no threatening growls or angry, warning whines. The dog was deadly silent.

She knew Specter was ready to attack. For the first time she wondered just what Specter had done for a living in his former life. Colby had said once that he'd probably been a junkyard dog. According to the old saying, there wasn't much that was meaner than a junkyard dog.

Eddy eyed Specter as he came around the car but when the dog made no move, he ignored him. He trained the gun on Diana.

"We got to climb to the top of the falls."

"Don't be a complete ass, Eddy. I'm in labor. I can't possibly climb up to the top of the falls."

"You got to. Harry said this is the way it has to be."

"Probably because Harry wants you to take the blame for my death. I'm sure he's got this all figured out so that he won't have to split the money with you."

"Move."

She started forward and then screamed. The cry was only partially faked. The contraction that went through her was strong enough to generate a very real shriek. Diana doubled over in pain.

The sound totally unnerved Eddy. He jumped and leaped back involuntarily. "Damn you, don't yell like that. Don't yell like that again."

"Specter, get him."

She wasn't sure what the dog would do. She had never given him permission to attack anyone. She didn't even know what constituted a proper attack command.

But Specter knew a threat to his mistress when he saw it. Her fear and anguish were more than enough to guide him. He sprang toward Eddy, fangs glinting in the starlight.

This time it was Eddy who screamed. He fell back, frantically waving the gun as a club. The dog's big body bowled him over. Eddy broke free for a moment, rolled on the ground and tried to get to his feet. This time he aimed the gun at the charging dog.

But Specter reached him an instant too soon for Eddy to squeeze the trigger. Animal and man tumbled over the edge of the rocky pool and into the churning water at the base of the falls. They both disappeared.

"Specter!"

There was a terrifying pause, during which Diana could see nothing in the cold starlight. The roar of the falls blanked out all sounds of a struggle. Then Specter's head appeared briefly amid the foam.

"Specter. Here boy. Come here, Specter."

He responded to her call, swimming toward her with great, surging movements. A moment later he pulled himself up out of the pool and stood shaking the cold water out of his coat.

"Good dog. Good boy. Come on, we've got to get out of here." Diana was halted on her way to the car by another contraction. When she got moving again, she yanked open the door and discovered the keys to the Corvette had gone into the water along with Eddy and the gun.

Diana's hands flattened on the roof of the car. She closed her eyes, leaned forward and whimpered in helpless fear and pain. She was stranded.

And then an image formed in her mind. It was an image straight out of her dreams.

The grotto. She would be safe in the grotto. She would be warm there. She would find comfort in that little hidden place. Her baby would be born where it was meant to be born and they would both be safe.

"No," she whispered to Specter. "I must be going crazy. I'll have to have the baby right here on the ground."

She looked about at the dark, uninviting parking area. Not a fetal monitor or an anesthetist in sight, she thought hysterically.

She would use her jacket as a receiving blanket. She rummaged around in the cockpit of the Corvette and found a flashlight. She began talking to Specter as she made her meager preparations.

"There's this tribe in Africa," she told him bracingly, "which has this thing about childbirth being a real macho thing for the women. They have to go off by themselves and have their babies all alone out in the bush. They aren't even allowed to have any friends around, let alone a doctor or midwife. Tribe's still surviving, so I guess it must work. Specter, I'm so scared."

But Specter wasn't paying any attention to her. He was staring out into the darkness, watching the pool at the base of the falls. His body was gathered for battle once more. He was eerily silent.

Diana raised the flashlight and swung the beam out over the water. At first she could see nothing in the white foam, and then she saw what Specter had detected.

Eddy Spooner was swimming slowly toward the edge of the pool. His movements were hampered by the heavy rush of water cascading around him. He had an object in his fist. The gun.

Did guns work after they'd taken a dunking? Diana had no idea, but it seemed to her she'd seen movies where the heroes had risen from the water and proceeded to let loose a hail of gunfire over the bad guys.

There was little chance Specter would get away with another attack on Eddy. Eddy would be prepared this time.

The only safety lay in the grotto.

Diana hesitated no longer. She didn't know if she could make it up the path to the cave entrance but she also knew she had no option except to try.

"Specter. This way. Follow me."

The dog turned reluctantly from his contemplation of Eddy Spooner and trotted toward her. Flashlight in hand, Diana started for the hidden path behind the falls.

She had no rain gear this time. She would get soaked and the night air was so very cold.

But the grotto would be warm.

"Where do you think you're goin', you bitch? Come back here."

Eddy started to clamber up the side of the pool—a dark, hulking menace from the deep. He moved slowly, awkwardly. Diana took comfort from the fact that he probably couldn't see her any better than she could see him. If she got into the shadows near the falls, she would disappear from his sight.

She kept the flashlight off until she was behind the falls. Specter was at her heels. She shut her eyes and cried out as another wave of pain went through her. The roar of the water masked the sound of her groan. She wouldn't be able to stay on her feet much longer. She must be in what the books called precipitate labor.

Specter crowded close and then darted in front of her as if he knew the way and wanted to lead her to safety.

The trip up the path was the longest struggle of Diana's life. Primitive female instinct alone guided her. The need to find a safe place in which to give birth was all that mattered now.

At the end, she was clinging to Specter, her fingers clenched in his coat. He had to drag her the last few steps. She knew she could not have made it without him.

But at last they were standing at the mouth of the cave. Diana paused, panting heavily. She did not dare use the flashlight to see if Eddy was following her up the path. She had to assume he was.

She moved into the dark cave and then turned on the light long enough to get her bearings.

"Over there, Specter."

The dog was already nosing along the floor of the cave, heading for the secret entrance to the hidden grotto as if he, too, sensed safety there.

Soul-shattering pain wracked Diana as she stepped through the hidden portal of the small chamber. She dropped the flashlight and fell to her knees. Instantly she was enveloped in comforting warmth. The heat from the pool was doing its job. She crawled farther into the grotto on her hands and knees. She no longer had the strength to spare to get back to her feet.

Then in the glow of the flashlight she saw Specter turn back toward the cave entrance and she knew for certain Eddy Spooner was, indeed, following.

"In here, Specter. Stay here, boy. We'll be safe in here." She no longer questioned that knowledge, but it was all she could do to get the words out of her mouth.

The dog returned to her side, hovering anxiously. Diana spread her coat out on the stone floor near the hot pool and switched off the flashlight. She couldn't take the chance that its beam might leak out through the entrance and betray her hiding place.

She fought to remove her clothing. Everything was damp, and she knew that only some of the moisture was from the spray off the falls. The rest was from her own body.

She bit back another scream as the next contraction peaked. She must already be heading into the transition phase, she thought. The pain was getting incredibly intense. She had been told that this stage would be the summit of difficulty.

"Difficulty" was another popular euphemism favored by instructors and books on the subject of childbirth preparation.

Translated, "difficulty" meant unrelenting agony. Jennifer from 301 had been right.

A scream of anguish filled Diana's throat. At the last instant she realized dimly she could not release it. Her cry might guide Eddy to the hidden grotto entrance.

Colby, where are you? I need you now. Come to me. Help me.

Specter crouched near her head, licking her face. Her groping fingers found his leather collar. She unbuckled it, her hand trembling with the effort.

When the next contraction hit she shoved the leather between her teeth and bit down on the scream that threatened to consume her. At the height of the pain she told herself it wouldn't matter if Eddy walked in, found her, and killed her. At least the agony would be over and done with.

But she couldn't let her baby die, too. She had to protect Colby's child.

It was then she devised a deadly little mind game. She would count to ten, she told herself, take the leather out of her mouth and then give way to the scream that would get her killed.

When she reached ten, she decided she could get through one more ten-second count without screaming aloud. When she reached ten a third time she made herself wait through yet another ten-second count.

Counting to ten became the only thing in the universe that mattered. She did it a fourth time, a fifth time and on and on while her teeth scored the heavy leather collar.

At some point she was vaguely aware of Specter barking loudly once and then deserting her. She wanted to tell him he mustn't make any noise, but she didn't have the strength to call to him.

She was in the middle of another ten-second count, her jaws clenched in agony, when a blinding light lanced across her pain-wracked body. She closed her eyes against the glare. It didn't matter. She couldn't handle anything except the pain.

"Diana."

Colby's voice pierced the red haze that surrounded her. She opened her eyes long enough to see his grim face reflected in the backglow of the flashlight he was holding.

"Knew you were alive," she panted. "Knew you would get here." The leather collar fell out of her mouth and her next shout of anguish filled the grotto.

"It's okay, honey. I'm here."

"Dad? Where are you? Where's Diana? Is she all right? Oh, Christ. Dad, she's having the baby."

"Trust Diana to try to do this on her own." But Colby's voice was infinitely gentle and soothing as he kneeled beside her. "Everything's going to be all right now, little amazon. I knew you would take good care of our baby until I got here. I knew I could count on you."

Diana let go, giving herself up to the urgent, overwhelming need to push that was suddenly hitting her. Everything would be all right now. Colby was here. She could hear him talking to her quietly and giving Brandon instructions. She didn't pay any attention to what was being said or done. Colby would know what to do. He always did. She concentrated on the job at hand. It was taking everything she had to get it done.

A few minutes later a new cry filled the little grotto. It was the lusty squall of a healthy newborn infant.

"She's here, Diana. Our little Tabby is here. Safe and sound."

Diana lifted her lashes and looked up at Colby. He was on his knees between her legs, holding his daughter in Brandon's denim jacket. In the glare of the flashlight Brandon held, she could see the brilliant expression of triumph and happiness in her husband's eyes.

"I love you, Diana."

"I love you, Colby." Diana relaxed. This time, she thought, Colby wasn't just practicing.

This time he meant it.

"You've got some visitors outside," the nurse announced as she took the sleeping infant from Diana's arms and replaced her in the cradle near the hospital bed. "Ready for them?"

Diana nodded, her gaze on her daughter. She still couldn't quite believe she was a mother. The door opened, and Brandon came in. He was followed by Margaret Fulbrook.

"Margaret." Diana stared at the other woman in delighted astonishment. "Good grief, you look fine. What are you doing out of bed? Are you all right?"

"Told you these young doctors don't know everything. Turned out I wasn't having a heart attack after all. All the fuss and pain was caused by something called a hiatal hernia. It mimics the symptoms of a heart attack and scares the daylights out of you." Margaret Fulbrook smiled at her. "How are you feeling, my dear?"

"A little tired," Diana admitted. "But mostly I'm frustrated. I've got a million questions, and every time I tried to get Colby to answer them last night he kept changing the subject."

Brandon grinned. "He was more interested in making sure you and the baby were all right than in answering your questions. Besides, after we got you two down from that cave, you kept drifting off to sleep every few minutes."

Diana had only fleeting memories of the trip down the path. She had been wrapped in a blanket supplied by the ambulance Brandon had summoned to the scene. Colby had carried her and one of the medics had carried little Tabitha. Specter was close behind. Diana had a vague recollection of Colby giving orders to everyone in the vicinity, but mostly she just remembered how safe she had felt cradled against him.

"Tell me what happened, Brandon."

"You mean with Harry and Eddy?"

"Right." Diana looked at him. "I assume you and Colby had no trouble with Harry?"

"Piece of cake." Brandon's grin had a certain very familiar male cockiness about it. "Dad says this time around I was his sucker punch." His grin faded slightly and his expression grew more serious as he continued. "But when we realized you were in danger, Dad went wild. I doubt if any car, even that old 'vette Dad used to drive, ever made the kind of time on River Road your Buick made last night. Dad really is a hell of a driver, isn't he?"

Diana smiled at the admiration in Brandon's voice. "How did you know Eddy had taken me to the falls?"

"Harry told us."

Something in Brandon's eyes made Diana raise her brows. "Willingly?"

"Sort of." Brandon hurried on with his tale. "Harry said Eddy was supposed to push you over the falls. But when we reached the parking area and saw the 'vette was already there, Dad didn't even start up the path that leads to the top of the falls. He said he knew where you were. The next thing I knew we were climbing a ledge behind the falls."

"Chained Lady Cave," Margaret said softly. "Incredible. How did you ever make it up that path at night while you were in labor, Diana?"

"I couldn't think of anyplace else to hide. Specter had bought me some time by attacking Eddy. He sent Eddy into the pool. But the next thing I knew Eddy was climbing back out again and he still had his gun. So Specter and I headed for the cave."

"Dad says Specter gets steak every Saturday night for the rest of his life."

"Specter will hold him to that, I'm sure." Diana leaned back against the pillows. "Hurry up and tell me the rest. Once Colby gets back, he probably won't tell me a thing. All he'll want to discuss is breast-feeding techniques and how to change diapers."

Margaret Fulbrook shook her head, her smile wry. "Everyone in town is talking about Colby Savagar this morning. As usual. He's more of a local legend than ever, after what he did last night."

"So, tell me what he did do last night. Brandon?"

Brandon leaned against the foot of the bed, his eyes alight with re-membered excitement. "I followed Dad up the path. He had a flash-light, and he seemed to know where he was going. The next thing I knew, we were at the entrance to that cave. I heard this scream from out of the darkness and at first I thought it was you. Then I realized it was a man. Then suddenly Eddy Spooner came flying out of nowhere, leaping at Dad. He was yelling like a madman."

"Oh, my God," Diana breathed.

"Spooner kept shouting something about how he wasn't going to let Dad ruin everything for him. He was nuts." Brandon shook his head at the memory. "The flashlight went flying. I ran to grab it. When I turned the light on Dad and Eddy, they were fighting right at the mouth of the cave. I thought for a minute they were both going to go over the edge. But at the last instant, Dad rolled free. Eddy went over the falls."

Diana sucked in her breath. "Is he dead?"

"Yeah. They pulled his body out late last night."

"That poor man." Diana shook her head.

"I always knew Eddy Spooner would come to a bad end," Margaret Fulbrook declared.

"He was nuttier than a fruitcake," Brandon said. "He was the one who played those pranks on you last summer, by the way. Except for the one Robyn played, that is. Harry told the cops all about it this morning."

Margaret walked across the room to admire the sleeping baby. "Spooner couldn't stand the thought that Colby Savagar was back in town and that he had really made something of himself and his life. Eddy resented everything about Colby, including the fact that he was dating you. He didn't have the nerve to attack Colby directly last summer, so he took out his hostility against you."

"Harry was smart enough to figure out he could use Spooner's resentment," Brandon said.

"And all for nothing," Margaret said, her voice sad. "It's true I changed my will, but I never changed the amount I intended to leave Harry. He just assumed I had. The bulk of what's left of the Fulbrook money, and I'll be honest and tell you there isn't all that much left, still goes to this hospital. I only put in a small amount for Brandon. I knew Colby would never tolerate my leaving his son very much. And he's quite right. Too much money spoils a young person."

Diana opened her mouth to ask another question, but before she could speak there was a commotion in the doorway. Colby strode into the room, laden with packages.

"What's going on in here?" he demanded. "I told you I didn't want her tired out."

"I was just filling her in on what happened last night, Dad," Brandon took some of the packages Colby was carrying. "What's in here?"

"Diapers, a used car seat from Brian McDonald and some odds and ends we'll need on the trip back to Portland," Colby explained absently. His eyes were on Diana as he walked over to the bed and took her hand. "How are you feeling, honey?"

"A little sore, but otherwise fine." She looked up at him with all her love in her eyes. "Thanks to you."

Colby grinned. "I don't know about that. You were doing okay on your own. You and that dog of yours." He fished something out of his pocket and dangled it in front of her. "I saved this for a souvenir."

"What's that?" Margaret Fulbrook frowned at the strip of leather in Colby's hand.

"The latest in modern pain control techniques for amazons in labor," Colby said. "Notice the teeth marks?"

"It looks like a dog collar!" Margaret exclaimed.

"It is," Brandon said behind her. "Diana had it between her teeth to keep herself from crying out."

"I was afraid Eddy would hear me and find the entrance to the grotto," Diana explained.

"Good heavens." Margaret Fulbrook smiled. "Colby isn't going to be the only local celebrity around here, Diana."

"Just what I always wanted to be," Diana murmured. "A legend in my own time. I'll have to be honest, however. If I had to do it over again, I'd make darn sure I did it the way it's supposed to be done: in a hospital, with all the latest state-of-the-art medical technology. And painkillers. Lots of painkillers. The amazon bit is for the birds."

But even as she said the words, she knew she had done it the way it was supposed to have been done, and when she met Colby's eyes she knew he understood that, too. When he had carried her out of the grotto last night she sensed something had changed in the small, hidden chamber. A sense of peace had descended.

Colby's hand tightened around hers. "I love you," he said, heedless of the others in the room.

"Practice makes perfect," Diana whispered.

Epilogue

At last he stood at the entrance to the cave. The roaring water was at his back, a heavy veil of glistening light that was no longer tinged with his blood. He walked slowly toward the hidden grotto, following the summons that had drawn him here.

He moved into the tiny, secret chamber and saw her waiting for him. She smiled at him with love in her eyes. She was holding the naked babe in her arms. Joy flooded through him because he knew that now they were free. She had broken the chains he had, in his arrogant rage, foolishly placed on all of them. He put out his hand.

She put her hand in his, confidence and trust and love welling up within her, washing away all the old fear and fury. They had been given a second chance, and she knew that neither of them would throw it aside. They knew now that they belonged together.

They belonged together for they dreamed as one.

He led her out of the hidden grotto, down the path behind the falls and into the light of a new dawn.

When they were safe outside, the warrior peered more closely at the naked infant and then he laughed at the wonderful joke the gods had played on him. The babe was not the son he had expected. It was a girl child.

When he looked down into the woman's eyes, he saw his own laughter reflected there and he knew he had chosen well.

He had vowed to teach her that she could not escape her destiny as a woman, but it was he who had learned the most important lesson. She had taught him how to love.

Colby came awake and knew at once that Diana was also awake. He sought her hand in the darkness.

"You, too?" he asked softly.

"Yes. It was different this time, though. There was a finished quality to it."

"The urgency was gone," he agreed. "I finally made it to the grotto. I mean, he finally made it to the grotto."

"And I was there, waiting. Or she was there. With the baby." Diana turned toward him, nestling close. "He was surprised that it was a girl."

Colby smiled. "I know. He saw it as a sort of cosmic joke on him. But he loves the baby. Almost as much as he loves the infant's mother. This time we both dreamed the exact same dream, didn't we?"

"Sounds like it. We set her free, didn't we, Col-by?"

"We set them both free. He was as chained as she was. They were bound together. They still are, but in a different way." Colby's hand tightened around hers. "Just as you and I are bound together."

"Nobody would believe us if we tried to explain what happened in the cave."

"No, and I'm not sure how much of it I believe, myself. But it makes a good story. We'll tell it to Tabitha when she's older."

"Do you think we'll go on having dreams about the cave now that we've lifted the curse?"

Colby gathered her against him, lost in her soft, luminous smile. "Honey, you might as well face it. You and I are going to be sharing our dreams for the rest of our lives."